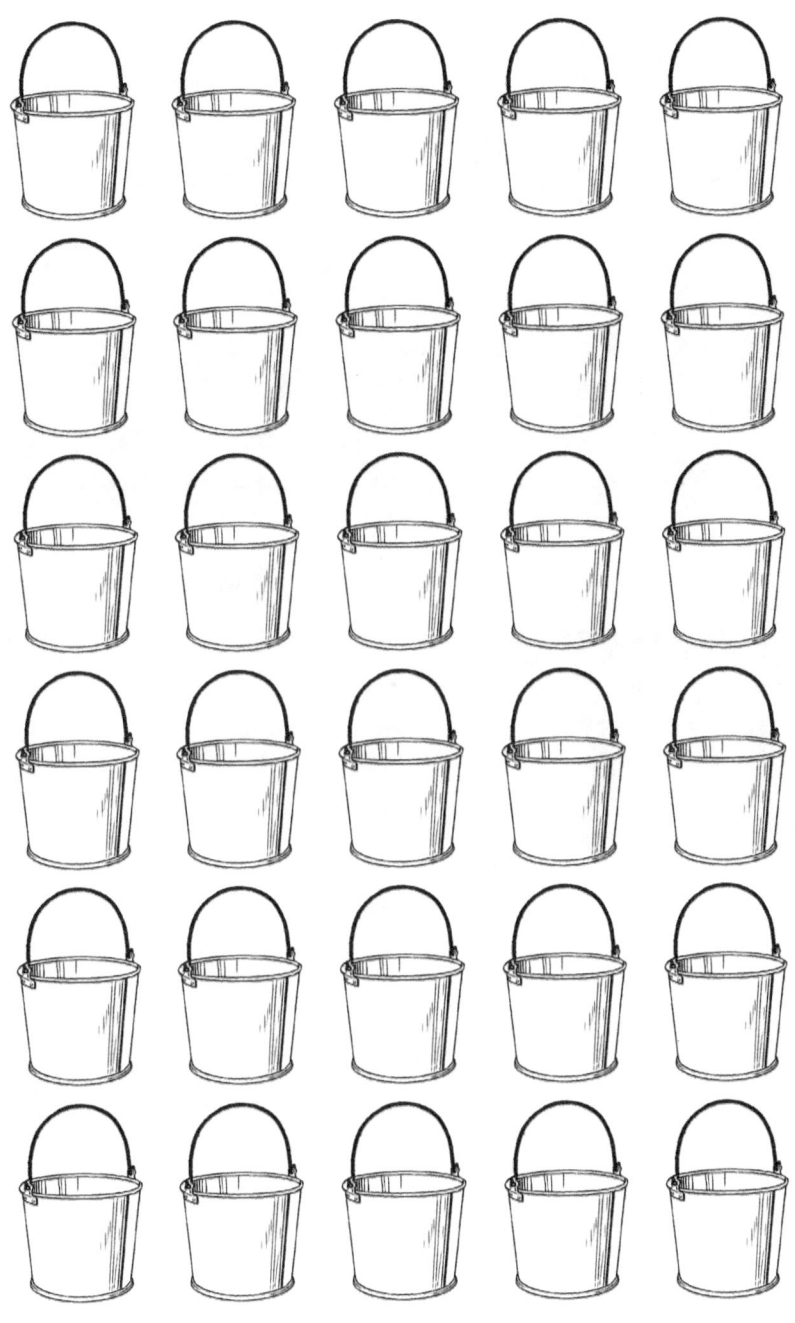

Pure Slush Books

July
August
September
2014

a Pure Slush compendium

First published December 2014
Edited by Matt Potter

Pure Slush Books
4 Warburton Street
Magill SA 5072
Australia
Email: edpureslush@live.com.au
Website: http://pureslush.webs.com
Visit the Pure Slush Store: http://pureslush.webs.com/store.htm

Front cover photograph copyright © Scott Liddell

ISBN: 978-1-925101-47-8

Pure Slush proudly features (both online and in print) writers from all over the English-speaking world. Some speak and write English as their first language, while for others, it's their second or third or even fourth language. Naturally, across all versions of English, there are differences in punctuation and spelling, and even in meaning. These differences are reflected in the stories *Pure Slush* publishes, and it accounts for any differences in punctuation, spelling and meaning found within these pages.

stories by

Guilie Castillo Oriard

Townsend Walker

Derek Osborne

Gloria Garfunkel

John Wentworth Chapin

Lynn Beighley

Andrew Stancek

Rachel Ambrose

Gill Hoffs

Susan Tepper

Jessica McHugh

Shane Simmons

Michelle Elvy

Len Kuntz

Michael Webb

James Claffey

Gwendolyn Joyce Mintz

Stephen V. Ramey

Gay Degani

Sally-Anne Macomber

Mandy Nicol

Margaret Bingel

Darryl Price

Teresa Burns Gunther

Matt Potter

Gary Percesepe

Nathaniel Tower

Kimberlee Smith

Vanessa Weibler Paris

Joanne Jagoda

h. l. nelson

July

Hot Water

by Guilie Castillo Oriard

Luis Villalobos uses hot water in the shower for the first time since he moved to Curaçao. The tropical rock where opening a car window feels like holding a blow dryer to your face. Where cold showers are as coveted as they're impossible. Even at 2 AM water won't go any cooler than lukewarm.

The mirror is still fogged up when he finishes dressing. Sweatpants, socks, the Timberland fleece he hasn't used since flying back from Mexico in May. His teeth won't stop chattering. And his head. Oh, his head.

Day three of dengue fever. Who knew a mosquito could transmit such misery? He supposes he should be thankful it's not malaria. But dengue comes in varieties. According to Stepan, the legal counsel at Ehrlich and the closest Luis has come to a friend in Curaçao, one of these varieties makes you bleed to death, Ebola-like. Luis's brand-new doctor did say that's not the kind he has. But her assurances sounded mechanical.

Luis doesn't handle illness well. Makes him feel vulnerable. Which he is, isn't everyone, and he understands this in the grooves of his subconscious the way he understands his forehand isn't as good as Nadal's and never will be. But in the heat of the game reality is malleable. Until it's Nadal on the other side of the net. Or, say, a deadly strain of dengue scorching your body.

15

He wants nothing more than to crawl back into bed. But Al has gone over twelve hours without a bathroom break. And without food. He's waiting at the top of the stairs, imploring with big chocolate eyes.

Vulnerability.

"Let's go take a leak, bud."

Al tears down the two flights, nails skidding on wood then on granite tile. When Luis makes it all the way down, nausea blooming like an oil spill under his ribcage, Al is already at the patio doors, wiggling his vast body in spurts, as if impatience is vying with remorse for making such demands on his human.

"Sorry, bud. Should've let you out earlier. Thanks for –"

It takes him a whole new step to realize his foot is wet, another for the why to sink in, and then only because of the smell. "Oh, fuck."

Too late. He's already left a pee-soaked footmark on the rug.

Al cringes, massive shoulders scrunched down to the floor.

"Sshh, it's okay." Luis runs a hand over the dog's trembling head, the silky ears. One has a corner missing. Al came with many scars; most have healed, or disappeared under the regrowth of blue-black fur. Others, like this one, no amount of good food or kind hands can heal. "My fault, man. I know you tried."

The dog dashes out onto the deck as soon as the door opens a crack and around to his favorite palm. Luis leans against the door frame, shivering in the 32-Celsius breeze, and listens to the splash of Al's stream. Sounds like the freaking Nile.

Laughter startles him. No, it's not Al, having suddenly acquired a taste for irony – or the human means of expressing it. Besides, it came from the opposite corner of the deck. But the sound is familiar, pleasingly so. And unsettling. Doesn't belong here.

It belongs to Pélagie Solak.

Must be the fever. He should've stayed in bed, let Al turn the house into a Turkish-market toilet, the kind you roll up your pants to enter and throw away your shoes when you exit.

Al's on the deck, bladder urgencies either satisfied or forgotten, ears perked as high as they go. His face – his whole body – rigid. Listening.

The laughter comes again, from behind the feather hedge of palms separating his yard from Vikram's. Al streaks past him and leaps like a cheetah into the greenery.

"Al!"

But the dog has disappeared. Behind the palms, Vikram shouts something. Metal scrapes on wood. Then Pélagie's voice – it must be her, Al's hearing cannot lie: "Al? Hey, Al! Whatcha doing here?"

Pélagie here. Today. He's not only not at his best but at his worst of worsts. Life has a dirty-bastard sense of humor. At least the palms provide cover. She'll be spared the sight of him quivering like hummingbird wings, turned into this – this wuss. He pushes an arm through the mesh of greenness, far enough, he hopes, that it can be seen from the other side. "Hey, Vikram. Sorry about Al."

"Luis?" His neighbor sounds surprised, but not particularly angry. "Is it the weekend already?"

"No, man. I'm, uh, not feeling well." He catches intermittent glimpses through the palms, mostly of Vikram's pool, just large enough, like his, to escape jacuzzi status. No humans. No Al. "Al, come on, boy. He didn't hurt – uh, anyone, or make a mess, did he?"

"No, no, it's all –"

"We're fine."

It's Pélagie speaking, and her voice sends his flesh into a new eruption of shivers. "Okay. Good. And, uh, hi."

"Hi, Luis."

"You know each other?" Vikram sounds understandably bewildered.

"Thanks to this guy," Pélagie says, and Luis imagines her scratching Al's chest, the pure pleasure on the dog's face. "Go on home, Al. Luis, call him."

"Here, boy. Al, come on. Let's go."

Nothing.

"I'll bring him around," Pélagie says.

Luis panics. There's dog pee in his fucking front hall. Will she smell it from the door? What if she wants to come in? But he has no energy to argue. All he seems able to do is call out a strong and determined, "Uh, okay. Thanks."

The front bell rings as he climbs back up on the deck. How the hell did she get here so fast? He throws the rug over Al's puddle – the handwoven cotton is already stained, already doomed. Doorbell rings again. Keys, where are his keys? Kitchen counter? There, on the bookcase. "Coming. Hey, thanks for –"

But it's not Pélagie. It's Milena. His lover. His boss. She's wearing a filmy blouse of big sleeves and big neckline, heels so high and slim he wonders, as he often does, about the miracle of physics that keeps her upright.

"Luigi, I just heard. I would've flown back sooner if I'd known." She pushes past him, sophistication wafting off her, and heads down the hall towards the kitchen. "Did they do a blood test? Dengue's rare this time of year. God, you must be feeling like shit. What's that smell? And where's your monster mongrel? Listen, I had Francelle make you some chicken soup. She's such a good cook. I might take her to Singapore with me, just for the – Luis, close that door already."

But he doesn't. Pélagie's coming down the walk with Al. They both smile when they see Luis, but only Pélagie speaks. "So this is your secret lair, Mr. Hotshot Tax Attorney?"

Luis wants to lob back the banter, but his glibness has gone the way of the woolly mammoth. Emotion is building at the base of his throat, and he realizes that what he wants, more than his bed or the snugness of his duvet, more even than to feel well again, what he *needs* is this woman's arms around him. Which is mad, beyond unhinged, not just because he's never felt those arms, has no idea how they'd feel, and how can he need something he's never had, but because Pélagie isn't just out of his league – she's a different sport altogether.

He takes hold of Al's collar. "Thanks for bringing him back."

Pélagie squints at him. "You look – not well. Bad cold?"

"Dengue." There's a certain pride in not being vulnerable to just any common virus. He kind of wishes it was malaria now.

The square of skin between her eyebrows furrows. "How's the fever?"

"Under control." He shrugs.

She comes closer, lifts her hand. Before he can back away or say anything, she's touching his forehead. Cupping his cheek. Small and cool, that hand quiets the tomahawk army that's taken up residence inside him. He leans into it, closes his eyes.

Milena's saying something from the kitchen. She probably found Al's puddle. She'll come looking for Luis, might be starting down the hall right fucking now, towards him, him and Pélagie and this suspended animation. And Milena has the instincts, the sensorial prodigy, of a lioness hunting. The question isn't *will she know*; it's *what will she do*. Luis's career is in her hands. He put it there, seven months ago.

Milena's footsteps are unmistakeable now. Pélagie's hand moves, begins to slide from his cheek. A sort of disappointed relief blows through him. And then, just as the door begins to swing wider, just as Milena's perfume begins to claim the air, Luis crushes Pélagie – so lithe, so scrawny, and yet so vibrantly alive against the arm he slips around her waist – to his chest and plants a lip-mashing, teeth-gnashing, make-the-fifth-grade-class-dork-proud kiss right on her mouth.

Al, with his usual disconnect from the complexities of human endeavor, barks in approval.

La Ronde /
Serge and Jimmie

by Townsend Walker

After Serge misreads an email (not an infrequent occurrence) he calls his boyfriend, Jimmie. "Darlink, is Serge."

"Like I wouldn't know your voice."

"Be nice, I be star, show you."

"You? A star?"

"Myron Fopnik new film. I have connection. Know wife. Gloria email this morning."

"Okay, read it to me." Jimmie knows to be patient with Serge and the language.

"Serge my sweet (she call me *my sweet* all time), talked to Myron last night about a role for you. We talked for a long time and read the script carefully. Not now it seems, but maybe later, after the shooting starts roles will become clearer."

"Serge darling, come over, come over now. I need to explain a few things to you about the business."

Like Myron, Jimmie is a film producer, but: shorter track record, more misses than hits, last movie couldn't find a distributor, actors are suing for wages, investor is beyond unhappy. That would be Salvatore Mancuso, aka Sal-your-Pal or Sal-the-Slayer, depending.

Serge jumps into his Miata, drives like he's in no-rules-India to Jimmie's bungalow in Venice Beach, leaps out of the car waving a print-out of the email. Jimmie is waiting by the gate, the middle of his slight pale body tightly wrapped in a strip of blue lycra, a racing Speedo, feet in matching flip flops.

"Hey, not even a kiss for your lover, my big Russian hunk?"

Serge lifts Jimmie above his head and plants a smacker on his belly. "You yummy bear, Jimmie."

By the pool, Jimmie explains Gloria's email. "You see where it says 'not now'? That means never. You see where it says 'maybe'? That means never. You see where it says 'later'? That means never."

"Why she not say that?"

"You have an email with three 'nevers' and they'll buy you a ticket to Newark for a crowd scene? Not going to happen, lover boy. But that's okay, I'll have you to myself. Come here, let Jimmie make everything better."

An hour later. Serge now draped in a zebra stripped robe; Jimmie in a leopard spotted one.

"Want to take a dip before lunch?"

"Serge have appointment."

"Cancel it."

"With Gloria. Maybe they change mind."

"Tell her you'll be late."

Serge frowns. "She my connection."

"Didn't you understand anything I told you about her email? I think you just don't want to stay."

Jimmie sulks off through the sliding door into the living room. Serge panics and runs in after him. "What you do with room?"

"A new friend of mine is getting into the decorating business and using the room to try out ideas. You don't like?"

The incongruity of the aluminum framed glass doors and the 19th Century Victorian interior clash with even Serge's sensibilities, never a strong suit with someone from Vologda. The walls are hung in pool table green velvet dressed with pre-Raphaelite portraits and medieval altar pieces; orange and red oriental carpets overlap on the floor and a tiled faux fireplace has been installed.

"Who this friend decorator?"

"Just a guy I met at Roosterfish. Remember, a couple of weeks ago when you had a late appointment. I got lonely, went down and had a couple of drinks."

"I suspicious, there more to tell Serge."

"You damn Russians never believe anyone. Reason you're here and not there."

"Well, I not tell you what Gloria tell me about other job." Serge plops down pouting in a red velvet covered wing chair.

"Look, there's nothing at all between Phillipe and me. I promise, cross my heart. What's Gloria's other job?"

"Myron tell her about lady in New York City want kill husband because he beat her up."

"So?"

The phone rings next to Jimmie's chair. He's startled someone's calling on his business line. "JBK Productions, James Kilburn speaking." Only a murmur is audible, from the ear piece. Jimmie's face grows paler and tighter, lips compressed to the size of a donut hole.

"Just a minute." He turns to Serge. "Excuse me a minute, can you wait out by the pool while I finish this call, important business."

Ten minutes go by; Jimmie listens, his cheeks become cavernous, his hand shakes. "Sal, look I'll have it for you next week. I promise. Yes, I understand what happens if I don't ... Yeah, Thursday, I promise Sal."

Serge, sent outside, has his nose up to the window, watching. Finally, Jimmie waves him in.

"I know, that Frankie. You no want me hear about plans for tonight."

"Listen stupid, that was not Frankie. It was about my last movie. By the way did you ever see it?" Serge shakes his head. "I thought so, even my lover didn't go. Thanks a lot."

Jimmie takes a deep breath, reaches for Serge's hand and leads him to the railed sofa. "Now tell me more about this lady in New York."

"Lady pay to kill husband."

Jimmie leans closer. "How much? A lot?"

"Gloria say Myron say $100,000. Big?"

"Yes, big … This guy have protection?"

"What mean, protection?"

"Like mob, political, you know, people with guns around him."

"Work for Goldman bank."

Jimmie moves in closer to Serge, put his arm around him, and massages his bicep. "So what's this guy's name?"

"Franklin Lincoln Cabot Three. He called Frank."

"What's he look like?"

"Why you ask questions?"

"You know us movie types, always looking for something interesting to make a film about. More details we get, the better."

"Gloria say sixty three, 250 pounds, pasty like dough face, curly black hair with shiver."

"You mean silver."

"Big nose like bird, shoes with dangle things, Prada Aviators, blue tint. He wear in rain."

Jimmie reaches over, grabs a pen and writes it down. "So I don't forget."

"And he lose kids."

"What do you mean he lose kids?"

"In park, go to big park and lose kids, need police to find."

"How did he do that? Oh, never mind."

Jimmie's cell rings. He looks at the number. Swipes to answer. "Not now. I told you later. Yeah, half hour."

"Who that, half hour?"

Jimmie is clearly uncomfortable, his body bobbles, hems and haws, shrugs his shoulders, finally arrives at an answer to disguise Phillipe's call.

"That was one of Phillipe's clients, wants to see his work. Thinking about having him do some rooms for her. She called earlier, I told her I wouldn't be free until two and here she is calling at one, wanting to be here right away and it was just hard to get rid of her, you know how these decorating clients can be. So demanding."

"I wait to see client. Maybe she need personal trainer."

"That's not a good idea."

Serge stands up from the sofa and installs himself in the red wingtip chair facing the door, arms folded, feet spread wide.

"I wait here with you, Jimmie, for Phillipe client."

Family

by Derek Osborne

Eddie's already up and on the 6AM ferry over to Hyannis. He told Anja it's to meet with a local chandler, but he's really meeting a jeweler from Boston, one with a small and rather expensive package. Max has a surprise planned for dinner.

The ring is more than a week overdue so the intimate moment Max had initially planned can't happen. The entire family has come to celebrate The Fourth – both sides – Rebecca thought it was time. The mood onboard is still a bit formal. It's an odd sort of comfort when Joey, Rebecca's younger brother, pulls Max aside and says, "My mom's gonna fuck with you. Do you really have cancer?"

Rebecca's sister, Connie (Consuela, when Mom says it) is there as well. She's nothing like Rebecca, small and shy. Her husband, Jose Ramon, has a forgettable handshake. He's spent the last two days taking the kids into town. There are six from the Perkin's clan and then Rebecca's two nieces. They're a bit confused over who is an uncle, a dad or a grand-dad, but they love camping out in *Gadabout's* salon and Anja has shown them where to buy ice-cream. There have been two closed-door sessions between Rebecca and her mother, one in muted English, the other, much louder, in their native Andalusian. "I do not want to talk about it," Rebecca says when he asks. Max finds it awkward calling a woman his own age 'la senora'.

He's meeting Eddie at Black Eyed Susan's. Jose and Joey are taking the kids for pony rides. As they pull away in the harbor launch it dawns on Max he is leaving the women alone. They're all in the cockpit having coffee. Rebecca is laughing; her mother is tousling Consuela's hair. At some point the launch is closer to town and further from *Gadabout*. They get to the dock and the kids take off. Max looks one more time. *Gadabout* sits quietly at her mooring, a slack line to the ball. The restaurant is just up the street. The Russian girl comes for his order. Eddie arrives a few moments later.

"Brother," he says, even before sitting down, "This guy knows his stuff." He's pulled out the case. The ring is a 5.5ct Oval Blue Sapphire, four pin setting, the band engraved in Elfish. "What does it say?"

"That's for her."

Eddie nods, then pulls out another case. "It's going to be some dinner."

"What the fuck," Max says, a little too loud, drawing some glares from nearby tables.

"You got me thinking," Eddie says. "We haven't had time to talk."

"I know."

"God is coming."

Max reaches across the table and takes Eddie's hand. "Sooner than later, I'm afraid." The last test results weren't good. "You're covered, you know, enough to buy *Gadabout*."

Max lets go of his hand.

"Maybe I and I am home as well," Eddie says, using his native Jamaican, referring to the legend of *Gadabout* having been built to help seven sailors find their way home. A boy at the next table is watching. He leans in to ask his mother a question. Seeing Max, she smiles apologetically.

"Just give me some space in the drawer," Eddie says.

27

They eat the meal in silence. The Russian girl comes back to ask if they are finished. There won't be a check. Max leaves a ten dollar tip. When they pass by the owner up near the register both men nod; they know one another from the clinic. Outside, it's one of those grand Nantucket days, warm sun and blue sky, painted wood doors, cobblestone street, carved colonial signs. Behind the shop windows are hand stitched leather iPhone cases for $700.00, a pair of sandals for $650.00. By the corner, the haunting eyes of a war-torn girl stare out of the original 3' x 5' McCurry photo – 1.7M.

"Who would write such a check?" Eddie says.

Max looks in through the plate glass window.

"Are we good men?" he asks.

"Yes," Eddie says, without hesitation.

A couple strolls by with two small children, pale, blond, nearly Albino, dressed in matching outfits of khaki and baggy blue cardigan sweaters. They all wear floppy beige hats. The slightest breeze might blow them away.

"Are you asking, are we good enough?" Eddie says.

"I guess."

"We will never be good enough."

He smiles his wonderful smile, laughs and claps Max on the shoulder. "This is why we need wives – to remind us."

Max looks back at the girl in the window.

"Hey," Eddie says, "We have a formal surrender this evening."

"You put it so well."

They also need to go meet with the realtor. It looks like they've found a place onshore.

Back at the boat, Anja greets them by the ladder. "We've had Fourth of July a bit early, I'm afraid."

"How bad," Max says, hoisting up over the rail. It's difficult.

"You couldn't hear them onshore?" Anja motions over her shoulder. "Becky has asked you not disturb her."

"And la senora?"

"In the galley. A good meal solves everything."

"And the others?"

"In the salon playing Parcheesi."

Max looks down the companionway. He can see the women gathered around, the game spread out on the table under the skylight. Connie seems to be fitting right in. Pam looks up and waves him off. The sound of pots and pans can be heard in the galley. He's hit with the smell of paella: lobster, clams, and mussels, fresh tomatoes and spices he does not recognize.

"Anja, could you please get my meds?"

After one OxyContin and two gin and tonics Max is feeling no pain. The kids are back; Jose Ramon fell off. They won't let him live it down. Max is sitting by the helm. The cockpit table is set with extensions to handle the crowd, a white linen table cloth waves in the wind. The kids want their own table down below. Jose and Joey volunteer to chaperone.

"Sorry," Max says, "All hands on deck."

He can hear Rebecca helping her mother. It's an ongoing commentary, sometimes in English, sometimes in Spanish. He's seen her exactly twice. She hands things up the companionway stair and then disappears. There's the hint of a smile, telling him not to worry. She's wearing a light green dress and sleeveless top, her hair is loose and her shoulders freckled. Over the dress is a tattered blue apron; her mother must have brought it. The day is ending, the harbor filled with tall white masts and graceful sheers, the town all gray shingle and lines of white trim, the marshlands crimson and gold. Eddie's brought out a Jadot Pouilly. Candles in glass chimneys, a board with bread, a big bowl of butter. Max calls them all to come up to the cockpit. Even the children get wine.

"To family," he says, "To loved ones here and gone, to this gadabout we call life."

La senora looks at her daughter. Rebecca is looking at Max. Eddie is holding his breath.

"And so," Max says, reaching into his pocket, "in order to bring our two families together …"

Rebecca catches her breath. "Max, don't."

"I have a proposal."

"Max wait!"

But he's already opened the case. The evening sun catches the sapphire perfectly.

"Shit!" Joey says.

Max is already over the table. He slides off the end and into the hatchway. Anja grabs at the candles. It's a six foot drop. Rebecca is down on her back, she isn't moving.

"Eddie, Mayday!" Max says.

Eddie grabs the mic hanging at the helm. His voice is steady, mechanical. "Mayday Mayday Mayday, this is sailing vessel Gadabout, Gadabout, Gadabout. Nantucket harbor, Nantucket harbor …"

The response is immediate, a young voice, the hint of an inner-city accent, "All vessels this is US Coast Guard, clear sixteen. Repeat. All vessels clear sixteen. Gadabout, state your emergency."

Max has climbed down, skirting Rebecca's limp body. The kids are all screaming. "Shut up," he yells. He's checking for vitals. Her leg is still hooked in-between the steps. He can't tell if it's broken. He doesn't like the angle of her neck.

"I've got vitals," he yells up on deck.

Eddie is calmly going about it. "Female, early thirties, fell down companionway stair, unconscious, four months pregnant ..." He turns from the mic, looking on shore. "They're manning the boat," he shouts down below. Max can hear the siren in town. "... possible broken leg," Eddie is saying, "possible neck injury ..."

Another voice comes over the radio. "Gadabout, Wind Song II. I'm an OBGYN en route. ETA two minutes. Do not move her! I repeat, do not move her!"

"You hear that?" Eddie shouts down.

Now other docs are checking in, six in all, one of them a neurosurgeon.

"Is that a psychiatrist?" la senora asks. She's more exasperated than anything else. "Sort of," Eddie says.

"Tell him to come, and after he examines those two he can look at me ... for giving my blessing."

There in the cockpit they all stop, trading glances. The Coast Guard boat is at full throttle, its siren up, weaving out through the anchorage, throwing a good-sized wake. The police are blocking off streets. There's a Medevac bus, its lights flashing, the siren loud, then soft, then loud again. The water amplifies everything. The Dock Master, his little work scow with the ring of old tires pushing a fat little wave, is going to reach them first.

"Was that my mother?" Her eyes barely open. "Mama, que dijiste?"

"She's conscious!" Max yells.

"I turned ... I spun so he wouldn't get hurt."

"I know."

Max squeezes her hand, smoothes out her hair, he can feel the swell of the other boats coming alongside. The Dock Master's face appears in the hatchway. Seeing she's awake, he blows out a sigh of relief.

"Yes, Max," she whispers.

"Yes what?"

"Mama dice que esta bien."

But then her eyes roll back, there's a tremor. She stops breathing.

"Becca?" Max says, "Becca?"

The Dock Master jumps down the stairs. "Let me in, Max. Move!"

He gently pulls back one of her eyelids. "God damn it!" Then he looks at Max. "We've got to get her flat."

"But they said ..."

"Fuck what they said. C'mon, hold her here and here. Keep her head in that same position ..."

Still Miserable

by Gloria Garfunkel

Still miserable Ralph here. These depressions take so damn long to get over. Chloe invites me to a barbecue at a friend's with a pool, but I lie that I have food poisoning and I sleep all day. Haven't seen her much lately as I'm still on a down slide, with that constant lump in my throat like I'm going to cry any second. She's really understanding. I don't know how she puts up with me. I can't put up with me. That's why suicide creeps into my thoughts constantly, though I've sworn myself to abstinence. I hang a flag on my porch to honor our veterans who all have it worse than me and shuffle back to bed and suddenly start crying about their families and fall asleep. At night, Chloe drags me out of bed to watch the fireworks from a hill in town and I can see it is beautiful but find it annoying.

"I wish you were back to your hypomanic self when I met you," she says.

"Me, too. Those were the days. They'll be back and you'll regret you said that."

Maize

by John Wentworth Chapin

Charles starts kicking when he feels the wave engulf his body. The surf rushes past him, through him. He's never certain whether he's caught a wave until the last moment when he finds himself hurtling blindly toward the shore, eyes scrunched tight against the salt. His chest and stomach scrape shells and sand in ankle-deep water as the last of the wave zooms up the beach, smoothing the sand in a blanket of foam. A powerful on-shore current pulls everything forward up the beach. There aren't many other swimmers out today, just a few body-surfers and the occasional wiry old person swimming parallel to the beach beyond the break-line. He has had his eye for a bit on two guys horsing around, laughing and shouting. They have spent plenty of time at the gym, these two, salt water dripping down cuts of lean, tan muscle.

Charles slogs back through the surf to the spot just seaward of the cresting waves. He has to keep from staring at the two guys. It's a heavily gay beach, so a little staring is okay, but creepy is creepy, no matter the flavor of the beach. Charles catches the next wave, a big one, and one of the gym boys rides it with him. They both land spluttering on the sand, laughing, not far from each other. The guy stands and then another wave catches him off-guard and pulls him down. He shouts something to his friend, but Charles pays more attention to the guy's arms, beefy and ringed in matching tribal tattoos.

Tattoo Arms skitters out of the water, escaping the next wave. Charles watches him retreat. The beach is crowded on this long Fourth of July weekend. *Independence Day* – Charles snorts to himself every time he hears it. He doesn't feel very independent. Rehoboth Beach is in Delaware, across state lines; Charles was warned not to leave the state of Maryland.

Fuck that. He didn't commit a crime. *The stupid fuckers in the police department and the mean fuckers in the prosecutor's office can go fucking fuck themselves.* This is what he told Stephanie as he drove east in heavy traffic across the Bay Bridge early yesterday morning.

"You're unhinged, Charles," she said. "Nothing good will come of this."

He was silent, perhaps one of the benefits of *unhinged*, certainly preferable to the kind of unhinged involving screaming and hurling feces at cars from the underpass. He saw a guy do that right next to the city jail. Ever after, when he drove past, he thought about that guy and wondered if the guy was just a lunatic who happened to be tossing shit under the overpass outside the jail, or if the location was somehow central to the story. Was he just out? Was he trying to get back in?

Stephanie continued, "Even if you didn't commit murder, you're committing a real crime now."

Even if you didn't commit murder. Charles didn't much like the way that sounded, so he tapped the 'end-call' button on the steering wheel and Stephanie disappeared. The button icon was red, an old-fashioned phone shape, like a little dumbbell. Phones haven't looked like that in two decades.

Everything's fucked up.

The other gym bunny floats on his back now, just out past where the waves break. He's wearing a square-cut dark yellow Speedo-y suit, trashy and immodest and hot. If Charles had a body like that, he'd wear the same suit.

"How's it going?" Charles says, eyes on the lumpy yellow island.

The guy laughs. "It's going."

Charles gets a good look at him; about 27, lankier than his buddy. "I'm Charles."

"And I'm about as a drunk as I have ever been in the ocean! Woo-hoo!" the guy chortles.

A wave catches them off guard, dousing them. Charles comes up sputtering and laughing. He treads water on the next wave, rubbing the salt from his eyes and spitting, waiting for the guy to come up.

He doesn't come up.

Charles looks around, swimming now, bobbing up to get a glimpse of the guy. He scans the shoreline to spot him walking or swimming toward the beach.

The guy is nowhere to be seen.

What. The. Fuck.

The brown-green water has visibility of only a few inches, so Charles can see nothing when he ducks under. He starts to feel a little panicked, and then he feels something brush against his leg. His first thought is the guy, and Charles dives down again, eyes open in the murky salt water, arms pinwheeling to see if he can find the guy.

Then he thinks – no, realizes – *shark*.

Charles freaks the fuck out.

"SHARK!!!" he yells, waving his arms, and then he just *swims*, panic overtaking him. Every head on the beach turns his direction, people rush to the waterline from the cluster of blankets and umbrellas.

As soon as Charles gets to his feet, he starts running, then turns around backwards in terror as he remembers the guy in the yellow suit. He scans the water for him.

"There is a guy out there – he went under and didn't come up!" Charles gasps, hoping to grab the attention of the nearest beachgoers. People near him shout into the water, trying to get the attention of the few swimmers out there to come ashore.

Tattoo Arms stands at the shoreline, brow scrunched, a beer in each hand.

A crowd forms around Charles and Tattoo Arms, and Charles repeat his story. "He told me he was drunk and then we got surprised by a wave – I mean, what I *think* was a wave – and then he disappeared. I felt something against my leg and –"

The crowd parts and they hear a commotion. Charles follows the gaze of the crowd; a guy leaping now through the waves toward a body tossing in the churning surf. Charles catches a flash of yellow.

Time slows: the crowd grows tighter. Two people begin mouth-to-mouth and chest compressions. There's no movement. No sudden sputtering of salt water and a sigh of relief from the crowd. New volunteers step in to take over the efforts. No sigh of relief from the crowd. After a few minutes of compressions, the guy in the yellow suit stops being a guy and becomes a corpse.

Distant sirens now pierce the air. People are crying or standing mouth agape. There is one very dead body sitting on the beach. Not a drop of blood.

"Did you *see* a shark?" a man asks Charles.

Charles shakes his head, no.

"Why'd you start yelling 'shark' if you didn't see one?" another voice shouts.

There are sharks around here. There most certainly fucking indeed *are* sharks around here – killer sharks. Tiger shark is the only name Charles knows, but he's pretty sure there are lots of varieties.

He was the last person to see this guy alive. This guy who drowned while he was right there, in front of all these people.

Charles hears another voice say, "Hey! Did you drown this guy and then yell shark?"

Only Charles isn't sure if the voice is inside his head or out. He's pretty sure it's inside, but what matters more, what panics Charles as much as the threat of a shark attack, is that he isn't sure.

Sincerely

by Lynn Beighley

Seamus sits across from me, holding my hand on top of the table.

"Jenn," he says, "Thank you for coming. I know you weren't supposed to." He pauses. "I've wanted to be alone with you for a long time." He rubs his thumb across the palm of my hand and I'm getting goosebumps. "I want ..."

"How's your dinner? Can I get you anything?" The perky waitress is back. She's smiling at Seamus. And at the camera that's aimed at us. She's ignoring me, which is refreshingly odd, given the attention I get every time I go out. Maybe she doesn't know who I am.

"Another round?"

"Oh, of course, right away!" There's a word for how she's acting. What is it? Oh, unctuous. She's unctuous. I think she's trying to schmooze Seamus and America.

She glances at me and mouths "bitch." She's not trying to be sneaky. It's exaggerated, so the viewers at home will know that she, like them, hate me. Seamus didn't notice, but Mike, the producer standing behind Seamus did see it, and he's pointing at Miss Perky. I'm supposed to confront her, I guess, but before I can come up with the beginning of an idea about how to react, she's gone. Mike does the shooting himself in the head with a finger gesture.

"You were saying? You want ... ?" I want Seamus to finish that sentence. He wants what? To take me home and make passionate, hot love to me? To get married and have 1.8 kids and a mixed-breed shelter dog? Dessert? What does he want?

"I want … to go to the bathroom," he says, destroying all my plans for either the next 12 hours or 50 years, depending.

I'm alone and the waitress returns. She puts my drink in front of me with enough force to slosh a few drops out of the glass.

"You don't deserve to be happy, Jenn. You're a whore and everyone hates you." She says this while smiling at the camera, so it doesn't have quite the impact she perhaps intended.

"Tell me what you really think. After you bring us a dessert menu," I say. And smile at her. Not a great comeback, but not too bad, considering. Mike shrugs, which I guess is better than suicide by index finger.

Perks huffs and stomps off. Seamus returns and kisses me on the mouth before he sits down. He picks up my hand again.

"Jenn, I want you to listen to me." What? What? Of course I'm listening. But he's not looking at me. He's staring at something behind me.

"I want what's best for you, Jenn. And, well, all those people who voted care about you. They think you should be with Bill." I am flabbergasted. I am gobsmacked. My mouth is open, but I have no words.

"Bill loves you. America knows it. You'd know it too, if you'd give him a chance." Seamus stands. "He's here for you. And you need to be with him."

Seamus is dead to me. Dead.

Mike is grinning like a loon. This was a setup. Well, every time the camera is aimed at me, it's a setup. So I'm not surprised when Seamus turns and walks just out of camera range to stand next to Mike, and yeah, there's Bill, plodding towards me like he does.

What do I do now? If I leave, I'll be hated even more. The show will love it, though, and I'll get more money for all kinds of things. If I stay, the show will love it, because everyone will keep waiting for me to yell or leave. And I'll make more money.

And I've gotten pretty fond of the money. I make money for selling pictures and giving interviews, and I get paid for every second I'm on camera. And now I wonder, what could I do that no one would expect? What could I do that would make me even more money because no one expected it and it would make me even more famous. Or infamous. What should I do?

There is no scenario I can come up with where I won't make more money. That's good, right?

Bill hands me a giant, and I mean GIANT box of Valentine's Day candy. It's July. And it's hot.

"Jenn, I forgive you," Bill says. "You don't need to apologize. Be very careful when you eat these candies, the label says they may contain shell fragments."

What to do? I sip my wine. I open the box. They look okay. I grab four pieces and stuff them all in my mouth.

"OWW, MY TOOF!" I yell, as I pretend to be in great pain. I slip off my chair and writhe around on the floor.

Storm Brewing

by Andrew Stancek

A storm is brewing. Mom is clattering forks and polishing glasses in the kitchen. A pot lid bounces on the floor like a drum but her humming continues uninterrupted. We used to sing that one together, full-voiced, and laugh. *In the Summertime When the Weather is High,* Mungo Jerry. "Life's for living, yeah, that's our philosophy." Been a while since we felt like singing together.

I'm so attuned to temperature, to barometric pressure, to moisture in the air, that I'd be a terrific TV weatherman. I'd just have to work on that bouncy manner, pasted smile and pretense that the temperature in Arizona or rain in Montana is important. This sensitivity to weather is something else I can't take credit for, another side effect of my illness and the concentration on flight, and now it's become second nature.

It's thrilling to hear Mom humming, her mind on something other than Adam, Adam, madamimadam. She must be so tired of me, my gift a curse. Back before the flying, when I was just a sick normal boy, she and Dad would sit together at the kitchen table and play Crazy Eights. She liked to win. Her tongue would wet the corner of her lips when she was about to put down a winning card and she'd laugh hard scooping up the pennies. She's a soprano, but her laugh came from deep within and was throaty, gurgly. She should have had another baby, a normal boy, or even better a little girl she could dress up and teach how to cook and sew. But I guess once I got sick, she and Dad didn't like each other well enough for another child. By then it was over between them. A friend might make her laugh, but she lost track of friends with her devotion to me, too. Maybe we should fly to see her sister. I'll just spread my wings and … A bad joke. I don't have the balance or strength to carry anyone and she wouldn't want to be carried. But she's never dated since Dad left and she should. I wonder if Professor Langeweile is married. He wore no ring and he made me laugh.

This storm is making me uneasy, low pressure and clouds gathering. My joints are sore, like I have growing pains, my eyeballs throb, muscles twitch, everything's out of tune. My nose is filled with the stench of rotting meat.

I wasn't supposed to figure out the flying, I think. It's just not right for humans to fly. In the Old Testament stories Mom read me, when the Israelites worship the golden calf or Assyrian gods, bang! they're hit with the wrath of God. Not a great analogy, I know. I'm not worshipping a damn thing but I still have this foreboding.

When Prometheus brought down fire from Mount Olympus, it could not be taken back, could not be extinguished, and he sure as hell was zapped for his sin. Ever-growing liver, what a nightmare. That's what the Church calls everlasting torment, I guess. Always in pain, always a body part growing, always living with the knowledge it'll get ripped out of you with a sharp beak, no blackouts and no anesthetic, always certain it will never stop, that is hell.

Fire.

Flying.

They're similar. If I'm guilty like Prometheus, then I'll have to suffer like he did. Does. For eternity.

Mom shouldn't be on her own right now. Even more so once I'm punished forever and she's lost me. She's a young woman still. In the movies divorced women date all the time and I'm sure she could find someone nice. When the tabloids were after me, wanting to find out every juicy tidbit, a pretty reporter put her small hand on top of mine and asked about my girlfriends and snorted when I said I didn't have any, that I was busy with birds and research and disease. I think if Mom hadn't been there, she might have offered to be my girlfriend for a night or two, to get a story, a sensational headline. Mom doesn't have Perthes, or a flying gift or a contagious disease, only a wingy son and she shouldn't have to live with pain and be alone.

When I close my eyes I see white lab coats and uniforms, and sometimes I don't even have to close my eyes. That thunder and lightning were so close to each other, it must be a tree in our backyard that was hit. I hope it's not the willow. I hope the birds are okay.

Someone's banging on the door, ignoring the bell, making the house frame shake. *After great pain, a formal feeling comes,* says Dickinson. Mom's not answering the door so I'll go see. I'm chilled, in a stupor. Time for letting go.

A Woman with a Cat

by Rachel Ambrose

"Seriously?" Blake demands of his car, jamming the key deeper into the ignition. The car's engine is making some kind of apologetic whining noise, perhaps as recompense for not starting up like it should. Sorry, boss, I can't today. I feel the need to empathize. I haven't really been the most reliable of employees lately myself, as I've been taking a greater number of sick days than usual, mostly because getting out of bed is harder these days than it really should be. After eliciting another high-pitched groan from the car, Blake turns to me. "I guess we're stuck," he says, running a hand through his thick hair. "You wouldn't happen to have AAA, would you?"

"Of course I don't," I say, feeling bad about it. AAA would be so helpful right now: just pick up a phone and wait for a tow truck. I should have AAA. "But at least it's a beautiful day!" I say, gesturing to the park around us. "And we still have wine from lunch!" We had decided to take the gorgeous July day and go out to the lake, where we brought sandwiches and a very good riesling and chocolates that slowly melted in our hands. But now that we are done and ready to head off to Blake's house for a little afternoon delight, the car won't cooperate.

Blake rolls his eyes at me. "Yeah, great," he says grumpily. "That'll be a good one, the tow truck showing up and both of us sloshed. Fabulous idea, Claire."

I open my mouth and close it again, hurt. "No, I suppose you're right," I manage to squeak past the sudden lump in my throat. "Sorry, just trying to lighten the mood a bit." I try for a laugh, but it comes out strangled and strange, catching in my teeth.

"Well, don't," says Blake. "Say, what do you want to do after this year?"

"Not sure," I reply, not liking where this conversation is going in the least. First he's scolding me, then he's asking me constructive questions about the future. This is going to end horribly, I just know it. "Maybe travel some? I haven't really thought about it."

"No, and I knew that that was going to be your answer," he says, sighing. "You just don't have any ambition, Claire. You're colorless. That's why I have never wanted to paint your portrait, because nothing could be more boring than a beige model in a white background."

I close my eyes and hear myself saying, "not even sepia?" while the blood pounds in my ears, and I knew it, I knew deep down that this was too good to be true, and I want to get out of the car now, before I start crying.

"No, Claire, not even sepia," Blake says, and I grab for the door handle and catapult myself out, the one thing I've done all day that feels like propulsion rather than stasis, and lurch in my pockets for my phone. I stab at the touch screen and listen to the phone ring at the other end, and whisper through trembling lips to my best friend, "Isa? I'm at the lake and I need you to come get me."

Twenty minutes later, after I've secured myself up a tree with the bottle of riesling and have deafened my ears against Blake's half-hearted apologies, Isa pulls up in her tiny car. "Fuck off, you bleeding turd of an asshole," she says calmly to Blake when he asks her for a jump. "Claire, disengage yourself from that tree and that bottle of wine, because I sure as hell am not getting pulled over on an open container violation. Go on, now, put it down and get over here." I toss the bottle in the grass, not caring that a small trickle of wine comes out, slide down the tree and stumble over to Isa's car. She has the radio blasting, and when she asks me where I want to go, I say, "animal shelter" and when she frowns at me, I say, "I want a cat."

More accurately, I want to be the kind of woman who has a cat, who holes up with her cat in her apartment that is artfully messy but altogether hers, well, hers and the cat's. Maybe that's my goal for next year, I think. To be a woman with a cat, to own the cat and the apartment and herself, utterly and completely. But to be a woman with a cat, you have to first acquire a cat. So off to the shelter we zoom, while I drink an entire bottle of Gatorade and make sure I have an ID and a pen, so that I can sign papers for adopting a cat.

An hour after that, we walk into the shelter, which smells strongly of animal and bleach and somehow, also, grease. Walking up to the front desk, I say to the lady standing there tapping on a computer keyboard, "Do you have any cats for adoption? Not kittens, full grown cats, maybe a tom cat," and she looks me up and down, and sniffs, but leads me into a room that is full to bursting with tabby cats, marmalade cats, fat cats and skinny cats. Looking around, I settle on one cat who's looking at me, quizzically, as though asking himself, what is she doing here? and he's huge and fluffy and the color of the pavement after a rain. The lady says his name is Diogenes and that he has been here longer than any of the other cats, and that he's terribly picky about his food, and I say, "that's fine, but so am I, so we'll understand each other."

Dildon't

by Gill Hoffs

I was meant to be doubling up with another woman for this client, but then Zhara fell asleep on the grass in the park. Her sunstroke means I'm working alone today.

Usually, I wouldn't mind. Usually, I'm happiest working one-to-one, or one-to-two, or three, or four, but with clients as companions, not my colleagues. It's more difficult to switch to fantasy work mode with someone present who you've borrowed tampons from and swapped whore-stories with.

But I'm not sure about this guy.

His eyes flick about too quickly, his voice pitches from high to low like his balls are dropping instead of swinging damp and hairy below a runty cock as he paces round the hotel room, watching me undress. It doesn't take long, I've only the thinnest of silk blouses on and a pleated black skirt that swishes as I toss it to the floor, and nothing underneath. With most clients I find my nudity empowering, but with this one I just feel vulnerable. He keeps licking his lips, more nervous than he should be for a repeat customer, and the thought of his tongue poking into my mouth or most intimate crevices repels me. I keep my heels on, as detailed in his form back at the office, and brush the tip of my index finger against the grotesque glans of a dildo, lumpen and purple and thick as a toddler's arm.

"Where do you want … me?" I draw out my words and lick my lips back at him, but seductively. I hope.

He pounces and I land awkwardly on the bed with him on top, penis stabbing me, sliming at the top of my thigh, my legs half on half off the mattress. I'm uncomfortable and unable to change position but murmur "Oh baby!" like it's just wonderfully erotic nonetheless. He will *not* be a repeat customer of mine. I'll be sure to tell Zoe to mark him down as a Never Again on my file when I get back to the agency.

"Dirty … bitch …" he mutters between grunts, thrusting at the palm tree I had Akisha trim out of my bush for the summer. I wonder if he knows he's not in yet, or if his runty cock is only used to pushing pudendas rather than pussies.

When he bites me, I scream.

"That's it, you dirty bitch. That's it."

There's nothing coquettish about how I push and struggle now, nothing to suggest I'm enjoying his assault in any way, shape, or form, but he's heavy, solid muscle under a layer of sweaty flab, and when I kick out my high heels connect with nothing at all. And from the way his breathing accelerates, curry fumes hot and unpleasantly moist in my ear, and the thrusting gets wetter against my pubes, I can tell he's enjoying my discomfort, my fear.

Meditations flood my mind as my shoulder pulses "Bite!" "Bite!" "That bastard's bitten you!" "Run away!" and he mutters something about my "tight little arsehole". *You cannot control the actions of others, only how you react.* Dead right. No-one from the agency will be calling me, let alone looking for me, for another hour or so. I am NOT putting up with this shit 'til then.

"Oh baby!" I fake a squeal. "Harder, harder, make me feel it. Give it to this dirty bitch. Give it to me!"

I cheer him on to climax, or try to, anyway, but the bastard slows and lifts his upper body up by pressing down on my upper arms. No eye contact, his type don't usually try to see *you*, just your body and all its possibilities, and I lick my lips and pout and take control of the situation as I lie trapped on the bed.

"Want to see this dirty girl get cleaned up?" I'm thinking a wank-scene in the shower would eat up some of the next hour nicely, and the hot water would soothe my shoulder. But he ignores me and stares at my neck like a farmer checking a chicken for Sunday dinner. Like he's working out how easily his hands would fit around it.

"You want to see me get *really* dirty?" From the twitch of his cock reviving against my thigh I gather it's a yes. "You want to see me fuck that dildo?" Twitch twitch. "I don't know if it can make me feel like you do ... maybe you could help this bad girl ... ?"

And he's off and lying next to me, just like that. I move slowly, slip back into sex-mode, though I'm sure there's blood trickling from my shoulder, and maintain the professionalism that got me into this particular escort agency in the first place. Lick my lips yet again, keep them slightly parted like I can't wait for his cock between them – yeah, right – and ease off the bed. He lies there on the burgundy covers, watching my body as I place my right foot on the bed, careful not to snag the heel on the sheets, and reach my right hand between my legs. I spread myself wide, as if butterflying a shrimp, so he can see the neat pink ridges, and moan when I pinch the fingers of my left hand together on what he probably thinks is my clit.

No twitch.

I lick my fingers.

No twitch.

Pick up the hideous purple dildo from the nearby dresser and circle its tip with my tongue.

Twitch.

Deep throat what I can of it, spreading my fingers wide along its length to make it look like it's further in than it actually is.

Twitch twitch.

Maintain the foot-on-bed-foot-on-floor position and, now the dildo's lubed up with saliva, stick the damn thing in like it's the world's largest Tampax. Both hands on the blunt end, hiding the length, half-shutting my eyes so I can watch him without making him feel too inhibited.

Twitch twitch twitch. Now it looks like a hard-on, only smaller.

I milk the wank for all it's worth, until my client moves on the bed as if preparing to come get me, and then I pull out the dildo with an unappealing (to me but going by his cock, not to him) *slurp*, change positions so I'm now kneeling on the bed with my knees well apart, bring the dildo to my mouth so I can drool plenty of spit on it, and lean forward, weight on one hand, so my arse is high in the air.

"What do you want to go where?" I ask, hoping he doesn't want to toe-fuck me as I can smell his feet over the dewberry-fragranced potpourri in the en suite. I wiggle the dildo a little to tempt him and wonder what Zoe would say to my idea of using the larger dildos as hand-weights if we ever go to a keep-fit class.

And he's at me from behind, thrusting, poking me without lubrication, without even fucking *warning* me. I move my legs, angle my buttocks so they take the brunt of his attentions, his balls swinging against them with every push, and I think "Okay, a bit of ice on my arse tonight and this is bearable" and how there's only maybe another forty minutes or so to go before I can leave but still consider this appointment 'kept' instead of run out on, and then – oh boy – then he uses one hand to pull my hair back hard and reaches with the other for my throat.

This is where our 'date' ends.

I have this one breath left and it's already burning in my chest and throat.

I won't be able to reach his head, his eyes, or anything similarly vulnerable from my current position. Nobody's coming, except, I surmise from his grunts, perhaps him.

I still have the dildo in my hand.

Reaching between my legs I stab awkwardly up and as luck would have it get him *right* in the arsehole *thwack!* He lets go of my hair and throat and squeals, and I feel the warm wet splatter of a satisfied client up my back.

I'm out from under him and grab my clothes from the floor as I strut to the door. I leave his room naked and stride down the corridor in my heels, like I don't give a shit who sees my wounds. And I don't. Then I walk to the lift doors, press the down button, and pull on the expensive top I bought for an ex's wedding and the skirt I know I won't wear again as I wait without turning to check behind me while my escape reaches me from the floor below. When I'm safe, I can cough and cry and swear and be weak.

Nobody comes after me.

My blouse and skirt are sticking to my back and shoulder. They're ruined.

But I'm not.

I add skirt – blouse – ice-pack – plasters to the mental list of things the agency needs to reimburse me for, along with dildo. And start thinking about whether Amsterdam brothels would really be better for me.

Tide

by Susan Tepper

This morning a woman near the oranges tries conversing with him by saying the market keeps the fruit aisle too cold. Pedersen only nods. It seems to give her a signal to go on talking. She isn't bad if women are your thing. When she knocks down an orange from the stack, and a bunch tumble after, he bends to help pick them up. She smiles showing a cracked front tooth; the angle such – that makes a woman look sassy. It won't help, he's thinking, smiling back and moving to the next aisle. Tide. He lifts it by the red handle.

On Fourth of July he'd lit some rockets in the park designated: NO BALL PLAYING, NO FISHING (in the pond), NO ICE-SKATING, NO PICNICS, NO DOGS, NO NUDITY. The sign didn't mention rockets. Pedersen had gone in through the hole he cut in the fence some months earlier; the one blocked by creeper, now, and poison ivy. He wasn't allergic so he didn't cover up.

The first rocket had failed. The second one zinged like a comet leaving its red tail in the black sky. Making him feel alive for the first time in weeks. Weeks since the grammar schools had shut for summer, his little darlings taken away. Shipped off to damp camp grounds and grandparents. Old gnarled hands grabbing them in attic hallways. He knew.

He was about to set off the third rocket, then decided to hold it. Pedersen wasn't sure exactly why.

He carries his Tide swinging it by the red handle – same color the rocket left in the sky. This summer being one long drone aimed at tearing up dusty villages. Places where people talk like they've got food stuck in their windpipes. Pedersen guffaws. The *oranges woman* comes around his other side from the cookie aisle. "It's Kismet," she says grinning.

"Yeah." He squints at the chipped tooth.

She looks down at his Tide. "Industrial strength."

He knows if he takes her home he will hurt her.

Risk and Reward

by Jessica McHugh

Sitting in the sacristy, Edward McKenzie slides his hand over the Lost and Found jar. He's here again. After a month of soldiering through fear, after battling demons that spoke in his mother's slurred voice, he's still here, thinking about the lipstick.

His last class at St. Anthony's ended earlier today, and though most of the other teachers lingered to praise their students' achievements, Father Edward bolted right after the bell, seeking the sanctuary of the sacristy. He survived teaching an eighth grade health studies class, and he wasn't about to push his luck.

Looking into the Lost and Found, the tube of lipstick shines purple amidst pale garbage. He plucks it from castaways, pulls off the lid, and twists the merlot shaft from the tube. He imagines sliding the creamy lipstick across his mouth. Surely a hint of color couldn't hurt, just a quick congratulations on a job well done at St. Anthony's.

His eyes roll upward as the tube nears his lips. "Tell me it's wrong," he whispers. "Give me a sign. Strike me down if you must."

As usual, God offers no reply. But Grandma Eleanor does. Standing in the sun-drenched corner of the room, she's barely visible, but her encouragement is clear enough. At the touch of the merlot lipstick, Edward is drunk on heaven. Waves of delight move through his body as he paints his lips, and though he knows every dip and curve, he looks into a communion plate to verify.

Or boast, he supposes.

You look lovely, dear.

Edward scoffs. "You have to say things like that, Grandma."

Chuckling, she replies. *I certainly don't.*

He gives her a grateful nod, but looking back at his reflection, he sighs, wipes the color off, and tosses the lipstick back into the jar. Slumping down at the desk, he massages his temples and begs the tears not to fall.

A knock on the door straightens Edward's back. He clears his throat, hoping the grief will disappear before he says, "Come in."

Thanks to the summer class, Edward is now used to seeing Nelson Wade in street clothes rather than the surplice he wears as an altar boy, but he's surprised to see him so soon. Entering the sacristy slowly, he gives the priest a small wave.

Edward smiles, but the boy doesn't reciprocate. He leans against the wall, his face somber. "Nelson, what's wrong?" he asks.

"I know, Father Edward."

"You know what?"

He furrows his brow and sighs. "I *know.*"

Grandma Eleanor stands beside Nelson, her hand on his shoulder and eyes fixed on Edward. She nods to her grandson, who sits down, his head bowed.

"I'm sorry, Father Edward," Nelson continues. "I didn't mean to spy – the first time, it was an accident. I saw you with the lipstick and –"

Edward holds up his hand. "You don't have to go on."

"I think I do," he says, stepping forward. "I stood outside this time. I watched you. I watched you put on the lipstick."

56

Edward turns away, shaking his head. Eleanor appears in front of him, smiling. Why, in the name of all that's holy, is she happy to see her grandson's biggest secret exposed?

"You don't have to admit anything to me, Father," Nelson continues. "You're close enough to God to know what's right."

It's a knife in his heart – painful if Nelson doesn't approve of his lifestyle, and worse if he does. Edward *should* be close enough to know what's right. But what Nelson says next dulls the anguish, like Grandma Eleanor's whisper as she tucked him into bed when he was young.

"I know it's not my place, but you don't seem that happy, Father. Maybe it's because you're not being true to yourself," he says. "You should do what makes you happy."

He looks over his shoulder at the boy. How could a fourteen-year-old so easily articulate what he's spent his entire life trying to grasp?

"I should go, but ..." He gives the priest a small smile. "With all the hearts you touch every week, Father, I figured you deserved to know that feeling, too."

Eleanor leaves with Nelson Wade. She seems to know her grandson craves her advice, but she says nothing. Nelson has already said it all.

The boy's voice resounds in Edward's mind, warming his heart. "Do what makes you happy."

Alone again, Edward reaches into the Lost and Found jar and pockets the lipstick.

Accidents and Emerging Seas

by Shane Simmons

"Hey," I look up to where the voice came from, "anyone sitting here?" An armful of tattoos points to the space beside me. Shaking my head, I toss Sandra's belongings to my other side and the guy sits down. Sat in a dark corner of this function hall, I'd been ordered to wait here while she went off to 'mingle'. Twenty minutes later and still waiting for her return, I go back to fiddling with my phone.

"Don't think I've seen you around, which department do you work in?"

Great, a talker.

"Oh, I don't work at the hospital. I'm just here with someone." Scanning the floor I spot her, standing by the bar with a crowd of shrilling women. I point in her direction. "The one in the red dress, Sandra."

"Mad Sand from A&E?!"

"Mad Sand?"

He laughs, "That's her nickname, *everyone* knows Sandra!"

"That doesn't surprise me in the slightest."

Rapping his fingers on the table, the stranger gives me the impression I'm meant to continue this conversation. I raise my voice above the pounding dance beats.

"Do you work in A&E too?"

"No," he shouts back, "IT, the department everyone forgets about. What do you do?"

If I could bore him enough perhaps he'd move on to someone else.

"I work for the National Trust, digitising their archives for an online library. I spend my day taking photographs of other people's photographs and –"

"Well I thought I'd be designing award-winning games by now, instead I'm telling people to turn their workstations off and back on, all day long!" Swilling the last drop of his pint he sweeps up my empty. "Fancy a top up?"

Whilst he's away, Sandra appears in front of me, eyes swirling under half-closed lids. At her side stands a thin waif in the slimmest, tightest jeans I've ever seen.

"Ahh babes, you're still here ... where I left you ..." she slurs, "This ... is Adam!" She directs her hand up and down his slight frame as if she's introducing the cheap prizes on a game show. "He's sing–" But the IT guy barges past carrying two fresh pints.

"Alright, Sand."

As he sits back down she furrows her brow at him. *"Who – are – you?!"*

He pokes my shoulder, "What did I say, no one knows who we are!" He turns back to Sandra, "It's Callum! We have met before!"

She glares at him, turns and gives me a crooked evil eye before snatching up Adam's hand and yanking him away.

"Well, she *is* called Mad Sand for a reason!" he shouts. "And that stick insect, gayer than a mouthful of cocks!" His right hand slaps down onto my left thigh and he chortles. I squirm around on the sticky plastic leather seat. "Huh."

To my right I notice a mound of jackets and coats which has built up on the edge of the seat, abandoned by those now cavorting the night away. I see Sandra grinding up against the stick insect from earlier, her bra straps glowing pure white under the dance floor spotlights.

"I dunno about you but I'm getting tired of shouting over this lot. I know a cracking bar up the road where the beer doesn't taste like watered down piss!"

As I say it I imagine curling up on the sofa, getting away from the music and all these people I don't know. "Cheers, but I think I'll call it a night. This music's giving me a headache."

"Ah, come on," he looks at his watch, "it's early!"

He strides up the road, "It's only a few minutes from here!"

Inside, the décor looks a bit poncy, low-lights, small groups talking over the murmur of quiet music, a world away from where we've come from.

"You ever tried any of these?" He points to the selection of alien beer bottles.

I poke my neck over the bar. "Tried? There's not one I've heard of."

He grins as he rubs his hands together. "In that case, leave the selecting to me!"

Soon he passes over a bottle, a chalice glass and leads the way to an empty table.

I scan the label, "Delirium Tremens? 8.5%? Pretty strong for a beer, isn't it?"

"Oh, there's far more potent stuff in here!"

All of a sudden the beer bladder strikes. I'll be pissing away the rest of the night.

As I saunter towards the toilets he calls after me, "You had enough yet?"

When I get back there's a different bottle, dripping condensation onto the table.

"Straff ... Hen ... I can't say – Eleven percent?!"

"Yep, this one will really knock your socks off!"

Inside the taxi each speed bump churns my insides. Gassy beer rises in my throat and I taste the sickening bile from my empty stomach. I belch, and wish I'd eaten something earlier on.

I trail him up flights of stairs until we reach the top. Keys jingle in a door.

"Make yourself at home."

I slump on the sofa, but the room swirls of its own accord.

He places a cold bottle in my hand and sits down. "Compared to the last one you had this stuff is virtually water!" His elbow nudges mine.

Picking up the remote, he channel-hops before landing on a station playing heavy rock music and proceeds to nod his head, tap his feet.

"You're Sandra's gay pal, aren't you?"

"Eh?"

"I overheard her the other day, said she was bringing her gay friend to the party. You are the guy she was talking about, aren't you?"

In a sobering moment of clarity, I realise I don't know this guy from jack, but he knows more about me than he should. I'm in his flat which is god knows where and I'm catching up on a game I didn't realise was being played.

I open my eyes wide. Take a deep breath. Squint, try to focus.

"Look, I really should be heading off. I thought that taxi was going to drop me off first ..."

"Aww, come on, at least finish your beer!" His left hand slaps down on my right knee and he takes another swig from his bottle. His hand still on my leg.

Which starts creeping so, so slowly, edging its way upwards.

I'm aware of every stuttered breath I take. I lift the bottle to my lips, take a gulp that sticks in my throat.

I turn to peek at him. He's staring straight at the television screen. Am I so drunk I'm imagining this?

His hand pauses, his fingers stroke the inner reaches of my thigh.

Leaping up, my beer spills down the expensive (for my budget at least) shirt Sandra had picked out for the night.

But he rises calmly. Takes the bottle from my hand and puts it down on the table.

"Best get you out of this, eh?" He smiles. His words, his movements are smooth and cool and undeterred by my abrupt reaction.

"Look ... I –"

He pops open the top button.

I spot the bulge, tenting his jeans.

"Fuck, fuck, fuck ..." I mutter under my breath as his hands close in. He unbuttons the last one and peels open the beery cotton from my skin.

"Come on." He takes my hand, leads me towards the hall.

As we pass the front door, he stops, twists the deadbolt. Flashes me a cheeky smile.

Plastic

by Michelle Elvy

Stevie rides fast. He glides along smooth straightaways and pedals up hills. He's in a hurry, but he's not sure why. She said she'd be there all day – so what's the rush? She said it casually – *come by later*. He really doesn't have to go there *now*. He should wait a while. He should take his time.

His feet pedal faster.

But when he arrives at No. 4 Rock Road and stands in front of the house, sweat dripping down his face and sticking his shirt to his back and chest, he really wishes he had pedalled his Schwinn slower. He's suddenly aware that he smells bad, and that his hair is dirty, and that he is so, so thirsty. He thinks he should ride back home, shower, and come back *later*, like she said – possibly walking. He doesn't even know what to say to her now that he's standing at her door. He runs a hand through his sweaty hair, turns to leave.

But the door opens and the girl standing before him smiles wide and says, "Stevie! I thought you'd never come!"

It's not her. It's Sylvie, her little sister. Relief and disappointment.

The last time he was here was four months back, in March. It was accidental that he came to this house that day, and it was because of Sylvie. He'd come across the small girl wandering up the road looking for her canary, and he'd helped her find it and then bury it in the backyard. He has not seen Sylvie since, so now he's not sure what to say.

"Are you coming in?" Sylvie asks. Her hair is in disarray, one bit flying up distractingly from her left temple, and she's wearing pajamas. Stevie has seen these before – it's the same pair of cat-and-mouse pajamas Sylvie was wearing that day in March.

He smiles. "Do you only ever wear those pajamas?"

"These are my lucky pajamas," she says matter-of-factly. She is tiny, and carries something of a Yoda-like wisdom about her that both intrigues and scares Stevie.

Stevie does not know why she's wearing her lucky pajamas, but before he can ask Sylvie takes his hand and pulls him across the threshold.

"You've come on the right day. I just made lemonade."

She leads him into the kitchen, where there is an assortment of flowers scattered across the table – roses, carnations, tulips, freesia, lillies. They are all yellow.

"These are for Yellow Bird," says Sylvie. "I am re-burying him today."

Stevie suddenly feels queasy. He buried this bird once, all muddy and mangled from bouncing off a car bumper. He does not want to bury it again. He can imagine this small girl – is she five or six, he can't recall – digging up the bones of her bird and burying him all over again, for whatever strange reason. He knows if this is her plan there will be no arguing with her. He does not know Sylvie well, but he understands her will. *She's a force of nature*, Ellie had once said, and on the day he'd helped bury Yellow Bird the first time, Stevie could see why.

But he does not want to bury this bird again. He does not want to bury anyone or anything again. He went last month to Lucky's grave with Manny – on graduation day. They had lain in the large patch of daffodils that surrounded their friend's grave, and they both felt something akin to peace. Finally. But he's not been back to the cemetery since, and he has no intention of playing undertaker or preacher again for this small girl.

Her Yoda eyes look up at him. Stevie wishes he could drink a large glass of lemonade and then just leave. He searches for the right words and opens his mouth to tell Sylvie he can't help her today.

He says, "How can I help?"

He's only ever been to this house twice, and both times he has meant to see Ellie but has instead found himself fully engaged with her six (or is she five?)-year-old sister. And both times it's been because of her lost canary.

"You can help pull all the petals off the flowers," she replies. He looks quizzically at her and she offers an obvious explanation: "Well they won't all fit on a bird's grave, now will they? We're going to scatter the petals over it. Like potpourri."

"Do you put flowers on Yellow Bird's grave a lot?"

"Pretty often."

"Some people use plastic flowers."

"Not me."

"They last forever."

"They're dead. And they don't smell like anything. And nothing lasts forever."

They sit at the table, pulling petals off the flowers and placing them on a large red plate. Sylvie seems content in silence, and Stevie does not feel compelled to talk either, though he wonders where Ellie is. He marvels at the peaceful nature of this small child, how singularly focused she seems to be on the mission at hand. He likes this kind of focus, the clarity of the moment.

"Why today, of all days?"

"Today is the four-month anniversary of Yellow Bird's death," says Sylvie. "I had him four months, then he died. I want his grave to be especially pretty today."

"Seems like a nice idea," says Stevie, but he's wondering whether the girl should just get a cat or a mouse to go with her pajamas. Yellow Bird requires a lot of care, even four months underground.

Just then the kitchen door opens and Ellie walks in. Stevie's glad to see her but then he remembers his sweaty shirt and dirty hair, and he feels clammy all over. To accompany his grime, his palms now exude a sickeningly sweet aroma from the flower petals. He feels Sylvie staring up at him with her taskmaster eyes.

Ellie approaches the table and stands next to Stevie. He hopes the floral aroma will cover his sweaty stench.

"Ready, buttercup?" says Ellie to her sister.

"Yes."

"Let's go then."

Stevie follows the two sisters out the screen door and into the backyard. When they get to the corner where Yellow Bird is buried, Sylvie hands Stevie the plate of flower petals. She goes into the shed and returns with a bag of mulch, which she spreads over what is a very large grave for a very small bird. She then dips her hands into the petals and lets them fall all over the grave. Softly, softly, they cover the ground, and as they fall Stevie feels silly for worrying about something so mundane as body odor. Sylvie is a tiny kid, but he can almost hear her heartbeat, huge and focused solely on loving this small dead thing in the ground. He realizes that Sylvie is the most extraordinary person he's ever met.

Later, sitting on the front porch with Ellie, he admits admiring a six (or is she five?)-year-old. "Your sister's amazing, you know."

"Yeah. I know," is all Ellie says.

He doesn't know what else to say. He doesn't know why he's here, or how he's gotten so entangled with Sylvie and Yellow Bird. It's their story, but somehow he's in it.

66

He's thinking of the million things he wants to say to Ellie when she breaks the silence.

"You're leaving?"

"Yeah. Florida. How'd you ..."

"Heard through the grapevine."

Silence again. He wishes Sylvie would show up. She'd say the right thing. She'd bring lemonade. Instead it's Ellie who speaks again.

"I just want you to know I think Rick's a complete knob."

"Oh." Woah. He did not see that coming. "Uh, yeah, me, too."

"Sylvie told me you suggested using plastic flowers."

He can't follow the turns in this conversation, if that's what you could really call it. Are they done with Rick already? He'd like to add a few adjectives on the subject of Rick. "Knob" is only the beginning – but it's a good beginning, especially coming from Ellie. "Ummm ..."

"Sylvie and I hate plastic flowers. Our mother used to have them scattered all over the house. So fucking stupid. She even had one of those little vases in her car – with plastic flowers – stuck down with duct tape. Don't know why. It's like no one told her she didn't have to be this stereotype, you know? The chain-smoking alcoholic redneck whose house and car look like she should live in a trailer park? And she uses plastic plates too. When I was little – before I could do any chores like wash dishes – we had plastic plates. Took me a long time to figure out she was too drunk to wash up after a meal, so she used disposable plates and silverware. Can you believe it? Born with a plastic spoon in our mouths."

"That's ... weird."

"So one day, I just got sick of it. Took all the plastic out of the house – spoonsforksknivesflowersplatesvases – and drove it to the dump. Our house is less colourful now. But Sylvie and I eat off our parents' wedding china."

Bitterness seethes through Ellie's chuckle.

"Where'd Sylvie get the flowers for the grave?"

"Martha Stewart's garden, next door." Stevie looks blank so she adds, "It's what we call the neighbor. She's like polar opposite to our mom – perfect garden, perfect house, perfect hair, perfect nails. Her name is Martha. But not Stewart. We just call her that."

Stevie is still trying to follow where this is all going when Ellie takes his hand. "Come inside with me," she says quietly. He thinks they are going back to the kitchen but instead they turn at the hallway and head toward the stairs.

Ellie's quiet footfall leads the way up each wooden stair, her toes showing just a tiny bit of pearly pink polish. Her shorts swish against her inner thighs as they barely touch with each step. A sweet-sour perspiration and fruity shampoo mingle in the air with Stevie's dried sweat. By the time they reach the landing, the hairs on his arms rise up softly and he feels the back of his neck prickle. He licks his lips and wonders if he has bad breath. But none of that matters when Ellie turns and pulls his lips down to hers. They kiss softly in the hallway, and when they finally reach her room and sit on her bed and she pulls his t-shirt up over his head, all he can smell is *her*, every molecule of her breath, her hair, her freckles, her eyelashes, the beads of sweat on her upper lip … He feels a singular focus wash over him for the first time in a long while, a clarity of the moment. He hears a noise downstairs and his mind flits briefly to Sylvie, but then he is back in this moment, where he stays the rest of the afternoon.

In the evening, Ellie and Stevie join Sylvie in the kitchen. She has made dinner. They eat mac and cheese on china plates and drink lemonade from Waterford crystal.

Rave

by Len Kuntz

In Austin, I find myself at a party where everything glows –
walls, ceilings, clothes, flesh, tongues, eye balls. I'm not
sure if what I'm seeing is real or if the Roofies I took are
kicking in. The floors rattle and bounce and keep jumping
up, as if they're trying to sit in my lap, even though I'm
upright, dancing in the middle of a crowded kitchen, with
Rylie, a girl young enough to be the daughter I never had,
who's wearing Daisy Dukes and a plaid shirt knotted high
above her belly button. The stereo plays country hip-hop, a
genre I hadn't known existed. DJ Rusty Crawdad spins
music on the kitchen counter where earlier a heap of dirty
dishes had been. Now he works the needle, or dials, or
some such things with one hand while the other makes
lasso motions in the air as a croaky-voiced singer growls,
"And I'm a Kid Rock it up and down your block, buy a
bottle of scotch and watch lots of crotch."

Rylie does a sloppy stumble into my chest. For a
moment I'm afraid she's either passed out, or dead, but
then she says, "Isn't this fruckin great," slurring hard before
biting my earlobe.

I met Rylie at Starbucks where she was working, where
she remade my double-mocha-ginger-spice-no-foam-chia-
tea-latte three times without ever getting it right. Rylie was
worried I'd complain to her boss, and as a favor, she invited
me to this country-themed "Rave."

I hadn't thought I'd come, but once I did, I hadn't thought Rylie would give me the time of the day, though upon seeing me, Rylie pressed her huge breasts against me and squealed. "I'm so glad you showed. You're, like, the hottest old guy I know." To wit, I thought: I hadn't realized we knew each other. I hadn't thought forty-two was all that old.

Rylie has a lot of friends who are just as gorgeous and as daft as she is. When not dancing, they huddle together, bobbing like skiffs, nodding quite a bit and tittering before any sentence is finished, even if someone's just remarking on the weather. One of them – Tessa – rubs the back of my thigh and squeezes my buttocks anytime I get near. She has diamond piercings over each eyebrow that glitter like bright, white halos. Earlier, as I was refilling my radioactive-looking cocktail, Tessa leaned in and whispered, "I bet you really know how to clean a girl's carpet."

The house we're in is a monster, containing millions of rooms and crawl spaces with their doors flung open, revealing couples engaged in all kinds of salacious acts, the participants oblivious to anyone or anything. Rylie explains it's the Sigma Chi fraternity, that their charter was revoked after a hazing incident involving a pledge and a goat in heat, and that the house has remained vacant since, except when people want to rent it for engagements such as this.

All night long Rylie hovers around me, clinging when she can, fawning and groping. Towards midnight, we end up in a room where someone's pinned a gigantic Confederate flag across one wall, with a twelve foot-long aquarium stationed on the other wall opposite it.

Rylie grabs my shirt placket and pulls me onto the bed. Her pupils are brown quarters, her mouth a trapdoor sprung open.

When she says, "It's now or never, Pappa," my stomach clutches, and I don't know if it's because of what she's inferring, or what she's called me.

The aquarium makes a steady gurgling noise that gets me dizzy. Bright, fluorescent fish flip through the gleaming clear water, leaving a trail of air bubbles in their wake.

"Kiss me like you mean it," Rylie says, tugging on my beard stubble. "Then fuck me like you don't."

I'm tempted, of course, but I push her away instead.

Rylie grabs fistfuls of my hair and yanks and yanks, shrieking like a cat with its tail caught in the garbage disposal. I think she's having an epileptic attack, or some such thing, so I pull her inside my chest, which is slick with Rave-induced sweat, and hold her there, as if trying to calm a frightened pet.

I say, "It's okay."

I say, "Everything's all right."

She asks me again to do things to her. She says she'll call me Daddy. She says that's what all the boys like.

I cup Rylie's hands. Over her head, in the tank, a rainbow-striped fish hovers by the glass, as if listening and watching.

"What happened?" I ask. "You can tell me. Go ahead. What happened to you when you were little?"

Seventh Inning

by Michael Webb

I wait for her to come to bed. It is the All Star Break, otherwise known as Christmas in July for the lonely / horny major leaguers who aren't selected for the Midsummer Classic. I try to minimize the distraction I cause, but it's always an issue, a week without me interrupted by sudden Daddy overload. Even if the team is home, I'm constantly leaving before they go to bed, missing activities, missing out, becoming an absentee father, absentee husband, just the guy who brings home the money that pays for the lessons and the shoes, the manicures and the brand name handbags.

She comes in, finally having addressed the last of the requests for water and stories and reassurances that permission slips were signed for the camp trip to the zoo tomorrow. I watch her prepare for bed, the television on silently behind her back as she brushes her hair out at her makeup table. I watch the way her Arizona State t-shirt flexes and moves with her body. She is still the woman I married, but somehow more refined. Children have made her more serious, thicker, more grounded. Someone to take seriously. She is as beautiful as she ever was. And she mentioned thinking about a third child, and my pulse thrummed excitedly at the prospect of trying to make that happen. Perhaps tonight.

"Lucasita called me this morning," she says.

"Oh?" I say, not knowing what to add.

"Yes, I guess she sees me as a mentor. Or something. All this is new to her. Being a mom, being a ballplayer's wife. All of it."

"I suppose it must be," I say evenly. Her voice is too bright for the conversation, like she is trying too hard to sound casual.

"She asked me if you were out last night," she says. She knows I wasn't. Yesterday, the first day of the All Star break I spent with her, going on the camp run, shopping for groceries, then odds and ends at Target before a spinach salad for lunch and the reverse trip in the afternoon. I probably wasn't more than a hundred feet from her the entire day. I feel a trap coming, like a high school boy trying to explain who will be supervising the party.

"You told her I was with you."

"Of course I did. And then she told me about the conversation you had with her in May. In the park. Do you remember?"

I picture Lucasita, Juan's wife, her tiny swollen feet barely touching the pedals of their gigantic car as they inched their way out of the player's parking area.

"I think so," I say carefully.

"She said you mentioned being out with him. The night before. You never told me you've been out with Juan."

"I haven't," I say softly.

"Why did you lie to her, Mark?"

"To support Juan," I say. On the TV, a computer-animated lizard is trying to sell me insurance. I swallow hard, suddenly needing a glass of water. Or a beer.

"What does that mean?"

"Juan's a teammate," I say, hating how lame it feels even as I hear the words coming out. "We support each other. We're brothers. I cover for him, because he saves my ass in the field. Saves runs, which lowers my ERA, which raises my asking price, which makes the money that pays

73

for our beautiful house," I say, standing up and moving towards the bathroom. "The money that pays for all those Manolo Blahniks you love so much," I say a little too loudly.

"That's not fair, Mark," she says, tugging at the tangles at the end of her hair. "And you know it. I could have gone to law school. I had the grades. I could have paid for my own goddamned shoes. If it's that fucking important to you, I'll sell the damn things on eBay. Are we that fucking broke?"

I pour myself the water, gulping it down in several long swallows, then sucking in a deep breath. She is staring daggers at me, her arms folded tight on her chest, the hairbrush flung aside, forgotten. "I'm sorry. It's not the shoes," I say. "I'm sorry I lied. I shouldn't have. I know."

"Say that to Lucasita," she spits bitterly.

"I know," I say quickly, my arms thrown wide as I stand against the bathroom door. "But I have to have Juan on my side. You have to understand, I can't sell him out. I can't sell him out because I need him to make plays for me. And I can't sell him out because I can't get a rep as a guy who does that!" My hands fall as I realize she isn't getting it. Or isn't buying it.

"A rep?" she says with exasperation. "A rep? What are you, a bunch of 12-year olds?"

"Essentially," I say. I think about Sam Madden, who I played with in New York, who could hit and field but was suddenly unemployable with one truthful interview too many.

"Listen, Mark," she says, standing up straight. I stare at her legs, bare and trim and perfect. "For however long we are here, Lucasita is my friend. You and Juan and you overgrown children can play your bullshit games with someone else. You don't lie to me, and you don't lie to my friend. Period. You know, Mark? That's going to be your daughter someday. Do you want some 22-year old shortstop lying to your pregnant daughter while he's out at a strip club?" I watch her pick her brush up and put it back on her makeup table, her motions fluid and precise like a dancer. I marvel at her beauty, two kids and still pretty as a schoolgirl.

She turns out the light, slipping under the covers and defiantly facing away from me. I stare at the TV screen, a busty fan flirting silently with a catcher in a shampoo commercial, the flashes of light playing across the Egyptian cotton sheets that cover her body, only a splash of hair emerging from the top.

"I swear," she says slowly. "I don't know why the fuck we put up with you."

"Ballplayers?" I say.

"Men," she says to the wall.

I consider getting up to go downstairs, but just continue to sit there, watching the All Star Game play out silently on the screen. Eventually, I think, someone will win.

From Under
His Nose

by James Claffey

The post brings a letter from the solicitors. The Bird sups the cup of tea as he reads the typewritten page, and when he gleans the message it contains, splutters the tarry brew all over the kitchen table. "By Jesus, I'll not let those bitches take the roof over my head." He slams the teacup on the table and makes a beeline for the O'Meara & McCarthy, Solicitors at Law, over on Casement Place.

Mary Igoe, with the lazy eye, perches on the desk, legs crossed, the *Irish Press* open and the radio playing the Gay Byrne Hour. The Bird's entrance sends her scurrying for the safety of behind the desk.

"How are you, Mr. Mahony?" she asks.

"Don't Mister Mahony me," he says, distracted by the one eye on the door and the other on his movements. "I want to see one of the chiefs."

"Oh, they're in conference," she says. "I can take a message and make an appointment for you."

"Appointment? For to have them steal the house from under my arse? Scutter them. Go and tell them I'm here and I'm not leaving until I see one of them." He sits in the old armchair by the window and grips the armrests as if an earthquake were about to rattle the crockery in the kitchen presses.

"I said," she says, "Conference. No appointment for you, so you'll have to make one and come back."

"Back? Back, while they're selling my home to the fucking nuns up the road?" His roaring echoes off the walls of the small office and a door opens and the bald, red-faced O'Meara of the practice emerges to see what the commotion might be.

"Oh. Mahony. Listen, if it's about the nuns and the old homestead, you've not a leg to stand on."

"You'd better explain something to me, and fast. I'll bloody open your skull if you don't," the Bird says.

"Come through, for Christ's sake. Come through, now."

The two men leave Mary Igoe one-eying the obituaries in the paper for new opportunities for the firm, and in the back office the Bird sits on the offered chair.

"Listen, your father was in debt. Sure the business was going downhill these past twenty years. He did a deal with the ladies in the convent and you're all right in the house as long as you like, but when you depart this world, the title passes to them, along with all that's in it."

The Bird scratches behind his ear. He's unsure at what he's been told. "Do you mean I can live there, but the nuns will own it when I die?"

"That's the long and the short of it, Bird." O'Meara shakes his head, holds both hands up in supplication, and says, "We're only carrying out your father's wishes, you understand."

"Why wasn't I told of it before this?"

"Aren't we only having the reading of the will this month," O'Meara says, smiling. "You'll hear it all again there."

"Bugger those old hens. They'll murder me in my bed to get the place sooner," the Bird says, standing up and making for the door. "Curse the pair of you in this bloody business," he shouts, as he departs without a backward glance at Mary Igoe, who's already spreading the news through the parish grapevine on the party phone line.

§

In the cubby where the mother kept the bread, he finds the stowed bottles and opens the first one to hand. Blue lights cracking black sky, the Bird holds his head to stop the buzzing from driving him mad. Ever since the day's post arrived with the news, ever since he discovered the nuns were on the deed and the parents had turned the house over to the bitches, he's emptied the bottle of Tullamore Dew, and is now halfway down the Smirnoff. "Vicious harpies," he says, the words a slurry of drink and venom. "And the business, too. Hearses, coffins, brass and silver fittings, all turned over to the Holy Roman Empire."

"I have my bicycle," he says, falling against the range in the kitchen. "I'll head off and find that French one, and sure we'll marry and that'll be the saving of me." More blue and black and on the way to the floor the Bird's head connects with the edge of the kitchen table and he opens a long gash that pours red on the linoleum. He sleeps fitful drunk through the midday church bells ringing out the Angelus, and some time after the rain hammers the windowpanes he groggily climbs to his feet and makes his way to the bathroom where he doses his head with mercurochrome and cotton wool.

Shock, and the specter of being swindled of his birthright combine to torment the Bird as he gathers the evidence of his morning's debauchery. He slings the empties in the dustbin outside the back door, the house number painted in white on the silver aluminum. He's a good mind to roll the dustbin down the road and fling it through the window of the convent, but he'll only end up in the barracks without any means to bail himself out. Across the road, two leather-jacketed punks creep along the path, their perfect Mohawks sharp-shadowed against the backdrop of concrete as they pass the police station.

Stutter-stepping down the path with his bicycle, the Bird is an underdog in the game of love. His ears tipped red by the brisk breeze, he sails off towards Hogan's in Clara, the rear mudguard rattling away as he maneuvers the potholes. At the corner of Main Street, McCarthy, the other solicitor, drives by in his brown Mercedes, the morning cigar dangling from his lips. The Bird haughs up a mouthful of phlegm and spits it at the passing car. "Cur," he says, and pedals away triumphant.

Still woozy from his overindulgence, he wobbles from side to side, puddles splashing his pants leg as he passes through the dirty rainwater. Off to the east the clouds darken, large, rolling cumulus, their promise of more rain nearing as they tumble towards the town. He knows the drink is behind his hopeless fantasy about Melodie and the possibility of her even being in Ireland. As his father used to say, "God loves a trier," and the Bird smiles to himself, the faint sound of his father's voice echoing in the street.

The Best Time
to Die

by Gwendolyn Joyce Mintz

Diane, who's been waiting, lifts her hand and waves when Aaron, with Phil in the passenger seat, drives up. She's sitting on the wooden FOR SALE sign staked in the lawn.

"I'd buy that," Phil says under his breath.

Aaron lets out a loud chuckle. "It's a shame you aren't taken with Diane," he says.

Phil's face colors. "I didn't mean to say that out loud. But since I've already said too much, I might as well add that she has no idea of what she brings to the world."

Nodding, Aaron lifts the handle, pushes open the door. He steps out. "That she does not. And that's what makes Mora crazy."

He shuts the door and greets Diane.

She stands and meets him in front of the car.

They chat. Then Diane heads toward the front door. Aaron raps his knuckles on the hood, gestures for Phil to join.

Phil opens the door, pulls himself out, heads, too, for the building.

It's just the three of them tonight. Mora had to work but Aaron had confessed (when he called the other two to invite them to his place) that he'd been prepared to ask her not to come.

"Your place looks different in the daytime," Diane says. "Bigger."

Aaron is twisting the key in the lock. "I only live on the bottom. My grandparents converted their house into two apartments when they moved," he continues as he opens the door. "They left it to me when they died." He gestures Diane and Phil in. "I lived with my dad's parents for a lot of my life. My parents were crazy; my grandparents, not so much."

His friends laugh.

There is no furniture in the living room except for a recliner pushed sideways against one wall. A green-plaid blanket is folded on the seat, a pillow atop it. Against the adjacent wall is a card table holding a lamp, a few books, a cup of pens and a stack of paper.

"I hope this is not your regular bachelor pad," Diane says. "Let me guess," she tells Aaron as she poses by the recliner like a game show model. "Daytime." She presses the lever and the chair falls back, leg rest up. "Nighttime."

"Exactly," Aaron replies.

She walks over to the kitchen area and peers in. "Your lap holds your meals?"

"Something like that," Aaron replies as he steps into the kitchen. "What I do still have is beer and wine. Any takers?"

They sit on the floor. Aaron, back against a wall, legs stretched before him, crossed at the ankle. Arms folded across his chest, he holds a bottled beer in one hand.

Phil leans against the recliner and Diane sits crossed-legged by the door. Both sip at plastic cups of Chardonnay.

"I can't believe it's July already," Diane says.

"I didn't think I'd still be here," Phil adds.

Aaron grunts. "You should be dead by now, huh?"

Diane tells Aaron that "just yesterday" they were forming this "Suicide Club."

"So what happens if a new year rolls around and you're still here?" she asks him.

Aaron shakes his head. He points the bottle at a piece of paper taped to the wall above her. "Every day I cross something off is another day closer."

Curious, Diane stands and reads part of the list:

Buy motorcycle – ride it to Tucson
Pay overdue library fines
Spend Valentine's Day with Mora
~~Call Aunt Lily~~
~~Give away/sell furniture~~
~~Pare clothing to 2 weeks – get rid of rest~~
~~Shred documents~~
Sell house
Have utilities disconnected

"Well, you *will* be here next year if you have to get all of this done," her finger points toward the one caveat.

Aaron rises, reads it and scratches the side of his head. "Don't have an answer for that." He returns to his place on the floor.

"How 'bout you Phil," Diane says, returning to the hardwood as well. "You have a date in mind?"

He shakes his head in slow motion. "Still working on the best time to die." He sighs. "Either of you feeling guilty?"

Diane shakes her head. "Not a bit. Not to sound mean but the people left behind cannot possibly hurt as much as the person gone."

Phil contradicts her. "I think everyone involved hurts."

"Is it so bad for you, Phil?"

He looks Diane full in the face. "My parents used to tell me that I could have what others have, but that's not true. People aren't big enough to look past the way others look."

"Amen." Diane interjects. "It goes both ways though."

"Yeah, well, I'm tired of being looked at like I'm the modern-day Quasimodo."

"Maybe you just need to ask someone out," Aaron suggests.

"I did. She said 'no'."

"Who?" Aaron takes his place back on the floor.

"Lindsey."

"Our server?" Diane asks.

"Yeah."

Aaron releases a breath. "I'm sorry, Man."

Phil shakes the apology away. "If I had to choose between you and me, I'd choose you too."

The laughter that follows is awkward but feels good.

"Maybe I've ignored just how much I'm hurting." He lifts the cup to his mouth and empties it. Setting it aside, he says, "I'm blabbering, aren't I?"

"Alcohol always loosens the tongue," Aaron comments.

Phil chuckles as he shakes his head. "I'm glad it's just us. I like Mora, but –"

"We all do, some more than others." Diane turns her attention from Phil.

"Ouch," Aaron says.

"We're being honest here," she responds.

He nods. "You're right. Objection overruled."

Friday

18

July
2014

Birthday Boy

by Stephen V. Ramey

It's my birthday. Fifty-eight glorious years. I roll onto my back. Plastic tarp crinkles. My bones ache. Light smears through the glass block window.

"Crap." I overslept. While the cops don't often check these basements, they sometimes do on their morning rounds. If I'm caught, I go to jail. I got my warning last week. I'm in the system now, albeit under an alias. They just assumed I wouldn't have ID. Now, I'm a notarized street bum. Be on the lookout. Disarmed and odiferous.

I won't pretend to have suffered the way truly homeless people do. I have some cash, an ATM card, keys to many things should I choose to use them. I bought a tarp the first day, having read on a blog that that's what to do when you're homeless. A backpack too. I'm actually pretty proud of how I've handled my walkabout; that's how I prefer to think of this foray onto the skin of New Castle's underbelly. Research for the novel, a stroll through my character's inner terrain.

Rose's voice pops into my head: *Oh, it's more than that.* Of course she's wrong. Just because Rose is pagan, does not make her wise.

I need to release the past if I am to find my path forward. It's been a month since Amanda's ghost shocked my senses clean. Cancer is a natural process. I don't want to live out my life as an invalid, don't want to be a burden for the people I care about, or rack up reams of debt. That's my truth. That's what I should cling to when I find myself peeing in an alley.

Which reminds me.

After relieving myself against the far wall – a process like squeezing glue from a bottle with a clogged nozzle – I wad the tarp into the backpack, ease open the door, and squint up a half-flight of steps to the street. *All clear.*

Outside, I reposition the padlock so the door looks intact. I can squat here for weeks if I play my cards right.

I pull the backpack tight between my shoulders and climb the steps, looking as if I belong. That was probably the most difficult adjustment. When you're newly homeless it feels like everyone is watching for an excuse to call the cops or beat you down. After a week or so, you realize you're invisible.

Most of the homeless are solitary by day. We disperse, scavenge, nap on benches by the library. When we do pass, it's like jungle cats. Our hackles rise, and we're ready to defend our territory even if we have nothing to defend.

At night, there's more community, small groups, barrel fires when the opportunity presents. Alcohol and drugs, but mostly companionship. We're wary, though, and when we bed down, we do so with one eye open.

I turn onto Mill. There's a seventies-style shopping plaza across the street. It hasn't been fully occupied since Anne and I moved to New Castle. I try to imagine shoppers, kids laughing, shops filled with consumer goods. Longtime residents tell us that's how it used to be. In moments like this, I understand their nostalgia. It's easier to look back than forward when you are dying.

The dumpster behind The Confluence has been picked clean, but I find an intact fast food bag in one of the trash cans. As I cross the bridge to East Side I toss cold fries to the fish and down a pair of chicken nuggets. Tent City is out of sight around the river's bend. *Come back when you are ready*, I recall the tent woman saying. I'm not ready yet.

A crowd has gathered at the day-old bread shop. Usually they roll out a shopping cart filled with stale product by 10 AM, but I'm not in the mood to fight over dry loaves. I continue past the shop. If you keep moving, the cops are unlikely to hassle you, and business owners don't get cranky.

A savory smell penetrates the cold-air sterility, a hint of lamb charring. I think of the three twenties tucked into my sock. *Four Brothers Bistro* is across the street. I can splurge.

One look at my dirt-stained jeans, the frayed hem of my shirt tells me otherwise. *Keep moving like a shark*, I think, only I don't feel like a predator, but a minnow.

I head back toward town. A bank sign flashes: *July 18, 84°, 11:38*. "Happy birthday, Stephen." I slide my wallet out – keep it in a side pocket, not the rear – and open it. Anne smiles from behind a plastic shield. I emailed her from the library the day after Amanda's ghost. *Gone fishing*, I typed. *You know that I love you, but it's come to that.*

I told her once that I had made a pact with my suicidal teenage self, that if things ever got unbearable I would just take off, go fishing, and sort it out in solitude. Having endured her own bouts with depression, Anne said she understood. I haven't seen signs of a search effort, so maybe she did.

"Hey S-Man!" A scrawny guy with a guitar slung over his shoulder hurries across the library lawn. Dave is a Desert Storm vet who's been homeless for a few years. As a street corner evangelist and talented vocalist, he does pretty well for himself. It's his temper, sudden like a storm, that gets him into trouble.

He meets me at the corner. His smile is missing no teeth; his eyes are polished stones inset into a hardened face.

"It's a glorious day, S-Man," he says. "Did you sleep last night? I didn't see you at the shelter." Dave tells me often that I should check into the Men's Shelter across the river from the Riverplex. Free meals, beds, hot showers. You have to get there early, of course, but they're good folks. I did stay a couple nights, but the required prayer and rigid scheduling turned me off. Plus, it would be one of the first places Anne might look.

We cross the street together. Gentle twangs sound from the guitar as Dave walks. A sweet smell wafts from the Cake Eater Bakery. My hunger erupts. I dredge my pocket for coins garnered from sidewalk scavenging.

"Don't waste your resources," Dave says. "The Presby is doing a prayer breakfast today. They probably have something left."

I stop. "It's my birthday." Coins press into my fist like the nodules in my prostate. I haven't told anyone about the cancer. That's part of a code I'm learning. We don't complain about problems we all have. You don't become homeless by accident.

"How much you got?" Dave says.

I count. "Dollar-forty-five."

He gives my shoulder a squeeze. "Let's get you a cake, man. On me." He flashes a twenty from a pouch inside his waistband.

A bell jingles as we open the door. Smells mix in my nose, cake, fried doughnut, boiled bagel. My mouth suds up. A display case holds cupcakes arranged on plates. *So many colors, all that frosting.* I can taste the sugar on my tongue.

Dave slaps the twenty down. "A cake for my friend."

The clerk frowns. She has blue hair today. "You want to order a cake?"

"Yeah," Dave says. "Make it say, 'Happy Birthday S-Man'."

"Ohh ... kay." The clerk takes out an order pad. Her eyebrow lifts. "Our cakes start at $29.95."

When Dave does not react, she sighs. "What kind do

you want? Chocolate? Red velvet? *Devil's* food?"

"Fuck you!" Dave erupts. He jabs his finger forward. "The Lord rebuke thee, foul temptress, instrument of Satan!"

The clerk presses a cell phone to her ear.

"It's cool," I say to the clerk. "It's cool." I wrap my arms around Dave. "Come on, let's go." I coax him through the door, and we hurry down North Street.

"Stupid," Dave mutters. "Stupid, stupid, stupid."

"It's going to be all right," I say. A siren sounds. I don't feel invisible now.

Concrete steps lead down to the right. Relief washes over me. *This is where I slept last night.* I pull Dave into the basement and close the door carefully, hoping the broken hasp won't show.

"We gotta lay low," Dave says. The whites of his eyes flash in the semi-dark. The acrid urine smell is overpowering.

"No worries," I say. "I know this place."

I unbuckle the backpack and spread the tarp into a corner. Dave leans his guitar against the wall. He sits beside me, stiff-backed with tension.

"It's cool," I murmur. "We're safe." I want to believe it's true. Dave's the one they really want. If they find us, it's Dave who is in trouble. All I have to do ... I stop that thought.

Footsteps pass. A fire truck siren sounds. Even so, I'm drifting off to sleep before I know it. That's one thing that is easier now.

The Trencher Mansion

by Gay Degani

The oaks and sycamores along the Old Road offer shade, but do nothing to alleviate the oppressive heat. Only when the hot summer sun falls behind the ridge on the other side of Riolito creek does Gus leash up Gracie and head out. It's the shadowy time of day – Gus hasn't even fixed dinner yet, waiting for sunset – so he decides not to trek down to the creek, but stick to the sidewalk. He's slow, and so is the dog, both of them old and drained of energy even though they've stayed inside all day in front of an oscillating blower fan from Walmart.

When Gus passes the Trencher mansion, he's surprised to find its faded gate gaping open. In the fading light, he squints at the yard's thick dry weeds tickling the bottom of the Shane Realty "For Sale" sign. He should tell his son to cut the grass – Mars works for that realty lady who has the listing – because if the Trencher goes up in flames, the neighboring bungalows where Gus lives won't stand a chance. Almost no rain since December, what the hell is going on with the weather? Windstorms in winter, polar vortexes back east, now severe drought in the west? "The gods," mutters Gus, "are angry."

A man in a flapping white jacket rushes down the walkway of the low-slung stucco cottage next door, aiming for Gus, setting off Gracie, who yelps and strains at her leash. The old man pulls her in and steps out of the way, but the man – the podiatrist or chiropractor, Gus can't remember which, with the pretty young wife, his brow now puckered with worry – stops and begs, "Have you seen her, a woman about your height and slender with light brown hair, maybe walking?"

"Hush, Gracie. Who? What's happened?"

The dog barks and hides behind Gus' legs.

"The front door was open, her purse on the kitchen table, but I can't find her," the man says. "Have you seen her? My wife?"

"You sure she's not taking a nap. Gracie, *heel.*"

Sam Martin shakes his head and pivots away, through the open gate and across the weedy lawn, up the driveway of the Trencher house.

"Hey!" Gus hollers, "You can't go in there. Nobody's home." The old man shambles after him, Gracie trotting ahead, Gus' heart speeding up, his mind jumbled with images of the woman dead, the man breaking a window, the mansion going up in flames.

"This is private property." Gus puffs toward the backyard. He hears the younger man calling, "Charmaine!"

Plywood has been nailed over sliding doors or maybe French doors, shards of glass and splintered wood barely visible in the growing dark. The younger man rattles the kitchen doorknob. Pounds the door with the side of his fist. "Charmaine?"

Catching his breath, Gus gasps, "She – she can't be in there."

The man turns toward Gus. "She's gone in before."

"She got a key or something?"

"Well no, but she finds a way in." The younger man studies the back of the house, his eyes glancing from window to window.

Gus wonders if she's the one who broke the patio sliders. "You can't go in there. We should call the cops."

The man takes a deep breath. "Look, we live next door. My name's Sam Martin. I've seen you walking your dog. My wife, she hasn't been well."

"You're a doctor?"

"Podiatrist. She does this sometimes, disappears. She's been coming here, and I don't want to call the cops if she's sitting inside in some corner, crying."

Gus lowers his head and then shifts his eyes toward Sam Martin. Reluctantly, he says, "Okay, but I'll go in too to make sure you don't take anything."

Sam Martin nods, then strides across the patio, glass crunching under his feet, to grab a tattered lawn chair and carries it back to the house, positioning it below a window. Using the chair like a step ladder, Sam puts a foot on the front of the seat frame and his other foot on the top of the back of the chair. It wobbles, but holds his weight as he presses the bottom part of the window upward and hefts himself inside.

Sam looks down at Gus from the open window, says, "I'll let you in so you can keep an eye on me."

He ducks inside and a few seconds later the kitchen door opens. "Can you help me look? If she's not here, I need to get in my car and search the neighborhood. I don't want to waste time."

"Is there something wrong with her?"

"No – yes. She's been depressed is all and sometimes she has this urge to get away. If you can look around down here, I'll go upstairs. She's usually up in the nursery." Sam scrapes fingers through his hair.

"The nursery?"

"She miscarried in January. You can bring your dog inside."

Gus shuffles into the kitchen, though he doesn't like it much, breaking into someone else's house. Then it hits him. She was pregnant. Lost a baby. His own wife had lost one too all those years back, and they'd waited a long time

91

before they had Mars. He feels himself softening toward the other man.

It's musty and dark inside, empty over six months, for sale for three or four. His son works for the listing agent and says she wants to sell to someone who'll turn it into a bed and breakfast, all part of her personal urban renewal plan for the area. Sniffing the stale air, Gus shakes his head. Whoever buys this place has his work cut out for him.

He peeks into the murky living room. Gracie runs her nose along the carpet at his feet. The drapes are open and the streetlights have flicked on outside, casting a blurry glow across the room. What was that by the window? A shoe catching the light?

"Hello?" His voice sounds weak and frightened to his own ears. What was her name? He clears his throat and says "hello" again, moving slowly into the room, pulling Gracie with him, cursing his old man eyes. He leans down. Grace snorts and picks up whatever it is in her mouth. He takes it from her, a crumpled bag, stinking of French fries.

Floorboards creak above his head, Gracie yelps, and he jumps. "Hell!" Dropping the bag, he hurries out of the room, not quite remembering where the kitchen is, stopping to glance into another room, dark and foreboding, with what he takes for headless shoulders at first glance, his mouth going dry, only to realize what he sees silhouetted against the window are dining room chairs.

Back into the hall, peering toward the front door and a staircase, he shouts, "Dr. Martin!"

A thundering down the stairs startles Gus. The dog lets out two sharp barks. Sam Martin arrives at the bottom, asking, "Did you find her?"

"No. Just an old French fry bag. Maybe it's hers?"

Somewhere in the dark house a door closes. Not a slam, but kind of click.

"What was –" asks Gus.

Gracie growls.

Sam hisses. "Shhh!"

Gus leans down and picks her up, clamps her muzzle, just as Sam grabs the older man's shirt and drags him to a door near the kitchen.

Sam whispers. "Wait here. Block the door." And slowly turns the knob. The door squeaks as it opens. Cool air gusts up. Stairs lead down.

Gus feels Sam's hand squeeze his shoulder and watches the young man descend into the blackness below. Gracie quivers in his arms. Gus takes one or two steps down and leans over to see what he can see. Nothing, so he takes another step. He wishes he had a flashlight, trying to do anything without –

Below there's a grunt and a scream, and the crash of glass and metal against cement and Gus is knocked against the wall, falls on his butt, a shock of pain up his tailbone, as someone rushes past him, up the steps, Gracie loosened from his grasp in hot barking pursuit. Above, running feet and Gracie's fury, then the slam of a door. Gus gasps for air, tries to pull himself up, feels a hand under his arm lifting him.

"You okay, old fellow?" asks Sam Martin.

"Gracie!" says Gus as he finds his feet.

They lumber up the stairs, the dog in the kitchen ranting at the backdoor. Sam searches for a light switch, flicks it on, but it doesn't work. He opens the door and they hasten out where a full moon glints in the glass scattered across the patio.

"Was that her?" asks Gus as he catches his breath.

Sam doesn't answer right away. He plops down onto the step, burying his head in his hands. "No. Just some kid."

Hot and light-headed, Gus pivots toward the backyard, and catches in the moonlight, just for a moment, a glimpse of his own long-dead wife.

Playing with the Big Boys

by Sally-Anne Macomber

To: Milton Flaxmill, Red Cow Publishing
From: Trudy Polaris
Date: July 20, 2014 11:57 a.m.
Re:

I don't know what it is about you Milton but you keep me awake at night! You're like the strong silent type except you might not be so strong now because you might also be dead.

I haven't heard from you for over 6 months so your death could be a distinct possibility. And my *Nuclear Fission in The Pyrénées* manuscript could be languishing in the bottom drawer of your desk. And maybe not even yours. It could be someone else's desk. Or your old desk that's been sent down to the basement for storage. Did you make sure you cleaned out all the drawers before you sent it downstairs? Is that an official policy at Red Cow Publishing?

These are the thoughts that keep me awake at night, Milton.

(Did you see how I didn't put anything in the subject line of this email? It's because – and it feels a little weird to admit this but well, I've admitted worse things – I'm a woman of mystery.)

Yeah, who would have thought, over-communicator-of-the-century Trudy Polaris actually keeping something secret?

Well, I have a lot of secrets, Milton, I'm just very choosy who I keep them from. Because I believe in human happiness and the pursuit of generosity.

Just in case you were asking yourself that very question.

While eating lunch at your desk and editing everyone else's book but mine.

Later:
So, now it's a little later (just in case you didn't know what 'Later' on the line above meant) and I've had my little barium enema pick-me-up, but things are still a little confusing for me here in the Tyrol – oh yes! we are still heeeeere, Milton, on the world's longest tax break, but that's so depressing I don't want to talk / type / write about it for one minute one second one millisecond longer – so I'm just going to do some freefall free associating while I type instead.

So. I keep seeing mountains all the time. I look out the window and I see mountains (we *finally* ate our way through the wall of fetta, and now I can never pat a goat on the butt in quite the same way again) and I can't help thinking of the mountains I wrote about in my book – the Pyrénées, those mountains on the French-Spanish border, if you care to remember.

Oh, how do I put it without sounding a little silly?

OK. The Pyrénées are sweet enough but I can't help thinking that maybe they're just the wrong mountains for me. That is God's truth. I look at the Tyrolean Alps and think, the Pyrénées just seem ever so slightly immature in

95

comparison. It's not their fault, it just *IS*, it's just NATURE, and you can't buck nature.

And the other day I was trolling the internet and I came across some photos of the Nepalese Royal Family and in the background were the Himalayas and I thought, those are *some* mountains, Trudy, and those mountains are truly deserving of your talents. Not those pathetic Pyrénées but those macho mountains, the Indian ones, the ones in Nepal, the ones at the top of the world.

That's really where I should be Milton, at the top of the world, not down here in Tyrolean Lego Land, but up there, with the big guys.

And then I thought, well, I bet nothing even vaguely nuclear has ever gone on up there, not in those pristine looking snow-capped mountains I thought, sipping my coffee. (I'd gone grocery shopping just the day before so we had some coffee again.) And I sighed, and my sighs last a good deal longer up here in the Alps because the air is thinner, and then my husband thought I had the hiccups and he burst into the room and pressed a gun to my head and the shock made me stop hiccupping.

(OK, that didn't happen that last bit, I'm just checking to see if you're still with me. If you are, please send me your reply in red, so I'll know you read this far.)

But these are the things that try me and I am positive they would not if I had some news from you. It's hard not being communicated with when you're a big communicator.

Later again:
I just looked it up on the internet and nothing even remotely nuclear ever happened in the Himalayas, not even close by, so I'm stuck with the Pyrénées. You are probably greatly relieved – yay, you say, no taking out *Pyrénées*

seven times from every page and replacing them all with *Himalayas* – but I can't help but feel disappointed. In fact, I just gave a big sigh and because the air really is a good deal thinner up here it really did last longer than I expected.

(I get the feeling you're not believing me Milton. Just another reason to come and visit and breathe for yourself!)

So now we come to the purpose of my email which is: the cover.

Because I can't get mountains out of my head, I'm thinking mountains might be good on the cover. I would send you some potential photos I downloaded but they're of the Himalayas – they're stalking me, those big guys, calling me to expose them! – so I wonder if we can't capture the essence of the Himalayas in the cover anyway. No one would know. It would just be subliminal, like one 25th of a second but longer and on a book cover. Just a flash of the Himalayas just to give people the idea. No one'd get hurt.

You could disguise them, of course, by moving them around. They don't all have to be of Mt Everest, you could throw in a few more of those other Himalayas too.

I like simple designs so here is a design that I am positive would probably work. You just need to make it bigger and in colour and glossy and mountainous.

(I know it doesn't look much but I'm really more after their *essence*.)

The latest Later:
I think I have been spelling 'fetta' when really it should be 'feta'. This is why I loathe spelling anything.

If you are going over some of my older emails to you, could you correct that please?

Up the Himalayas!

Trudy

To: Leonard Strauss Jr., Red Cow Publishing
From: Trudy Polaris
Date: July 20, 2014 1:32 p.m.
Re: !!!!!!!!!!!!!!!!!!!!!!!

Frohe Weihnachten, Herr Strauss!

What a coincidence that I should be talking to Frau Erdbeeren just yesterday in the Fleischerei and she mentioned she has a brother in Boston … who works in publishing … and at Red Cow Publishing, no less … as the Dialect Editor / Janitor!

I was immediately struck by your job title – though less by the words *dialect* and *editor* and more by the word *janitor*.

I am wondering if you have a key to the basement where the editing staff keep all their old office furniture. And if you could look through the drawers of the old desk of Milton Flaxmill? And rescue a manuscript of mine that I am sure is gathering dust in the bottom drawer.

The manuscript is called *Nuclear Fission in the Pyrénées* (since renamed *Nuclear Fission in The Pyrénées*) and I would be eternally grateful if you could find it, read it, cross out every mention of the word *Pyrénées*, and replace them all with the word *Himalayas*.

Doing the same on the title page would be good too. Though please keep my name – Trudy Polaris – wherever it is mentioned.

(I have not seen one example of messy Austrian penmanship since we moved to the Tyrol earlier this year in a bid to improve our tax standing, so I am sure you would do all the crossing-out and adding-in in a neat and steady hand.)

Then please take the manuscript up to Milton Flaxmill's desk and put it in his In-Tray.

I'm sure his old desk is there in the basement.

As you will see by all the exclamation marks in the Subject of this email, my request is very important.

It's been a terrible and stressful last few months (perhaps Frau Erdbeeren has already spoken of me?) but I am determined to put all this negativity behind me and move forward, ready to embrace the anticipation of my success.

There is also the added incentive of a financial reward for your troubles. I can cut you in on an amazing Europe-wide gourmet cheese distribution deal.

Speed is of the essence here too, so just a quick message telling me you received this email, took the elevator (or *lift*, as I usually say) down to the basement, found the desk, unlocked the bottom drawer, pulled out the manuscript, changed all the mentions of *Pyrénées* to *Himalayas* including the title page (and in a neat and steady hand), then took it upstairs and deposited it in Milton Flaxmill's In-Tray, would be good.

If you are speaking with Frau Erdbeeren soon, please thank her for me, and tell her I have contacted you. She seemed very concerned that I did so, and I would hate her to think I had not followed up on her good advice.

Given the possibility that Milton Flaxmill may have left the building, left Red Cow Publishing, left Boston or even left this mortal earth, what do you suggest would be a wise next step in that eventuation?

Thanking you in advance, for a job well done!

Grüß Gott,

Frau Trudi Polaris

Discipline

by Mandy Nicol

"I knew Persephone would like the Colonel," says Mum, feeding another sliver of KFC to the Pomeranian perched on her lap at the dining room table.

"I thought the chicken was for you," I say. "I thought you wanted it for lunch. *Your* lunch. I wouldn't have gone out of my way to get it for the bloody dog." Seph licks Mum's fingers clean and I stand beside the table, ready to scoop the spoilt little mutt off the table if she decides to help herself to her special meal.

"There's no need to speak like that Nadia, and it was a small detour off the highway. How much did it add to your trip back from Melbourne, five minutes?" Mum wipes her fingers with a serviette, then uses it to delicately dab around Seph's mouth.

"It was more like half an hour, actually." I tear some meat off a drumstick for Peregrine, drooling and overlooked under the table. "It wouldn't normally bother me but I have to finish embroidering the logos on all those shirts for the pub. They want them tomorrow."

"Well that's not my fault."

"I didn't say it was, but ..."

Mum slaps her hands on the table. "If you'd listened to me you'd have had plenty of time to do the shirts! You'd have been here instead of gadding about in the city with

Charlie all weekend. You can't run around like a teenager and expect your business to look after itself, Nadia."

She pauses for breath. She's yanked me off cloud nine and I turn to escape but I'm too late, she starts up again.

"Now, if you had your brother's business sense you might get away with it, but with the best will in the world you're no business manager and you never will be, so if you're running behind, don't blame me." She shakes her head. "We all told you at the start that you'd have to treat it like a business and not some fancy little hobby you pick up and put down as you please. Discipline, that's what it needs, and if things are falling apart that's what it'll come down to, so you can quit blaming me."

I stare at her for a good ten seconds. "Nothing's falling apart, Mum, and I'm not blaming you for anything." I step into the kitchen and take her pill box off the fridge, make sure the Monday compartment is empty. I don't like it when her face turns beetroot. "How about a nice cup of tea?" I call out, flicking the switch on the kettle.

"No thank you, I wouldn't dare waste any more of your precious time."

"All right then." I turn the kettle off. I'd much rather immerse myself in memories of the weekend.

I scarper down the hall to my workroom, which is actually the spare room, which means I get to hear her talk to the dogs about how I never listen, how I'll never learn, and how I'll be sorry when she's dead.

I pick up the box of shirts waiting for their logos.

And I wonder about that sorry bit.

Heat Rises

by Margaret Bingel

July in the city is a humid, sticky time of the year, but the weathermen claim the heat wave should be over in a few days. Ned and his mother are drinking iced tea while standing in the back doorway of his apartment, Ned with one foot on the back stoop, his mother's head sticking just outside. Nadia gnaws on an ice cube, belly flat on the kitchen linoleum.

"Ned, I wish you'd get an air conditioner. This weather is no good for a dog. Look at her," Nora points to the dog, now growling as she tries to crack the cube. "Dogs don't sweat, you know. You should take better care of her."

"Mom, she's fine," Ned says, keeping his eyes on the waves of heat undulating the sunset. "I keep her watered, she pees a lot, it's alright."

"Watered? Ned, she's not a plant!"

He rolls his eyes. She needs to stop panicking, he thinks as he steps back inside to get more tea from the fridge. His mother follows him to the kitchen, still talking.

"Have you been taking her out on walks every day? Have you been remembering to feed her? How is your physical therapy, is she keeping you on your feet? You know you have to keep moving every day or else your muscles will atrophy again, and you don't want that, now do you?"

Ned pours more iced tea into their glasses. He puts the pitcher back in the fridge.

"And how is work going? Are you still able to work? It's ok to push yourself, but not that hard."

"Mom, I work as a translator for a juicer company. It's not like I'm going to get finger strain typing Spanish. And since I work from home, there's no need for me to leave the house unless I'm going to the store, or if I have to take Nadia out on a walk."

Hearing her name, Nadia lifts her head to her owner, and wags her tail. If Nadia could have human thoughts, with words instead of pictures, she'd tell him that he left the fridge door open again. Instead, she steps away from her ice cube and nudges Ned.

In the month he's had her, Ned's memory hasn't grown better so much as it's now easier to prompt him when he's forgotten something. Figuring she must've been a service dog school drop-out, he has no other explanation for Nadia's intelligence and intuition for when he's misplaced objects, left his shoes untied, and now, left a door open. Every time she pokes him with her nose, Ned picks up on his mistakes.

After closing the door and patting Nadia on the head, his mother asks, "Why aren't you seeing a therapist for your depression?"

He looks his mother full in the face. Ned can't tell her that he prefers suicide to therapy, and the last thing he needs is another chattering harpy in his life not listening to him.

"Mom," Ned starts, "you need a man in your life and you need to leave me alone."

Nora places her glass of iced tea on the kitchen counter and leaves before he can say anymore. When he hears his front door snap shut, he wonders if he said too much. But she needed to hear that, he rationalizes. He faces his kitchen window and looks out at the sunset.

Wednesday

23

July
2014

All That Trouble

by Darryl Price

Hey, Doc, did you hear? They tell me I'm going home pretty soon. Probably next week, next week sometime. I won't know what to do with myself.

I'm going to miss you, Doc. You've been a real good friend to me, which to all but us chickens seems like a funny kind of thing to say to someone in your position, I know, but I mean it. You've kept the fox at bay.

Well, this isn't the final goodbyes or anything remotely like that, or is it, nope this is just the same old routine point of the day where I tell you all the things I've been meaning to express this week, like always. What are you going to do with all those papers, Doc? Burn them?

It's going to be lonely.

You know I started one of these yesterday but it got accidentally thrown out, so now I keep them under my pillow – for safekeeping.

It was something to do with the moon. Oh yeah I think I kind of remember it now. It's when I got in trouble with your staff for chasing the moon that one night. I don't know. It just seemed like the right thing to do then. The moon was so big and bright and I needed that kind of company, so I went outside to get a closer look, but the moon's a tricky customer, Doc. Just when you think you'll be able to tap her on the shoulder and ask her name she appears somewhere else, higher, farther away. It's frustrating. Still I was attracted to that particular moon that night for sure and felt like I had to go to her. So I did. I didn't mean to cause all that crazy trouble. In the end it was more trouble for me than anybody else because I had to swallow all those pills and be watched every second of the rest of the night. I felt like a dog chained to a doghouse. And I still never met that particular moon maiden, if you know what I mean. Maybe one doesn't so much get to meet the moon as be allowed in its presence. Jesus, that's a lonely thought there.

Well, anyway, I do appreciate all your help. I know I'm going to be just fine. It might be a little rough in the beginning – because really I don't want to have to talk with anybody, but what if someone asks me a question? I guess I'll have to deal with that as it comes.

I've got a little money saved up, a little money left, so I should be able to buy some groceries and pay the electric bill.

Do you think I'll ever be happy, Doc?

Maybe I should get a dog.

Quelle Surprise

by Teresa Burns Gunther

Rachel unfolds from the cab at Pier 39. It's July 24th. 6:00 pm. San Francisco has wrapped her gray shawl around the day, dropping the temperature into the 50s. Susie's not waiting in front of the Aquarium as agreed. Rachel grits her teeth and texts *where r u?* Susie responds *w/the seals!* Rachel passes shivering tourists along the wooden wharf. Screeching seagulls swoop for easy pickings. A juggler packs up his machetes and bowling balls while a homeless man terrifies tourists with his outstretched, distressed hand; a kid who needs voice lessons entertains Japanese tourists with a red guitar, the case begging.

Susie appeared last night as Rachel stepped into the bath. She'd worked late at the office parsing the tax return of a faux investor-lawyer who secreted pilfered millions into phony accounts he created using his daughter's SSN. Rachel peeked through the curtains to find her cousin with suitcases on the porch. *Damn.*

"Surprise!" Susie shouted, hair hacked all different lengths like she'd had an argument with a blender.

"We don't want any," Rachel said, holding Stella whose barks became whimpers of joy. *Traitor.* "Why are you here?"

"Visiting. Remember? I called."

"Yes. And I said no."

"Rach," Susie laughed as she wrestled her bags inside. "You're so funny!"

Rachel knew she should tell Susie to leave. Her last visit involved a party while Rachel was working that left her apartment a mess, the liquor cabinet empty, and jewelry gone missing. But, Susie is 50% of her remaining family tree.

"One night, Susie. No guests."

Rachel finds Susie ogling sea lions with two men in tow. She's 27, a fluttery package of curves. Her hacked hair dyed an odd "champagne" color stands on end in a frigid wind that drags the evening into the 40s. Rachel made Susie leave the house with her this morning, planning to meet for a goodbye dinner after work. Susie's dressed the part of tourist in shorts and goose bumps, her lips colorless with cold. She's bouncing on her toes, hands fluttering as she talks, acting out a story starring herself. When they were kids Susie's stories tricked Rachel into believing Susie was exciting, complex. But she's learned that her cousin is like the Russian nesting dolls Rachel's father sent in lieu of a 7th birthday visit. When taken apart, the dolls reveal themselves in new costumes, growing smaller and smaller, to their baby core. Susie adopts different personas but when you get to the heart of her there's just a little girl incapable of organizing herself into a woman's life. Rachel's heel drops into a crack in the walkway; she wrestles it free, regretting agreeing to meet at Fisherman's Wharf, a tourist trap she usually avoids.

Susie introduces Rachel to her catch, farm boys from Indiana. Steve is short, buff and tan with hair and teeth bleached white. He's wearing crisp jams, sandals, and a tight *Frisco* sweatshirt. He's an actor working his way to LA and stardom. Kevin is tall and lives in San Francisco. He looks like a farmer; lean, square-jawed and freckled in jeans and leather jacket; a software engineer.

"Don't tell anyone," Kevin says. Young techies are the latest whipping boy for SF's housing shortage and skyscraping rents.

The sea lions stink but Susie, like Steve, is enchanted. "They're *so* cute!" She hops, pink sneakers slapping the wharf. Susie's "between jobs," a space she occupies more each year. She has little money but probably paid a fortune for her huge tourist sweatshirt, identical to Steve's. She links arms with Rachel, who towers over her, and poses on tiptoe for Steve to take her picture while Kevin slyly checks out Rachel's legs. "Oh Steve! Thank you!" Susie beams, like he's just cured Ebola and turns the camera on him. "Give me your number and I'll text these to you." She winks at Rachel and whispers, "You can have the tall one." Susie promised to find Rachel "a manhunk" before leaving town. Given Susie's penchant for guys with compasses set south of trouble Rachel suggested she leave well enough alone. Her resolution for July is *be open to new experiences* but Susie's *surprise!* slammed that door last night.

"I just have to pet those seals!" Susie says, looking for a way onto the floating haul outs.

"They're *sea lions,* and wild, and protected. They can be nasty," Rachel says, but Susie waves her off. "Excuse her," Rachel tells the guys. "She's judgment impaired."

"See!" Susie says. "I told you Rachel has a great sense of humor!"

Rachel shakes her head. "You know that's code for *my friend's a dog,* right?"

Kevin, *the tall one,* throws his head back and laughs, a rib-rattling *hahaha.* It wasn't that funny. "That's what *I* was figuring." He wipes his eyes. "But you're not. A dog. I mean

..." He coughs. "You're ..." He shoves his hands in his pockets and turns pink.

"Very attractive?" Rachel suggests.

He smiles, saved. "Yeah."

"Thank you." Rachel gives him the once-over. Her gaydar says he's straight.

"Isn't it amazing, they're cousins too. And from Indiana, like me?" Susie says, like this meet-up's on Mars. "We should celebrate!"

"I have work to do." Rachel points to her watch.

"Well, we have to eat." She clutches Steve's and Kevin's arms. "All four of us!"

Outside the Crab Pot restaurant, Susie frowns at the menu. "I don't know." She taps a long, green fingernail against her teeth. "It's mostly crab." She makes snapping pincers of her fingers.

"Quelle surprise!" Rachel says. "Are you allergic?"

"No."

"Vegetarian?"

Susie lifts her chin. "I'm a cutetarian."

Rachel won't ask.

Steve the actor does.

"It means I only eat *cute* animals."

"How weird of you," Rachel says.

Susie strikes a pose and waves a hand over herself. "Well ... you are what you eat!"

Kevin laughs like she's a riot.

Steve claps. "I just love that!" He's not even acting.

"Maybe," Rachel says, "we can find you some deep fried kitties."

Steve looks alarmed, but Kevin grins. He's getting better-looking.

Inside, fishing nets with faux crab and lobster drape the restaurant walls. When the waiter comes to their booth Susie says, "Four Cosmos, please."

"Coffee for me," Rachel says. "Remember, we agreed it's an early night?"

"I'll have McCallan, neat," Kevin says. That's Rachel's drink. He takes off his leather jacket. His T-shirt says *"You can shoot yourself in the foot in any language, C++ allows you to reuse the bullet."* This makes Rachel laugh, which earns her another grin. "Most people," Kevin says, sliding closer, "don't get it."

Rachel stands before the restroom mirror and smooths her dark hair, pleased at how smart she looks in her fitted blue suit. But if she's so smart why is Susie staying another night? The door flies open. Clearly Susie thinks bathroom visits are a group activity.

"Kevin likes you," Susie says, touching up her lipstick. "Admit it. I did good! Found us each a man our size." She laughs at this, her eyes bright. Their dark blue color is the only proof they share DNA. "Steve's so hot, and an actor!" she says, like this is a rare find. "You must feel it."

"Feel what?"

"The chemistry." Susie puckers her lips and smiles, delighted, perhaps at some new idea of herself. Rachel just nods, sad to think Susie might never turn her enthusiasm to some true and lasting effort. Like what? Rachel mocks herself, a mortgage? Working for the IRS?

Susie steps close, serious now.

"I know we didn't have much time together Rach, but I've agreed to drive Steve to LA." As if fearful Rachel might argue, she adds, "He's paying for gas."

Rachel thinks she should talk Susie out of it. It's clear she's clueless that Steve's gay. But her face is so bright, so full of hope. Rachel tries to remember the last time she opened herself up to that.

Morgana Malone and the Mystery of the Manna from Heaven

by Matt Potter

"Morgana Malone?"

I turn and see a young man, high cheekbones on a thin face and short dark hair atop deep brown eyes. He's looking at me through the open driver's window of a shiny, dark blue car. It's cold and the sky above is that depressing pale grey we all grow to know and loathe over the Australian winter. No rain, just cold and grey and dull dull dull. But it's a quiet suburban neighbourhood and we appear to be the only two people around – me on the footpath and he in his car with the engine still running in the middle of the street.

I stuff the leaflets back into my cotton hold-all – it's too cold to do two things at once – while I talk to this charming man. I want to know how he knows me.

"Morgana?" he asks, his eyebrows aquiver. And he smiles. "You must be, it's your hair, it's so … *orange.*"

I brush my hair with my hand, which is past my shoulders now, but it unsettles the beanie on top of my head – I hate beanies but it's keeping my head warm – and the hat falls to the ground. So I bend down, and the cowl neck of the thick jumper looped across my chest swoops down in front as I pick the beanie up off the footpath.

He lets out a large whistle. "Whoa! It *is* you, that racing stripe is so sexy!"

I stand up and do the usual cramming of the beanie on my head, pulling it down over the grey-brown regrowth. I want to have my hair dyed again by a professional hairdresser – as opposed to an amateur – but it's taking a while to earn the money. And I've had a lot of bad luck job-wise (and bad luck life-wise) since I stopped working as junior admin officer at Grigor's therapy practice way back in … oh, April … and then Ludmilla moved out and moved in with her kitchenhand cousin Sergei and then –

"No, don't cover it up," he says, "that stripe is hot! Opi was right, you are one sexy mama." Leaning his elbow on the window frame, he grins. He has no gaps in his teeth.

When I stepped outside this morning to deliver more junk mail – my savings are running out and I don't have any other job and it gets me out in the fresh (cold, dull dull dull) air and I get a lot of knuckle exercise with all the folding beforehand plus I thought it would be a good way to meet single men – I had not expected the third degree (if this is the third degree, though, it could be the first, second or fourth degree instead) from a young man with short dark hair, deep brown eyes and all those teeth who also knows my name and who also might be single.

But I can't help it, it comes from nowhere. "I'm probably as old as your mother."

"Yeah?" He reaches forward and the engine stops idling. (He must want to talk to me, he's stopped dead in the middle of the street.) "How old would that be?" he says, and settles back into the seat.

"Forty-seven," I say. "Today, in fact. I'm forty-seven today."

"Yeah? Dang, me too! It's my birthday today as well. I'm twenty-three."

I pull the strap of my hold-all further on to my shoulder. "It's really your birthday today?"

"Nah, just kidding," he says, and grins again. This guy, he's a great grinner.

"Me too, I'm just kidding too," I say, though it actually *is* my birthday today, and I *am* forty-seven now. I'm just trying to forget. "Do you want me for something?"

"Are you busy?"

Am I busy? Well, I could be busy, I think, wondering what his plans are. If he's stalking me then yes, I'm definitely busy. But if he wants to get to know me and buy me a drink and whisk me away to somewhere that's sunny and warm and not dull dull dull grey, then no, I might not be so busy after all.

"Well, I'm stuffing letterboxes with advertising for *Knights of the Polish Cross* sauvignon blanc," I say, half-flashing him a tri-fold leaflet sticking out of my hold-all, "if that counts as *busy*." I step off the kerb and hold-all swinging against my hip, cross the three metres to the car.

"Opi is right – you are a *damn* fine woman, Morgana Malone."

I'm standing by the driver's door now, hands in the pockets of my corduroy trousers. "Who's Opi?"

"Opi. You know, Julius Rubinstein, from where you used to work." But he says it Germanically, *Yoo-lee-ess*. Yoo-lee-ess Roo-bin-shtine.

"Oh, Mr Rubinstein!" I smile, happy to remember my favourite patient at Grigor's therapy practice, and I rock back on my heels. "No one can carry off an eye patch and toupée quite the way he can. How is he?"

"Good," he says. "Okay," he says. "Well, not too good really," he says. "A bit fucked."

Mr Rubinstein is sitting up in bed, his toupée perched further back on his head so it looks like it's revving up for a take-off, and his eye patch removed, a darkened sewn-up hole where his eye once was. A nurse holds his wrist with one hand and with her watch in the other, checks his pulse. Which strikes me as old-fashioned (isn't there a robot to do this?) but then, with a toupée and eye patch and all, Mr Rubinstein is an old-fashioned kind of man.

"It is lovely to see you, my dahlink," he says, smiling against the pillows. "You and your lovely orange hair, just like my late, dear wife."

"And it's lovely to see you, too," I say, but it's not. A tube reaches in through his left nostril and a drip is attached to his right arm. And his skin is grey, near to translucent, and it's the middle of winter and a little chilly on the ward but sweat beads on his forehead, and his arms and the skin stretched across his collarbone are shiny with sweat. Even in the short time since I last saw him – an everyday sight until I left the job in late April – he's older and thinner and frailer and closer to the end.

I sniff and the room smells of sickly-sweet old man sweat but I smile at him anyway. I don't know whether to kiss his cheek or hold his other hand or what, so I just stand at the end of the bed. Which allows Seth – his grandson, the one who found me walking the streets delivering *Knights of the Polish Cross* junk mail – time to open the folder at the end of the bed and glance over his medical notes.

"My grandson is makink sure I have the best care in the hospital," Mr Rubinstein says. "He is a *brilliant* medical student and he will be a *brilliant* doctor. But seeink you is the best medicine, my dear, always the *best*."

I smile again. I'm smiling but I don't know what else to do. There's no reception desk separating us and now I'm just the visitor, not the person printing invoices and picking up the 'phone and doing all the things Zebadie didn't have the insight or interest to do. I'm just someone who was picked up on the street by a man half her age and whisked in for a visit.

116

The nurse returns Mr Rubinstein's hand to the mattress and taking the medical file from Seth's grasp, opens it on the tray table beside the bed and scribbles inside the folder.

"It's Morgana's birthday, Opi," Seth says, ignoring the nurse. And he winks at me.

"How old are you today, my dear? Not a day over twenty-two!"

"Forty-seven," I say. And to Seth I say, "Actually, it *is* my birthday."

"Yeah, I know," Seth adds. "It's *my* birthday too."

Mr Rubinstein yawns, his mouth full of big yellow teeth and a furry, white tongue.

"You need to drink more, Opi," Seth says. "Keep your fluids up."

The nurse wheels the tray table over Mr Rubinstein's legs, and taking a plastic cup filled with water and a straw from the bedside cabinet, plonks it down on the tray table.

"I just thought you might like a visitor, Opi," Seth says. And then to me, "Opi talks about you a lot."

"You need to keep your fluids up, Mr Rubinstein," the nurse says, patting his leg. Then she slots the medical notes back in their wire cage at the end of the bed and, white shoes squeaking on the lino, walks out of the room.

Mr Rubinstein opens his eyes wide and lifts up his arms, as if beholding something. "Such a vision," he says, I think to me.

"She was hard to track down," Seth says.

"You must come back and visit me when I am feelink better," Mr Rubinstein adds. And closes his eyes. Then he opens one, just a little. "Beauty always makes me feel better."

"Was I really that hard to track down?" I ask, as we walk out onto North Terrace to the beeping horns and gear changes of Friday mid-afternoon traffic. "Did you have to go to the police or scour the 'phone book or the electoral roll or dental records?"

I look at Seth side-on – high cheekbones on a thin face and short dark hair atop deep brown eyes. And am struck by how much he looks like Grigor. And he's a doctor too.

"No," says Seth, looking into my eyes and grinning again. "Wanna go back to my place for a birthday fuck?"

Hazard

by Gary Percesepe

Seven months after his divorce, a man steers his rented Cadillac Seville down the narrow lane of a manicured country club, positions the car so that it is facing the eighteenth green, and cuts the engine. He touches a button and four windows glide down leather doors, letting in the local air, and with it, a flood of memories.

Playing alone on a sultry July afternoon at his New England club, Gary Hollow had it at one under par on the thirteenth hole when it occurred to him that his wife may be having an affair. Dropping his bag to the ground, he fished a clean white handkerchief from one of the side pockets, and blotted his brow. Just yesterday, one of his firm's senior partners had remarked that he was mildly surprised at how reasonable Savannah had been. They had been in the library in the tort section, researching negligence in the Shinnecock tribe case. Gary started to speak, he'd been filling the air with explanations and aimed to continue, but Vanderslice placed his hand gently on his shoulder and said, "Son, save it. You've made the common mistake of thinking your divorce is interesting."

He and Savannah had been best friends in college. They were part of a touring Princeton ensemble that performed at the tall steeple Congregational churches of Vermont and New Hampshire. Savannah was a soprano, he a baritone, part of a group of eight perfectly matched voices that sang French madrigals and holiday music. Gary was taken in by Savannah's long, willowy frame, accentuated by a floor length cross-back jersey maxi which she had toughened up with a military parka and Doc Martens. With her pancake makeup and thick mascara, Savannah looked like Morticia Addams, had Morticia been a blonde. It was a joke between them, Gary holding her pale arm aloft in the Princeton touring van, kissing it in two inch intervals as the others cheered, and he proclaimed to her, only half joking, "Cara Mia!"

Gary placed the handkerchief back in his bag, pulled his driver, and stepped onto the manicured tee box. As he rehearsed his swing and tried to visualize the way he must shape his next shot, he saw instead Savannah in her skinny jeans, and then the way she applied night cream to her pretty face before climbing into bed next to him. One day soon that stops, Gary thought. And someone else will watch her move in those jeans, through the Italian restaurant or pottery shop and into her car, into the seat beside him, knowing at the end of the day he can remove them from her slim hips and watch her apply her night cream and count the seconds till she presents herself to him in bed.

He placed a white tee into the ground and wondered, how had they come to this? Just last month, lying in bed on a Sunday morning, he and Savannah had rehearsed a half dozen scenarios – married too early, two miscarriages, Gary's meddlesome mother who had never approved of her son's wife's couture, the numbing routine of a young New England associate at an historic Boston firm, with longer and longer nights at the office and fewer opportunities to spend time together. When they spoke of these things that Sunday, their tone was one of sweet reason, doctor conferring with lawyer, as if they had simply missed a question on their SATs. Married young, divorced young. They would both go on. She in pediatric medicine, he at the firm. It was far from tragic. With all that was terribly wrong in this violent crazed irrational world, their problems didn't amount to much, even to them. They would use a mediator, one not from his firm. They would go on as best pals. No fault, win win, the ideal way to play it.

Gary smashed his drive, starting it over the right side of the fairway, a high arcing draw. He shouldered his bag and tried to reason things out. If Savannah was really having an affair, everything changes. But why? Because deceit alters things. But why? Why should it matter to him? The marriage is over. Yes, but facts matter. But if she denied an affair, he would have to establish the facts, which means an investigation. Does he want that? What if nothing happened? What are the grounds of his divorce, now? Is there a case that can be built?

He reached his ball. It had landed in the middle of the fairway, 270 yards from the tee box. He has 150 yards to the back of the green where the pin is tucked in the far left corner, guarded by a large bunker. A sucker pin placement. Gary took his stance over the ball, made a few waggles with his eight iron. He concentrated on the shot before him, a shot he had executed a hundred times or more.

But he had a corrupt swing thought, disturbed by the nagging suspicion that Savannah is seeing someone at work, and he came over the top on the shot, slicing the ball into the trees. He walked angrily after his Titleist. It had come to rest two inches from a tall maple. Trees line the right edge of the fairway on this old Donald Ross course, and he was in jail. With no other option, he took a five iron, punched out into the fairway, chipped onto the green, and two putted. Double bogey. Just like that, one over par.

Gary pulled his ball angrily from the cup and walked briskly to the ball washer at the fourteenth hole, a long par five. He pumped the ball up and down in the bright red washer, trying to remember the name of the guy Savannah had mentioned a few months back, a young intern at Boston General, the brother of one of her partners. Or was it a nephew? A guy who'd shown up with his stethoscope and blood pressure kit in a red and yellow Sesame Street lunchbox. What was his name? Halverson or Halverton. One of those. He had met him, Gary recalled. It was at an office party when he picked Savannah up at work one night when her car was in the shop. Deferential as hell, this kid doctor had been, he remembered that.

He took the ball, dimpled and gleaming white from the washer, and promptly dropped it into a small patch of mud. Cursing, he washed the ball again and placed it, still wet, in his pants pocket. On the tee box, he took a few rehearsal swings, smooth and rhythmic, and addressed his ball. He hated the thought that something had been hidden. That he had been so *not knowing*. He was not vigilant enough with Savannah, then hadn't bothered to put up a real fight for her. But why? Why had he allowed this Sesame Street kid to come between them? He had failed to *defend* her!

Sotto voce, he hummed the Emperor's Waltz. Imagining himself gliding alone around a polished dance floor, he took the club back slowly, loaded his weight onto his back leg and haunches, and made a full turn. But his right elbow flew open and he sliced again, his ball peeling like a banana and landing in the next fairway. He hit a smothered hook from the rough, managing somehow to reach the green in regulation, but then three putts from thirty feet. Furious with himself, he took his bogey and moved to the fifteenth hole.

Where he had a revelation. If Savannah *is* having an affair with Halverson or Halverton then she has surrendered to him the moral high ground.

All through their marriage Savannah had been the faithful one, the one whose steadiness guided their marriage, the one who had sacrificed her career while he advanced at the firm, the whimsical wife turned reluctant scold, who had tried to make babies while falling behind the pace in med school. And of course! It made sense that she was now the very soul of reason, now that she had proven unfaithful at last. But now he knew!

Sensing his advantage, and with the natural rhythm he had mastered as the captain of the Princeton golf team for two seasons, Gary kept his left foot grounded on the turf, felt his spikes grab and hold, his lower body stable and quiet, while he rotated his upper body in a powerful coil and lashed at the ball, unleashing a beauty, a long powerful draw that split the fairway 290 yards out.

He struck a perfect approach shot to the center of the green and drained the five footer for birdie. Back to one over par.

He birdied the next two holes and arrived at the eighteenth hole one under par. The eighteenth is a long par four, uphill, to a green that cants from top to bottom. It is important to keep the ball below the hole on the approach shot. Too deep and one finds oneself in a steep greenside bunker where it is impossible to get the ball up and down. Gary Hollow cranked a soaring drive up the fairway. His ball came to rest 160 yards from the pin, where the fairway meets the first cut of rough on the left side.

There was grass between his club and the ball. Not a good lie. Gary placed his gleaming seven iron behind the ball, hovering it over the grass, careful not to ground the club. He rehearsed what he would say to Savannah when he got home, all possible ways into his conversation about Halverson or Halverston. Halliburton! Ha! He waggled his club and tried to visualize the shot. He saw the lovely form of his wife, naked under the sheets, the sheets of Halliburton, the line of her long legs beneath the thin percales, the look of ecstasy on her face, and backed away from the shot. He shook his head and tried to empty it of every thought. Let the nothingness enter your shots, he recalled his Princeton coach say. The swing is the man. Relax, and feel it.

But as he built his stance and addressed the ball, his swing thoughts again were banished by the thought that he once had a wife and now he does not. The simple logic of subtraction: two minus one. Gary recalled the look on Savannah's face when he presented to her on their first anniversary a diamond necklace with matching earrings. He had taken care with its purchase, scouring the stores at the mall trying to find something that would fit his law school budget. The young woman who had wrapped the gift in silver striped paper had beamed up at him and told him what a perfect selection he had made for his wife. His *wife*! How proud he had been of that word, how delighted he was with Savannah, the way she moved around their small apartment, carrying toward him two gold-rimmed teacups she had found at a church rummage sale, their tiny treasures. One morning, he'd carelessly dropped one into the sink, breaking the handle. Late for court, he'd thrown the cup in the trash. That night he came home to Savannah seated at the kitchen table, holding the cup and a tube of epoxy. Were you going to tell me? she'd said.

He flailed at the ball, his swing ugly as a collapsing lawn chair, and caught it thin. Too much club and he'd airmailed the green. From where he stood, looking unsteadily from his moistened eyes, he could not tell if the ball had found the bunker. If he managed to land it in the grass beside the trap he could still save his par.

Gary Hollow trudged up the fairway to the green, stabbing at his eyes. Captain of his golf team, student government president, rising young associate sure to make partner, he understood nevertheless that he had lost Savannah. When he confronts her about Halverson – over what, a Sesame Street lunchbox? – she will look at him, in

that way that she does, smile her Morticia smile, and say,
"Gary, you are so sweetly dumb."

*Now, alone at dusk in the gleaming white Cadillac, Gary
remembers that day as if he has never left it. He scans the
eighteenth green, as he had scanned it that day, raking his
club through the tall grass, hoping for a break. Overhead, a
lone red-tailed hawk had soared, its broad wings beating,
searching its quarry. As he'd reached the crest of the hill
that day, Gary saw his ball at last, sitting like a poached
egg, buried in the hazard.*

In the Bathroom
at Arby's

by Nathaniel Tower

It's been a month since Samford discovered he wasn't a clone. Unless of course the doctor was lying, but Samford saw no reason why he would. Since watching the doctor die in front of him, he has been on the run. He hasn't spent two nights in the same city. Today he is in Nashville, taking a shit in an Arby's bathroom. Greasy food has always sent Samford straight to the shitter, and he hasn't been able to eat anything that isn't greasy for the past month.

Samford had been eating his meal, a regular roast beef sandwich with curly fries, when his bowels started to churn. He ditched the sandwich but grabbed the box of fries and headed to the bathroom as fast as he could, clenching his cheeks on the way. He didn't even have time to line the seat with toilet paper before plopping his hairy ass down on the black rim. The shit flew right out, like a barrage of missiles out of a big ass cannon. It would've been humiliating had anyone been in there at the time. Luckily, it is 3 in the morning and listening to Samford take a putrid shit in an Arby's bathroom is the last thing on anyone's mind.

Samford's still hungry as hell, maybe even hungrier now that his bowels have been cleansed by the grease invasion, but he wants to clean the outside of his ass before introducing more fries to his system. With the curly fry box still clutched in his right hand, Samford prepares to wipe, hoping the single-ply toilet paper will be adequate for removing the fresh mess. As he peels off a piece of toilet paper, he feels the roughness with his fingers and wonders if maybe it will rub the serial number right out of his ass.

The doctor's revelation has bugged the shit out of him for the last month. Why would they put a serial number on all the non-clones? What is the purpose of this tracking? And just how extensive is the tracking? Does someone know he's taking a shit in an Arby's bathroom while holding onto his curly fries at this very moment?

The door swings open and pounds against the tile wall. If the door had opened with less force, Samford probably wouldn't have heard it. But this noise is impossible not to hear, and so Samford hears it and opts to delay his wiping. Instead, he lifts his ankle-trousered legs as high into the air as he can. He isn't sure what there is to be paranoid about. It's an Arby's bathroom. People use it to piss or shit. That's all there is to it.

Samford listens as the person he presumes to be a man unzips his pants. A gentle waterfall trickle of urine pings against the porcelain of the urinal, like the man has some kind of kidney or prostate problem. Surely the man can hear Samford's strained breathing if Samford can hear such a delicate tinkle.

The toilet flushes and the pants zip back up. The sound of water gushing from the sink comes next, followed by the roar of the hand dryer, one of those high efficiency ones. It occurs to Samford then that he hasn't heard any footsteps. This bothers him to no end. No one walks around silently in an Arby's bathroom at 3 AM. Not unless there is some serious reason to remain silent.

In spite of Samford's incredible feeling of unease, he decides to take a bite out of one of the few remaining curly fries. He can't resist. Those fries are just that good. Besides, the hand dryer will drown out the sound.

The moment that Samford's teeth clamp down on the crisp seasoned fry, the stall door kicks open. Samford sees a mirror image of himself standing right in front of him, a curly fry clenched between the man's teeth.

"What the fuck, man? How 'bout some privacy?" Samford mumbles through his fry-ridden mouth.

Samford is neither embarrassed nor afraid. He recognizes the man immediately. It's that stupid bastard who'd been in bed with him and the woman with the clone brochure. This is the first time Samford has seen this man for six months, and Samford is again appalled by just how ugly he is.

"Wipe your ass and get up," the fake Samford says.

"You're a clone, aren't you?" Samford asks.

"I said wipe your ass and get up."

Samford leans to the left and begins wiping with his right hand. The grease-soaked cardboard slides through his buttcrack and the remaining fries spill into the toilet.

The clone laughs. "You dumb ass. Wipe with the TP, not the fries. I swear. You reals have no clue sometimes."

This is the first time Samford has been called a *real*. It's the first time he's heard the term. Even when he was training for the clone Olympics, such a word was never used. Suddenly, Samford wonders if he was the only real in the clone Olympics.

Samford lets the box fall into the toilet and starts wiping with the toilet paper. He winces as the rough paper scraps across his delicate flesh. He wonders if clones have problems like this.

"Hurry up. Your ass doesn't have to be immaculate. Let's go."

The clone grabs Samford and pulls him off the toilet even though there is much wiping still to be done.

"Where are we going?" Samford asks as he is dragged out of the stall, his pants around his ankles and his junk flopping like a bloated fish out of water. The clone continues to pull Samford, not allowing him to snatch up his pants as they exit the bathroom and enter the Arby's dining area. It doesn't matter though. There are no diners. The cute girl with the nose piercing behind the counter who took Samford's order doesn't even seem to notice his junk waving at her as the clone drags him outside.

"Where are you taking me?" Samford cries as the clone throws him on the curb. The concrete is warm against his bare ass.

"Shut your mouth, Sam," the clone shouts. "I'll do all the talking. You just listen." The clone lowers his voice. "Look, I need your help. You're the only one who can help me."

Samford is relieved by the sudden change of tone. "I'd be happy to help," Samford says. The clone offers a hand and pulls Samford to his feet. Then the clone reaches down and grabs Samford's pants. In one quick motion, he pulls them up to Samford's waist, covering his real genitals.

"So what exactly do you need?"

"I said no questions!" the clone yells before striking Samford in the face. The blow sends Samford through the glass pane of the Arby's front door.

"Get up, now!" the clone yells. He doesn't help Samford this time. "Stop being a pussy. I won't have my real be a pussy."

Samford slowly stands. He is frightened of the clone's power and temper. He wonders why *he* isn't that strong.

The clone grabs Samford and tosses him in the trunk of a white Ford. As the car speeds away from Arby's, Samford's body is flung around the spacious trunk. Still, Samford is glad to be riding in the dark and not up front with the ugly, menacing clone.

Roadies

by Kimberlee Smith

I don't know where my husband Dean is, and I'm not that interested in finding out right about now. I am transfixed. This is what I watch my mum Maybell pack up for our baby daughter Etheline and for herself: bottled water, canned sausages, two serrated knives, adult diapers size medium, lime cordial, several bottles of gin, a case of instant oatmeal and boxes of sultanas to go with it, cases of pureed baby food, peanut butter, wet wipes, kitchen-size plastic rubbish bags, her Ouija board, disposable baby nappies size six-to-nine months, plastic jugs filled with tap water, her favorite blanket, a fishing pole and lures she fixed from chook hackles, and the toy rattle Dean made for our daughter from dozens of real snake-tail rattles.

They're ready to roll and I know where they're going. If I could ask Mum one question at this moment, it would be, *Why did you wait so long?*

I don't remember the last time I was this excited. Like bouncing off the walls excited. She is heading out on a road trip to find her ex-husband, who also happens to be my daddy, who also happens to go by the name of Brother Tom Bend. He is a preacher. But not just any preacher.

He's also the founder of the Signs of Holiness Supreme Divinity Evangelical congregation. He and Mum traveled all around the continent spreading the word as soon as they were married. She was sixteen years old, and he was twenty-two.

They had me a year later and then of course I went with them. He took us with him on the evangelical gypsy caravan until one day we settled down so I could go to a proper school like regular kids. I was twelve, thirteen. Mum was good at schooling me at home, so I caught up all right. Then Brother Tom left. I've been waiting ever since to find out why. And Mum? She's been, well, mum. Never could get her to talk about them breaking up. Maybe on this trip I'll finally learn the real truth.

Brother Tom doesn't know he has a granddaughter. She's his first grandchild, and she's going to be his only. That's on account of me being his only child and that I died the same day my baby was born. She arrived in the living world by Caesarean section seconds before I arrived in this afterworld. It was a snakebite. Pardon. Snakebites. Multiple bites, one snake.

Brother Tom has some current events to catch up with; he has no cellular phone that we know of and the places he travels are generally so remote they're off the map. And to add to the alien nature of this whole situation, we haven't physically seen him since I was sixteen. Brother Tom told me I was old enough to take a husband of my own, so we were to take care of each other – and my mum – from then on.

Maybell – who is now Etheline's sole guardian – and Etheline are about to hit the road this arvo after tea. They're taking my old Jackaroo with bald tires and a petrol gauge that's perpetually stuck on one-third of a tank, no matter how much you fill it.

The snakes Dean left behind were well cared for and could be left alone for months. Mum slowly lowered the temperature in the room she relocated them to and dimmed the lights so they would naturally be inclined to hibernate. She fed them plenty of the mice Dean raised as food and then put the rest in brown cardboard boxes and let them loose in the bush. She locked up the house, and left the snakes behind. Can you imagine if the neighbors were to ever find out?

Etheline's bouncing every which way strapped into her car seat, sucking on the rattle Dean made for her, and having a good giggle now, but considering the driving trip to find Brother Tom will take weeks I reckon little Etheline's mood will turn in short order. Yet Maybell knows exactly what to do to soothe her.

Brother Tom is revered for his serpent handling, which is illegal here in Australia. All my life I saw him handle serpents and he was bitten probably a dozen times. Lost two fingers. Never once went to hospital. The bites just cured on their own.

Mum handled at least as many serpents as Brother Tom without being bitten. He believed she had been anointed by the Holy Spirit. She allowed him that. But she understood the serpents' nerves, and they picked up on it. Fell floppy as rag dolls in her hands.

What Mum's gleaned from members of the church is he's parked his caravan at Kununurra, in the Kimberley. It's an inhospitable place, where barramundi jump right out of the rivers and bite you in the ass and crocodiles drag you down under in the billabong and drown you before they tear you up for tea.

Kununurra is "God's country": unspoiled and virginal. The most pristine place on earth.

But Brother Tom's always had the passion to convert folks to his beliefs – it's in his head and in his heart and nobody can change the way that man operates. You'd figure he might want to find a way to save his family before taking on the rest of the world, but then again most people

132

would rather take on the rest of the world than tackle their most intimate problems.

Mum's headed toward the Red Center. She's passed over the North Bourke Bridge and is heading toward the banks of the Darling. She's always wanted to see Uluru for real, and now she's going to have her wish come true, sleeping under the stars in the shadow of the rock, marveling at bands of wild camels, and eating skewered emu cooked on the barbie, all the while taking care of a baby and in the wake of having lost most of her family. For a woman who spent her adult life following her husband around, she sure does have a will of her own and an adventurous side. I never did know for sure she could do it alone. I'd rather she didn't have to, though. I wish I'd been able to share that with Mum while I was alive.

Now, Mum's been driving for about eight hours and finally is stopping. A place called Trilby Station that advertised "outback accommodations" on a roadside sign. There are caravan hookups and I bet this is the first time Mum will have missed the old caravan we lived in for so many years.

She's only stopped to refuel, give a bottle to the bub, and change her nappy. I wondered why Mum brought adult nappies but now I know too much. She hasn't had to stop to use the loo since she's been driving. Dear Lord. She's a woman on a mission, being maybe more passionate about this trip than Brother Tom could ever dream of being about his religious calling. And our sweet little bub, she knows her mum and daddy – albeit her highly distracted and fidgety daddy – are right here with her, looking down on her. I've tried to connect with Maybell as well, but with no success. It seems as if something is blocking our connection.

I reckon by the time they reach their final destination, Etheline will have cut a couple teeth and be able to sit up all by herself. She will know how to clap her hands and play peek-a-boo. But she still will not know what it's like for her mum to hold her. I hope it's a very, very long time before she and I are reunited in my world.

Family Values

by Vanessa Weibler Paris

"Don't rely on others for your happiness," I start. "You're responsible for your own happiness."

"Never admit weakness," Iris says without missing a beat.

It's a game Iris invented. She comes up with a topic, and then we ping-pong back and forth until someone is stumped or gives up. Tonight's topic is "Family Values (Things My Family Taught Me Without Me Even Realizing It)."

"Don't vote Republican," I offer.

"Everything you do reflects on your parents," Iris responds.

"If it's worth doing, it's worth doing well," I counter.

"Emotions should be kept private," says Iris. Sitting at the kitchen island, she's licking blackstrap molasses off the serrated blade of a steak knife. She does it every morning. Blackstrap molasses, she tells me, is full of iron and calcium. Full of *strength*.

"If you're not five minutes early, you're late," from me.

"Don't stand out," says Iris. "Conform."

She dips into the jar and licks, dips and licks, running her tongue over sharp silver teeth as the molasses stretches slowly, thickly along its edge. I watch, as always, for a burst of blood, but there is none. "Doesn't it hurt?" I'd once asked. "Yes," she'd replied, nothing more.

I can think of more – *you are expected to attend college, what goes around comes around, you can succeed at anything you put your mind to* – but fold instead. Iris likes to win.

This woman, when she met me for our first date, looked like any other woman on an evening date: little black dress (standard, slimming), dramatic eye makeup (sexy, smoky), and crimson lips.

What I didn't know then was this: That wasn't Iris on a first date, that was just *Iris*. Even now, at my kitchen island, she's in full eye makeup, with a tight black top, jeans, and bare feet with black toenails.

It takes a while to get to know someone.

"I'm an artist," she'd shared that first night. Weeks later she opened a closet and showed me the pieces of her first exhibit. She'd collected dozens of x-rays of broken bones, then arranged them into a glowing new person. Completely whole, and entirely broken. A body that, if real, might collapse hollow and clattering into a pile of shards if poked hard. "The left hand was mine," she'd whispered close, another night, when we weren't talking at all. "I used a hammer. I screamed." My left hand, on her thigh, shook.

"I actually kind of like skinny guys," she'd mentioned that first night. Now she warns me not to eat too many wings when I go out with Bobby and the boys; she doesn't want me to put on weight. She stuffs my baggy clothes in the laundry and stocks the drawers with new ones, small ones that show just how thin I am. She asks me to pull up a sleeve or hoist up a pant leg so she can touch the bone beneath. "I wish I could hold it tight," she says, making a circle of her thumb and forefinger, wrapping them around my forearm or ankle, straining to touch their tips. "If it were just a little smaller ..."

We haven't had sex yet. She says it will be soon.

I hear a tiny gasp and turn around. Iris is looking at the knife, smeared with black and red, and blood stains her mouth like crimson lipstick.

"Kiss me," she says, and I do, pressing on her softness as she leans into my sharp.

"You taste bitter," I whisper. "But I like it."

"Because it is bitter," she responds, circling my wrists hard with both hands, "and because it is my heart."

Wednesday

30

July
2014

The Getaway

by Joanne Jagoda

It's 5:30. If I see those damn green numbers one more time I'm going to puke. Why doesn't the time go faster? I'm packed though it took me all night. I splurged on a few new outfits and that sexy one shoulder black bathing suit, but I'll regret it when the bills come. Oh hell, for once I don't care. David is picking me up at ten. I've got to keep busy until then. I'll pay bills, dust and water the plants.

I need strong coffee. The twins won't be up for another hour. They're going to their summer jobs and will be gone before David comes. It's better this way. Robin is still giving me a hard time about him. This pile of magazines keeps getting bigger, but I don't want to throw them out with the articles about their grandfather's company. It's been exciting. George has been interviewed on the news and written up in all kinds of newspapers and magazines. He'll even be on 60 Minutes next week. I didn't know he has been working on this top-secret project for years, a sophisticated rocket receptor system known as Project Octopus. Israel used a similar version, their Iron Dome, in the Gaza War in 2012. I read that the new system is more advanced as it intercepts medium to long-range rockets from a much further distance.

Lucky for us George is so successful. He's covering the girls' tuition. It's been rough since Paul died. Without

George and Lillian's help, I would've lost the house, and I don't know how I could have paid their college bills.

I'll put stamps on these bills and shower. I'll wear my new fuchsia cropped pants and a tight black tee-shirt. I only need to tussle my hair and add a sporty cap in case David has the top down. I hope he does even if it's cold. Lucky he was able to get away mid-week. I didn't want to be gone from the girls on the weekend.

"You look cute Mom. Have fun and be good."

"Thanks Cassie. Grab my suitcase and bring it downstairs."

"Uhhh ... what **do** you have in here? Rob, Mom's going for two months. What's for lunch Rob?"

"I made you a peanut butter sandwich. Mom, I don't like him. You can cancel. Say you're sick. Say you came down with a rare disease that's catchy. Come on Cass. I'll drop you at BART."

"Oh Rob, I just don't get your attitude ... And don't SLAM the door."

Why is she so against David? She can be so unreasonable. I love this picture of the four of us in Maui. Oh Paul, I miss those fun times when life was simpler.

*   *   *   *   *

Nobody on the street, just that utility truck again. I feel like I'm being watched. I'm usually the "watcher." I'm going to get to my car from the basement. There's a back door to the street. Good I left my car four blocks away in an alley. Those assholes don't trust me. If this operation I've been working on for months isn't successful, they'll go after me. I'll be fish food in San Francisco Bay. When I found out yesterday the final testing won't be complete for a month, I had to cancel my plans for the kidnap to happen today while we're in the Napa Valley. My employers were not happy. I explained to them that I have to keep cozying up to Anne for this all to work and things can't be rushed, but they don't get it.

I'm glad I ditched that shitty rental for this BMW convertible. This charade is getting to be a chore though I suppose sleeping with Anne today won't be a bad perk of this assignment. Once this assignment is complete, I'll leave for South America and disappear. With my flawless Spanish, I'll blend in easily and have plenty of money to enjoy. Hopefully Grandpa George will give up the specs promptly. I won't relish hurting Cassie, though I'll do what I need to do.

Ah Anne, in another life I could have loved a sweet thing like you. Oh, she's opening the door before I can even ring. She's waiting for me. Sweet foolish girl.

"Hi David. I like your sporty cargo shorts and Giants cap."

"Hi darlin', and you look adorable. Give me your suitcase. Whoa, you didn't tell me we're going for a month."

"Very funny. I wasn't sure what to bring so I brought everything."

"Want to hear the lads from Liverpool?"

"I love the Beatles."

"You know all the words but you're way off key. Here we are at the Sattui winery. First we'll taste some of the Sattui wines. I'll get us a bottle of whichever you like and we'll picnic on their grounds."

"I like their merlot the best."

"Good choice Annie. Their 2011 Napa Valley Merlot is outstanding. Ready for lunch?"

"My tummy is growling. While you pay for the wine, I'll get in the deli line. So much to choose from. Mmmm, the roast turkey looks good, some cheeses, that broccoli raisin salad and a long baguette."

"And I'll find us a picnic table in the shade."

"This spot is perfect. I love looking out at the vineyards. It feels like we are in France, instead of an hour and a half from San Francisco. Mmmm, taste the broccoli salad. It's so good and this brie is …"

I know I'm being watched. Maybe it is the two men at the table over to the right who look like rednecks with big beer bellies or that olive-skinned man to the left in the '49er cap. Got to get away from here. It's too exposed. My employers obviously don't trust me or maybe somebody else wants the plans to Project Octopus.

"Let's go, Ann."

"David, why rush? I'm still eating."

"No, got to go NOW. We have spa appointments. Finish eating in the car."

I'm checking the mirror. Good thing Anne is oblivious. She's absorbed in the beautiful scenery of Highway 29, the oak trees lining the road and the acres of vineyards. Can't blame her for that. Seventeen miles to Calistoga. I booked mud baths at a fancy spa. Nice to spend money that's not mine.

"Never had a mud bath. I'm glad we're next to each other. Ohhh, it's squishy. Very warm."

"You're in volcanic ash. Great healing powers." *It's even making me relax. Maybe I'm just being paranoid about someone following me but I'm a pro at this business.*

"It's so fun to be in tubs next to each other. Then massages. I feel like a pampered princess."

§

"David, this hotel room is elegant. I'll be back in a minute."

"Annie, I thought you were tired. Very nice, your lacy black nightgown."

"It's been a long while David. I've been uh … looking forward to being with you."

She's an awesome lover. I'm such a shit to use her. "Let's get ready for dinner. I have reservations at Bouchon, a world class restaurant, Michelin rated."

"That sounds fantastic. I'll just shower, but first I want to check on the girls."

"Hi Cassie, how was work?"

"Fine. Having fun Mom?"

"I had a mud bath and massage. We're going to a fancy restaurant. I feel like a princess. Can I speak to your sister?"

"Uh, well she's not here."

"She was supposed to come home from work and stay at Denise's with you. Where is she?"

"Mom, I promised I wouldn't tell."

"Cassie, I'm not amused."

"She went over to Patty's house. They're going to a rave in the Mission later tonight."

"A **what**?"

"A rave. She'll kill me."

"Now I'm pissed."

"Let me try to call her Mom."

"Anne, you're going to wear a hole in the carpet. Relax, she's fine." *Robin's a little shit.*

"David, I have a right to be worried. She's just … There's my phone!"

"Cass, did you reach her?"

"Mom, it's Rob. Can you chill? I'm not going to the rave. I figured out it was a crappy thing to do. You have to give me a little space. We're all going to a late movie. Heard you had a mud bath. Oooh yuck."

"Thanks Robin. Love you honey and uh ... glad you checked in."

"David, come here. You were right. I shouldn't worry so much."

"Mmmm, Annie, I do like your kisses. No more fretting over Robin. We better hurry or we'll be late for our reservation although ... mmm, yes, you do have the nicest bum and perfect breasts. While you're showering I'll be outside by the pools."

I thought I saw that olive-skinned man on a lawn chair by the pool. Is that him in the deep end?

Hijinks Ensue

by h. l. nelson

Dear Diary,

Oh my god, I'm dying, this is so hilarious. I just returned from a StrollerFit class, where Robin, Julie, and I wrapped dolls up in baby blankets and put them in our strollers, then we pretended to trip and dump our "babies" on the ground, pull up our shirts to "breastfeed" without covering up, and be obnoxious and competitive "new moms" about our babies' height, weight, and head measurements. The other women caught on after about twenty minutes and insisted we leave. But, it sure was a riot! We collapsed in my car, crying from laughter. It was one of the best things we've pulled off in the last two months.

Let me back up, though, because you, dear diary, have no idea how the hell this all began. I shall enlighten you, then I must be off to my painting class at 2 P.M.

As soon as school let out in early June and we all found ways to busy our children, like summer camps, jobs, and visits to relatives, Julie, Robin and I started meeting at my house. Robin and Anne had had a falling out for the hundredth time, this time because Anne swore Robin stole liquor from Anne's cabinet. And Julie, of course, just followed along. I'm pretty sure she dislikes pampered Anne and her bleached butthole as much as we do, but she's just quiet about it. Anyway, Robin later told me that she had actually taken the alcohol, which I thought was hysterical. My hatred for Anne has blossomed over this latest installment of 'Anne's Winter Wonderland'. This year, she seems hell-bent on making us all her personal slaves. I told Anne to stick the party, all the hors d'oeuvres, the goddamn ice sculptures, the Alpine mountain of Swiss chocolate she's having flown in, up her perfectly bleached asshole.

So the three of us had my house to ourselves all day, and I had decided that we needed to start our own Moms' Revolution. When I said the words "Moms' Revolution," a slow Cheshire-cat grin spread across Robin's face and Julie's eyes bugged so big I thought they would pop out of her head. Exactly the response I thought I'd get. For a week, I'd been staying up late in my art room and planning out our revolution.

One night, Brandon had come in behind me without me hearing. I don't know how long he'd been standing there, but he said, "What do 'Perfume to Piss', 'Mutilated Machines', and 'StrollerShit' mean? I slammed my laptop down and said, "Why in the hell did you sneak up on me like that?"

He folded his arms. "Look, Joan, I don't care what kind of weird stuff you're writing or whatever, we just haven't talked much for a while and I thought I'd see if you wanted to spend some time together. I guess not." Then he left before I could answer him. The truth was, I barely thought about him anymore. He spent most nights at work, so the kids and I had learned to get on without him. This made me feel sad. Years we'd spent tied at the hip – trying weird restaurants like the Pho Florence, the Thai / Italian place that was open for four months; making love in crazy places like the exit hallways of malls; curling up together every evening on the couch. When did we stop doing these things? After the kids were born, of course. I totally understand why people get divorced more often after having kids – they're super stressful.

145

Anyway, I decided I would make up with him later. The work I was about to do with the ladies was important.

So, to loosen us up, Project Mutilated Machines was first up. That was about a month ago. It had already started to get hot outside. We piled all of Robin's kitchen appliances on her back veranda. Robin had brought one of her own, the dreaded Foreman grill. It was awkward, seeing all that metal and plastic splayed out in the afternoon sun. Like prostitutes at a barn raising. For a minute, we didn't know what to do. They both looked at me. Then, I said, "Fuck it" and swung the Louisville Slugger down onto the juicer. Jagged bits of plastic flew in all directions. Julie covered her eyes and Robin war-whooped. I must say, it felt good. It felt damn good.

By the end of it, we were screaming at the top of our lungs as we pummeled the sad machinery. Julie yelled, "No, I don't want to host another dinner party for your boss who loves burgers! I fucking HATE – GEORGE – FOREMAN!" punctuating each word with a smash of her bat into the small black appliance. Robin, green-kneed, was punishing pieces of her bread maker that had attempted escape onto the lawn. Her ponytail had fallen and she looked crazed with her bugged eyes and spittle on her bottom lip. It was like Nazi Germany all over again, right here in Palm Valley. But the Jews were made of plastic and metal.

Afterward, we surveyed the destruction, smoothing our hair and re-tucking our blouses. We felt a new respect for each other. I could see it in their eyes. And for ourselves. There was no going back.

A week later, we walked into the mall like it was a normal day, just three women shopping together. Stopping at the food court, we ordered Cinnabun rolls and ate them standing up, the sugar making our lips stick together. I hadn't eaten sweets with such abandon since I was a kid.

146

We yelled at passing teens and 20-something boys, hooted and hollered, "Hey, you want some of this?" A security officer peered at us, but didn't do anything. What was he going to do? Forever 21 was having a sale on thongs, so after sugaring up, we sauntered in and asked the checker to go to the back and look for items we each wanted. Like a fur-lined velvet zipper vest in size 4, for me, a red sequined scoop-necked halter top in size 6 for Robin, and a champagne-colored velour jumpsuit in size 2 for Julie. I told her we'd tried on all of these pieces the weekend before, so they simply had to have them in stock.

When she'd gone in the back after some convincing with a fifty dollar bill, a perplexed look on her face, we dug into the huge bin full of thongs and stretching them out between our fingers, we shot them across the store at each other until the checker returned. Well, Robin and I shot them at each other and Julie. Surprisingly, the checker came out from the back with almost exactly what we'd asked for. That gave us a good laugh. Even though none of the sizes fit us, of course, I paid for the items to immortalize the day.

At The Gap, Robin and I pretended to be mannequins, except Mannequin Robin tweaked Mannequin Me's tits, as I stuck them out proudly. Several teens stopped, laughed, and snapped pictures.

Hanging around until near closing time, we finally headed to Macy's. Kendra let us in, a big smile on her face. Brandon and I had made her and Kurt get jobs last month so they can really understand what it means to work. She hates that job, and I don't blame her. I remember working retail, too. She whispered that she had cut the feed to the security camera in the beauty department, said it would look like it was a technical glitch. Perfect. And no, I don't feel guilty at all about having had Kendra help. She has to learn that this "beauty" industry is a load of fucking bullshit. Buy this cream, primp that, lose the fat. She's started to look at me differently, act more respectfully. She and Kurt, both. It's been good for my relationships with them, overall. This makes me happy.

What we did was we dumped all of the Dolce and Gabbana, Juicy Couture, CK perfumes into a plastic container, leaving a little in the bottom of each bottle. Whew, it smelled like all the chicks from a whorehouse and a strip club got together in the same room. Then, using a funnel, we filled up the perfume bottles with our piss. We'd each been collecting it for a week. Even Julie thought this prank was funny, but she's allergic to most perfumes. Man, I wish I could see the faces of the women who buy our eau de toilet.

I have to pick up the kids from their jobs soon – Kurt from Scoops ice cream and Kendra from Macy's, but it's been real, dear diary. I'm going to take them to the beach for being such awesome kids lately.

Love,

Joan StrollerFit-Champ-Beat-Your-Appliances-and-Urinate-In-The-Beauty-Industry's-Bottle Colderman

August

Quixote Always Loses

by Guilie Castillo Oriard

The Curaçao branch of Ehrlich Fiduciary operates out of an eighteenth-century *landhuis* that's been declared a World Heritage site. As far as the island government's concerned, this alone justifies outrageous rent – which does not include maintenance. The sprawling plantation house is all high ceilings and French doors and wide verandas and hardwood shutters. The parquet floors, waxed every three months, make the clack of Milena Durant's favorite Jimmy Choos echo through the halls. When she's working late she goes barefoot, which has made her privy to much she shouldn't be. Information is mighty currency.

But the grapevine isn't infallible.

The best view in the building, hands down, is from the south side of Wing B. Milena's office, to be exact. Caribbean blue in sky and sea fills three quarters of the window behind her desk. The riot-colored buildings of the Handelskade – that cupcake Amsterdam, the unofficial icon of this tiny and otherwise unknown island – fill the remaining quarter. A bright cruise ship, Royal Caribbean judging by the size, perches today like overripe fruit in the middle ground.

The view is wasted on the two people in Milena's office. She's paging, somewhat vaguely, through a yellow legal pad. The man sitting across the desk from her, Ehrlich Group CEO Rowan Barry, has turned his chair sideways, and seems deep in contemplation of the shirt buttons straining over the zeppelin of his belly.

"Is this going to be a problem?"

Milena looks up, but he's still gazing at his stomach. A touch of mutiny creeps into her reply. "Why would it?"

He sucks on his lower lip. "You and I don't often clash on judgment issues. I thought you might be ... disappointed."

"Disappointment implies gain was expected. I've nothing to gain from who takes my place. Surprised, yes. Not disappointed."

"He was your hire. You did expect –"

"He was *your* hire, Rowan. Remember? I wanted to hire that ballbreaker from London to replace Stepan as Legal Counsel and make *him* Managing Director. You were the one who insisted on Luis."

"He's Latin. The Mexican market is going to hell. Someone like him, with his connections, his track record, can make all the difference."

"Which explains why I'm surprised."

Rowan taps his thumbs on the tautness of his stomach, a pensive drumroll. "He'll be a great MD. One day. When he's not so raw. So full of –" He tilts back the granite block of his head, looks for the word he wants – which, apparently, isn't *shit* – in the ceiling beams. "Idealism. Pipe dreams. You know what I mean. You were, too, at one point."

"So were you. All of us."

He looks at her. "An MD can't be a Quixote."

"He'll grow out of it. We all –"

"I have ample faith he will. What I'm saying – what Group is saying – is not *yet*. You need to name your successor. You need to begin the transition. Stepan is chomping at the bit to get started."

Milena leans back, and her chair creaks a complaint. "You spoke to Stepan? Already?"

"We had to know if he was on board." Rowan's lids droop to half-mast.

Why did she think there was still a chance, that her window – Luis's window – was still open? "He'll leave, you know."

Rowan uses the corner of a post-it pad to clean under the nail of his thumb. "He's bluffing."

"It's the only reason he came here. To be MD. He'll have nothing to stay for." And he'll blame her. He'll think it's because of that stupid fight. Her tantrum over that woman. He'll think she's punishing him. Which wouldn't be so farfetched if it was anyone else.

Her mother defined love as wishing for someone else's happiness more than you wish for your own. Over the last month, Milena has had to come to terms with the fact she might be – no, is – in love. The worst kind.

The kind without a future. (She's leaving, Luis is staying.)

The unrequited kind. (She's no naïf.)

The kind where none of the above makes a whit of difference.

And the only thing she has to give that might have any value at all to him – her current job – isn't, it's been decided, hers to give.

Rowan rests an elbow on the desk. "Luis wants to leave, let him. But I'll bet you next year's NOPAT he won't. I'll bet you this year's *and* next year's."

"What if he does, Rowan?"

"He's too proud. How would he explain leaving Cabrera y Machado in Mexico City for this nine-month stint in the Caribbean? He won't be happy, sure, but he'll finish his contract."

"And if you're wrong? Are we willing to lose him?"

He studies her with those half-lidded eyes. Frog eyes. Cold eyes. "Are you? How far would you go to avoid losing him? If this were your call, would you hand over this office – *your* office – to Luis? Now?"

Luis, who still cares so much about Doing The Right Thing. Luis, who refuses to grasp the basic give-and-take that keeps this business running. Luis, who has no guile in his soul – not even enough to realize how transparent his Man Of The World act is. Luis, who expects the world to function according to karmic rules or something. Being completely objective, all emotion aside, all personal involvement – even if objectivity isn't something she feels capable of right now – there can only be one answer.

"No," she says, and the guilt feels like the Devil whispering in her ear.

"Good." Rowan stands, stretches. Nonchalant. Heedless of the lives lying in shards around him. "Look into that replacement for Stepan, will you? The – what did you call her? The ballbreaker?"

"She's with Ernst & Young now. Legal for LatAm. We'd have to offer her diamonds and pearls to get her here."

"Would she consider MD in a couple of years? Stepan wants to go to Luxembourg. You know he turned down Singapore? Said he's had it with tropical weather."

Her stomach turns a triple axel, lands wrong, doesn't quite recover. "What about Luis?"

Rowan shrugs. "A little competition won't hurt him. Might even help him."

Luis will hate – no, revile her. But that won't be as bad as knowing the damage she's inflicted on his career. Because her fucking him did, in fact, fuck him over. If she hadn't been sleeping with him, she'd have made damn sure he was ready. Instead, she coddled him. Didn't push hard enough. Didn't coach him the way she should have. Not in the office, anyway.

Perhaps she can still help him. Not that he'll ever know, or believe it if he did. "I agree, Rowan, that Luis isn't ready now. But he'll be a kick-ass MD one day, not too far in the future. Ehrlich would do well to make sure he doesn't leave us before then."

Rowan acknowledges that with a single nod. "Sounds good. But at what price, Milena?"

"Forget about that London woman. It won't work, and she'll be ridiculously expensive. Wasn't the Brazil Legal Counsel looking to relocate? He knows Stepan. They'd work well together." And with his Compliance background, Milena feels he's unlikely to have MD ambitions. He won't be a rival for Luis.

"It's an option."

"A good option. It'll make it easier to convince Luis of staying."

Rowan nods again, noncommittally, and turns to go. That's it, that's all the assurance she'll get. Now she has to find a way – and the balls – to break it to Luis.

With a hand on the door, Rowan turns back. "What about Singapore?"

"What about it?"

"The Latin American market, especially the Mexican market, has strong ties there. Treaties and such. Lots of opportunities. Something to consider, perhaps."

Milena feels cold creeping up to her face. "You mean – Luis should go in my stead?"

Rowan chuckles, dry as winter-chapped lips. "I don't want him running a branch, but you think I'll give him a position in Group? No, Milena. I meant a – I don't know, a directorship or something. Get him to run a few projects, get him involved with sales maybe. Or he could work with Asian clients. Something new for him."

"He knows Asian clients. He was in Hong Kong for two years with HSBC." Her head is spinning.

"Just an idea, Milena." He winks at her, opens the door. "You could come up with something interesting for him there. If you wanted to."

Rowan, the bastard, always manages to find that most secret hope: one's most contemptible temptation. And then he holds it out, a careless child squeezing a baby chick, daring you to do something, anything, before he squashes it to death.

Typical Rowan, the bastard. Find that most secret of hopes, then go for its jugular.

La Ronde /
Jimmie and Sal

by Townsend Walker

The phone rings in Jimmie's Bungalow in Venice Beach. It's Sal.

"Jimmie, sweetheart, how's the leg?"

"How the fuck you think it is?"

"I heard you broke it."

"Heard I broke it? What are you, some kind of pathological sadist?"

"Jimmie, Jimmie, let me explain things to you. I had to do that, had to."

"No, I don't understand why you had to break my leg."

"But, since I like you, it was a clean break, no? It'll heal quick. I even asked this doc I know what kind of break heals best, and my guys called 911, didn't they. That's the kind of friend I am."

"Sal, you have so missed the point, I don't believe it. Why did you <u>have</u> to break my leg?"

"I thought you knew. You have some time?"

"That's all I got these days."

"I lend you money. You don't pay me back. I ask and ask. You don't pay me back. If word gets out that there are no consequences when Salvatore Mancuso doesn't get paid back, what kind of business is he running? You see?"

"But you were an investor, you were an owner. I didn't borrow money, you invested in a movie production. Big difference."

"You said, and I remember things like this, you said 'Sal, my friend, I have this fantastic script, if the Weinsteins or MGM knew, they'd snap it up in a minute. But I'm giving you this opportunity. I want you to think about it as a loan with a guaranteed interest rate of 1000%."

"That's the way we pitch out here. Where you been?"

"Well where I been is that if you don't come up with something by the end of this week you're going to need a wheelchair, not crutches my friend."

"Look, I got this opportunity for you to cash in big time, say $150-200K."

"Opportunity? Sounds like I gotta do something to get my money. Not exactly precisely how this business works."

"Well, you wanna hear about it or not?"

"How much you say?"

"150-200K."

"Speak to me."

"This dame in Manhattan, Park Avenue, is paying to off her husband cuz he beats her up."

"You need a hit man. Me, I'm a money man. I lend money. I take risks most banks wouldn't even let walk in the door, much less open your mouth. What do I know about hit men? I run a legitimate business activity."

"Okay, okay. I just thought maybe this was a way I could pay you back."

"Jimmie baby, I gotta run, call you back, maybe I'll drop by later. You gonna be there?"

"Where the fuck you think I'm going with a busted leg? Clubbing? I don't think so, and you wouldn't believe how unfashionably shaped and colored casts are. I wouldn't be seen outside with it."

§

Jimmie hobbles into the kitchen to make a sandwich, opens a bottle of Grey Riesling to wash it down, goes out to the pool with the bottle (no glass) and a ham sandwich. Thinks to himself: awful look tan line I'm going to have with this cast. Then:

"Damn him to hell," to himself.

"Damn him to hell," louder.

"Damn him to hell," to the sidewalk.

The gate opens, the Sal-your-pal demeanor is on display: wide grin on a broad face, kind blue eyes, ruddy cheeks, blond hair slicked back. Sal has a square head sitting on a square body, tailored suits that make him nearly (stress on nearly) suave. Today he's sporting a tan suit, Super 200 wool.

"Who you damning to hell in here?"

"Oh, it's you. No one, no one, just aggravated by this fucking leg."

"Well, to show you where my heart is I brought you some flowers. Roses, sent up from Ecuador, this guy says. You imagine that, sending flowers on a plane all the way from Ecuador. That's got to be what, 5000 miles?"

"Well, maybe three. You want some wine? There's another bottle in the fridge. Glasses are in the cupboard."

Sal comes back out from the kitchen with two glasses and wine in an ice bucket. And some roasted almonds.

"The living room, what are you starting up, a bordello? All that velvet and wood."

"Nah, friend of mine, decorator, experimenting with stuff. I said he could use it."

Sal flops down in a lounge chair next to Jimmie; claps him on the leg.

"Shit!"

"Sorry, didn't notice. That's the bad one, huh?"

Under his breath: "This will pass. This will pass. This will pass."

"I made some inquiries."

"And?"

"We can probably do business, but you gotta understand, there's a fifty percent discount on whatever the dame pays."

"Fifty fucking percent?"

"What can I say? Standard. You want me to break the rules of the game. No, of course you don't."

"Like I have a choice."

"That's the spirit, my friend."

Sal moves closer to Jimmie and whispers. "Now you tell me everything I need to know to find this guy and the dame with the money."

"The guy's name is Franklin Lincoln Cabot III."

"So what's he look like?"

"Big guy: six foot, maybe a little less, 250, pasty faced, big nose, curly hair."

"What color?"

"Black, I think."

"You think? What's he do?"

"Gotta get back to you on that one?"

"Excuse me. You gotta get back to me? Did I hear that right? You, who are giving me this gift to pay back what you owe me? You do have some idea of how many people there are in Manhattan?"

"Yeah, yeah. I know."

"What else do you know?"

"He wears blue tinted Prada aviators, rain, snow and shine and he loses his kids in the park."

"Well now Jimmie my lad, you haven't told me jack-all. I'd suggest you get more information before I even want to think about accepting this job as partial payment for what you owe. Capice?"

"Yeah, I understand, Sal. I'll get back to you, tonight, promise."

"While you're at it. How about the name of the dame who's making the payoff? I'll leave you now to go to work."

"Sure, tonight, promise."

On his way out Sal raps Jimmie's cast with the butt end of his pistol.

"Sayonara, sweetheart."

Under his breath, "Fuck you."

Jimmie hustles to his computer looking for Cabot. Not hard to find, works at the Goldman, had a society wedding. Photos of Frank and Madge at benefit functions. Jimmie pays (not insignificant amounts) for phone numbers and addresses.

Three hours later.

"Sal, Jimmie. Here's the scoop."

"Let's hope you got it right this time. You got a lot riding on it."

Things We Can't Explain

by Derek Osborne

Max had never asked God for anything, he never felt he had the right, not during the war, nor that night off Hatteras when he was sure the sea would take them, not even when Maggie lay dying. But that day as he watched the Dock Master beating Rebecca's chest, the Coast Guard EMT's opening their packs, the smell of oxygen – he prayed – it wasn't their time. Leaning against the companionway ladder he had closed his eyes and pleaded and begged and promised he'd do anything, anything so long as they lived.

And so they did.

"I wasn't sure about the color," he says, looking about the room they've converted for Rebecca's recovery. It's the house he and Eddie went to look at that July 3rd morning. Rebecca spent nearly a month in Boston General. They flew her back to Nantucket earlier this week. The room they've set up was originally an enclosed sun-porch off the back deck, a sweeping view of the harbor, but now it's equipped with a hospital bed, a nightstand, a small sitting area with an entertainment unit and a big brass telescope. Max is hoping the telescope will give Rebecca something to do, satisfy her natural curiosity, *snooping*, la senora would say. It will be her place for the next three months. From the porch they can see the entire harbor and most of the waterfront. The break in her fibula (the sudden crack that loosed the tiny fragment of bone which travelled up to her heart) will need at least six more weeks to heal. She had been without breath for less than four minutes. By all accounts the baby is fine. It's a hot August morning; at least there's a breeze.

"It is very nice," Rebecca says, though he knows she's being polite. She can only take a mild pain suppressant due to the pregnancy. Max has broken his share of bones and he knows the discomfort. Anja's doing a terrific job with massage oils and flower essences and every homeopathic remedy in the book. Eddie comes by in the afternoons and plays his guitar. They've flown in an acupressure specialist. Max doesn't care what it costs.

La senora turns her nose up at most of it, though she did gave Anja a check, in secret. "If all that nonsense helps so be it," she said at dinner, and then, when she and Max were alone, "This is not your fault. She's been getting hurt like this ever since she was small. A regular tomboy." It's interesting how her English becomes quite good when they're alone.

"And how are you?" Rebecca is asking. It's not hard to see how much the past few weeks have taken out of him. The cancer is spreading.

"I'm fine."

"Liar."

"I am. I have everything I've ever wanted."

He's forgotten Andi is sitting in the other room. Rebecca glances in her direction.

"You two still need to talk," she says, "This has all got to be very hard for her."

Andi is pretending she can't hear. The painted gray floorboards and windowed walls bounce the sound like a drum.

"Andi," Rebecca says, "can you please come here for a moment?"

Max has been avoiding this ever since that day in the hospital, the day he got confused. He's watching his

169

daughter walk across the room. She glides, like her mother did. Maggie studied dance when she and Max were in school. Grace seems to have come naturally to their youngest.

"Give me your hand," Rebecca says.

The air is still ionized from the morning squalls. All of the French doors along the porch are open, the sun rushing in. It's Sunday, the boats out in the harbor are leaving and some have their sails set; less experienced owners stay under power. The big mega-yachts won't go until after lunch. For them, Newport is only an hour or two away.

"I've ordered a motorized chair," Max says, indicating the telescope. "It will lift you up to the eyepiece ..."

"Max," Rebecca says.

He looks at his daughter, taking a deep breath.

"Guys, I'm okay," she says, but the tears are already coming. "I am."

Max is standing on the other side of the bed. He comes around. At 5 ft 4 she barely comes up to his chest.

Rebecca is still holding her hand. She looks up at Max. "I am not," she says, matter of fact, speaking to Andi. "I have just met the love of my life and now I am going to lose him. My baby will never know his father."

Max has closed his eyes, slowly shaking his head. He's never been good with these things.

"I'm just so angry!" Andi says, breaking away and stepping back toward the open doors.

Max knows what is coming next. He can see his daughter looking around. She has always had a habit of throwing things.

"Not the telescope!"

She had indeed been eyeing the scope, but instead grabs the spindle back chair beside it and in one fluid motion has it over her head, coming down in a slanting arc and catching the edge of the open door beyond. The chair

170

and the glass explode as she falls to her knees. La senora comes rushing in. Max raises his hand to her to stop.

"I'm just so angry," Andi says, fists clenched, emphasizing the word. "I know Mom's been dead almost eight years but shouldn't I hate you? (This to Rebecca) Shouldn't I be pissed at both of you? (Then at Max) You've acted like two spoiled brats with no concern for anyone … like children … like …"

"Like people in love?" la senora says from the doorway. "As if there will be no tomorrow."

"Fuck it," Andi screams, bringing her fists to the floor. She is still kneeling among the splinters and glass. She does not mean la senora, more like she is cursing the room, the house, the island, as if her screams might be heard by everyone, everywhere.

"Max, give her a pillow."

Max grabs one of the pillows from the bed and shoves it underneath his daughter just as she comes down again but it's too late. They all hear the crush.

"Fuck you," she growls, raising her fists again and bringing them down again on the pillow this time. "Fuck you."

The pillow is bloody.

"Go on," Rebecca says, practically cheering her on, "Beat them all. Beat them for me."

Eddie and Anja have come into the room.

"Smash them to pieces," Anja says.

All Eddie sees is the blood and the screaming.

And Andi is really screaming, "Fuck you! fuck you!" and flailing at will. She growls like a dog. The pillow is starting to tear. Max is trying to gauge the extent of her cuts as she lifts and pounds the pillows. He decides it can wait. The others have circled around his daughter there in front of the bed.

"It's not fair," Rebecca says, raising her voice.

"It's not," Andi says.

"It's just not fair!" Rebecca yells.

Max wants to run from the room. By the look on Eddie's face, he's thinking the same thing.

"Fuck it," Andi says, bringing both her fists down again.

"Fuck it," Anja blurts out.

"Fuck it," the three of them say in unison as Andi starts swinging her clenched fists like a club.

"Fuck it," the three of them say again.

It's becoming a chant. "Fuck it ... Fuck it ... Fuck it ... Fuck ... It ... Fuck ... Fuck ..." Andi is getting tired but doesn't quit. She doesn't see the blood. The pillow has long since died, its guts spilling out over the boards. She's pounding a bloody corpse. "Fuck it," she says, now out of breath, barely able to talk. "Fuck it." With one final effort she rises, bringing her open hands up over her head, collapsing over what's left of the pillow. "Fuck it," she whispers, eyes closed, completely exhausted.

Max looks up at Rebecca. She's crying but also glaring, indicating their daughter. In that moment, this is suddenly how he thinks of her, their daughter, he sits down on the floor beside her – the glass is everywhere – and gathers her into his arms.

"Daddy, please don't go."

For the first time in his life, Max cannot fix this. He looks up again at Rebecca. In less than six months they have lived a lifetime. He remembers, they both remember, that first night on the boat. He had told her he wouldn't. He was sure then he would beat it. Eddie and Anja are holding each other. There's this look on Eddie's face; it's finally sinking in.

"I think we should all get married on Labor Day," he says, surprising even himself.

Andi looks up as if he's gone mad.

"I agree," la senora says. "It will be a beautiful double wedding."

"Oh god," Rebecca says in her best Brooklyn accent.

"I will see to everything," la senora adds. "And tonight I am cooking paella."

The Dread of the Jewish High Holidays

by Gloria Garfunkel

Ralph here. I forced myself to go to the Cape with Chloe for two weeks. My boss at Orwellian balked about the short notice and so I told him I'm so stressed out he can chalk it up to sick time. I'm covered by the Americans with Disabilities Act. They all know I'm bipolar anyway, it's obvious, and they can't fire me for it. They have to make reasonable accommodations, so fuck them. I drag myself into work bolstered by vats of caffeine no matter how bad I feel. I deserve this break.

The ocean and long walks on sand mellow me out, waves of peace washing over me as I lie on the sunny beach. There's a cool breeze but the sun is hot. Nirvana. This is how I feel when I'm stable, except for a little bit of irritability and dread when it gets dark.

As the days are getting shorter, I try not to think about the Jewish holidays in the fall, having to beg God to let you live another year and being held accountable for all your sins on Rosh Hashanah and Yom Kippur and the ten days in between. What a fucking depressing religion. I often just want to pray to God to strike me down dead right there and get it over with. I hate having to beg for my life every year, especially when I'm depressed and not sure I want it.

The biggest problem with bipolar is that you spend most of it miserable and only a very tiny smidgen of it euphoric which you lie to your doctor doesn't exist because you don't want her to medicate it but your fast speech and "flight of ideas" give you away every time and up goes the dose of Lithium to smack you down to bland.

I'm lucky that Chloe is so tolerant of my moods. I think I'd be dead already without her. But I'd never do that to her. She's the best part of my life. She brings me peace, whenever possible.

Mauve

by John Wentworth Chapin

The woman in front of Charles argues fiercely: "My father was the greatest man *on the planet,* and no one *ever* ... my *mother* didn't even appreciate him. He was a *great* man." She shouts this at the bowl of mashed potatoes and plastic tumbler of iced tea on her cafeteria tray. They do not argue back.

This has been going on for several minutes. Charles lifts his own tray off the rails and maneuvers around her, heading for the salad bar and the desserts.

"Hey. HEY! No cutting."

Charles turns; Mashed Potato Lady stands frozen, both hands clutching her tray, dark eyes glaring in his direction under furrowed brows.

"I didn't *cut,*" Charles corrects her. "I passed you."

"YOU CUT! You were behind me, and YOU GOTTA WAIT YOUR TURN."

The buzzing chatter of mealtime has quieted around them. Mashed Potato Lady's feet are planted firmly: dingy pink espadrilles with raveling hemp soles.

"You were having an important conversation. With your food. I didn't want to interrupt, so I went around you," Charles says, quietly.

MPL shouts again. "YOU CAN'T CUT. Everyone hasta wait their turn."

Flecks of amethyst spittle sparkle in the institutional glare. A week ago, he would have resigned himself to trotting back in line behind MPL, but there's only so much grinning and bearing that Charles can take.

Charles goads the woman. "Everyone's father is a fucking asshole." He narrows his eyes at her – don't fuck with me, the eyes say. "Pull it together," he hisses and turns back to the salad bar.

"You can't *cut*," he hears her grumble.

Then she's silent: she is mollified.

Good job, Charles tells himself. His therapist advised him to recognize his feelings and he is doing it –

Something wet and heavy hits Charles' shoulder and neck, then drops to the floor. Charles knows it's mashed potatoes; at his feet, a melamine bowl clanks to a rest.

The room is now silent. He turns to find MPL scowling at him from the same spot, lightened tray wobbling in one hand. Charles sees options:

a.   take the high road: apologize and move back behind her

b.   take the tolerable high road: turn back around and ignore her

c.   take the middle road: scrape the mashed potatoes off his t-shirt and fling it in her general direction

d.   escalate this motherfucker

He drops his tray on the rail and walks the few steps in MPL's glowering direction. They are the same height, so he gets face to face. He says, "I am not about to put up with your *shit*." He takes the tumbler of iced tea from her tray and pours it on her head. The liquid is a deep, rich purple: grape juice, not iced tea as it seemed.

She sputters and wipes her face with one hand. "You're a cutter!" she shrieks. She whacks Charles with her tray, a firm two-handed tennis backhand. He deflects it with his

177

forearm, glaring at her juice-streaked eyes; the tray falls to the linoleum.

"You're a fucking crazy person!" he barks, and as she reaches to claw at his throat, a pair of young staff members wearing St. Bernice's institutional violet polo shirts jog toward them across the linoleum.

The lavender walls blend into windows filled with a late evening sky.

"We don't use the word *crazy* at St. Bernice's," the therapist says. She's one of many; he doesn't think he's seen the same one twice.

Charles says, "I suppose we don't throw mashed potatoes, either."

"You're responsible for your own actions," she said.

She's aggravatingly robotic. He shoots back, "How would you *like* me to have responded?"

"How would you like to have responded?"

"Exactly as I did, except I wouldn't have slipped on the grape juice," he answers. His tailbone is killing him. For this and a multitude of reasons, Charles wishes he'd chosen pills over booze. Drinkers are unkempt, unsteady, unpleasant, unresponsive: they're just nasty. It's like bunking with the homeless. Pills would have given him a higher-class environment. He didn't even realize until after he'd admitted himself that there are residential programs for eating disorders and internet addictions. *Way* better.

She doesn't accept his answer. "What would have happened ... if you turned the other cheek?" She says this more like it's a quiz than a question. Clearly, there's a right answer.

"It was unkind of me to call her crazy," Charles admits. "But she threw food at me and she was out of control."

"So you felt it was your job to teach her a lesson."

"She threw mashed potatoes at me!"

"If she fell and got mashed potatoes all over you by mistake, what would you have done?" The therapist waits a moment, but Charles doesn't respond. "You probably would've helped her up, right? Same outcome, different response. She bruised your ego and you retaliated, Charles. It triggered you. Until you see that, you will be a marionette, jerking and dancing."

"So I should just let people walk all over me?"

The therapist sighs, disengaged. "We don't have space for people who interfere with other residents' treatment. Delaney seems to think you were insulting her father. I don't think you appreciate the greater implications of your actions here, in this facility. You are restricted from the cafeteria. We can reassess in two days."

The cafeteria is nasty, but he doesn't like being punished; it's a matter of pride. "I don't belong here," he says.

The therapist nods. "You are welcome to leave at any time."

Charles says, "No, you don't understand. I'm not an alcoholic."

The therapist touches the folder again, almost longingly. He can see that she wants him to leave. "If you don't belong, why are you here?" she asks.

"I know that's an alcoholic cliché, right? But I just want you to know that it's true. I quit my job and I admitted myself to this place because ... I thought I needed a reset. To get away for a bit."

"You checked yourself into St Bernice's as a vacation." The therapist looks around her at the relentless, sad, institutional lavender.

"I didn't do my research very well," Charles admits. "This was the wrong place. Plus, I hated my job."

"I don't think it requires a whole lot of wisdom to recognize that when you find yourself in the wrong place, you should leave." She closes a lavender folder that matches the walls.

Charles says, "You mean the job? Or you mean you're throwing me out of rehab?"

"I was in rehab until this afternoon," Charles says to the bartender. He chews the cherry from his third supergay cocktail.

"Rehab sucks," she answers.

Charles nods. "I didn't really belong there."

"It worked for me, I mean," she says. "I took pills. Three weeks in rehab and never looked back."

Charles says, "I went because I thought being with more fucked-up people than myself might be enlightening. It was just crappy." Charles studies her; she isn't very high-class clientele. He thinks he might have been wrong about wishing for pill rehab.

"Maybe you'll go back when you're ready," the bartender says, shrugging. She slides a vodka with grapefruit juice and cranberry seltzer in front of him and he takes a sip. An older woman two stools down has been punching buttons on her phone and squinting at the screen in the dim lighting. She leans across the empty stool and taps Charles on the forearm.

"You're not supposed to tell a bartender you just got out of rehab while you order a drink," she whispers, overly loud. Charles doesn't respond, but she winks, and he realizes it's a joke. He also knows it was meant as a joke because she is laughing and Charles and the bartender aren't.

"Good point," he says. He hoists his glass to the woman and she leans across to clink cocktails. It's dim in here, but the woman's garish clothes – is she really wearing a purple and magenta paisley caftan? – light her up like Vegas.

"I can tell you're not a drinker. Anyone who drinks knows to stay away from the grapefruit juice," the woman says. "It'll tear your stomach up before you can crawl in your car and get a DWI."

Another joke unlaughed at by Charles and the bartender.

"I like your bracelet," she says, pointing at his wrist.

"I got it in India a few months ago," he said. It is a cheap stretchy thing with little squares of polished coconut shell. "I think it looks like shiny chunks of Toblerone."

The woman laughs harder than the comment deserves and slaps the back of the empty stool. "I like you," she announces, to the bar in general. "My name's Deonna. How would you like a job?"

Now, *this*, thinks Charles, is crazy.

Unmended Fences

by Lynn Beighley

My dad is twitchy. We've managed to get out without a camera pointed at me, and yet he's nervous. What is he up to?

"What are you up to, Dad?"

"Uh, well ..."

Crap, there is something with which he is up to with. Something like that. Last time, it was letting the *You Tell Me* people film me in bed. Could this be worse than that?

And it seems like every time I'm in a restaurant, something horrible happens. God, it's true. First, Bill Plover fell in love with me, then I went out with him because America told him to and because I'm an idiot, then we went out again because I wanted money and he tried to propose, then Seamus asked me out but set me up to run into Bill because he wanted money. I look around for the cameras or Bill. Or Seamus. Nope. Just my dad.

"Princess ..." he says.

Yes, this is going to be bad. I grip the edge of my chair and wait for it.

"The thing is, I've fallen in love. I've asked her to marry me and she's said yes."

Oh. Well, that's not so bad. I look around for the cameras again, but I start to relax while he raves about his beloved. Maybe this time it'll be a nice dinner.

Here's the summary:

1. Her name is Gloria. She's a widow. He met her online a month ago.

2. She's a vegan nudist who enjoys taxidermy and snowboarding (presumably while dressed).

3. They are IN LOVE and don't see any reason to wait.

And I'm smiling. Dad is glowing. He tells me she's going to join us in a few minutes. I don't see a downside. He's happy, she can't be in it for his money, because he doesn't have any, and maybe with him involved in his own life, he'll stay out of mine.

He's sitting up straight, now, the nervousness gone. He orders a bottle of champagne and a dozen oysters. Which I'll be paying for.

"JENNNNNNN!" Someone is shrieking. Arms grab me from behind and wrap around me like tentacles.

And she's here. She releases me and I turn. Dad introduces us, although there's no reason for him to. I get my first look at her.

She's cute. And she's taken care of herself. Maybe a bit overcoiffed, with puffy blonde hair. Killer tan (but well, nudist, I guess she gets a fair bit of sun). She looks sane. And in spite of her enthusiastic mauling of me, she seems quite nice.

We sit and talk as the champagne arrives. I'm relaxed in a way that I haven't been in six months. Now that the whole *You Tell Me* crap is over, maybe life can get back to normal. Or even better than normal.

"Jenn, we're so happy you'll help us out like this," Gloria gushes.

"I just want to see Dad happy, Gloria." I'm a bit perplexed by the word "help".

"Pookie, see? You had nothing to worry about!"

"Uh, I didn't ask her yet, Honeybear," Dad mumbles, looking down. Dad's face turns red.

"What? Just say it."

It comes out in a mumbled rush. "Bill, your Bill's my

best man. Because we get a free wedding and honeymoon out of it."

I can't speak. I reach in my bag and start digging around for some cash. Gloria starts chattering.

"And you're my maid of honor, Jenn! I have such a gorgeous dress all picked out for you."

I spit out, "hell no." I throw a handful of cash on the table and leave.

I'm not sure how I manage to make my way to my apartment building, but I do. I collapse on my couch.

I guess I've slept, because it's dark. My doorbell is ringing.

"GO AWAY DAD," I yell. But the doorbell keeps ringing. I go to the door and I jerk it open.

It's Seamus. That bastard.

He's holding a bouquet of what looks like weeds (complete with dandelions). Stands there, shoulders slumped, the dimple on his left cheek nowhere in evidence.

"Jenn, God. I'm such a dick. You have to forgive me."

I grab his arm and pull him in, and then I pull him even closer. He drops the flowers as he wraps his arms around me in a hug I hope never ends.

Vtak Ohnivak

by Andrew Stancek

They say the whole house went up in a flash. The bombs at Hiroshima and Nagasaki evaporated matter, nothing left, and this sounds something like that. This is my neighborhood and I remember the house. I've been to Hank Johnson's parties on this street and I helped put out a fire, an ordinary kitchen grease fire, three doors down, some years back.

An ordinary lower middle-class suburb, fields at the north end and a mixed, poorer neighborhood at the other. No more crime than anywhere in America today, unexceptional in every way. No famous sons and no national headlines until now.

I studied chemistry in college. I understand fire, causes, accelerants and retardants. Fire is my life, you could say, and I'm fascinated by it. I've set fires and I've put them out. I paid my dues, started part-time like everybody, but was good enough to get promoted to a full-time firefighter job, and if I'd carried on, would have had a good shot at becoming Chief. Now I earn every penny the insurance company pays me, save them a fortune, you need a logical, disciplined mind and the ability to sniff something wrong if you're an investigator, and I am damn good at it. Facts is what I deal with, no kooky conspiracy theories, UFOs or sightings of the Virgin. Everything in my life has always had a logical, rational explanation.

Until now.

When the stories first started coming out, I laughed, like everyone else. Yeah, right, of course an ordinary American kid has mastered flying. No aids, no contraptions, no tricks, he just flies. Never been done before and no logical explanation for it. He says he just figured it out. All over the TV, the internet, the tabloids and everyone says the same thing: it's real. Everyone says it cannot be, but it is. This kid is flying. I watch the TV, the videos, the whole shebang and I can't see what the trick is, and neither can anyone else. It doesn't make sense that there is no trick.

The kicker for me is that this isn't a kid out in India or someplace like that, not even California, Land of the Kooks, but here, in my own neighborhood in Maryland. My own backyard.

Well, I have a life. I am bugged by this stuff; quite frankly, when something makes no sense, it upsets me. I like an explanation. But I'm not one to obsess. I've probably seen the kid around, even before he became famous. His father hadn't been around for a few years, I'm told, the marriage broke up, but I think I may have said hello sometime. The mother's face is kind of familiar, one of the thousands you meet in a mall or a restaurant and nod at because you know you've seen them. For a while there are TV vans on that street and paparazzi, and when I go into Smitty's to buy ice cream, I see tabloids with Adam's face on the front cover, and flipping through channels I sometimes see him soaring through the air, or some bozo explaining what it must mean, but I don't pay that much attention. Lots of fires around, keeping me busy. The economy is in the crapper so people losing their homes and businesses figure the insurance company is stupider that they are, and they can walk away from the wreck of their lives with a few thousand dollars. I'm the hired gun who says no.

After a couple of months the neighborhood settles down, hardly any commotion in front of the house anymore. I read an article that says that if Adam Zajac teaches us to fly, we'll cut our dependence on oil, won't need cars and planes and trains, but it's all balderdash. Even if the kid is doing it, he's not teaching anyone, isn't explaining how he does it, other than "merge" and "commune" and no one's about to sell their car and fly unaided to Florida with those instructions.

But now there is no house. A hole in the ground is all, not even the foundations but the lawn is still as green as ever. In my work I examine physical evidence: brick, timber, furniture. The ground isn't even charred the way we understand charring. I'm working with the cops, of course, nobody is any wiser than anyone else and probably soon Homeland Security will come in and take over. The rumors are flying around anyway, even if Adam Zajac isn't. He's gone, poof, and so is his mom, in addition to the house. Martians took them, I heard, little green men in a UFO. And considering what we've already seen with our own eyes, the kid soaring, that's just as plausible as anything else. Maybe it's past the time for men of science. I can't trust my eyes. If a kid can fly, then maybe there are Martians abducting humans and incinerating houses in ways never experienced by science.

My brother sent me a Slovak folk tale by email. Our neighborhood flying miracle kid, he was of Slovak heritage. In this tale, a magical bird, Vtak Ohnivak, brings blessings and doom. He's a phoenix. He self-destructs, burns up, and then resurrects. So maybe Adam was a phoenix and that is why he could fly and somewhere in the world, or maybe on Mars, he's now resurrected. Makes as much sense as anything I've seen with my own eyes.

The other rumor flying around is that two armored cars and a limousine with government plates pulled up to the house in the middle of the night, that there were bangs and that our government used a secret substance to evaporate the house. Like drones. They have Adam now, and he'll teach them to fly and be a secret weapon.

I prefer the magical bird.

Friday

8

August
2014

At the
Bistro D'anglaise

by Rachel Ambrose

"Claire, this is your mother. Are we still doing that lunch date today? Call me," my mom's voice chirps at me far too early in the morning. It's a Friday, so usually I would be working, but Mrs. Hatfield has taken her yearly two-week vacation to Bora Bora, and the office is closed. In some ways it's nice: I don't have to slink around the office trying to get away with wearing as little as possible, and it's a good rest for me as well. But it does leave me with a lot of nothing to do, now that Isa has moved back in with me and Charlotte has moved out. And ever since last month when I broke up with Blake, more time on my hands has not been something I particularly like. It mostly leads to bouts of crying and, after, staring at the grubby gray ceiling in my room for long periods of time.

Hence the lunch date. I call Mom back and let her know that, yes, lunch is still happening, to which she replies, "Oh, good, I was hoping you'd say that, I'm going to be bringing someone along for you to meet, you'll love him."

"Excuse me," I say. "Him?" I had been under the impression that we were meeting at a cute little French bistro downtown for some much-needed rosé and chatter. Why does a man need to be involved for that? It seems like an intrusion.

"Trust me, darling," my mother says in a weird,

whispery tone, like she's keeping a secret from herself. "Dress up nicely and do something about your hair, it'll be fine."

I am armed with misgivings and do the precise opposite, slinging my hair back into a messy bun and putting on a paint-splattered dress that's a half-size too big for me. At the last minute, though, I add a few wooden bangles and a swipe of blue eyeshadow, just for appearance's sake.

Upon arrival to the restaurant, I take a look around and find Mom in a corner booth sitting across from a suave-looking olive-skinned man in a button down shirt. She catches my eye and says, "Claire, darling!" as I walk up to them. I wave back and she pats the seat next to her saying, "Claire, this is Frederico de Vera, he curates the art museum downtown, I thought it might be fun to bring him along." She takes a pull from her wine glass as a waiter fills mine and I nod in Frederico's general direction. Another art-world person? Didn't she know that I was just getting over Blake? I manage a "lovely to meet you," before diving into the menu.

"Your mother tells me that you dated Blake Easton for a while," Frederico says.

I almost choke on my wine before sputtering, "Yes, yes, for a couple of months, but it wasn't serious."

He surprises me by saying, "This may not be of much comfort, but I always thought his work sucked."

I find myself letting out a little chuckle, and I haven't laughed in so long that the sound almost shocks me. I look up and take another look at this guy – aquiline nose, slatey eyes, youngish, with an elegantly cultivated streak of gray in his hair. I raise an eyebrow. Maybe I don't have to hide in my rosé today after all.

Over lyonnaise salad and vichyssoise, Frederico stands up to the claims Mom made about me loving him. He lacks Blake's magnetism, but he's charming and funny and

190

intelligent, three good points in his favor. I'm wondering, though, why Mom brought him along. Then he surprises me at the end of lunch, when we're all lingering over truffles and berry pavlova, by saying, "You know, I could really use a personal assistant at the gallery – you wouldn't be interested, would you?"

"Um," I reply, furrowing my brows and thinking of poor Mrs. Hatfield, but then I think of how stuffy the office can be and how boring my job actually is. Maybe this could be just the push that Blake was talking about, and I find myself nodding, a smile stretching across my face. "Yes, I am most certainly interested!"

"Fantastic," Frederico replies. "Come in on Monday for a test run. Livia, who's my personal assistant now but she's leaving to go to Paris, will train you. Keeping track of me isn't all that hard, but it does require a fine attention to detail."

I try not to gulp – at least if I'm awful at it, Monday was only an audition. I might even be good at it, who knows? "I'll be there at ten," I say, downing the last of my wine.

Where might one buy a fine attention to detail?

Callus

by Gill Hoffs

"What does your mother think you *do* for a living then?"

"Well –" I start to answer and he cuts in with "Ha! I suppose I should've asked you WHO do you do for a living!" and cackles out a laugh revealing dark fillings in his back teeth and thick yellow scum on the meat of his tongue. I imagine accepting a French kiss from this man – that curdy saliva being thrust into my mouth and the sour taste of it – and have to sip my tea quickly, despite its heat, to rinse the squirmy feeling away.

We are in a coffee shop near Deansgate, a decent one with the prices drawn in dusty white chalk on a giant blackboard behind the counter, the elegant angles of the 7s and 4s and the extra serifs on the 1s suggesting the European mainland was the baristas' original home. The whole place smells of fresh coffee and gingerbread and I regret hustling this noisy prick into a place I could've reserved for time off and rare rendezvous with real friends, if I'd known how nice it was inside.

"So d'you get to fuck anyone famous? Anyone I know? Hey – d'you fuck anyone from Creatlesby and Bartlette? You fuck my boss?" I can see him imagining some kind of powerplay with his unfortunate superior on Monday, his eyes narrowing with cunning, and swiftly shake my head, no. I *have* fucked his boss, imaginatively and enjoyably (for me, I mean – for my clients, enjoyment is a given), but the day I confess my client list is the day I leave my life, and by that I *don't* mean retirement, but for good.

This prick's my worst nightmare made real, with added halitosis and hair tufting out his nostrils, crusted with the yellow-white escapees of a million sniffs. I don't know how he knows about my life, or recognised me on the street – sure enough of himself to shout to me across the Saturday crowds hustling in and out of the Arndale Centre, "I know *you*! You're a callgirl!", obnoxious enough to demand an audience and explanation of my life – *my life* – with a broad Manc chatter of "How come you ended up shagging for money then? Watch too much 'Pretty Woman' as a kid, did you?" but here we are, in the emptiest café I could find, out of the bright heat of a northern summer's day, having a conversation I hate.

I am SO glad he's gay.

Previous iterations of this discussion or interrogation or lecture (depending on the dickhead burning with so much curiosity he just *has* to confront me, any or all of these descriptions could apply) have usually ended with a request / appeal / demand for a freebie. A quick lick / suck / fuck in the toilets or his car or a room nearby or even a full-on 'date' to a stuck-up sister's wedding. Not one of these awful encounters has ended in ejaculation, to my knowledge. Certainly not at my hands (or crotch or arse or tits or mouth). Thankfully this is unlikely to be an aspect of my career choice this droning tosspot will want to experience.

So far I have admitted nothing. My steaming Earl Grey (with milk – I know, I'm a disappointment to the human race) is my shield and I'm grateful for the café's air conditioning and how it allows me to sip and blow and cradle the mug in front of my face and hide while I gather my thoughts.

"Is all this sex the reason why your skin's so good? Do you even have to go to the gym to maintain that *fabulous* body? Or is it the sperm – you know, I read that cum facials are the key to staying young and gorgeous even into your forties – and champagne? I bet that's all you drink on your 'dates'," for goodness sake, he even wriggles his fingers in air quotes when saying 'dates', "it's alright for *some*."

And he sniffs so the clots of snot on his nose hair quiver and vibrate.

I wish my phone would ring or the fire alarm would meep or some fucker with an Uzi would run in and hold the baristas up. Just something, anything, to shut this nasty bastard up.

I slurp instead of sip my tea, savouring the bergamot, keen to make a noise of my own, and drown out some of his.

"What about your bits?"

Sweet jesus.

"Do you use some kind of salve to keep you supple down there? Stop the johns rubbing you the *wrong way*," and he sniggers at his attempt at a joke, "keep you limber for their timber?" And he's hooting and slapping the table now, the baristas looking over at this dickhead and his cringing companion.

If I 'drop' my drink in his lap, will he fuck off home?

Noooooo …

What if I dump it in mine? 'By accident.'

Maybe when it cools down a bit.

Yes, that's the plan.

I keep blowing on it.

"Whatcha going to do when your looks go? Soon your boobs'll sag, your looks'll go, and *then* what'll you do? Which of your sugar daddies and sad cases will put Cristal in your fridge and a cock in your hole then?"

He is really quite exquisitely offensive and I wonder if he's like this with his friends, if, indeed, he has any.

"What do you do for kicks? Are you vanilla on your days off?"

His voice is getting louder, grating in my ears, and one of the baristas, a woman with the dimples and generous smile of a young Tori Amos, keeps glancing over at our table.

"I mean, my careers advisor always told me if you do what you love you'll never work a day in your life." Fucksake, really? You're bringing out *that* old chestnut? "So I s'pose that's the real question, huh? Are you doing what you love instead of *who* you love? Huh? Huh?"

And he raises his eyebrows and nods at me like he's swallowed the collected works of Freud, Jung, Oprah, along with a box of fortune cookies, and is belching out words that should mean something in that order but really don't.

I blow my tea.

"Are you, like, callused?"

Now it's my turn to raise my eyebrows. Surely he doesn't mean …

"Like, vaginally?"

The barista is very still at the counter.

"You know what I'm getting at? Have you done it so much that you're, like, hard down there? Tough? Not that I'm an expert on ladyparts!" He's laughing again. "But that amount of sex'll surely get you calluses. Do you use moisturiser to keep you feeling right?"

Then the kicker.

"Do you have to pumice?"

And at this I cannot take his jibes and awful questions any more. The Earl Grey is out of my mug and onto his in one swift desperate action.

He squeals, I gasp, and the baristas applaud.

One shows him out, stuffing a bunch of paper napkins in his hand as they open the door, smirking at his discomfort. The Tori lookalike beckons me to the counter. As she makes me another drink, she offers me a brownie "On me" – oh, I wish! – and says, "My dad's been invited to my mum's wedding, and he needs a hot, classy date. How might he get a hold of you?"

And I smile at her, pinch a chunk off the brownie, and consider my day complete.

Sunday's Child

by Susan Tepper

Blisters on his heels. *Payless*. His feet are killing him. "You buy discount, those cheap sneakers that look good, you take a hit," he says getting out of the car.

He's back at the mall with the idea of returning the sneakers. Carrying them in the original box, receipt and all. *Payless* being at the cheap end of the mall where the kids shop. A cool spot. No expensive boutiques, no Bloomingdales, no snotty bitches toting mounds of high end shopping bags. Just Payless and a DQ and a GNC and some junk jeans stores. A *Life is Good* store that went out of business. Only the name remains on the glass. The kids like this end of the mall.

Pedersen enters through a side door, stopping to watch some real small kids dancing around on a musical mat. The more they dance the more music comes from that mat. Not a great sound but the little darlings just love it! The mothers, mostly fat and ugly, stand around talking to each other.

Tucking the sneaker box under his arm, he strolls toward the DQ. He'll have a dip cone. The chocolate in the big poster photo looks undernourished; like they didn't give it enough cocoa bean. "Is that dip chocolate dark?" he asks the DQ girl.

Behind the counter she has on heavy glasses and a stupid blue hat with red trim. The hat matching the rest of her uniform. She doesn't seem to understand the question 'cause she just stands there with her mouth dropped open.

"The dip cone," he repeats. "Do you dip into dark chocolate?"

The girl shrugs. "It's not white chocolate. If that's what you mean."

Damn! Pedersen is starting to sweat, feel nervous. Pulling on his shirt collar. "Dip me a large size vanilla cone, OK?"

Without answering, she moves like an ice cream robot. She takes a cone from the cone dispenser holding it under the soft serve spout. The vanilla comes out in a high swirl. At least she doesn't short change on the amount of ice cream. He's seen them give half that much and charge for a large serve.

Now he watches her do the fast upside down dip. At least she does it correctly. The new ones don't have the technique. It can be a mess. He pays, and she hands him one napkin.

While he eats his dip cone he wanders toward the mat kids. They're the same group: two blondish girls, a chubby girl about three years old, and a little dark boy of about five or six.

"Moosie," the mother calls out to the boy. At least what sounds like moosie to his ears. Pedersen can't make out half these foreign names. He decides it's a bad name for this boy who will turn out magnificent. He has the features and the compact, sturdy frame. Thick black hair. Moody eyes. A natural stud. You can't go around with a name like that, he's thinking.

He bites off some of the hardened chocolate, not as dark as he wanted. It tastes waxy. Then wiping his mouth with the napkin Pedersen strolls toward the mother. He stops a few feet away from the music mat. Catching her eye. He smiles and she smiles back. He catches some gold in her mouth. "Cute kid," he tells her.

The mother smiles wider.

"You ever thought about using him for modeling?"

The mother sort of brightens, waving fleshy braceleted arms around in an excited way. "You mean like the American Idol?"

"Well, yeah, sort of. Without the singing part."

He watches for a reaction. There is none. She's waiting for the payoff. Wants a big one. Pedersen sees the saliva forming at the corners of her mouth.

Paradiso Monday

by Jessica McHugh

He's surprised by how fast he found a gay bar. Venturing out of town doesn't usually stir his anxiety, but he's never made the journey to the city in high heels before. After parking in front of the Paradiso Club, Edward McKenzie tucks his crucifix under his dress and looks in the rearview mirror. The neon lights from the club sprinkle his face in pinks and oranges as he smears on a fresh coat of lipstick.

It suits you, sweetheart.

Eleanor pats his hand, her nails like withered roses compared to the brilliance of her grandson's. For his first night out, he's worn his boldest and most un-Edward outfit, dazzling with jewels and crisscrossing stripes of fuchsia and flame. The shift dress doesn't quite fit, but he's utilized a sweater to cover the loose spots wider hips would fill. Combing his fingers through his new wig, he frames his face with blond curls. Maybe he's not as beautiful as he could be, but when he smiles, he doesn't see Father Edward McKenzie, and that's all that matters now.

"This is it," he says to his reflection. Looking to his grandmother in the passenger seat, he purses his lips and exhales a quivering breath.

Do you want me to come with you?

He does, but he shakes his head. "I'll be fine on my own."

I've always known you would be.

She squeezes Edward's hand and disappears, but her warmth remains. He feels it even as he sets a tapered toe on the asphalt of the Paradiso, encouraging him. There aren't many other cars in the parking lot, but he didn't except many people to visit the club on a Monday night. Maybe if it goes well, he'll come back on a weekend.

He doesn't need Eleanor to remind him: one step at a time.

A Lady Gaga song pumps from the speakers inside the bar. For a moment he imagines it's Kay Starr instead, her silky song filling him with the confidence he feels at home. But the real rhythm soon takes hold and he sashays into the Paradiso.

"What can I get you, honey?"

He sits at the bar, blushing at the bartender's term of endearment.

"Ginger ale, please," he says, surprised by the natural femininity in his voice.

The bartender sets down the glass and pops a straw into the bubbling soda.

"On the house," he says with a wink. "This is your first time here, right? I think I'd remember a face that beautiful."

Edward bites his lip. He can't recall the last time someone complimented him on his appearance, if ever. He nods and watches the bubbles rising in his glass.

"What's your name, honey?"

Rather than looking the bartender in the eyes, Edward stares into the mirrored wall behind him. When he replies, "Eleanor," he really believes it for the first time.

"Pretty name," he says. "You live around here?"

Heat blooms in his cheeks. "There aren't places like this where I live."

The voice ringing from the corner is slurred but powerful. A drunken shuffle accompanies the stranger saying, "Then maybe you should come here more often."

Stinking of vodka, he oozes onto the bar stool next to Edward, wobbling. He finds the man familiar, but his slumped position and rumpled hair reminds Edward more of his mother, Betty, downing bottle after bottle at Shady Acres Nursing Home, than any man he knows. Leaning into Edward, the stranger's stench intensifies with a cackle.

"You know, this isn't a lady club."

The bartender shakes his head. "Cool it, Charlie. Everyone's welcome here."

The man laughs and pushes the hair out of his eyes. The name and another glance are all it takes for Edward to recognize Charlie Kitner, a parishioner from St. Peter's.

Fidgeting worsens his sweating palms. Edward hasn't spoken more than the few words necessary for communion to Mr. Kitner since the supposedly heterosexual married man confessed his attraction. He tilts his body away, sipping his soda in silence.

"You're a pretty thing. A little old for my taste, but that's not a dealbreaker."

Pointed in the opposite direction, Edward says, "If this isn't a lady club, why would you be interested in a lady?"

Charlie slaps the bar, punctuating his laughter. "You're a quick one. The truth is, I'm kinda like this place. Everyone's welcome," he says. "Let me buy you a proper drink."

"This drink is proper enough, thank you," Edward replies. "And I should be going anyway."

"You just got here."

Digging into his purse, Edward mumbles, "It was a trial run."

The bartender leans on the bar and says, "You don't have to go. If he's bothering you, I can kick him out, or send him back to his table. I've done it plenty before."

Sidling up, Charlie exhales boozy breath against Edward's ear. His dangling ruby earrings swing, and his neck prickles with goose bumps when the man purrs. "Yeah, make him send me back to the corner. I've been bad."

He instantly regrets getting angry over the man's brazen attitude, as well as giving him a clear view of his face when he snaps his head around. But most of all, he regrets the words he fires at the drunk. Charlie's eyes widen when Father McKenzie says, "It sounds like you have lots of sins to confess."

Edward watches the wheels turn in Charlie's foggy brain until he whispers, "Father McKenzie?"

Edward shakes his head as he places a five-dollar bill on the bar, and stands from his stool.

"Don't leave on my account. The night's just begun." Charlie's chin juts out as he smiles. "I won't tell anyone I saw you. Just like you won't tell anyone you saw me. Right?"

"Of course I won't."

He pats the barstool. "So sit down. Finish your drink. Let's pretend we're strangers," he says, looking Edward up and down. "It looks like you have a hell of a story to tell."

Edward's stomach turns. *A hell of a story* is right. Confidence drips down his face with his foundation. And though fear and doubt rise again, he doesn't let it show. When Charlie Kitner's hand slides up his arm, the knot in his stomach fires burning bile up his throat, but instead of doubling over, he shoots the man an icy glare and pulls away.

"Hey, you know how I feel about you. Whatever you are, whatever *this* is, it's okay. You don't have to be afraid of me," Charlie says.

Squaring his shoulders, Edward puffs out his padded chest and declares, "I'm not afraid."

"You're not going to give me that 'priests are celibate' crap, are you? We both know what you came here for."

"You're wrong."

Charlie rolls his eyes. "You frigid or something?"

"No, I'm just not interested."

Squinting, he huffs. "In sex?"

Edward's reply is more resolute than he'd thought possible, especially in Eleanor's voice.

"In you, Mr. Kitner."

While Charlie sits dumbstruck, Edward whips around, his golden hair bouncing as he strides to the door. Exiting the Paradiso, his body burns with pride, his cheeks aching from the strength of his smile. Inhaling the brisk August night, he's never felt so powerful. His calves burn as he strides to his car, the clacking from his high heels louder than the bass line pumping from the club. He won't be surprised if his strut cracks the pavement.

His joy survives the entire drive back to town. It isn't until he's home, removing his dress, that he realizes the possible danger he's welcomed by refusing Mr. Kitner. Sitting down on his bed, he rolls a rosary through his fingers and begs for Grandma Eleanor's advice.

The only Eleanor to visit him tonight will exist solely in his terrified reflection.

Opportunities /
Escapes

by Shane Simmons

"New opportunities available. Location: SCOTLAND."

It's rare that anything on the notice board at work catches my eye (even if I had been told to pay more attention to the various signs that litter it). Someone must've had a cleanup of the usual out-of-date guff and there, pinned in the centre, is a mostly blank A4 sheet which I'm certain I've never spotted before.

"Enquire with your manager for further information."

The vagueness of these so-called 'opportunities' piques my interest, but for all I know it could be anything from a cleaner's position to the search for a new head honcho.

Scotland.

Mark was half-Scottish.

Perhaps that is what made me stop to take a look. I wish Sandra had never put him back there, in my consciousness. But who am I kidding? She didn't reinstall him. He'd never entirely left it in the first place.

Out of the corner of my eye I spot Malcolm, my line manager, approaching. He doesn't break his stride as he passes. "Bit silly, getting us lot to put that up there. But you know what they're like …"

§

I spend the rest of the morning thinking about *things*. About this job, where I am, where I'd rather be. What I should or even could be doing instead of being tied to a desk for most of the day. I check over scanned images for the archive one by one and I wonder where all my ambitions had disappeared to. And Mark once again crashes in on my thoughts.

I wonder if he ever thinks about me?

I catch myself grimacing in the faint reflection on my computer screen. I must be the last thing on his mind.

God, would he even remember me?

Just as I turn to exit the coffee shop, one hand grasping a brown paper bag containing a cheddar and ham toasted sandwich, the other wrapped around the obligatory midday coffee (always with one extra shot of espresso), I bump into Malcolm.

"Fancy joining me for lunch?" he asks.

It's a sun-drenched summer day and I really fancied taking up a bench over the road and watching the river. Instead, as he goes to order I spot a solitary empty table. The one by the swinging toilet door.

I don't mind Malc, he's quite a down-to-earth guy. Dull as dirty windows, but decent nonetheless. You could say he was part of the reason I got this job in the first place, what with his wife and him being good friends with Uncle John and Aunt Patricia.

But that also makes him one of the few who know the truth about my parents' demise. I can't help but feel that sometimes he looks at me in that sort of way. Head tilted slightly to the side, lips wincing under big cow eyes, reeking of unnecessary sympathy. I've never been one for sympathy. I didn't need it when they were here, and I certainly don't need it now they're gone.

Sitting down, he takes a bite and mumbles with his mouth full, "Best salmon and cream cheese bagels by the way!" He wipes the crumbs from his mouth and swallows. "Seen your John and Pat lately?"

"Not recently, but I keep up to date with them on the phone."

"We've not visited in a while. Really must head up their way one weekend. Nice neck of the woods."

Munching through our respective lunches, the surrounding hubbub doesn't make up for the slightly awkward silence.

"What's the deal with that new sign on the notice board?"

"The Scotland one? Goodness knows, I've not bothered looking any further into it. It's hardly as if anyone down here is going to ask about it."

Fat lot of good that was. I put down my sandwich and scratch the stubble on my chin. "So, no ideas what they're looking for then?"

With his coffee cup to his lips, one eyebrow raises higher than the other. "Why are you taking an interest in it?"

"Oh, just intrigued. You did tell me I should pay more attention to the notice board ..."

"I did, but I genuinely didn't expect a single soul to enquire about that." He rests his elbows on the table, leans across. "You're not thinking of leaving us, are you?"

Am I?

What *are* my intentions?

"I've long been meaning to have a little one-on-one chat with you," Malc continues. "You've been here well over a year now and we really haven't had much chance for any sort of appraisals. You know, snowed under with this never-ending backlog for the archive ... Do you know, there's talk of merging with English Heritage and taking on their archival inventory! We're nowhere near through our own yet!" Malc can make excuses as well as anyone trained in management can.

"You've slotted in well and really, we didn't expect much from yourself during your probationary period, but overall we have been impressed with your efficiency, as well as the quality of your work. Makes a change to have some young blood on the team." Seems he's adept with back-handed compliments too.

Back outside thin cloud cover masks the sun. I shake my head – "No thanks, I don't smoke" – to Malc's offer of a cigarette before he lights up as we stroll back to the offices. "You know, I lived in Aberdeen for a bit in my youth. Grey buildings, grey skies. It was always wet and miserable up there. Stay there long enough your skin starts to turn grey too!"

And back at my desk I think it over. Why *did* I ask about that notice? What's made me consider the remote possibility of leaving here? I've not got such a bad setup. What, if anything, is out there for me?

I notice a flashing light on my silenced phone. *No go tonite. Gf not going out now.* I sigh, relieved Callum's inconvenient girlfriend has forced him to cancel tonight's secret sordid session.

So, what *is* keeping me here?

Aunt Patricia and Uncle John. Two gravestones I can't bear to visit. A sister I couldn't care less about. A cramped flat and a job that pays my way but ticks too few of the boxes. Sandra. A fuck-buddy I know barely anything about. And memories.

Memories of a guy who's long gone.

And there's nothing. Nothing else at all.

I stroll over to the notice board. Hold my phone up and take a photo of that piece of paper. I upload it and stare it on the computer screen, wondering just what it's about. And if this is my opportunity to escape.

Just what I want to escape I'm still not sure of.

Cake

by Michelle Elvy

"Hey, haven't seen you around a while." Manny looks up from under the hood of an SUV, studies his friend as he enters the garage. The glare of the sun is behind Stevie, but Manny would know his walk anywhere.

"Yeah. Been kinda …"

"I know." It's always been this way with the two friends. They can finish each other's sentences or not say anything at all. They could spend all afternoon as boys, catching crabs down at the end of Spa Creek, and never say a word. In later years, they could drink a whole bucket of beer at the same dock, lying in the hot sun next to each other. Silent happy afternoons.

But now Stevie wishes Manny would let him talk, let him tell him everything about the last few weeks, how things with Ellie began so suddenly and now seem to have reached a momentum that won't stop. Stevie is scared of what he's feeling, of where this is heading, of whether his feelings for Ellie will keep him from going to Florida.

"You still goin' though, right?"

Manny puts down a screwdriver and walks to the folding chairs. Sits down and pulls out his smokes. He looks up at Stevie, his head cocked sideways, and grins. "You think I don't know what you been up to?"

Of course Manny knows. Of course he knows about her. Ellie. Stevie has not slept in weeks. He dreams of Ellie day and night. He's been dreaming of her for years, it turns out, but those were dreams he pushed away. Those are not the kinds of dreams you can let take form. Now, for the last month, he and Ellie have been ... Have Been. Yes. Have. Been. That's as far as he can get because he can't name it but he knows whatever 'it' is is something that could be, yeah, love.

He walks over to Manny, sits on the folding chair beside him. Manny pours a coffee from the pot, burnt and stained but still with something passable in the bottom. He pours Stevie a cup, too. They drink coffee from Styrofoam for a few minutes, Manny smoking and leaning over, elbows on knees.

"See that piece of shit?" Manny nods toward the truck he's been working on.

Stevie shifts his gaze to the huge vehicle. Even from his vantage point from across the room, he can see it's almost new. Shiny. Midnight blue, almost black. Silver detailing.

"Owner's been in the shop every other day. Says we need to fix the motor. Fuel leak, he thinks. We been over it and over it. Nothing wrong."

"I don't get it. What are you gonna tell him?"

"That he bought a piece of shit car in the first place. You know what those cost? More than your college fund, school-boy. That's how much."

"And there's nothing wrong with it?"

"Nope. Fuel leak. Fucking idiot. Only thing wrong is that it gets ten shitty miles per gallon in the first place."

Stevie laughs at Manny's practical side. No room for flash in Manny's world. Manny's a hands-on kind of guy. A wild heart, sure, but a no-bullshit friend.

Stevie drinks more brown sludge. Wonders what he can tell Manny about Ellie. But Manny speaks first.

"So, Romeo."

Stevie drinks the dregs, studies the rim of his Styrofoam where his teeth have marked it ever so slightly.

211

"She goin' with you now?"

"Wha ...? – No." Stevie hasn't put this into words since he and Ellie started being Stevie-and-Ellie, but he knows as soon as Manny asks that he will leave next month alone. That, whatever This is, it will end when he leaves Maryland, and that even if he and Ellie haven't spoken of it, they both know. So he clears his throat, says again, louder now, "No."

"I been wondering."

"Yeah. Me too. I can't even believe we've been ..." He hasn't spoken to anyone about Ellie since she led him up her stairs for the first time last month. The only person he's spent any significant time with since then, besides his own family, has been her sister Sylvie. He has been at their house almost every day for a month.

"Her sister's kinda amazing," he says. And he realizes as he says it that this is not what Manny expects to hear.

"Her little sister? That little blonde kid?"

"Yeah. It's hard to describe. She's like Yoda in an even smaller package than Yoda. She's hilarious, and sweet. And she makes me feel ..."

"Woah. Wait. You talking about Ellie or her sister?"

"Her sister. Sylvie. She's an amazing kid."

"So that's why you spend more time with Ellie, huh? You are re-living your *yout*!" Manny says it like a wise guy from Jersey.

"Na. It's hard to explain."

"I can play Jenga with you, man."

Stevie laughs and punches Manny's arm.

"But I can't suck your ..."

"Hey." Stevie can't tell if Manny has stopped on his own or if he cut him off. Either way, he and Manny both shift in their seats, feeling uneasy.

"Seriously, though," says Manny. "You've had a thing for Ellie for ... forever, I guess."

"Yeah, I guess so." Stevie grins to himself.

"You guys ever talk about …"

"No." This time Stevie knows he's cut Manny off. He doesn't want to hear the rest of that sentence. He doesn't want to hear Lucky's name. Lucky, who died in January when a car flipped and spared all of them, but not Lucky. Lucky, who was Ellie's boyfriend. Lucky, who was his and Manny's best friend. Lucky. Unlucky Lucky.

Just then Ellie walks through the door. Manny sees her first, stands up. She's wearing red shorts that swish a little, and a white tank top. Nothing special but enough to make him feel unclean, greasy. His dad's shop is always greasy, of course. But he instinctively looks at his fingernails as Ellie enters the cool of the garage.

"Hey you grease monkeys," Ellie says.

Manny hasn't talked to Ellie much all year. He saw her here and there during the school year but after graduation he didn't go looking for her. He'd seen Rick too, but he didn't want to talk to Rick. With Ellie, he always *wanted* to keep talking to her, but he was lost for words. What would he say? What *could* he say? It had been a shitty year for all of them, and nothing was going to change that. He and Stevie had kept close. But with Lucky gone, they'd lost some kind of glue that stuck them all together.

Stevie stands and points to the white box in Ellie's hands. "What's that?"

Ellie smiles. "Cake."

She pulls off the lid to reveal a small chocolate frosted cake with yellow icing sculpted around the edges. In the center is piped, in fancy scrolling, *Manny*.

"Happy birthday," says Ellie as she places the box on the table. When she pulls out a joint, Manny's smile grows wider. "For later," she says, and places it in his palm, folding his fingers around it. Manny looks down at Ellie's thin white fingers wrapped around his oily hand. She's cupped one of her hands under his now, the other on top.

She's holding his big ugly fist in her small hands, and she squeezes. She says again, "Happy birthday, Manny."

She releases his hand and steps back. The release washes over Manny and he knows now that all those things he didn't know how to say will never be said. That with this one small cake and those two hands wrapped around his, Ellie has found a way to fill in all that time, all those months of not knowing how to talk to each other. He knows they'll keep surviving the year that's impossible to survive. And he feels grateful – a catch in the back of his throat. Such kindness in those small white hands. Such sweetness.

Such friendship.

Manny turns to the coffee pot, his eyes hot. He shrugs his shoulders and sniffs hard, pours three small Styrofoam cups of coffee. He hands the cups to Stevie and Ellie. They push their cups into the air, into the space between them.

Manny looks at his two friends. Stevie, who is leaving. Ellie, who's come back.

He holds his cup of stale coffee high in the air. "To Lucky!"

Their Styrofoam cups smush together.

They eat cake.

Jerrod

by Len Kuntz

Outside of Akron, driving a beater car on Interstate 71, I pick up a hitchhiking dwarf.

Ordinarily I would never pick up a hitchhiker, but August in Ohio is a scorcher and I feel bad for the guy, not to mention (and this is me being judgmental, if not also bigoted) I don't see as how he could pose much of a threat.

He seems effervescent, amped up, both surprised and giddy that I've stopped. When he jumps in, sweat flicks from his forehead and splatters the dashboard so that it looks as if it's been crying.

"Thanks, pal," he says, holding out his hand for me to shake, which I do, trying not to cringe at how warm and moist it is. "Name's Jerrod."

There's still a bit of caution lingering in me, and I don't feel like telling him my name, so I lie and tell him I'm Clint, because I've been thinking of Clint Eastwood's *Dirty Harry* films for some reason.

"Where're you headed?" he asks.

"Don't know."

Jerrod laughs, a huge *I-just-fucked-your-wife-in-the-ass-last-night* laugh. "Come on, man."

"Okay, how about I'm on my way to Akron. You?"

"Akron," he says, disappointment scrunching his forehead. "Sure, Akron, that's my target as well."

So we're both drifters.

Much to my chagrin, Jerrod's a talker, blathering on about everything from Obama's daughters to the evolution of country music, how it's really just pop music without Auto Tune or lines about Hoe's and bling, and right at once I'm sorry I picked him up.

Then he starts with the questions: *What do I do?* ("Really? You lucky fucker, you actually have enough stashed away to just up and quit?") *Am I married?* ("You did the right thing, Clint, cutting the cord. A hag cheats once, she'll do it till she dries up.") *Why am I going to Akron?* ("Going to see your Sis, huh? You two must be close. I had a sister once, but she ran away at age *tennn*. Can you believe that? She hasn't resurfaced since.") *What kind of music do I like?* ("Bullshit, man. Nobody likes everything. Wait, so you like country music, I mean *real* country, Conway Twitty and Loretta Lynn?") *Who did I vote for in the last election? Have I ever seen a ghost? Do I wish I'd had children? Do I like spareribs? How many bodily scars have I got? Do....?????*

It takes thirteen years or more until we finally see the road sign that says, **Welcome to Akron**. And underneath: **Home of LeBron James**.

"Shit," Jerrod says, suddenly anxious as a junkie, "Can you believe they're still loving on LeBron after he pulled that stunt and dumped the Cavs?"

I tell him I don't follow basketball.

"Fuck you don't."

I tell him I don't follow *any* sports.

He leans forward and turns to look at me, his face lit with astonishment. "Are you serious?"

"I am."

"And you're not gay?"

What if I was gay, I want to say. *What if I was gay, I* want to say, *and I pulled out a gun and put a bullet through your waxy forehead. What if I was gay*, I want to say, *so what? At least I can reach the dinner plates in the cabinets.*

216

But then it hits me that I've sunk to his level. Wait, that's bad, too. More bigotry on my part.

"Look," I say, "would it be all right if I let you off here?"

Jerrod's expression resembles a wife who's been told that her ass has grown fatter than her twin sister's. "At a truck stop?"

"We're in Akron."

"Can't you just take me where you're headed?"

"Where my sister lives is a residential area."

"So? Do I not look *residential* enough for you?" Jerrod holds his arms out, palms facing me, as if he's in a stick-up, and I notice in a flash, both how short his arms are, but also that he has huge hands, with fingers long enough to stretch across the entire radius of my throat.

"Hey," I say. "Easy, tiger."

Jerrod is panting now, breathing hard, his square jaw lowered, his eyes black bats swirling.

"No sweat," I say. "I can drop you there."

Jerrod blinks, blinks and blinks, and I wonder if I should ask if there's something wrong with him, but I don't want him to get more agitated.

"How far away are we?" he asks.

How should I know? I have no idea where I'm going, or where the residential sections are, yet I lie and say, "About twenty minutes."

"What's your sister's name?"

"Tawny." *Tawny. Why Tawny? Because it's the first thing that popped into my head and I once had a grade school friend whose sister was named Tawny.*

"She a good cook?" Jerrod asks.

Uh oh. Now he's expecting to be fed.

"Hey, Jerrod, this is all a surprise, you know, my stopping by. She might not even be home."

"That's not what I asked."

What did he ask? Oh, yeah. "Honestly, my sister's cooking sucks. You'd be better off eating dog food."

"Man, I'm starving."

"We can stop at McDonald's."

"Thing is, I'm broke, flat-busted."

"My treat."

"Really?"

"Yeah."

"Cool."

Jerrod smiles at me for the first time since I picked him, but I notice he's wringing his hands. I wonder if maybe the guy really is a junkie, though he doesn't look pale.

It's harder than you would think to find a McDonald's in such a big metropolis, but I do eventually. Jerrod doesn't want to do drive-thru, though. Inside, there's no line, which I'm grateful for. When Jerrod steps up to give his order, he takes a pistol out of his pocket and aims it at the stunned, teenage Hispanic and says, "Unload your till. *Now!*"

I try to remember where my own gun is, then realize it's back in the car.

"Hey, Jerrod," I say.

He tells me to shut my pie hole. To the clerk he shouts, "Hurry up! This is loaded," wiggling the snout of the pistol at the poor kid's nose.

When I turn to make a run for it, Jerrod swings his arm in my direction, aiming the gun at my crotch.

"Whoa!" I say.

"Clint, this was your idea," Jerrod says, enunciating too perfectly, clearly trying to set me up in the event this episode is somehow being taped.

"I had nothing to do with this."

"Now you're going to try and lie," Jerrod say, whipping the gun back toward the befuddled teller, then back at an obese couple who've just entered, telling them, "Get the fuck out! And find some fucking treadmills!"

The teenage clerk hands Jerrod a bag of bills in a McDonald's bag meant to hold a few Big Macs at most. Fives and Tens dangle over the lip of the sack.

"What about the change?" Jerrod says. "I want the change, too."

Once the till is completely emptied, we flee the place, Jerrod pushing my right ass cheek. "Hoof it! Cops'll be here soon."

When we get back in the vehicle, I'm so nervous I can barely slot the key in the engine.

"What's your problem?" Jerrod asks.

"My problem? You just held up a McDonald's!"

Jerrod waves the gun at me, and I notice how it smells like dirty underwear.

"You want I shoot you?"

I swallow. I think; it's been an interesting ride, my life these last few months. "Go ahead."

"Are you fucking nuts?"

"Shoot me if you have to, but I'm not driving."'

"I'll do it."

"Fine."

"Fine? Are you an idiot? You want to be dead?"

As if acting reflexively, I slam my palm into Jerrod's forehead and his skull smacks against the passenger side window. I stiff-arm him in the face again, and again. The gun plops on the floor mat. Jerrod starts whimpering.

"Why'd you do that?" he asks.

"Because you're the fucking idiot."

"But you don't understand."

"Get out."

"It's my girl. She needs an operation."

"Get out."

"She was born the wrong gender. She knew all along she was a she, I mean, he was a she."

"What?"

"Leslie wants to become my girl for real, but it's an expensive procedure."

When I pick up Jerrod's gun from the mat and aim it at him, he squirms.

"Get out now," I say.

"You ain't going to shoot me. I know that."

I fire a bullet into his leg. Jerrod squeals, shouting, "What the fuck, man?"

"I'll shoot again if you don't get out."

"All right. Fuckin' A, all right."

"And take your money."

"I will. Okay. Just don't shoot me again. Fuck, man, you actually shot me."

After Jerrod crawls out of the car, I peel away, tires screeching, rank smell of burnt rubber rising in the cab. I see a glimpse of Jerrod in the rearview, him squatting down near the kid's play area, obviously in pain. I floor the accelerator and get the car doing fifty and start thinking where I should dump the vehicle, wondering what Dirty Harry would do in a predicament like this.

Eighth Inning

by Michael Webb

I am standing outside, on the tiny balcony of my hotel room, feeling the breeze come in from Lake Michigan. Below me, taillights race away down Lake Shore Drive, Friday night lovers hurrying to a tryst, parents rushing home to see children off to bed, families headed off for the weekend. I watch them drive, standing there in a t-shirt and shorts, thinking about Don Henley's lyric that somebody's going to emergency, and somebody's going to jail.

There's nothing preventing me from getting dressed and going out. Every city, Chicago included, has steakhouses and bars and strip joints that will entertain a lonely man well into tomorrow. But I know better than to do that. The inflection point where that is worth both the effort to become presentable and the price to be paid the next day is different at 32 than it was at 22.

My phone, plugged into the wall on the bedside table, begins to warble. I glance at it, and then activate the FaceTime feature. My wife's face appears, her face slightly reddened, her hair loose, her eyes darting around the room. She probably just scrubbed off her makeup.

"Hi."

"Hello sweetheart. How are you? How are the kids?"

"I'm fine. Kids are good. Cuddle Bug misses you. I told her you're home Monday, and she said, 'how many day that?' I told her three, and she said, 'that too many day, momma'."

My heart pounds softly for a moment. Along with the massive paychecks comes equally large helpings of guilt.

"That's cute." She still alternates being wary upon my return with wanting so much attention crawling inside my skin would not be enough.

"Yeah," she says. Her eyes dart to the right, then center on me again. "Lucasita called an hour ago. You're not with Juan, are you?"

"No, hun. We all split apart when we got back to the hotel."

"If you see him, tell him to call his wife, OK?"

I try to imagine a situation where I would see Juan before the bus tomorrow morning. Yes, we play a game, but it's still a workplace. We don't hang out in each other's room and braid hair.

"Sure, hun."

"Marcy called and I bought a table for the art museum fundraiser."

I sigh, trying not to be audible. Another night of sitting around in uncomfortable clothes with people I don't like.

"I know, Mark," she says, picking up on my annoyance. "But Marcy is a good friend of mine. And she says I might get to be on the committee next year!"

I try to think of a reason why I should care about that. I paste on a smile. "That's great, hun. Did you watch?"

"The game? No, babe. I had to wrangle the kids, and then the phone hasn't stopped all night."

On some level, I am still 12 years old, trying to show off.

"How did it go?" she says, setting the phone flat to reach for something out of view. I can see the lights above her head, and a sliver of brown belly where her shirt gaps above her pants. She starts gargling with mouthwash.

"Not too bad," I say. "No runs charged. But we lost."

I only earned one out, and allowed 2 inherited runners to score, tying a game at 6 that we lost 9–7. In baseball logic, though, no runs were charged to me, so it was a fine day. I know she only really cares about outings that damage my stats, and thus my future earnings.

She leans over, her shirt and the shadow of one breast filling the screen as she spits out the mouthwash. I think about the easy, smooth way she moves, the way she seems put together, all curves and soft angles, by some higher, more intelligent power. I feel a stirring, my heart thrumming again at the impossible beauty of her, the way gravity pulls me to her, my heart as helpless to the laws as a comet.

"I have to go, hun. I promised Luca I would call her back. Talk to Juan, hun. OK? Love you!"

The picture disappears, and I say "I love you," to myself in an empty room.

I know I'm not going to talk to him, and she should know that too. Men aren't like that. It's one of the rules. And ballplayers certainly aren't.

I think about the throb I feel, the ache for her body, the need, her belly still taut and firm. The glow is fading now, my lust rapidly cooling in the air conditioning. I don't have to be alone tonight, if I don't want to. Everyone knows the bars where the groupies hang out. Or there are the escorts, or there are …

I stop myself. No there aren't, I think. You're not going to do that. You're not going to go chasing, trying to rut like an animal. You're going to turn on the TV, set your alarm, and go to sleep. I look around the room, remembering the nights she used to send me naked pictures of herself to get me through 4 nights in Cleveland, and I pick up the remote control. One of the PBS channels is showing something about Churchill. I turn the volume up, and open the minibar for some M&Ms.

Endangered Species

by James Claffey

The granite of the church sparks diamonds in the sunshine and the Bird takes a good look all round to make sure nobody's watching. He undoes his fly and streams his widdle into the outside holy water font. Quick as can be he slips his mickey into his pants and before he can zip up again a lorry slams on the brakes and he almost topples into the font with fright.

Back on the bicycle he pedals out the gravel driveway of the church and makes for Hogan's in Clara, hoping the fresh late-summer air will clear the fog from his head. Since the reading of the will he's spent more time out of the town than in it and his trips to Clara always bring him hope of seeing Melodie once more. He'd give his last euro to hear her play the tin whistle the way she had the night he first noticed her.

The fields he passes are busy with workers harvesting barley and wheat, the combine harvesters chewing up the crops in great mechanical bites. From the top of a nearby machine a farmer gives him a wide-arced wave. The Bird tips his hat, the handlebars wobbling a bit under his grip. The Clara Road is birdsong and clouds of raised dust, the scents of summer sultry and reminiscent of childhood when he'd take the road almost every day on his way to his favorite fishing spot. As a small boy he would spend weeks casting flies on the slow water, the trout and perch rising relentlessly to the bait. Lately, his fishing tackle gathers dust in the house not his own, and as he crests the first hill and the glint of river water catches his attention he feels a pang of not guilt, but deep sadness, knowing his summers are no longer plentiful and the gray hair continues to arrive.

A gutted cottage in an unkempt field reminds the Bird of his grandfather, a poor cottager who had been arrested by the police in the late months of 1920 and remanded on suspicion of being in the IRA. Only a letter from the local monsignor testifying to his character spared him a long spell behind bars. God, his father loved telling the story at Easter in the pub, always on the touch for a free pint or two. This, the Bird thinks, as he watches two swallows swoop into the shell of the cottage, might have been the very cottage his grandfather was arrested inside. His father said it had been somewhere on the Clara road, before the village proper.

The real criminals weren't the police who arrested his grandfather, he thought. No. The real bastards were the solicitors. The sting of the solicitor's words as he formally read the will and thus granted the deeds for the property to the nuns acted like a stone in the shoe for the Bird. He couldn't make it through even an hour without cursing his parents and their desire to add only further to the convent's wealth. If he could land that bloody Mother Superior with his long gaff, drag her by the bleeding throat onto dry land and gut the bitch …

"Come here to me now," he says, grabbing for the swallowtail that flits past his head, the bicycle teetering beneath him. He swipes and swipes again and misses, again and again. The flimsy creature is impossible to catch, and reminds him of Melodie and her own evaporation from his life. Strange, how one moment Life can be full of the wide acres of possibility, and the next as constricting a space as a coal cellar. He pushes down hard on the pedals and into the loneliness of the open road.

§

Hogan's is empty, the quiet deadly. The barman polishes glasses taken from the dishwasher, the only sound the squeak of the floorboards he disturbs with his motion. The Bird nods and orders a pint. The man fills the glass over half way and sits it impassive on the countertop. "It's like ripples in a pond," the Bird says, eyeing the settling liquid. The man simply nods, reaching for another wet glass to polish. After a minute he tops off the pint and sets it on a bar mat in front of the Bird. "Slainté," the Bird says, foaming his upper lip with the head of the drink. No answer.

"Will there be music this week?" he asks, running his eyes across the chalkboard near the door. He doesn't see the name of Melodie's group listed.

"Only what's there. Read it for yourself," the barman says, placing another glass on the counter, gleaming.

"Thanks for that. I see it all right. D'you see the group with the French girl at all?"

"French girl?"

"Melodie, her name is," the Bird replies, eager to engage the man in some conversation.

"Haven't seen hide nor hair of them this side of Easter," he says.

"Pity." The Bird sips the pint, watching the second hand on the clock stutter its way around the dial. All's fair in love and war, my arse, he thinks.

The pint drained, he plucks a note from his pocket and leaves it on the counter.

Outside, the threat of showers seems real enough as dark thunderclouds roll across the horizon. The Bird clips both trousers and pushes the bike along until he swings into the saddle and rolls towards home. Off in the distance a corncrake's plainsong catches his attention and he smiles to himself at the rare bird's song. He knows what it is to be running out of time, like the corncrake, a victim of modern life and changed farming techniques. The Bird and the corncrake are blood brothers, two of the wounded of this world. Like the corncrake, the Bird needs only the one mate, and like the poor bird in the distance, he is frantically seeking her out before the last few grains drop through the narrow neck of life's hourglass.

Peace and Utter Joy

by Gwendolyn Joyce Mintz

A 'Back-to-School' event at the restaurant / bar where they work keep Aaron and Mora from making the meeting. It's Sunday besides. Diane has suggested that she and Phil take in a movie.

"Not in the mood for death and drinking," she tells him.

As they stand in line for tickets, Diane slips her left arm around Phil's right one.

It is a friendly gesture, he knows. Still, he says, "I wonder if guys are wondering how I scored you."

Diane leans over and kisses him on the cheek. "Wonder what they're thinking now."

Phil finds no malice in her face. "Did you do that because you pity me?"

Diane shakes her head. "Nope. Got a new motto: I'm gonna die, no need to lie."

"Kind of corny."

"Maybe. But if I felt pity for you, I would've kissed you on the lips."

Phil rears his head back, groans. Looking again at her, head tilted to the side, he pleads in a playful manner, "Please feel pity for me."

Diane giggles. Moves closer, leans against his arm.

Phil is buoyed by her sweetness and the moment swells around him. A moment he never thought to have: one of peace and utter joy, a beautiful woman beside him.

Monday

18

August
2014

Wounds

by Stephen V. Ramey

"Hey, Mac, wake it up." Something prods my side. A tinted window blunts the light, but the sun is still hot on my face. I turn away from it.

"Come on, Mac, I don't got all day." Another poke.

A bus driver leans over me from the aisle, light blue shirt, narrow tie, nametag I can't read. I rub my eyes and sit straight. Usually I'm a light sleeper, but lately the ache in my hip has been keeping me from getting any real rest. I'm constantly fatigued.

"Yinz can't sleep here," the driver says. He points to a *No Loitering* sign amid the glowing ads along the bus' angled ceiling. I smell his cologne, pungent like Old Spice only fruity.

"I bought a ticket." I wave my pass book. One of the tricks Dave taught me was to buy a bus pass book and ride around all day. It's safe and more comfortable than a concrete floor.

The driver shrugs. "Look, Mac, I don't mind hauling yinz around – ain't like we don't have empty seats – but don't get on this bus again 'til you wash off some of that stink. I get complaints." The four or five passengers are looking at us. It makes me itchy.

"Don't make me call the cops, Mac."

"Okay, sure," I say. "I'll get off."

The driver returns to the front. I grab my backpack from

under the seat and stand. My knee nearly crumples. I've had some issues of late. All this walking is wearing me down.

The side door accordions. I spill through it to a sidewalk on the edge of downtown. A flyer taped to a metal light pole catches my eye. It's me, shaved, round-faced, almost smiling. *Have You Seen This Man?* There's more, but I don't bother to read it. Fat chance anyone's going to recognize me from that photo. My beard is like a bird's nest now, and my cheeks have lost their plump. I still wear glasses, but they're taped, the frame bent across my nose.

I shamble toward the Riverplex. A woman with a little girl crosses the street to avoid me. I don't take offense, in fact what I feel is relief. No need to be on my best behavior for ten or twenty strides. And my hip really aches now. The pain has spread into my lower back. I need to find a space to bed down even though it's barely noon.

East Washington is busy with traffic. Hot smells, metal smells, a hint of blue exhaust.

"Stephen?" The voice comes from several yards behind me, husky and female. It sounds like Rose.

I step into the crosswalk. An SUV rolls to a stop a foot from my shoulder. Chrome winks. I continue across the street.

"Stephen."

I move across the Riverplex as fast as my hip allows. Only when I turn behind The Confluence do I sneak a look back.

There's no one there. I continue around the corner into the wedge between buildings where they keep the dumpster. The scent of rotting vegetables greets me. Shade cools my head. I relax despite the smell. I probably smell worse.

I pull the tarp from my backpack. This is as safe a place to bed down as any on short notice. The dumpster will block me from view if someone walks past.

"'Sup," a man says. He's tall and slightly bow-legged, with a leathery face that recalls the Marlboro Man. He must've followed me.

He comes closer. "This your digs?"

"Public space," I say. "No one owns it."

The stranger snorts. "I got snipe, you want ..." He flashes a baggy holding partially smoked cigarettes.

"Don't smoke," I say.

"Square's fine by me," he says. "I'm new. Know any good squats?" His eyes roam the alley, the dumpster. He chuckles. "Guess not, huh? How long you been on the street?"

"Long enough," I say. I spread the tarpaulin on the ground, keeping one eye on the stranger.

He strolls casually to the opposite wall. "Mind if I sack here?"

"Free country," I say. I don't mean it, but what can I do? He's bigger than me, meaner than me. I guess I could abandon the alley, but that would only reveal my fear. Plus Rose could be snooping around out there.

He settles down against the wall. His eyes close. I wait until his breathing is slow and steady. Then I lay down, using the backpack as a pillow, and close my eyes too.

Sunshine. Anne, laughing, runs to me through a field of grass. Her eyes shine with the same chlorophyll. I brace to catch her.

Something presses down. Breath squeezes out. I try to roll. An arm pulls around my throat.

"Where do you keep your stash?" Of course it's the stranger. I squirm, but he knows his leverage like a wrestler.

"Give it up," he says. "I know you got something." His forearm compresses my neck. A pen knife glints.

"Sock," I choke.

He rolls off, keeping the knife in view. Wheezing, I pull up my pant leg, roll down the sock, and peel two twenties from my ankle.

He licks his lips. I toss the bills. He scrabbles to get them before the breeze. I think of running, but he's between me and the exit. *Stupid wind.*

He tucks the cash into his pants. "That all you got?"

"Yeah." I spread my hands.

"Why don't I believe you?" He motions with the knife. I climb to my feet, back pressed to the dumpster.

"Empty your pockets," he says.

I turn out the left and let coins spill. He doesn't chase, doesn't bat an eye.

"And the other?"

I sigh and pull the wallet free.

He reaches. "Thought I saw a bulge."

I make a break. Pain flashes. My hip locks. The stranger tackles me before I reach the alley mouth. Breath flushes from my lungs. My palm stings. Asphalt bakes my cheek.

"You dumb fucker," he says. His fist pushes against me. I feel a new pain beneath my ribs, sharper, deeper.

He rolls off. I sprawl forward, but my side hurts so hard I see stars. My whole body goes limp. I reach for my gut, and blood coats my fingers. *Stabbed.* A sense of wonder comes over me. For an instant I revel in the thought of life leaking out, but that makes no sense. It's only a pen knife.

The stranger stands and harvests my wallet. "Three bucks? You have got to be kidding me, Einstein." He takes a bankcard from its slot and holds it to the light.

"Fuck," he says, and tosses the card down. "You ain't going nowhere." He glances at the plastic insert. "This your girl?"

I nod. Pain throbs through me.

"Alive?" he says.

"No," I say. Tears cloud my eyes. The thought of this man harassing Anne, touching her, makes me groan.

"Sorry for your loss," the stranger says. He tosses the wallet into the dumpster and strolls away as if nothing has happened.

How can anyone do that? How can you stab a man and walk away? And then I think, *How can I just walk away from Anne?* Maybe I deserve this, maybe I'm meant to bleed out in an alley with no one the wiser.

The sun creeps overhead. I feel its heat, yet I'm cold inside.

A man appears from the head of the alley. He walks toward me, using a cane. *Step-click-step.*

Is this God? The other guy?

"You're hurt." His voice is soft. He kneels down and feels my pulse. "I'm going for help."

"No." I push onto my arms. The wound tears and pinches as if the knife has slid into me again. My elbows collapse. I sink down onto my belly.

"You need a doctor."

"I'll be okay." *No doctors, I'm done with doctors.*

"I can't just leave you here," the man says.

"Please," I say. "It's only a flesh wound." I try to chuckle. It hurts.

"My name is Frank," the man says. He grasps my shoulders and helps me sit.

"St – Jimmy." I picture Jimmy's broad smile, hear his laugh. He would stick his fingers into my wound if he caught me posing as him. *How's that for funny, Stephen?* He doesn't like people stealing his material.

"Is there someone I can call?" Frank says.

"No. It's ... complicated. Just help me up, I'll be fine."

He shakes his head, eyes fixed on my bloody shirt. "If you insist on being stubborn, at least let me bind your wound. I was a medic once. I'll bandage you up, and then you can decide where we go from there."

He extends his hand, and I grasp it between my own, wincing at the sight of dried and half-dried blood on my fingers. He does not pull away, and a surge of gratitude flows. Frank is the opposite of the bus driver. They cancel each other out.

He leans back, and I pull myself to my feet. I wonder what the ducks on the river must think as we exit the alley, me leaning heavily on Frank, Frank leaning on his cane. I think of my blood smearing his suit jacket, my grime embedding in the fabric. It disgusts me.

"Sorry," I mutter.

"It's nothing," Frank says. "I have other suits."

Unravelling

by Gay Degani

Sybil is naked in her bed, sleeping off Margaritas, her windows open because of the heat, the air as dry as ash, wildfires in the nearby hills sucking up oxygen. The shouts are part of her dream – a dream in which she scrambles down the corridor of a speeding train, children and old men blocking her way. She leaps over dogs, shoves conductors into seats, then finds herself clinging onto a window ledge outside the passenger car, sand and wind blasting, mountains hurtling, and all the while, there is yelling, yelling, and now barking …

She wakes up. The barking doesn't stop. Neither does the yelling, the unfamiliar voices quickly familiar. Ian Shane from next door and – is that Gus' son, Mars? Of course it is. Ever since Ian's mother and Mars jumped into bed together, the tension between lover and son has crackled every time they meet. Sybil grabs her robe from the floor and glancing at the clock – 1:00 AM – she scurries into her living room to peek from behind the curtain.

Light blazes in Ian's bungalow, his windows flung up because of the heat, while Gracie barks in Gus' open doorway as the old man stumbles past her onto his porch. Then, as Sybil watches, Gus tumbles down the steps, landing on his side on the sidewalk. She's out the door, hurrying to him, shouting "Mars! Ian!" as she goes.

235

Reaching the old man, she stoops down. He groans, "My hip, my hip." Gracie whines and sniffs.

"Is it broken?" Sybil glances over his crumpled body, hollers, "Mars, come help!" The courtyard is silent, empty. The eyes of a coyote glint from the middle of The Old Road. No one is rushing out to help.

"I'm calling an ambulance," she says to Gus. "Do not move."

She straightens – her bones creaking – and hurries up Ian's steps, pounds on his door, opens it.

Ian is rolled into a ball on the floor, arms and hands bloodied, the glass coffee table shattered. Mars stands over him, fists clenched. She shivers in spite of the hot night air, keeps her voice low, but firm. "Mars, your father's fallen down. Go outside and see to him while I call an ambulance."

He pivots toward her, his face bewildered, and mumbles. "He's okay. I only hit him once. Not that hard."

"Go take care of your father. Now." She pushes him toward the door and he goes, slowly, reluctantly.

Ian, wearing only boxers, is unfolding on the floor. She leans over him. "Are you cut? How bad?"

He extends his arms, both dotted with small cuts and a thin slash along the side of his shoulder about two inches long. Bleeding, but not gushing.

"Okay," Sybil says. "Stay still. Let me call an ambulance and then we'll see how bad it is. Where's your phone?"

"In the bedroom."

Sybil tightens the raincoat she grabbed before driving Mars to the hospital. In the emergency waiting room, Mars slumps over his knees in the chair opposite her, his face concealed in his hands. He's been this way for the better part of an hour. Gus and Ian are beyond the swinging doors and Ian's mother is on her way.

"They'll be all right," Sybil tries to reassure him. Ian will, she knows, because his wounds are superficial. She doesn't know about Gus. Broken hips often lead to decline in the elderly, she thinks, forgetting that Gus isn't all that much older than she is.

The door to the waiting room whooshes open and in stumbles a nervous, disheveled woman, and at first, Sybil doesn't recognize her, but then recognizes the designer handbag Ian said he spent $1200 dollars to give his mother, money he doesn't seem to have and ridiculous since she pays his rent. But it *is* Rita Shane hesitating in the doorway, despite the messy hair, the sloppy sweatpants, the tattered t-shirt, all polish and brisk professionalism gone.

"Mrs. Shane." Arranging a reassuring look on her face, Sybil leaps up to greet the real estate agent, but the woman doesn't see her as she marches toward Mars and throws herself at him, falling against him, pummeling with her arms, growling obscenities. A male nurse rushes forward and grabs Rita Shane by the shoulders, trying to pull her off Mars while a voice calls for help over the intercom. Sybil stands frozen, her mouth forming an 'O'.

Mars doesn't move. Lets her beat down on him, even as the nurse and security guard pull Rita Shane off him. The woman holds up her hands to show she's done and backs three or four steps away.

Sybil looks at the guard, hoping he takes the woman to some security office to cool down. But after the two of them confer in whispers, he puts a hand on Rita Shane's shoulder and nods.

Rita Shane glances past Sybil as if she were no more than a hat rack, and wags a finger at Mars, but when he doesn't look up – he's studying the carpet squares at his feet – the woman heads through the swinging doors. *To see her precious son* is the thought that flashes through Sybil's mind.

The nurse crouches down beside Mars who shakes his head and shifts toward the wall.

The nurse returns to the emergency room while the security guard heads down a corridor toward the lobby and only then does Sybil find her feet and return to her chair and sit down.

"Mars?" she says gently. He doesn't answer, but lifts himself from his chair and moves trance-like across the waiting room and through the door into the night.

She picks up her purse and puts it on her lap. She folds the handle over itself, then lets it go. She rummages for her phone and wraps her fingers tightly around it. She has no one to call. She drops it back into the purse and puts the purse back on the floor. Stretches her legs.

These are the times she thinks about Jamie. If Jamie were here, the two of them could form some kind of shield around Mars. They could stand guard and protect him from – who? Sybil pulls her feet in and tucks them under the chair. Himself? Of course. A middle-aged man who needs someone to protect him. It certainly wouldn't be Gus. She sighs, picks at her peeling nail polish. Men are more fragile than people think. Tougher than women on the outside, but inside. Why else do they die first?

These are the things she would explain to Jamie. About men. Some men. Most men. And about women like Rita Shane. How they tumble through life blinded to the faintest outlines of love and kindness, self-worth and contentment. And what good is having earned wisdom if there's no one to listen? Jamie had been a tenant too, but they'd become friends, the young mother with two little darlings and an irresponsible husband. The windstorm that blew through the Old Road at the first of the year toppled more than just trees. Then her mind wanders to the other missing woman, the one who lives on the other side of the Trencher

238

mansion. Charmaine. Like with Jamie, no one knows what happened to her. Sybil shivers. Reminds herself that Jamie took her car, her kids, she has an aunt in Oregon.

A doctor, Sybil can tell by his confident stride, comes in from the emergency room and says to Sybil, "Are you Mrs. German?"

"No, I'm not." She stands up, holds out her hand. "I'm Gus' landlady and a friend."

"What happened to his son?"

"Oh. He – he went out for some air. Is Gus going to be alright? Did he break his hip?"

"I really need to talk to a member of the family."

"Okay, I'll see if I can find him, but Gus is okay, isn't he?"

The doctor nods, his mouth an impatient frown. "Yes, yes. Lucky for him, it's just a bad bruise, but have his son talk to the nurse when he shows up, will you please?" He turns and quickly disappears behind the double doors.

Exhaustion takes Sybil by surprise as she sinks back into her chair, her only thought, *If Jamie were here, I wouldn't be all alone.*

I would have the strength to go out and find Mars German and drag him back.

I will do that.

In a minute.

She breathes in and out.

In and out.

Musical Moments

by Sally-Anne Macomber

To: Milton Flaxmill, Red Cow Publishing
From: Trudy Polaris
Date: August 20, 2014 8:03 a.m.
Re: Creative Tension

Phew! I am just back from rehearsal and am brimful of energy so I thought I would write to you again Milton. *Fortune favours the fortunate* (is that the saying?) so I have decided to burn the Tyrolean voodoo dolls and make my own fortune.

I have long been fascinated by the works of the absurdist Eugène Ionesco. (You know, the Romanian playwright who wrote mostly in French? I met him once, on a tour of Parisian nursing homes – oh, it's a long story, Milton, but I will spare you the dramatic details because I have such *extraordinary* good news.) My favourite work of his has always been *Rhinocéros*, ever since I first read it as an eight year-old on an accelerated learning programme. Perhaps you know the play?

Well, I have been feeling especially musical since we arrived here in the Tyrol, the air is so fresh and creamy, and I had the strangest dream a little over a month ago – strange I did not mention it in my last email to you – but in the dream, I was touring the local zoo and was struck by a singing rhinoceros. This image was so strong it stayed with me after I woke up, and then while I was eating my morning Alpine muesli I just started singing gibberish.

"What are you doing? Singing Romanian?" my husband said to me across the table, his mouth half-full of half-chewed Old Viennese imperial omelette. (His manners have deteriorated the higher we go in altitude, it's crazy! And what makes the omelette so Old Viennese imperial? Strawberries!)

But it was like an epiphany. *Rhinocéros* the musical! (Except I called it *Rhinocéros¡*) I bribed old Klaus next-door to milk the goats and wrote the musical in a day and an evening, 10 songs and the music and the script. (Though don't they call the script *the book*, in musical theatre circles? Milton, I have *so much* to learn!)

My husband fed me mushrooms and schnitzel and Edelweiss Schnapps when I called out for them. I was like Beethoven possessed, but at a higher altitude and possibly with a more subtle (or *subtler*?) tuning fork.

And luckily I've met a few musical people up here in the Tyrol, mainly through my ill-advised attempt at *dirndl* catwalk modelling (those laces on the bodice do *nothing* for an uneven cleavage) and within a few days we had the show cast and a rehearsal schedule mapped out ... and then came the bombshell. Some well-meaning schmuck on the next mountain over was doing exactly the same! except he was mounting the 1990 musical version of *Rhinocéros*, called *Born Again* (What a stupid title! No wonder it completely passed me by!) and first staged at the Chichester Festival. (In fact, I may have seen it then: I was in Chichester in late 1989 and stayed a little longer than intended due to an extended airline pilots' strike. Which may explain the strange dream I had about the singing

241

rhinoceros just over a month ago, which I think I forgot to tell you about in my last email.)

So it was back to the drawing board. Or rather, the harmonica. (The rooms are a little smaller than you might think up here in our Tyrolean hideaway, and even a keyboard is impossible to fit into the cramped music room, once you squeeze past the kettle drums aka *timpani*.) So I bribed Klaus to come back again to milk the goats (I told him he was going to be famous one day for knowing someone famous) and rewrote most of the songs in another all-day-and-night session, throwing out only one of them and adding two more because I was on a musical roll. I have based this new work on Ionesco's *Les Chaises* (or *The Chairs*), set it in Andalusia rather than the original Paris and called it *!Sillas¡ !Sillas¡ !Sillas¡* (which is *Chairs! Chairs! Chairs!* in español).

Which brings me to the point of my email: the dedication in *Nuclear Fission in The Pyrénées*. I know I originally dedicated it to my son i.e. *For my son*. Luckily, I only have one son, because changing the dedication would then prove even more difficult.

Given the influence I am now feeling since I immersed myself in Ionesco specifically and the Theatre of the Absurd more generally, I would really like to rewrite the last third of the book in a more absurdist fashion. But I am going to spare you that particular heart attack and say that instead, I would simply like to change the dedicatee to Eugène Ionesco, and I would like the new dedication to read,

ytidrusba etelpmoc ni
retsaM eht rof
ocsenoI enèguE

Don't worry about the possible psychological impact this betrayal of a thirty-year promise will have on my son. I will square it with him with some ice cream.

The only thing that can top the genuine creative excitement I am experiencing at the moment, is an email from you.

Yours, and passing no value judgements,

Trudi Polaris

To: Leonard Strauss Jr., Red Cow Publishing
From: Trudy Polaris
Date: August 20, 2014 1:27 p.m.
Re: Absurdities

Schöne Grüße im Sommer, Herr Strauss!

I wrote an email to Milton Flaxmill earlier this morning and of course, have received no reply as yet. Though I remain ever-hopeful. Of course, I have also not heard from you since my email *to you* dated 20th July either but that was my first email to you and so, of course, you have a little catching up to do re neglecting your email replies to me.

Are you reading this as diligently as you can?

The reason I sent Milton an email is because I advised him I want to change the dedication of *Nuclear Fission in The Pyrénées* (originally *Nuclear Fission in the Pyrénées* and soon to be, if you did as I asked in my last email, *Nuclear Fission in The Himalayas*) and I want the new dedicatee to be Eugène Ionesco, whom I know is Milton Flaxmill's favourite playwright. I made up some crazy story about writing and rehearsing a musical version of *Rhinocéros* which is just the silliest thing to contemplate but there you go: I'm a career writer in for the long haul.

And I think the new dedication will get me in good with Milton and speed this editing process up.

(Don't ask me who I had to do to find out he's a fan of Ionesco: just know that it involved a lot of grinding. The bad thing is though, I had to change my whole story because some wacko on the next mountain over came up with the very same story to impress *his* publisher. Jeez, this writing / editing / publishing world is a small place!)

So where do I come in, you ask? Or rather, where do you come in, I say.

Well, *Nuclear Fission in the / The Pyrénées / Himalayas* was originally dedicated to my son Boy. (Short for Boysenberry, a now rather embarrassing I-was-a-hippy-for-18-months reference to the bush under which he was conceived, though he prefers people to think *Boy* is short for *Boyd*, so please, when you meet him, don't tell him I told you his real name is not *Boyd* but *Boysenberry*. He can be a little temperamental about it.)

So I had to come up with some pretty amazing thing to sway him from suing me for breach of promise, now that the dedication is going to Eugène Ionesco, so I told him you had promised him an internship at *Red Cow Publishing*.

Boy is on an athletics tour of the US at the moment and hits Boston tomorrow. He has blue hair and is in a wheelchair. He will be easy to spot because he is the über-talented shotputter.

His other particular skill is with languages, which you as the Dialect Editor / Janitor will probably find useful. He does not take up a lot of room and loves Boston accents.

(You will probably find an appropriate intern-sized desk for him in the basement, which you as janitor would have the key for.)

I see your sister Frau Erdbeeren quite often in the street. I would like to thank her for giving me your email address but usually she is in the distance so I just see the back of her disappearing head.

Grüß Gott,

Frau Trudi Polarissen

Purple Elephants

by Mandy Nicol

"Read it again and tell me what you think," Mum says, bouncing around in her chair and waving the letter at me. She's moving about so much that Seph jumps off her lap and trots over to the heater to edge Peregrine out of the warmest spot in the house. I snatch the piece of paper from Mum with one hand and use the other to cram the last piece of toast and vegemite in my mouth. This stifles any swearing at the breakfast table. I scan the page.

> *Dear Mum,*
>
> *Sorry I've been a little lax with my letter writing these past months, but you can imagine how hectic my life is over here in the 'Big Apple'.*
>
> *Anyway that's all about to change. I have some great news ... *** drumroll *** ... I've decided to come back to Australia!*
>
> *I've had an idea banging around in my head for ages and it's getting more and more insistent. I know it's time to act now. It will be a life changer, that's for sure, and it will involve big family decisions but it will benefit us all, I'm sure of it.*
>
> *I'll go through everything with you when I get home, which will be some time before*

*Christmas. When I have the exact date sorted
I'll let you know so that Nadia can pick me
up from the airport.*

   All my love,
   Anthony

I toss the letter on the table. "I have no idea what he's talking about. He doesn't actually say anything except he's coming to Australia."

Bloody prick, he wants to sell the farm.

I jump to my feet, nearly knocking my chair over backwards. "You'll just have to wait till he gets here to find out," I say.

Mum folds the letter and feeds it into its envelope. "We'll all have to wait, you mean. He says it involves all of us. At first I thought he wanted me to sell the farm, but now I'm not so sure." She tucks the envelope into her cardigan pocket. "It's not as if he needs the money, and where would you and I live? Plus there's old Jack's lease on the land, he can't just up and move his crops and cows at the drop of a hat."

No he can't, can he? I hadn't thought of that.

I smile.

Mum looks over at the dogs, clicks her fingers and pats her thigh. Seph opens one eye but otherwise takes no notice. Peregrine waddles over. I think I'm feeding him too much. "Of course I could set it all in motion," Mum adds, turning back to me. "But it would be months before anything could happen."

I stop smiling and gather up the dishes. "You wouldn't really consider selling the farm, would you?"

"Of course I would, if it was for the best."

I'm not as careful as usual with her butterfly teacup and she winces when it clinks against the plates.

"Still," she says, "Anthony could have anything up his sleeve, you know what he's like." She stares out the window, through the driving rain, probably remembering a cherub-faced boy playing with his toy tractor in the yard.

I remember that boy throwing rocks at me.

"You're right, Nadia, we'll just have to wait till he gets here to find out what his plans are. In the meantime we'd better get his room ready. For a start you could make some nice new curtains, he's a bit old for purple elephants."

The dishes rattle and clunk as I thump them back down on the table. "Hang on a minute, he's not getting his old room back, that's my sewing room. We don't even know how long he'll be here."

"Of course he can have his old room back, and there's no need for you to look at me like that. I've told the three of you that your rooms will always be here whenever you want to come home." Mum shakes her head at me as if I'm a naughty toddler.

I feel like a naughty toddler. I want to stamp my feet and start squealing. But I don't. I just say, "You never told me that, because *I've* never left."

Ned Makes Friends

by Margaret Bingel

Nadia slows to a stop. The smells outside make her nose wiggle, and she can smell the stink of other dogs nearby. She squats down next to a bush and urinates. An unsuspecting squirrel on the ground is almost hit by the hot stream of piss, and it runs away, chittering insults.

Ned tugs on her leash one more time to get her moving, her legs sluggish from the heat. He doesn't want Nadia to get too fat at home, and besides, the walks in the park are really great exercise for his legs and lungs. Ned moves a lot more confidently now, hardly a limp left in his legs while he promenades down the concrete walk of the city park, the afternoon haze making everyone lazy and dull. Even so, the park is full of people lying about, or playing games on the grass.

Once Ned was comfortable with Nadia, he looked up places for the two of them to go so they can both get some exercise. At first he was ok with just sitting at home, surfing the Internet, but Nadia demanded more than just walks up and down his neighborhood. The vet told him that she was only 3 and needed more play time, preferably outside. So, Ned found a dog park within reasonable walking distance for both of them, and he makes it a point to bring her out every day.

Ned sits down on a bench to rest. The humidity is thick enough to coat the back of your throat with thirst, and luckily, Ned had the wit to bring water for the two of them. He forgot about it last time, and Nadia was so tired he had to carry her home. Now, if it's too hot out, Nadia sits crossways through the doorway, not budging until she hears the faucet run.

Ned pulls a bowl out of his rucksack and pours water from a plastic bottle into it, then pushes it towards Nadia. While she laps up the water, he pulls out an apple and bites into it, careful not to let the juices run down his chin. There is a comfortable silence between them, the man and his dog, and with it, Ned feels time move slowly, each second like a drop of molasses dripping out of a bottle. So much better than the break-neck speed towards death he was feeling at the beginning of the year.

"So much better than in a long time," Ned muses aloud.

Once Nadia is done drinking, Ned packs the bowl and the bottle in the rucksack and holding her leash, walks over to the dog park. He enters the fenced-in area where all the other dogs roam and unclipping her leash, watches her run wild with the rest of her kind, free and uncaring. Sure, she's just a dog, Ned thinks, but she has a much better sense of the world around her than he, a human, has ever had.

"Look at dem bitches go, amirite?"

Startled, Ned turns his whole body to face the man towering over him, gleaming white teeth shining through a wide smile.

"I know ma girl Daisy sure loves dem odda bitches. Look a' dem, sniffing asses like it was a meet n' greet."

Ned says, "Or at a Yankee Candle Shoppe."

The big man roars out his amusement. He offers his hand out to Ned.

"Jeffery."

"Ned," and they both shake hands, Jeffery's cool against Ned's. Ned looks the man full in the face, and sees a jovial sparkle in his eyes, and a friendliness that inspires him to talk.

"My Nadia is that beagle over there, rolling in the grass. Who's your Daisy?"

"Ma girl is dat Rottie over there, shittin' on de Pug."

Ned looks over, aghast, but sees that Daisy, who is clearly not a puppy, sitting on top of another dog. Ned looks back at Jeffery, who is laughing even harder.

"Made ya look, didn I?"

"Yeah, you did, Jeffery."

Later, after handing Ned a copy of his business card, Jeffery whistles for his dog, releashes her, and walks away, waving goodbye to his new friend.

Ned looks down at the business card. Jeffery invited him over to a party at his house over the weekend. And, Ned thinks, what the hell just happened?

Time in the Well

by Darryl Price

Well it's no use. I belong behind bars. Not real bars, but bars that are walls, walls that are made out of row after row of huge, hulking trees. I want to come home to you, Doc. This real world stuff is not for me. I know you thought I could do it, but I'm just not made for the everyday living stuff. It scares me.

Put me in a circle any time.

All this jagged running around tires me out. I feel like a bumper car.

And I still miss someone.

That's never going away, is it? I'm just going to roll through life like a shell on a beach, subject to the whims of weather and not much else. Why? What did I do but love someone? Is love its own crazy punishment? I just want to be left alone – by love and everyone else.

Look, Doc, I admit I'm a long, strange case. I didn't ask for it. Well. I guess you didn't ask for it, for me, either, so maybe life's got it in for you, too.

At any rate, I know what you are going to say: you've got to get on with your life. Am I right? Okay, let's try it your way. But if I end up in a ditch somewhere, it's going to be your fault. No, I'm sorry, Doc, I don't mean to blame you. It's just that I don't feel a part of things any more.

At the grocery store I might as well be a vegetable or fruit.

At the movies I watch the chairs.

Outside I'm looking for the exit signs between trees to some other world than mine. The sun, the wind, these mean nothing to me, except to let me know they can slap me around.

Okay, things are spiraling as you put it so often and I've got to stop that kind of thinking in its tracks, so how about a story?

Once there was a little boy who could walk through walls. No one knew how he did it, not even the little boy. It just happened one day and then it always happened. At first all his friends took real delight in this fact. They made him do it over and over, but eventually they began to not ask to see this amazing trick of his. In fact they began to shun him for it. Soon he had no one to talk with or play with and this made the boy lonely. He would crawl into a wall and stay there for hours at a time. One day the little boy heard someone yelling for help, like this, "Help me, oh anyone, everyone, my girl has fallen down a well and can't climb back up!" Well, the boy sprang into action and walked right down through the walls of the old well and with only his arms and hands visible gently lifted the scared little girl to the top inch by inch until she was safe in her mother's arms once again. No one thanked the boy. They all left in a big rush, squeezing and kissing the missing child over and over again until the boy who could walk through walls was once again left completely alone. The stars came out before all his tears had dried. Suddenly there was a warm feeling in his left hand and he looked down to see the girl holding his hand. "Come on, Silly," she said, "everyone's waiting for you." After that, with the girl always nearby, the boy began to do all the normal things that boys his age do, and soon he forgot all about walking through walls. As a matter of fact he never brought it up again.

See there, Doc, a happy ending for all. Even if I can't have my own happy ending I'll give it to someone else.

Surely that's worth a readmission to the greatest show on earth. Let me know.

I'm spending way too much time in the well as it is.

Working on
My Jokes

by Teresa Burns Gunther

The orange sun lingers on Malibu's horizon. Susie's skin is tight from sun and sand; her eyes burn with saltwater tears. She hugs her knees, knocks her forehead against them, *fool, fool.* She sits up, dries her eyes and reminds herself that heartbreak is good for artistic development.

When she gave Steve a ride to LA to pursue his dream of acting she had no idea she'd end up in television. It was an old friend of Steve's who helped Susie landed a role in a soap: *nasty nurse.* She owes everything to Steve. The thought washes loneliness over her like the wave foaming up the shore. She wants to call Rachel, her go-to person in a crisis, though there's a good chance her cousin will say something to make her feel worse. Rachel's *on the spectrum*: odd to rude. Susie knows she doesn't mean it, that deep down she has a gentle heart; but her words can bite.

In July, while visiting Rachel in San Francisco, Susie met Steve and his tall cousin Kevin. A double cousin double date! Steve hugged Susie, called her adorable, and Susie recognized instant love on Fisherman's Wharf. They are so well matched: both from Indiana, blond, short, a little lost, and oh how they love to laugh. And Kevin was perfect for Rachel, who's 5'9" and says *tall men are in too short* supply *ha ha.* 6'3" and he even found Rachel's unfiltered comments amusing! That night, seeing the sights,

Susie was proud, for once she was the successful cousin bestowing favors.

Rachel told her she was crazy when she'd offered to drive Steve to LA, but Susie figured she had nothing to lose and Steve to gain. They'd had great fun cruising the California coast, surrounded in beauty, laughing, *happy, happy*. But when she'd crawled into his motel bed that first night in LA, telling him how she loved him – she cringes remembering – he'd jumped away, pulled a pillow between them, his long-lashed eyes wide with alarm, then pity. Oh they'd talked it all out. She understands now, though at first she tried to believe he was just confused and might change his mind. But today, Steve introduced her to his new boyfriend. Susie made happy noises, forcing her face to smile as she took pictures of them, grinning and holding each other's hands.

Susie watches the sun disappear and when the *scary scary* in her center starts squirming up she throws caution to the red horizon and calls Rachel. Comforted by her cousin's crisp voice she blurts out her news about Steve.

"When did you figure it out?" Rachel asks.

"You knew?" Susie asks. "Why didn't you tell me?"

"I thought it was obvious. But you always tell me not to rain on parades."

Susie considers this. As usual Rachel's right. She compliments her on her restraint and tells her about the sunset. Rachel steps outside and describes her own sky then asks about Susie's show: *As The Sperm Turns, ha ha*. Susie begins to regret calling but asks how it's going with Kevin. Rachel tells her they went out but he never called.

"Oh, no. What did you say?" Susie asks. Rachel's smart and beautiful, until she opens her mouth. It's not that her observations are wrong; they're just not always … necessary.

"Nothing. We had fun. I'm working on my jokes. That's my August resolution."

Susie groans.

"I can be funny. He laughed. Well," Rachel sniffs. "He *said* I was funny."

"Funny, good or funny … strange?"

Susie hurries home, shivering through the incoming fog, her worries shifted now to her awkward cousin.

After dinner, a shower, and a big glass of wine, Susie calls Steve.

"Hi Sugar," Steve says and Susie wishes, just this once, that he could sound the tiniest bit blue. She misses being the perky one. As they chitchat she looks around her small apartment noting the mess, as if Rachel and her disapproval are surveying it too. Steve teases her to reveal the next twist on her soap. He only watches it for her, which makes her love him even more. She laughs and scolds him and reminds herself they're *friends, friends*. Then she tells him about Rachel and Kevin.

"You shouldn't phone after 9:00 p.m."

"God, Rachel. Don't answer if you don't want to talk!" Susie snaps, then softens her tone and tells Rachel what she learned. "Kevin called but you never answered. He told Steve he even left a note on your porch."

"He's lying," Rachel says. "I have voice mail."

"Think about it. Why would he lie to Steve?"

"Good point," Rachel concedes, then she's quiet, Susie hears footsteps, a door opening, the dog barking, Rachel murmuring *Stella, Stella,* now scraping noises. "Okay," Rachel finally says. "His note's under my doormat, but I didn't get any phone messages."

"Well, maybe he got the number wrong," Susie says. "Stop being so logical, Dr. Spock." Rachel doesn't answer. Susie pictures her, head tilted, eyes moving, *thinking, thinking.* "Are you still there?"

"What should I do?" Rachel asks.

"You're asking me for advice?"

"Do you have any?"

"First tell me I did good."

"Why?" Rachel asks. "Nothing good has happened yet."

Susie laughs. "Just say it." They go back and forth, the tug of war lifts Susie's spirits.

"Ok. You did good," Rachel finally admits. "Now what should I do? Though why I'm asking you –"

"Stop," Susie says before Rachel's words destroy her little satisfaction. It's silly but she's savoring it all the same. *"Be smart. Figure it out,"* she says, mimicking Rachel's rational advice. Susie says she has to go practice her lines, realizing it's the first time with Rachel that she ever got to hang up first.

Morgana Malone
and the Mystery of
the Family Trust

by Matt Potter

"Don't look at them!" Jane says, tucking them under her chair.

I lean sideways in my seat and peer at her feet.

"Don't look at them, I said! I don't even know if I can stock them." Jane opens her folder on the table – "papyrus," she notes, "imported from the Maldives," – and taking out a business card, hands it to me.

NOT made in China, I read.

décor • clothing • collectibles, I read underneath.

… for the incredibly discerning, I read under that.

Then, *127a King William Road*.

"It's a nightmare getting stock not made in China," Jane says, picking up her chai latte. "A nightmare!"

She puts her cup down on the table again with a clink, rattling the plates left over from lunch – black quinoa and juju bean salad for her (the Monday lunch special) and haloumi, lettuce and drizzled macadamia oil focaccia for me – then slides a foot across the tiles and into the open.

"They're made in Tibet," she says, "of bamboo and yak leather. But which Tibet? *Chinese* Tibet or *Tibet* Tibet?"

The brown strips across her feet are crinkly, but so too is her skin – nothing covering them but the yak strips and blue with winter cold.

"And isn't the Dalai Lama from *Indian* Tibet?!" she continues. "These are the decisions I'm faced with. You are lucky you don't have a career or a husband or children or a new business to set up."

I gaze around the café, and sip my double strawberry milkshake through a straw as sugary strawberry syrup wafts up from the glass. Pale sun streams through the window, a reminder that spring – has it really been that long? – is not far away. Almond trees have already blossomed and the apricot tree in the back garden of the house I rent is smothered with white flowers. (Ludmilla, my former housemate, visited only yesterday and eyed the blossom, dollar signs spinning in her head as she calculated how many buckets she would need to strip the free fruit from the lower branches in a few months.)

I pull my cardigan closer across my breasts.

"But we need to talk about Mum and the cake shop," Jane adds. "When was the last time you saw her?"

I shake my head. "I've sort of been keeping to myself lately."

Jane runs her fingers through her hair. Which is naturally auburn, not unlike the colour I thought my hair might turn out when I had it dyed orange.

"Mum can't keep the cake shop up much longer," she says. "She's seventy-two and on her own and she needs help."

(When we were growing up I always wanted hair like Jane's. Everyone loved it. *Jane has such gorgeous hair, so thick and auburn and shiny*, was a comment her hair always earned. I wanted hair like hers, so everyone would envy me.

Now of course, with my dye growing out and the grey-brown roots expanding across my head, I have hair people feel sorry for.)

Jane clears her throat then looks straight at me.

"And you don't have a career or a husband or children or a new business to set up or even a job so you'll have to be the one to take over the cake shop because I *do* have a career and a husband and children and a new business to set up." Jane breathes out. "*NOT made in China* won't set itself up, you know, and it's a business that I can well see will change the face of modern retailing."

I suck more double strawberry milkshake through the straw, my slurping noisy on the bottom of the glass. And then mention the unmentionable. "Why doesn't Mum sell the cake shop?"

Jane's mouth is a big 'O'. And then she gulps and collects her breath. "We'd never get what the cake shop is worth if we sold it in the current economic climate. And the cake shop is a family business. It'd be dreadful if it went out of the family. And let's face it Morgana, you stopped temping in January to work in your ex-husband's practice, and you left that *months* ago and *you're* not doing anything else so *you're* the obvious one to step in and help Mum." She purses her lips, and raises an eyebrow. "It's no different from when we were kids and we worked there on Saturday morning. She's seventy-two and on her own, and she needs help and it's time you stopped being so selfish and started thinking of others."

"But I'm seeing someone. We're talking about moving in together."

"And you know I've always had a head for business," Jane says, snapping the stud on her papyrus folder from the Maldives shut. "You know I know a lot about these things."

"So why don't *you* step in and work at the cake shop?" I suggest, assuming she's completely ignoring my news. "If anyone can keep it afloat, you can."

Jane sits back in her chair. "So who is this person you're seeing? Even though you're *sort of* keeping to yourself and don't have time to see your own mother."

Hmm, now I have to tell her.

"Well, you know," I say, "he has a bright future as a doctor and he's very good-looking and comes from a wealthy family and he's twenty-three."

"Twenty-three!" Jane says. "That's disgusting. You're old enough to be his mother." And a moment later, her eyes widen and raising an eyebrow again she looks directly at me and asks, "Is he good?"

A tall man with wavy brown hair and wearing a dark blue suit stands in the middle of the café and is looking at us.

"Is he good?" Jane asks again.

The tall man with wavy brown hair and wearing a dark blue suit is now two tables away.

"Are you just going to ignore me, Morgana?"

I snap my head to look at her because she never calls me Morgana and today she's called me that twice. I changed my name to Morgana a decade and a half ago and she's never –

"Susan?"

"Yes," we both say.

I look across the table at Jane. Who is now touching the ends of her naturally auburn hair.

The tall man with wavy brown hair and wearing a dark blue suit says, "You're both Susan?"

"No," we both say.

"Susan is my former name," I say, sounding very formal.

"And Susan is my new name," Jane tells him, and then looking at me across the table, she points at the business card she gave me and says, "for business purposes. It's on my card." And she flips over the card and there it is plain as day, *Susan Green-Baye*, her new name, which is actually my old name, with her husband's surname hyphened on the end.

"But *Susan Green* is my name."

"It *was* your name but it's not now, it's mine." And she smiles up at the tall man.

No one says anything. Perhaps the tall man's name is Susan Green too.

The tall man looks at me and then at Jane. "So which Susan used to be married to Grigor Smiroveich?" he asks.

"*She* did," the new Susan Green hyphen Baye says. "That was a looong time before I was ever Susan."

The tall man smiles. "Then this is for you," he says, and places a white envelope in front of me. "Have a nice day."

He hasn't cornered the next table over and I know what it is.

"What is it?" my sister (it's easier to call her that now) asks.

I pick the envelope up and without opening it, start ripping it into pieces. "Just Grigor still trying to get more money out of me for his cancelled wedding," I say.

"Don't look to me if you need money because I haven't got any," she says. "I have a husband and children and a business to support." She waves her hand in the air to signal a waitress.

I stare at the envelope and its contents, now a messy white paper pile on the table.

"It's all part of my business strategy," the new Susan continues. "Which I would not expect you to understand because you don't have a head for business like I do."

My eyes blur. She's expecting me to say something but I'm not going to say anything. What I want to do is shove the messy pile of paper down her throat and make her eat it.

"I went to a business specialist – she's very New-Agey – and she said *Jane* was not a good name for a businesswoman but *Susan* is."

The words are stuck in my throat. I breathe out and the paper flutters on the table. I can't look at my sister. So I look past her and out the window and I see Seth standing on the footpath: he with the bright future as a doctor who's very good-looking with high cheekbones on a thin face and short dark hair atop deep brown eyes and comes from a wealthy family and is twenty-three. I'd asked him to meet me after lunch. And my heart lurches inside my ribcage because, if ever I need rescuing, it's now.

"I had to take a bottle of sand from a place that's special to me but I didn't have any time to go to the beach so I just took a bucket and spade to the local kindergarten and got it from their sand pit. She's a sand reader."

I pick up my handbag from the spare chair beside me.

"And you weren't using your old name any more and it's a free country," she adds.

I stand up and look down at her. "I was hoping to start a new life again and I thought it might be nice to start by getting my old name back."

A waitress watches me as, high heels clacking on the floor, I head towards the door and a grinning Seth standing outside. I smile as I stop at the counter.

"Please send the lunch bill to this address," I say, handing the waitress the *NOT made in China* business card my sister gave me. "And mark it, *Attention: Susan*."

Q

by Gary Percesepe

How did I meet her?

We were both members of an online community, where writers from around the world would post their stories, poems, and essays, and comment on the writing of others. I cannot remember if she commented on my work first, or if I commented on hers. But I do remember reading one of her stories, which was an alphabet of desire. She wrote as someone who knew about the messiness of human relationships, and sex – connected and disconnected from love – but more, she seemed to understand the smallest calibrations of the human heart, how restless we are until we find – what? What is it that we are looking for? I didn't know either. But reading her stories, I began to name what it is that I wanted in this life by her name, Q. I wanted her. I didn't know her. But her writing knew me, had interrogated me, flushed me out, and called to me.

Having someone take the time to read your work, and make a telling comment, one that strikes at the core of what you intended to say, what you meant, someone who gets every feint, every gesture, every subtle characterization, every plot point, every word choice – is so rare. Everyone reads and writes from somewhere – all writing is contextual. Every writer wants to believe that he or she writes for some*body*.

John Updike once famously described his imagined or ideal reader as a teenage boy who happens upon one of his books on the dusty shelves of some library one afternoon looking for literary adventure. Updike found me in this way. But nothing could prepare me for Q, who somehow came to me through my work. She read me all the way through; she read me in every way that a reader can read you, and get you.

Being read by someone you do not know is strange. She sits somewhere with your work in her hands (on her screen?) in a place, in a time, in a setting that is unknown to you. Then one day, magically, she posts a comment on your work. You see her picture (as on Facebook), a picture of the person who has commented on a piece of writing so deep in your heart, so interior, that it is embarrassing to you even that you have posted it, but now here is this woman, a stranger, really, an amazing beautiful stranger (from her picture) who is telling you that she loves your work which, let us imagine, took you two decades to write, it was so painful, and let's say it was a portion of a memoir, or later a poem that you tossed off, let's say she read your poem of New York longing.

And off to the side of my poem Q wrote:

> an anthem shaped to fit into the city's skyline: love it. The juxtapositions of images uniquely yours and full of yearning. Horn & Hardart may never return, but won't you come home to us, Gary?

Right there, with one comment on a poem, she took an axe to the frozen sea inside and she had me then, though I didn't know it at the time. It would be a month before I met her, for drinks in Manhattan when I was in town. We met at an Italian restaurant I had liked once upon a time, but on this night there was construction outside and the restaurant was empty and there was only the two of us and we twittered away, two writers chirping, and I had been interested in another woman, also in New York, and still had a wife at home, and wanted to be (and was) on my best behavior, but we went on talking, and I thought, she is easy to talk to, she is full of heart, she is small, petite, I could fit my arms around her waist and carry her off, and the waiter kept asking and I kept declining to eat until exasperated they wanted to close the restaurant at 8 pm – this was Midtown Manhattan! – and Q exploded at the manager (I watched, amused – 90% heart, I calculated, the rest, fire), who responded by flicking the lights on and off, and just like that she had done it, what hadn't happened in so long, she ignited another fire in me (I had been in love three times in my life), one that smoldered for a month, until we met again on the roof of her building and she walked me through the edits she had made to my novel and I tried to listen while I studied the shape of her face, strands of her dark hair blowing in the breeze on a cool day in May. Then, in June, I waited for her outside a trendy restaurant in Greenwich Village. A pretty girl sat next to me on a bench outside the restaurant. She was vaguely European and smoked furiously on a small cigarette while we watched the weather. A storm was approaching. The wind was picking up, and the sky darkening. The Euro girl asked if I was waiting for someone and I said yes. Then I saw Q, walking toward me. I got up and went to her.

I keep trying to go to her. But there doesn't seem to be a way to be together, or at least no way that I know. The time is out of joint. No way is open.

Samford, a Motel 6 Couch, and the Blonde Woman

by Nathaniel Tower

Samford is feeling rather horny, which is a good thing because he has found himself on top of a blonde-haired woman on a couch in the lobby of a Motel 6. There is no one behind the desk, and the blonde has her hands down his pants. It's the first time he's been with a blonde woman. At least he thinks it is.

The blonde is quick and efficient. She lifts her skirt and has his real human penis inside what he thinks must be her real human vagina within seconds. It all happens so quick that he's not even sure how he ended up with his boner inside the hottest woman he's ever seen in a Motel 6.

She doesn't scream or moan or grunt or anything. It's the most silent act of fornication ever. They might as well be in a library or a church. The springs in the worn-out couch don't squeak or creak. Samford constantly looks over at the desk to see if the concierge – if they even call them that at a Motel 6 – is back there watching him. He doesn't think the concierge will break them up or call the cops. Hell, the scumbag would probably video tape it and have the whole event up on YouTube before Samford even blows his load.

At the precise moment Samford thinks about blowing his load, his load blows inside the blonde. The blonde smiles and nods and pushes him gently to indicate that he may get off her. There is no indication whatsoever that she has enjoyed herself even in the slightest, but Samford has to ask. "Was that good for you?" To his knowledge, this is the first thing he has ever said to her.

She keeps the smile on her face. "It wasn't bad for me." Then she pulls his pants back on for him and drops her skirt. They both sit up on the couch just as the concierge walks in.

"Do you need a room?" the concierge asks.

Samford looks at the woman in a panic. Will she want to share a room with him after that?

"Nope," she says before he can say anything. "He already fucked me, right here on this couch. In fact, his sperm has already swum up and fertilized one of my eggs. I can feel the baby growing in my belly."

Samford half-swallows a laugh, but he really does find it funny. He could see himself with this woman.

The concierge doesn't laugh. "Don't fuck with me," he says. "I'll have you two thrown in jail. Now, do you want a room, or not?"

"I'm not fucking with you." The blonde smiles. "I was fucking with him." She slaps Samford right on the thigh and squeezes, his erection returning even though the touch isn't affectionate.

The concierge picks up the phone. "That's it. I'm calling the cops."

The blonde stands up. "I wouldn't do that if I were you." Samford expects her to pull out a weapon, but there's no way she could have one on her.

The concierge begins dialing. Samford looks back and forth between the woman and the hotel worker. The blonde's stomach gurgles and begins to expand, within moments the size of a watermelon. "What the fuck?" the concierge says and the phone slips out of his hands.

The blonde's stomach continues to expand. She props one leg up on the couch. "Get ready, Sam," she says. Samford glances up her skirt and sees an arm emerging from her unpantied crotch.

"What the hell?"

"Just get ready!" she shouts. It isn't angry or even really a panic.

Samford holds his arms out, ready to catch whatever is coming out.

"No, just get out of the way."

Samford dives on the floor and watches a full-grown human emerge from her vagina. The thing slides out but isn't goopy at all like he would expect. Then again, it hasn't had much time to ferment in there.

The full-grown man hits the couch first and then bounces on the floor. The blonde lets out a relieved sigh. The concierge sprints out of the Motel 6. Samford stares at the man who possesses every single one of Samford's features down to the tiniest imperfections.

The man stands. "What the fuck are you looking at?" he says to Samford. The voice is familiar, but Samford doesn't think he sounds quite like that.

The blonde looks at Samford and smiles. "Your work here is done. You can go now."

Samford stands and stares at her. He wants to say something, to ask if it hurt, to ask why him, to ask if he needs to stay and raise it with her. Then he hears sirens approaching. Questions will only lead to answers he doesn't want. He bursts through the Motel 6 doors and sprints off into the night.

Kununurra

by Kimberlee Smith

She's been on the road for a month, my mum Maybell, on a trip that wouldn't take anyone else in the world more than a fortnight, and that'd be with plenty of stops along the way. She's traveling from our home in Sydney to the outskirts of Kununurra in the Kimberley region, where, she's been told by members of her old congregation after belabored inquiries, that Brother Tom Bend set his sights on finding a particularly sinful and barbaric aboriginal tribe he believes he can save through prayer and deliverance. Brother Tom is her ex-husband and my daddy. We hadn't seen him in a handful-plus of years.

Mum never did explain why. Maybe by the grace of God she'll find him, and I cannot wait to find out what stirred her up to do such a thing. For whatever reason she's searching him down, her curiosity bled over to me and I'm getting impatient following her as she travels with my bub, Etheline, who's exactly seven and one-half months old today. I'm not understanding Mum's tactics of stalling a trip that she started out hell-bent on finishing in record time. If she hadn't a burning need to get to him as fast as possible she never would have traveled eight hours her first day on the road wearing an adult diaper so she didn't have to stop at a dunny.

The closer she gets to him, the more side trips she takes, meandering across the country to see everything there is to see and even what I would consider a colossal waste of time.

She's driving my old Jackaroo that has over 392,000 kilometers on it. The petrol gauge is stuck on one-third full no matter how full the tank is. And no one either bothered to or, I hope, wanted to pop out the Tom Waits tape I was listening to the day before I died. Since Mum turned on the music to drown out the silence of the drive, she's been signing along with every song, knows all the words. But she most loves his version of *Waltzing Matilda*. It was her favorite song before hearing Tom Waits sing it, and I don't think she knew he was my favorite singer. I wish so bad that right now I could be there riding shotgun along with her. The longer I've been gone, the closer to her and the bub I feel.

> *and the ghosts that sell memories*
> *want a piece of the action anyhow*
> *go waltzing matilda, waltzing matilda*
> *you'll go a-waltzing matilda with me …*
> *… and his ghost may be heard*
> *as you pass by that billabong*
> *who'll come a-waltzing matilda with me*

The lyrics go more or less like that. Not the way they were originally written, and I don't believe she's even hearing the words she's singing, but she knows them perfectly, each and every one.

After driving for eight hours, Mum stopped at Trilby station in Louth where she fished along the banks until the sun went down, unaware that a toxic phosphorescent bloom had killed off most of the fish this past summer and the ones that remained were horribly poisonous (she thankfully

272

didn't hook one fish but had an extra gin and lime cordial that night, "Bob's your uncle!" she exclaimed to herself with too much hilarity as she poured herself another, while the bub slept straight through it, thankfully), then slowed her pace on day two, driving half the distance where she explored a used-books store and spent a dollar on a copy of *The Thorn Birds*.

She stopped at the Bandicoot Bar Hotel for the night and ended up staying for two, getting to know the locals, of which there weren't many. Most folks were like Mum, passers-through on their way somewhere else. The first night, Mum brought Etheline in her pram into the pub, and fed her mushy peas and fish she pulverized with the tines of her fork, taking extra care to pluck out a few bones that were as thin as a strand of hair. The bub absolutely loved it, bobbing her head like a cockatoo and clapping. Mum read her new book while she ate a cheeseburger with fried egg to soak up the gin and lime cordials she drank as daintily as she could, for appearances' sake. They had such a fine time and slept so well, snuggled up on a mattress as small as a camp bed, Mum decided to do it again the following night.

It took her over a week to reach Uluru, and she stayed there for *three* nights. She bought mozzie nets to cover her and the bub's faces, and the bub kept fussing to pull hers off. She was trying to eat the mozzies. This is not a good sign. But Mum knew that the venom that killed me had surged through Etheline's bloodstream and gave her a taste for insects and animals in general. She gave in and took the net off the bub and let her have her way with the mozzies. Etheline became so adept at catching them and popping them in her mouth and grinding them down with her slippery pink gums that Mum wasn't bothered by the pests anymore and she took off her net as well.

§

By the time they made it to Broome, they'd been three weeks on the road. I'm getting a feeling that Mum is procrastinating because she's apprehensive about seeing Brother Tom after all these years, how he's going to react, but more so how *she'll* feel. She loved him as much as the sun, the moon, the stars, and everything in between. That's what she used to tell him and me. I kept my mouth shut and never corrected her that the fact is the sun is a star, because that's not important. What is important is that I believe she *never* stopped loving him that much. She's afraid and I don't blame her one bit.

Today is the last of five days they've spent on Cable Beach. The bub is transfixed, watching the camels lope along the shoreline. Mum brought the baby backpack along for hiking and whatnot. *Whatnot* at Cable Beach means strapping Etheline into the backpack and taking a camel ride at sunset along the beach for an hour. The bub lays her head on Mum's shoulder and smiles and coos for the whole bumpy hour they ride along. It's one of the most beautiful things I've ever seen. All the tourists are taking pictures of the unlikely pair of travelers, promising to send copies back to Mum when their travels end. The bloke who runs the operation there asks Mum if he could use their picture in a poster for advertising purposes and Mum blushes like a schoolgirl.

"You hear that, you cheeky little monkey? We're going to be famous!" she says to Etheline, who pats Mum on both cheeks and puckers her lips to kiss Mum all over her face.

"Da, da, da*mum,*" the bub says, sounding as if she's imitating the drumbeat in a parade.

Mum's face lights up as bright as the fireworks over Sydney Harbour on New Year's Eve and she turns to Hugo, which is the name of the bloke in charge.

"You hear that? Her voice cracks on the last word and she's got a smile as wide as the sea. "She said my name. First time. She called me grandmum."

"So how you going now?" Hugo says, then laughs and shakes his head.

"Better than I been in a long while. Tell you that much. I live for this little one, I do," Mum says.

"She's a doll, no doubt you do. You two traveling alone, hey? Giving her mum and dad a break?" he asks.

"Naw. I wish. Her mum and dad, well, they passed right when she was born. It's the two of us, just us two," Mum says. She looks over at the bub, who is reaching out to pet the camel they rode. He dips his head toward her and makes a motorboat noise as his floppy lips rumble.

"His name is Ghan. I can tell he really likes you, darlin'," says Hugo to the bub. "Not true with all folks. He's a discriminating camel."

Hugo looks at Mum, who is squinting her eyes and has a hangdog face as she looks right to the sinking sun. The sky is the color of fire and amethysts.

"Sorry to hear that, ma'am. Sorry about your loss," says Hugo as he moves closer to Ghan and rubs his neck, but Ghan is leaning down to Etheline.

Mum doesn't acknowledge this. It's understandable. I'm surprised she said anything about the accidents, she hasn't told a soul about it. The thought of it must be painful enough for her; I cannot imagine her mustering the strength to say it out loud, *My daughter died from a lethal snakebite right before the bub was taken from her womb. Emergency Caesarean. It was just me and her widower, Dean, and the bub. A few months after, Dean was killed in a plane crash. Transporting those snakes that he bought and sold for business. That trip was the one he finally was able to get rid of the coral snake that killed my daughter. He died on the way home to us.*

That's just not a conversation you can have with anyone. I bet it'd be easier to talk about it with a stranger than someone who knew us, but that's relative. I can't imagine a person even revisiting that story in their own head, never mind enunciating it out loud.

"How 'bout that, ma'am. Ghan likes the bub more than he likes me, and I live with him!" says Hugo.

"She has a way with animals taking kindly to her," says Mum.

Hugo pulls on Ghan's reins and Ghan makes a squeal in protest then gives in. Hugo makes a comment about feeding time and says "Git" to the camel, who looks up at him and follows him back to the stable.

Mum carries the bub in her arms to the car and straps her into her safety seat, then wipes the sand off the bottom of her own shoes. She leans into the back of the car and whispers, "I love you, Etheline. As much as the sun, the moon, the stars, and everything in between." Her eyes get all misty and she is as happy as I've seen her since I left.

This evening, after one more hour on the road, they hit the mark of traveling for an entire month and finally enter Kununurra. Mum drives along the Ord River and then through about forty kilometers of farmland. The air dark as wet ink is dry and warm and smells like mango and sandalwood. Stars pepper the sky. Etheline sleeps with a smile spread across her face. Her pale blonde eyelashes flutter from colorful dreams.

Mum talks to herself out loud.

"After brekkie, I'ma put Etheline in her finest dress ... the one the color of the inside of a shell. All that pretty cotton lace around the hem. And white socks with lace to match. And shiny little white booties with the ribbon ties." She laughs, not heartily but wistfully.

"Soles of those shoes never gonna wear out. By the time she's walkin,' she won't fit in them anymore. Maybe I'ma get them bronzed. Put them up on the mantle. I'ma put on my best dress, too, now that I'm thinking of it."

I think it's time. I think she's ready.

Trypophobia

by Vanessa Weibler Paris

Every day I go to work and leave Iris behind. Home, alone.

What I know about Iris: She's fascinated by bones. Broken bones. My bones.

What I know about Iris: Like her floral namesake, she is beautiful and bewitching.

What I know about Iris: She is the first woman who has kissed me. Who has said she loves me.

What I know: She loves her art more than she'll ever love me. Or herself.

What I don't know about Iris: Is what I don't know about Iris. Yet. Or ever.

"What will you do today?" I ask this morning, as I'm drinking my coffee – lightened with skim milk, per Iris, instead of my former heavy cream. I've spent my life trying to gain, to stop being Slim Jim and finally become Jamie, but Iris likes me this way.

"I'm working on a new series," she says.

"More bones?" I ask.

"In a sense," she tells me.

"Broken?"

"In a way."

"What's it called?"

"Trypophobia," she says, licking blackstrap molasses from the blade of a serrated kitchen knife as she does every morning. "But that's all I will say. I can't talk about it until it's finished."

I go to work and spend my breaks online, learning the word and finding the pictures of the holes. Lotus pods and honeycombs and hair plugs. I take my phone into the bathroom and crouch in the stall, searching more. Crumpets and lava rocks and Surinam toads. Bone marrow.

Bone marrow.

I click through page after page after page, enlarging them. Zooming. Sweating. Goosebumping. Someone flushes and I grab the toilet paper roll, leaving a damp spindly handprint behind.

All day long, I can only think of the holes.

I sit in meetings and talk on the phone, and shiver: envisioning the holes. I drive home and kiss Iris hello and sit down to something low-fat and low-calorie for dinner, and shudder: imagining the holes.

"Drink your water," Iris says over grilled salmon and steamed asparagus, pushing my glass closer as though it's out of reach. "You don't drink enough water."

"I'll drink it," I say, and I do. And then I drink another. And I wonder how it stays in. I am full of holes, my ears and my nose and my penis and my pores. There's water everywhere, I think, pouring a third glass. And it keeps seeping in and leaking out of everything.

I drink my water, imagining Iris filling a dropper with bleach and squeezing it drop by drop by drop onto my bare skin. The flesh would sizzle as each hole formed, and she'd do it carefully, systematically, starting at the center and working her way out outward like a flower blooming. It would burn down to the bone, making marrow external.

Would it hurt, or feel like relief?

Eventually I'd be covered with them, round and neat like office hole-punches, and liquid would start to ooze out. It might be red or it might be yellow or it might be the clear water I'd drunk. It might be fears or it might be feelings or it might be words I can never say.

I chew my fish and sip my drink and listen to Iris hum. It takes me a few seconds to recognize 'Coin-Operated Boy' by the Dresden Dolls.

I picture a lotus pod, riddled with holes like a showerhead. The cluster of seeds, loose but secure. Bulging, sharp-tipped, staring like eyes and poking like breasts.

"Are you okay?" Iris asks. She reaches out, touches my arm and I shriek.

Saturday

30

August
2014

Eli Dangott

by Joanne Jagoda

"Liat, are you there? *Ma nishma?*"

"I'm good. We are about ten minutes from you sitting in a Starbucks on Judah St. How's it going Eli? Still up on the pole?"

"Liat, you sound just like an American teenager."

"I've been studying Cassie's voice, and you know I'm good with accents."

"It's blazing hot up here and I'm sweating like a pig in this utility man get-up. This must be one of the five hot days of the year in this city. I wish I was at the Beach in Tel Aviv with Dafne. I'm sick of listening to Cassie and Robin bicker, but I guess that's what teens do. The shopping trip to Stanford is a 'go'. Damon has his team in place. We've been monitoring him closely. Everybody ready?"

"Yes, I've got my transmitters set in place. Travis and the boys are waiting for your signal to take Cassie to the safe house. And don't forget your credentials. Anne will want to see them."

"May I help you? Do we have a gas leak?"

"Anne Donaldson?"

"Yes, that's me. What do you want?" Her voice is sharp and suspicious.

"Anne, please call Cassie and Robin." She opens the door but not all the way. She is looking at me as though she recognizes me but can't place where she has seen me.

"Girls, come to the door, NOW."

When they hear their mother's no-nonsense tone, they join her silently by her side. They are puzzled why a tall, olive-skinned, sweaty utility worker is standing at their door.

"My name is Eli Dangott. I'm not a utility worker. I'm the grandson of Holocaust survivors and a member of the Mossad, the Israeli equivalent of the Secret Service. Here, you can verify who I am."

Anne scrutinizes my identification in its leather holder and quickly reads the letter from Homeland Security which vouches for me. She shakes her head and hands the credentials back.

"I don't understand. What do you want with us?"

"Let's sit, and if you don't mind a glass of water would be appreciated." I take off my hard hat and strip off the neon vest and gloves and wipe my sweaty face with a bandana.

"Thank goodness I can take this stuff off. It's hot out there today." I pull out my cell and send a quick text to my team: *We're on. Get moving!*

Cassie hands me a glass of water, and I take a long sip. "Let me start by telling you why I'm here. I work closely with your Homeland Security as a liaison from the state of Israel in matters of national security that affect both of our countries."

Robin interrupts, "Are you a spy? Like James Bond?"

She doesn't get the urgency of the situation. My team is coming to get Cassie in ten minutes, and I need to get everyone on board. My tone is harsh. "Let me go on. I've been closely tracking the movements of David Lewis, whose name is actually *Damon Southeby*, since Interpol flagged Homeland Security when he entered the country from Canada using a fake passport. The state of Israel was alerted when it became apparent from his emails and phone chatter he was going to obtain the plans for your grandfather's Project Octopus by kidnapping Cassie and holding her for ransom. Israel has to be sure that Project Octopus doesn't land in the hands of our enemies."

Anne is incredulous and her face is reddening. She stands up and points to the door. "I don't believe any of this. Maybe you should leave NOW."

The twins giggle out of nervousness. Robin tells her mother, "Mom let him go on."

Anne stares at me. "Wait. I do know you. You look really familiar. I remember now. You were in Calistoga. Next to me at the pool. I noticed you watching me."

"Yes, I was there tracking you and your uh … David. Other members of my team were keeping a close eye on your girls. We've been tempted several times to whisk you all away into a safe house, but we felt it best to let this all play out."

Anne grabs a heavy pottery vase from the coffee table and stands up ready to hurl it at me. Her instinct is to take the girls and run out of the house.

"Why have you been following us? Are we in danger?"

Robin pipes up. "What's this about anyway?"

"Anne, put the vase down and sit. You, Robin and Cassie are the targets of an elaborate plot but we are doing everything possible to keep you safe. You know that George Donaldson's company has developed Project Octopus. There are many foreign interests who would do anything to get those plans."

Robin interrupts again, "But Grandpa's work has nothing to do with us."

"I'm afraid it does. Let me be frank with you. Damon Southeby is a foreign agent working for a terrorist conglomerate who wants those plans at any cost. His idea all along was to get close to your family and kidnap one of you girls as ransom."

Robin points to herself and has a triumphant smirk on her face, "See ... I knew it. I knew it. There was something off about *David* or whatever the hell his name is."

"Your instincts were right Robin." Anne lets out a pitiful sob, stands up and runs into the bathroom.

I hear her retching. I knew this would be a shock for her. Cassie follows her mother into the bathroom to check on her while Robin eyes me suspiciously. After ten minutes, she returns wan and spent with Cassie holding her hand tightly.

She sniffles, "How could I not know he was a phony. I thought I was in love with him."

"Anne, Damon is one of the slickest agents in the world. He cultivated you and studied your habits like a cunning hunter and preyed on your vulnerability. Your family was the perfect target. There are Homeland Security agents briefing George and Lillian now. Our engineers in Israel have developed fake blueprints which will be used for the ransom. We have an agent we have brought in from Israel to take your place, Cassie. You are the one who is going to be kidnapped."

Cassie gasps and Robin grabs her sister's hand and doesn't let go. "How did you and that horrible man know everything about what we were doing today? That's creepy."

"I don't have time to explain more right now Cassie."

Anne has little blotches of color on her cheeks. "That ... lying, scheming asshole. I want him to be caught. What can we do?"

"We have to work quickly. The shopping trip to Stanford will take place as planned, but Cassie's double will stand in for her. She will go in the car with you, Anne, and Robin. She will enter the Apple store supposedly to select her new computer, but Anne and Robin you will leave her there and go to Macy's. We suspect the Apple store is where the snatch is going to take place. Robin, mention you need to get stuff at Macy's on the drive over, and you need your mom's help. Damon has your car bugged. Be aware of that. You and our agent should argue like you usually do with your sister."

Robin looks at her sister with tears in her eyes. Cassie is white and silent.

Anne, Cassie and Robin start when they hear knocking. Eli opens the door. A young woman walks in who is a dead ringer for Cassie at a quick glance: auburn curly hair, wearing denim shorts just like she has on, an identical San Francisco Giants tee shirt, and is her exact height and similar build.

"My name is Liat, and I will be taking your place, Cassie."

Cassie is sobbing, "I ... I ... don't want you to get hurt."

"Cassie, you don't have to be concerned about my safety. I'm well-trained, an expert in martial arts and have hidden transmitters in my shoe, my bra, my necklace and even the bracelet that David got your for graduation."

Robin pipes up, "You even sound like Cassie."

Eli interrupts, "Liat will brief you on the plans for today. Cassie, pack a few things. We are taking you to a safe house overnight."

"What?" Anne and Robin answer together.

"Cassie will be perfectly safe, enjoying a nice swimming pool, video games, movies and will be guarded 24/7."

Liat stands up like she is leading a class. "This is the plan ..."

Gingerhead Man

by h. l. nelson

Dear Diary,

I may have really fucked up this time. I just got back from a night at the karaoke bar ... and somewhere else afterward. I'm in my art room, not wanting to get into bed. What the hell am I thinking? But I suppose it was so pathetic that Brandon would probably just laugh. He mentioned two nights ago that he hasn't felt the same way about me for a while, so I think I'm scared he's going to ask for a divorce. The conversation started when he saw some pictures I took of the girls and me at that StrollerFit class. Thank God he doesn't know about the Piss Perfume escapade. I don't know, he hasn't said anything, but he may be snooping around in my art room. Anyway, knowing that we're having issues ... why I did what I did, I have no idea.

The karaoke bar is in this Mexican restaurant. Being so far from Mexico, you can imagine how horrible the food is. All the cooks are Asian. I'm not sure why we go. We eat the chips and salsa, which isn't horrible, and drink the bottled domestics (no tap, of course) while lazily watching the untalented singers and their hideous renditions of 'Pour Some Sugar on Me' and 'Love Shack'.

So the girls and I were buzzing, eating chips, and chatting and a very red-headed, suited man I had never seen there before stepped up to the mic. He cleared his throat and the first strains of 'How Do I Live?' by Leann Rimes flitted through the restaurant. I elbowed Robin and pointed at the stage. She rolled her eyes and took a swig of her Shiner Bock. I smiled and turned back to the stage. I wasn't going to admit it, but I was intrigued by this ginger stranger and wanted to see what he could do.

The song began and he was surprisingly good. He had his eyes closed for most of the performance and really belted it out. And he got quite a bit of applause, whoops, and whistles. And not just from me. When he was finished, he turned red due to the applause, kept swiping his hand over his sweaty, receding hairline. As he exited the stage, I caught his eye and reflexively smiled at him before I could look away. He had a nice smile.

"You like that guy?" Robin smirked. Julie looked back and forth between us.

"Oh, I don't know. He's all right. Kinda sweaty." I turned back to the bar, trying to look nonchalant, and took a sip of my beer.

"Uh huh, I saw how you were looking at him and I –" she teased, but stopped because Julie had spilled her drink down her shirt.

"Dammit, Julie! Are you that drunk already? Ugh. Joan, I'm gonna go help her clean her drunk ass up. Hold our seats."

"Okay," I said, as they swayed to the bathroom. Obviously, they were both sauced and I would need to keep my wits about me so I could drive us. I also knew that Robin would try to pick a fight soon if we didn't get some liquor in her.

Two giggly teenage girls were giving 'Like a Virgin' a go onstage and I was checking my cell for messages from Brandon or the kids when I felt someone to my left. I looked over and Gingerhead was standing there, looking like a deer about to be creamed. I smiled quick at him, but he stood in the same position with the same facial expression for a good 15 seconds. I was starting to get creeped out and glanced about for an escape route in case he started stroking my hair and making goose calls.

"Sorry, hi. Do you mind if I grab this seat?" he said.

"Uh, hi there. Sure." I could grab my bottle and knock him over the head if he started dancing the Macarena on me. God help him if he did.

"I, uh, noticed you enjoyed my performance," he said, signaling the bartender. "Scotch and soda, please. No lime."

He seemed saner when he ordered his whiskey without lime, so I relaxed, leaning back in my chair.

"I did. You sang it well. I'm not a Rimes fan, but I liked your rendition." I noticed a lighter, circular area of skin on his ring finger. Pointing it out, I asked, "Are you married?"

"Oh, no. I'm a, uh, widower."

I got the impression he was lying, and I was a tad tipsy, so I said, "Haha, good one. The ol' 'I'm a widower'. How's that one working for you?" and I turned away from him. I mean, really, I was a total hypocrite. Here I was with no ring on my finger – I'd taken it off after the conversation with Brandon – and I was giving this red-haired stranger hell.

"Oh, wow. Uh, I'm sorry. I didn't mean to make it sound like a line. I don't really use lines. I hope you have a good night."

He turned to leave, but I grabbed his arm. "Look, I'm sorry. I'm bad at this. Please, stay."

"Okay. So yeah, I'm bad at this, too. I've never really dated much at all. My wife and I were high school sweethearts. Together for 31 years." He looked down at his beer and I could tell he was trying not to get emotional. But he looked up and smiled at me. I would be lying if I said it didn't make my heart beat quicker.

Before I could say "bad Mexican food," I had hiked it to the bathroom to check on the girls – Julie was sick and needed to get home. Robin was pissed but didn't want to leave Julie, so I grabbed a cab for them. Then, somehow I ended up following Gingerhead out of the bar. He never once asked if I was married. He probably assumed I wasn't, since I made such a big stink.

I felt guilty. I'd never cheated on Brandon before. But sadly, more overwhelming than the guilt was utter nervousness. Walking to my car, I tried to remember if I'd shaved everything, put on enough deodorant, worn sexy panties. I came to the conclusion that the panties I had on weren't my sexiest, but also weren't the granny panties I wear when I have my period. And the few-day-old stubble down south would just have to do. I could casually tell him I was growing it out for a waxing. Or like one of those long, thin beards that guys sometimes braid. Braided pubes … Okay, no, I wouldn't tell him that.

I sniffed my armpits while driving and wrinkled my nose. Ew. I had some perfume in my purse. Sitting at the traffic light, I sprayed it then so I wouldn't douse his bathroom in the stuff. Digging in your purse for something while driving and then putting it on while driving is a skill, let me tell you. My car smelled like it was looking for a good time.

We got to his place, a small apartment on the east side. Not a horrible neighborhood, but certainly not the best. He helped me out of my car, which was sweet. Then we hiked it up to his 3rd floor apartment. I was hoping the walk would dissipate some of the perfume, but the heat from my underarms only made it stronger.

His place was immaculately clean. Way cleaner than any bachelor's pad I'd ever seen. I figured his wife must have trained him pretty well. He offered me a drink and I went to the kitchen with him to help him make them. You know, just in case he was actually a weirdo. Though I was now in his apartment, alone with him. So, perhaps I wasn't the smartest person in the world. I glanced around for pillows and lampshades made of human skin.

He poured me a red wine and made a scotch for himself. We took our drinks to his living room. I didn't want to set mine down anywhere, due to the cleanliness. I didn't see any coasters, so I just held it. It was warm in the apartment; the ice in my drink had started to melt. Condensation dripped on my blouse.

I could tell he wasn't used to bringing women to his place. His forehead was shining again, and he kept tripping over his words.

"So, Joan, what do you do for money – I mean, career-wise?"

"Well, I stay at home mostly. My kids are teenagers, so I look after the house."

"Oh, uh, are you independently wealthy? I mean, sorry, that's none of my business."

He looked uncomfortable and took a big drink from his glass. He fumbled it and most of it ended up on his shirt-front. His face burned bright red.

"Dammit! My wife bought me this shirt – I mean, it's a favorite. Let me go clean up."

After he loped to the bathroom, I contemplated leaping off of his balcony. Instead, I moved over to his record collection. He had quite a few. I saw many singers who I admire, including what looked like a Miles Davis that I had never seen before. I couldn't tell for sure because it was in a semi-opaque plastic cover, so I put my drink down on the shelf and took the record out to get a better look. I was admiring it when he returned and said, "Oh, no! That can't be out!"

Startled, I bumped the shelving unit, spilling the contents of my glass all over his albums.

"Oh, shit!" we both yelled in unison. It was the most in-sync thing we achieved the entire night. He ran to the kitchen and came back with a few dish towels, handed me one, then grabbed records off the shelf and wiped them. I helped. I would have laughed at the scene if I hadn't been appalled at spilling the drink.

"Oh my god, I'm so sorry," I said, as he surveyed the damage. A few sleeves were bubbling up in places.

"Hey, it was a mistake." He was surprisingly calm about the whole ordeal, which turned me on. Obviously, I was still tipsy.

"I know how I can make it up to you," I said, and sidled up to his side. His face blossomed red again.

Thirty minutes later, it was over and he was crying. Let me back up. I don't mean the sex was over. We didn't even get that far. We kissed a little – awkwardly, I might add. Then he put his hand on my right boob in the typical go-for-the-tits-way-too-early move that many guys are so fond of. And he just burst into tears and pulled away. I was uncomfortable and cold, so I put my shirt back on and perched on his bed.

"I'm sorry," he said. "It's not you or your breasts. They're just so different from my wife's."

What the hell? I thought.

"Not in a bad way!" he continued. "Feeling them just reminded me how much I loved … still love, her. I can't do this. I'm sorry."

I gave him a hug, told him not to worry. Then he showed me out.

So, that was it, diary. Three months on this new crazy journey Temple started me on, and I'm in bed with a strange crying man. I need to reassess my situation. Time to shower and go lie in bed with another man who's become a stranger to me. I hope he doesn't cry, too.

Joan Disillusioned-With-Love Colderman

September

The Bonaire Feel-Good

by Guilie Castillo Oriard

There's a new bounce in Luis Villalobos's step this Monday morning. He takes the sweeping stairs to the Ehrlich Fiduciary building two by two and dances a Rocky Balboa victory hop, face lifted up to the morning sun, at the summit. The wind in his ears could be the roar of an adoring crowd.

The receptionist pushes one half of the glass doors open for him. Was she watching? Well, what if she was? He gives her a big smile. "Bon día, Rochandra." He's making an effort with Papiamentu, now that he has a private tutor. Of sorts.

Rochandra looks him up and down. "Bon dia i bon siman."

Bon siman. He always forgets that on Mondays. Not just *good morning* but also *good week*. What a lovely custom. He's never seen it anywhere else; maybe it's unique to Curaçao.

Curaçao. He came so close to leaving without giving this island a chance. He'd have missed so much. His dog Al, for instance. And Pélagie.

"There's a package for you." Rochandra brandishes a clipboard. "Will you sign for it now, or shall I send the messenger up later?"

"Now's fine. Danki."

She hauls a FedEx box onto the counter and hands him the clipboard. "Had a good weekend?"

He scans the spreadsheet of incoming correspondence for his name. "More than good, actually."

Rochandra is leaning on the counter, the picture of an eager fifth-grade gossip – notwithstanding the gray hair and the fact she weighs roughly four times the average fifth-grader. "What did you do?"

"I, uh ... I went to Bonaire."

"Bonaire?" Maybe it's the way he hesitated, or the way his gaze slid away from hers, but Rochandra is looking like a hyena that's just spotted a wounded gazelle all alone in the savannah. "I never pegged you for a lover of peace and quiet. Why would you go to Bonaire?"

"Well, I –"

"Oh, you're a diver! I forgot, yes. And? You loved it, no?"

"Yes, it's –"

"Your dog must've missed you. Poor thing, left all alone."

Normally, Luis finds Curaçao's corporate informality refreshing. Right now, though, he's missing the distance that deference provides. It's unsettling that a receptionist should know so much about his life. "He went with me. Sorry, I can't find where I'm supposed to sign."

He pushes the clipboard back to her, but she doesn't even notice. She's staring at him, quite literally agape. "You took your *dog* to Bonaire?"

He forces a smile. "Rochandra. Where do I need to sign?"

She lifts an eyebrow, miffed but not chastised, and flips with exaggerated gestures to another page. "Right *here*. Where your *name* is."

When he's Managing Director – the announcement should be made any day now – he'll hire a new receptionist.

As he hands the clipboard back, something catches his eye. "Is this date right? This package came in on Thursday?"

She barely glances at the page. "If that's what the manifest says."

The package most likely contains incorporation documents – which might've generated immediately collectible revenue if delivered last week. No point in belaboring the issue; not today, not with this attitude. He thanks her again, doesn't get a reply.

His Bonaire feel-good is fading fast.

He'll bring up the mailroom at the Efficiency Development Team meeting. He rescheduled it for today; he and Al had to meet Pélagie at the airport at three on Friday, so he took the afternoon off. First time he's done that since he arrived in Curaçao back in December. But it's Labor Day today. US banks will be closed. Plenty of time to catch up.

His phone rings as he walks to the elevator. Fifty bucks – fifty thousand – say it's Milena again. He expected a big scene and put off telling her about Pélagie longer than he should have, but she's been surprisingly mature about the whole thing. Until Saturday, when she lost it. Forty-three missed calls over the weekend. Voice mail, texts, even emails asking, pleading, then finally demanding he call her back, all of which greeted him this morning when the plane landed and Pélagie returned the Blackberry she confiscated on Friday. That was the deal: no expectations, no cheesiness, no Ehrlich. *The financial world does revolve without you*, she said.

For an adrenaline-soaked moment at the airport, the calls panicked Luis. But knowing Milena, it's either plain jealousy – somehow she found out he was with Pélagie – or more bullshit about the MD announcement. She's theatrical, wants it to come off all Cirque de Soleil. Useless, and moot; everyone already knows the job is his. But she's still MD now. He'll drop off his things in his office and go find her, make some sort of amends.

The elevator arrives with a muted ding. Before the doors open, he hears Rochandra's internal line buzzing and her voice, sans the mood, when she answers. "Bon dia, dushi. Oh, he just – he's going up now. But – he's already in the elevator. I can't –"

It's got to be Milena. Luis calls out, "Someone looking for me?"

He hears the clack of the receiver being returned to its cradle before she replies. "No. No one."

Could he have misunderstood? No; there's no one else here. This is bordering on insubordination. Anywhere else in the world he'd call her on it, but Curaçao has quirky labor laws. He's watched Milena jump through the most unreasonable hoops to avoid employment litigation. Best to take it up with HR first.

Goodbye, Bonaire feel-good.

But he'll be back. Pélagie goes at least once a month to check on the shelter there. He's pretty sure he earned a standing invitation after his performance this weekend. He catches his own eye in the elevator mirror. *Tiger.*

No, it's not the sex. It was good, *he* was good, which doesn't always happen when he's that into someone; he seems to do best on casual between-the-sheets encounters. Less pressure, maybe. Lower stakes. Not that this – this *thing* with Pélagie is going anywhere. She's been very clear, if not very vocal: she has no inclination for romantic entanglements. He senses an old hurt there; he's an idiot for not leaving it alone. But she says it's all about the now. You, me, here, why not. She's big on the fact of coincidence, not its significance.

The self-serving ego-trip junkie in him insists she's right.

He committed to the MD job here for two years; spending even just a fraction of that time with Pélagie will make it not just bearable but memorable. And after …

Well. She knows he's leaving. It's not like he's lied, or made any kind of *promises* –

The elevator doors slide open to Wendolyn's smile. A frantic sort of smile.

"Morning. Not good, by the looks of you. What's wrong?"

"Wrong? Nothing!" Her voice is pitched higher than usual, and her grip, as she takes hold of his arm, feels jittery. "But there's, uh, something I need you to look at. It's on my desk."

"I'll be right there. Let me leave this in my –"

"Do that after. Super urgent, uh, loan agreement. The bank's waiting."

She's tugging on his arm, which had a better chance of working without the backdrop of Rochandra's cheekiness. "They can wait ten seconds more," he says.

"Please! It's –"

And then he hears the shouting. Milena, from the direction of his office. The direction Wendolyn seems bent on keeping him away from. The grip of her hand is so tight his shirt is wrinkling. "Wendolyn? What's going on?"

She says something, but he's already moving past her towards the sound of Milena in full-blown rage.

"I don't care if the email came from GOD HIMSELF! Take this shit down *now*! How dare you, how FUCKING –"

Luis comes around the corner and the scene freezes into a diorama. Josinelle, Stepan's elderly assistant, cowering just inside the door to Stepan's office and clutching, incongruously, a bouquet of red balloons. Behind her, even more incongruously, Stepan himself standing on his desk, next to the dangling half of a CONGRATULATIONS banner. The other half is still taped to the top of the window frame. More red balloons, still tied together in threes, litter the floor under him. The new legal intern, whose name Luis can't remember – has he even met her? she looks completely unfamiliar, but then so does

303

everything else right now – stands by the whiteboard on the opposite wall. Someone spent a valuable chunk of time drawing a two-tone poster on it, which the intern is – was – erasing. Only the lower right corner remains; a too-large exclamation mark surrounded by childishly cute stars and pointillist umbrellas that Luis assumes represent fireworks. It must've been drawn a day ago, at least, because the ghost of the foot-high letters is still all too visible.

Congrats, new MD!
You deserve it!

Milena stares at him from the doorway, fury melting like butter on a griddle. "Why the bloody fuck didn't you return my calls?"

La Ronde /
Sal and Lana

by Townsend Walker

Sal's been calling back to New York to get in touch with Dmitri Ivanovich about this hit job. Dmitri did a couple of things for him earlier in the year, but the last job was botched badly. Supposed to hit the guy in the knee cap, cripple him for good, broke his leg instead, clean break and now the guy is up, walking, and got such religion from his physical therapist that he's entered the New York Marathon.

So Dmitri owes Sal big time. Sal figures with this much ownage he can get D-Man to do the job on this Wall Street guy for peanuts – south side of 20K – and pocket the rest of the 250K. He'll get back what he lost to that dumb ass producer Jimmie Farley. What a flake. He can't believe he fell for the pitch. Last time.

Dmitri hasn't been answering his phone. Goes to voice mail, then, *This mail box is full. Call later.* Middle of all this Sal got a call from his mother in Queens. "Salvatore, caro, your papa's not doing so good. He wants he should see you one last time."

"My Papa wants to see me? See me? You gotta be kidding. Twenty years ago he said *Get out of my life, I don't want your shadow to cross my face, even after I'm dead and don't know it.*"

"Mio figlio, he's dying. He's thinking, maybe he was too hard on you. You were young, a bit wild, no?"

"Yeah, but I still don't want to see him."

"For me, Salvatore, for me. Come for me, your Mama. I want him to die in peace."

"Okay, I come for you, not for him, for you, and I make nice."

Plus Sal can check up on Dmitri, nail that sucker. Get him to do the job while he's there and collect from the Park Avenue dame.

Sal got on the plane yesterday morning and landed at JFK last night. He's staying in Manhattan. See the old man, sure; sleep in the same house, not gonna happen. Hit the hotel bar, had a few, stayed late watching a shimmery jazz singer; so this morning he's getting up slowly and late and the green sequins scattered on the bed shining in the morning sun are hurting his eyes. He rolls over and a sequin digs into his butt. *Shit.* He's awake; he remembers to call Dmitri. No, first coffee, then Dmitri.

A woman answers, lilting English accent. Sal stumbles a "Sorry, I misdialed;" checks the number; dials again, same accented woman's voice. "I was looking for Dmitri Ivanovich. This was his phone, sorry for the trouble."

"It is Dmitri's phone, or was. I'm his sister, Lana Cameron."

"Was? You said was?"

"Indisposed, as they say. Rather permanently, I fear."

"What happened?"

"Something we're not at liberty to speak about."

Her voice is quickly charming Sal into indiscretion.

"I had some work for him."

"I've taken over some of his affairs. Perhaps I can be of assistance."

Sal's thinking: voice like this, I'd like to see the rest of her. He arranges to meet at two in Astoria Park on one of the benches facing Ditmans Boulevard, near the clump of trees.

"I'll be waiting – grey / brown suit, blond hair."

"Me – jeans, heels, also blond, I'm thinking longer than yours."

Sal visits his father who, thankfully, is asleep. He sits by the bed next to his mother for an hour, squeezes his father's hand, "Take care Papa," kisses his mother and restrains himself from running out the door.

At 1:45 he's on the bench in the Park watching passersby. The September sun is still warm and there's a pale breeze off the river. He misses this part of the year back here. California is too same-ol' sometimes. A cluster of people, looking like they all got off the bus together. A blonde emerges; she looks around at the benches, nods towards him and strides across the lawn. This is Lana, oh my god. At least six feet tall, the long hair, peasant blouse (filled out), painted-on jeans, turned up cuffs, silver ankle bangles and five inch heels. She stretches out her hand; the wide red mouth is smiling a welcome, the icy blue eyes are not.

"I say, I wasn't sure what to expect from a Salvatore Mancuso. I'm pleasantly surprised."

Sal, momentarily nonplused, stumbles through something complimentary without saying what he is obviously thinking. *Would this be good in bed, or what?*

"So, tell me about Dmitri."

"A vow of silence there, I'm afraid. I can reveal that I understand why you may have phoned him."

"You're his sister? Him, I could hardly understand. You speak English better than me. And the name, Lana? Is that Russian?"

"Svetlana, Lana. Spent time in London, attached to the Embassy. You've heard of FSB, successor to KGB? Doing a spot of freelance now."

"So you know about all of this, what Dmitri was doing? What to do? How to do it?"

"Trained by the best."

She brings her hands up and puts them around his face, pulls it toward hers. He's thinking, *what kind of game is this? Okay, play along.* She stops an inch away and whispers, "Who, where, when, how and how much?"

He likes this attitude in business. Sal relaxes; he's found his hit girl and she's hungry. He tells her what he knows about a woman who wants her husband dead. He beats her and loses their kids in the park.

"Met her last week, friend of a friend, told her I'd take care of it."

Sal describes the target as an important guy at Goldman Sachs in Manhattan. Six foot three, 250 pounds, pasty faced, silver hair, Armani suits and ties. Prada Aviators, blue tint. No names.

"To answer the other questions: wherever you want, as soon as possible, however you want, 25K. Deal?"

She cocks her hand and slaps him on the cheek. Hard. "You're a cheap bastard."

"What the fuck?"

"Sal. I know the market is 50."

"Okay, 50, and to show you I'm not trying to take advantage, there's a hot new club over in the Meatpacking District, *Le Bain*, pool in the middle of the dance floor. Dinner at *Betony*. Meet you there at eight."

Before setting out, Sal had the hotel concierge arrange the evening, in case she looked as good as she sounded. And he was not disappointed.

"You're not too much of a bad fellow."

At eight-thirty, Sal's waiting at *Betony*; looking up at the gaudy gold ceiling panels, looking over the crowd huddled around the bar. He doesn't see, but hears her arrival: forks hit plates, bus boys drop trays of dishes. He looks up: Lana is sashaying across the floor toward him. A dress of pearlescent, diaphanous silk panels swishing side to side: promising to reveal, at the last moment, swinging back. He looks around. *Eat it guys, she's mine tonight.*

Dinner goes quickly (it seems that way), even after three hours: waiters hover, dishes are placed, emptied, removed, glasses filled and refilled. As they leave, she takes his arm and coos, "Very nice, Sal. Delicate forceful flavors. My compliments."

The door at *Le Bain* opens to thumping music. They're led to a private VIP lounge. Not Sal's doing. *Has she been here before? Did the concierge arrange it? The tip was generous.* Not complaining, only wondering. A bottle of Cristal is on the table, opened, poured in two glasses. Sal sits back, sips his champagne, Lana beside him, same relaxed posture, legs akimbo. She whispers, "Sal darling, I did a little research on our target after I left this afternoon. I don't think you told me everything."

"I knew we'd see one another again, so maybe I forgot some stuff."

"How silly of me, of course, that's it."

She clinks her glass against his. "And then there are the aspects that weren't quite accurate – bloody wrong in fact."

"Huh?"

"Pour us another glass. We should start with the description; no one in the New York office fits it."

"Details, details." Sal slurring his words now; thinks the champagne's getting to him. Not having the effect it usually does. Getting groggy, not sparkly.

She leans against him, her lips touching his ear. "Salvatore Giuseppe Mancuso, you are a foolish lad to think I would let you skim the fee. Fivefold difference, I think not."

Sal slumps over.

"I too have contacts on the West Coast." Lana presses a button beside the sofa. Two men appear.

"It appears my friend doesn't handle drink well. Your choice lads, East River or the Hudson."

In Our Lifetime

by Derek Osborne

Already the caterer and preset crews are busy. The wedding will be this Sunday. It is a beautiful late summer day, winds from the southwest at 10 -12, a deep blue sky and the island dull green and gray. Anja correctly read the writing on the wall last month when Andi had her meltdown. She's called in a bunch of favors from her 2nd Unit production subs. It pays to have good relationships in an industry full of snakes, not to mention the bragging rights for producing one of the hottest Hollywood weddings of the year in less than five weeks. People have flown in from everywhere. La senora is writing checks faster than the FED.

There is no such thing as an old, established Latin American family having a quiet, intimate affair. Combined with three more families on the Perkins' side the immediate guest list is topping one-fifty. Then there are all those friends who want to say goodbye but don't know how and Max thinks this might be a graceful way out. Throw in a few dozen show-biz folks and a few politico must-invites and, voila, it's up to three hundred. Add another fifty in servers, sous-chefs, bartenders, security, traffic control, sound and lighting, video, three helicopter pilots (it is an island) and don't forget the orchestra (twenty-three of Glenn Scott's best) – seat all the guests in five (count them) deluxe tents and the back lawn from the house to the water suddenly looks like Gatsby's in town. Even for Nantucket it's all pretty cool.

As expected, the paparazzi are out in force. If anyone is wondering where Rebecca gets her mischievous side they needn't look further. La senora has ordered a dozen Super Soakers, those monstrous water-pistols that jet out thirty feet, and pulled from her former life all the necessary skills in recruiting a young militia prepared to die for the cause. There are eleven nieces and nephews, ages ten to fifteen. For ammunition she has stockpiled five-gallon tins of grape juice. The children have permission to patrol the marsh and shoot on sight. For added measure, she has ordered a gallon of commercial-grade indigo fabric dye to enhance the juice. The troops have gone through rigorous training.

"I'm going out to the boat," Max announces after lunch. "I need some peace and quiet."

"I am coming with you."

"The hell you are."

"The hell I am not."

Rebecca has had on a walking cast for nearly a week. Her new name is *Ahab*.

"How will you get up the ladder?"

"Slowly."

Anja gives Eddie a look.

"I will take you both out," he says.

Down at the dinghy pier they notice two men unloading a Zodiac full of camera equipment. With Rorschach patterns of blue on their face, they look like they might have been shooting a remake of *Braveheart*. Rebecca starts laughing. She is dressed in a set of baggie sweats and a hoodie with glasses, and the men are so deep in their argument as to what went wrong and who is to blame they don't notice. Their money shot hobbles by unnoticed. Eddie pulls at the outboard and they are off. As a precaution, he speeds toward the west side of the anchorage and the Coast Guard Station; they'll double back behind the other boats.

The harbor is filled with cruising boats. It's the last week of the season. *Gadabout* needs more than a football field of room to swing on her mooring so she sits somewhat off from the others, out at the east end of the anchorage and in sight of the house. Nicky, one of the older nephews, has outfitted one of their dinghies into a kind of grape juice gunboat, complete with twin Super Soakers and several water balloon depth charges. The crew wear red bandanas and black t-shirts (la senora's idea); Anja made sure to alert the police and the Coast Guard. They patrol the perimeter of *Gadabout's* mooring, challenging all comers. Once in the cockpit, beneath the canopy, Rebecca and Max will have all the privacy and quiet they need. With the house so buzzed it's been hard to be alone. They both crave and fear this moment, impossible to know what will come; they have yet to have "the talk". For Max it will mean surrender; it will mean the cancer has won. For Rebecca, whenever she even gets near it, her entire being goes into a kind of stasis, a billion stabbing needles. She worries how it might be affecting the baby.

"Let's go down to the cabin," she says once they're on board.

"You want to revisit the scene of the crime?"

"I had not thought of that."

"If you fall again we'll never live it down."

She starts laughing. Just then a gust lifts the canopy. The same wind ripples the water's surface and swings the boat. *Gadabout* groans and sunlight pours into the cockpit. "We never did get to go sailing."

It's a test, a small regret compared to others. She waits to see how it affects their mood.

"Well, we can't have that. Especially on a day like today."

Max jumps up and heads down below. Rebecca sees the ICOM radio light up on the helm. He reappears and pulls the mic off the binnacle.

"Unit seven, unit seven this is unit nine, unit nine. Come back."

They have developed a code knowing the paparazzi will be monitoring the channels. A young girl's voice answers the hail.

"Unit nine this is seven switch channel C."

There are ninety-six channels to choose from. They have selected five and given them letters, choosing which to use at random. The children love this more than anything. They use Rebecca's favorite word – skullduggery. Max has to admit he's getting a kick out of it too.

"Christina?"

"Yes Uncle Max."

"I have a high priority mission for you, need to know, only."

"That means it's a secret, right?"

Christina is all of nine.

"Yes," Max says, looking at Rebecca, "it's a secret."

"Oh goodie."

"Tell Eddie and Anja we want to go sailing."

"Uncle Max, can I come?"

It's Nicky, Pam's oldest son. Pam, Maxes sister, has brought her entire brood, and, being farm kids, they have all been a great help. Max forgot they would all tune in.

"Yes, Uncle Max, can I come too?"

Now it is Pam, herself.

"Me too, Dad."

And Andi as well. Rebecca grabs the handset.

"Listen guys. Your Uncle Max and I came out to the boat to be alone. We realized I have never had the chance to go sailing on Gadabout. We wanted Eddie and Anja to come along as crew. Now that your Aunt Pam and Cousin Andi want to come I think that is also appropriate. How about we have a kid's sail tomorrow if the weather is nice? And Nicky, as head of security you must remain behind today so we can make the proper arrangements."

Max nods approval. Various disappointed mumbles of "okay" and "I guess" come over the handset.

"Can we come?"

It's a stranger's voice. Max is guessing their code wasn't too hard to crack. He takes the mic from Rebecca.

"Person requesting to tag along identify yourself."

"Just an interested party."

Whoever it is, judging from the accent, they're Italian. Another voice crackles on the handset.

"Interested Party, Interested Party this is US Coast Guard Nantucket Station, repeat, US Coast Guard Nantucket Station. Honor protocol and identify yourself."

For a moment the handset is dead.

"Ah, we are tourists visiting your lovely island."

The Coast Guard comes back. "Interested Party I repeat, identify your craft and position."

Rebecca is wearing that smile she gets whenever she knows she has won. Max is truly touched; they don't have to do this. The "Interested Party" has gone silent again. Nicky is pulling away and heading for the dinghy pier to pick up the others. The Coast Guard returns om the handset.

"Nantucket Harbor and all Interested Parties this is US Coast Guard. Be advised the yacht Gadabout is leaving the harbor. Be advised all unauthorized vessels approaching the yacht will be stopped and searched. We advise all Interested Parties to have their passports available. We advise all vessels have the proper number of floatation devices aboard, proper fuel management systems installed, engines inspected for the current year, craft registration documents in order. Any vessel in violation will be seized. Repeat, any vessel in violation will be seized. This is US Coast Guard, out."

"Gadabout, out."

Max is touched by what the Coast Guard is doing. He looks down at Rebecca. At first he thinks she is also

315

appreciating their special treatment but sees something else is coming. She's trying to hold on but it's no use. He sits down beside her, places the flat of his hand on her belly. The tears begin, and when they do Max also loses control. So, he's thinking, the time has come. He grabs her and buries his face in her thick dark hair. There is no one else there to see them, no one else to comfort or worry about. And there is no one else to hear, so they allow this moment, the one they've been dreading, and there in the safety of *Gadabout's* cockpit come all the regrets, all the would haves and might have beens, all they now know will be certain. There is a strange, god-like wonder in it, what this child will mean not only for them but for everyone, what they must do to prepare.

"Thank you," Rebecca says after a time. She is laying on her side by now, her head nestled in Max's lap. Max can see the others approaching in one of the dinghies.

"My angel," he says. By the time Eddie and the others arrive they have dried their eyes and washed their faces. Max goes to the rail and greets each one in silence. He waves an acknowledgement to the kids in the grape-gun boat. He's hoping he'll have the strength to go with them tomorrow.

After the adults are on board he gives the command to raise all canvas. They will be sailing off the mooring, not a small feat and certainly not a maneuver for novices, but to seasoned sailors, aficionados, it is an act of both skill and purity. Eddie knows the drill. With Max at the helm, Andi and Anja man the winches. Pam tails the lines, coiling them in perfect order along the deck, a term all yachtsmen refer to as "Bristol". Rebecca sits silent. *Gadabout* glides past the other anchored yachts, their owners on deck, some with grand smiles and others looking like deer caught in the headlights. It's not every day a ninety foot ketch runs by your rail so close you could reach out and touch it. They're even flying the chute between the main and mizzen, a mass of billowing white, the bow of the boat cuts a clear path through the harbor. The Coast Guard's gunboat waits on station just outside the harbor's narrow entrance. Nicky and his fresh faced pirates follow astern. A lone photographer stands at the break-water, waiting for just the right moment when the boat and the lighthouse align with the blue and gray town behind, a once in a lifetime photo.

"Once in a lifetime," Max says to Rebecca.

"Our lifetime."

Gadabout heels. They are at sea.

Saving the Life
of the Dead

by Gloria Garfunkel

Every year I get into a Mixed Mood Episode, agitated and depressed leading up to the Jewish holidays. Rosh Hashanah and then 10 days of guilt-ridden repentance and then Yom Kippur, the final trial of whether you will live or die. Always irritable and act my worst this time of year. Eat lots of nonkosher food, especially bacon. Turn on the TV and drive a lot on the Sabbath. I'm daring God to kill me already. I drive extra fast. But that only leads to speeding tickets.

Chloe's mom and sister are here from Chicago and we're taking them out to lunch and dinner. I have to be on my best behavior which is torture because I'm in an irritable Mixed Mood Episode with a short fuse. We make small talk. I ask Chloe's sister about school. She's in ninth grade and in high school shock so she has plenty to say to fill in the conversation gaps. She's an adorable, skinny blonde, a smaller version of Chloe. Her mother is restrained and quiet. Preoccupied. Half in and out of the conversation.

Finally she says, "Chloe tells me you have bipolar. It's a terrible illness. You know it killed my husband. You know you two can never marry. The gene pools on both sides would make all your children bipolar. What a terrible legacy of doom to lay on them. You two should get out of this relationship now."

318

"You wish we hadn't been born, Mom?" asks Chloe.

Total silence for the rest of the meal. Chloe drives her mother and sister alone to the airport and doesn't say much when she returns.

"My mother still thinks she can save my father's life," is all she says. "She thinks it was her fault because they fought a lot."

Chartreuse

by John Wentworth Chapin

Eastern Antiques is a play on words: located on Eastern Avenue but filled with statuary and vases from Vietnam and Japan. Deonna, the owner, announces loudly to all new customers and window shoppers that the double entendre is fabulous, but she can't take full credit because it was Eastern Antiques before she bought it, back when it was filled with corroded brass fittings from ships dismantled in the Baltimore harbor a few blocks away. Now the shelves are lined with rows of identical porcelain laughing Chinese Buddhas, brass meditating Cambodian Buddhas, and decapitated stone Thai Buddhas.

"People *crave* them!" Deonna cackles. "How's that for irony?"

Charles sees a different irony; the stuff is certainly Eastern, but it's hardly antique. A few sumptuous Afghan carpets hanging from hooks in the back, beautiful but new, along with wooden tables made from medieval-looking temple doors salvaged from India – true artifacts but still newly made. The only actual antiques are locked in glass jewelry cases along a counter, and half that stuff looks faux-distressed. That's Deonna: antique and faux-distressed.

They unpack two wooden shipping crates. One more lies unopened; Charles and Deonna will be here late into the night, if the last couple of occasions are any indicator. She gets a new shipment every couple of weeks, and this is the third time Charles has helped her unload. He doesn't mind – she springs for Chinese food and they talk and he's getting paid and this is so much better than everything that has happened to him lately. When the customers are gone, she'll crack open a couple of bottles. Last time, they started with Grand Marnier and moved to a chablis, tonight it's Chartreuse. Mornings after are a wee bit rough, but they are entirely worth the feeling of being engaged in the world rather than worrying about how to be engaged with the world. Charles looks into his crystal ball and knows that this is exactly where he should be right now. Deonna is garish clothes. She is witty repartee. She is last-minute change of plans.

"This is a bigger shipment than usual," Charles says.

"I never know what I'm going to see until I unpack. Sometimes it takes three months, sometimes it's here on the next boat ... Every day is Christmas!" Deonna cackles, overly loud.

"Any idea what this is?" Charles says, pulling out a large round object swaddled in crinkly wrapping, more like magazine paper than packing paper. It's lightweight for its size.

"*Careful*!" Deonna shouts. "No bugs. This packing shit is full of bugs, so keep it in the crate."

No bugs, but there are flecks of dirt all over, as though someone packed raked leaves in there. Deonna explains that the thing he unwraps is a yaksha head – a guardian spirit. It has exaggeratedly vicious features and vibrant colors, more demon than spirit to Charles.

Deonna says, "Let me know if you see a – oh, YAY!" She suddenly throws raffia everywhere from her crate. She lifts a stack of day-glo green cloths, tied in a bundle. "They're here! I LOVE these! Look at them! OH!"

She holds it out for Charles's inspection. The fabric shimmers and melts in her hands like mercury.

"What is it?" Charles asks.

321

"They are – really, you don't know? Well, hold on a second!" Deonna bends over to suck down the last of her apéritif, gives Charles a sloppy excited pat on the hand, and then dashes to the storeroom clutching the silks.

Charles continues with the half-dozen yaksha heads in the crate that need unwrapping. One is heavier than the rest, and Charles feels something moving inside. He flips it over and finds there a plastic container stuffed into the hollow cavity. He pulls it out; inside rests an acid green velvet pouch, the sort of little bag you'd expect to package cufflinks or expensive liqueur.

Charles shakes from the bag, gently onto the glass counter, two things: a tiny plastic zipper storage bag with a tablespoon of cut, colored gemstones and a dark, brown-green brick the size of a deck of playing cards, wrapped in saran wrap and a healthy dose of tape.

Gems and something that is probably not chocolate.

He looks up. Deonna stands in the doorway, shoulders bare, wearing a thin piece of fabric wrapped around her midsection, the silk acting as a halter top and pressing desiccated old breasts against her bony chest. She stares at Charles and the bag and its contents.

It's weird. He's gotten plenty of weirdness from her over the last few weeks, but this is something new. He imagines her pulling out a revolver and wasting him on the spot. But where would she keep it? She's practically naked, which is making this all the weirder.

She saunters over to him, the tops of her breasts firmly tourniqueted in place and the bottoms swinging freely against the thin fabric. "If you think you're going to grab my stash, you've got another thing coming."

Charles begins to stutter a response.

Deonna picks up the brown-green brick. "But if you want to help me make brownies, we're golden."

"It's – what is it?"

"You've never seen hash before?"

322

Charles shakes his head.

Deonna says, "I don't approve of the look on your face, Judge Judy. It's for my personal consumption."

When Charles thinks of all the things that he cares too much about, the things that upset him, the things that set him off – well, this certainly is not one of them. He says, quietly, "No. I don't care."

"Well I think you do care, from what I can see," she says. "Your body language is all tense and you're getting defensive. I get high sometimes. That's the deal."

"It's more that I didn't expect to find a velvet bag of contraband inside a demon's head."

"Yaksha. They're benevolent guardian spirits. It's kind of a joke that – my contact put it in there."

Hilarious, Charles thinks. *Nothing funnier than a droll smuggler.* "What's up with the gemstones?"

"I can get a lot more for them here than he can over there. I grease his palm with cash and he greases mine with hash. Ha! That's a poem!" she crows as she grabs the Chartreuse and pours them both another shot.

Charles waves goodnight to Deonna and fumbles with his car keys. He's never smoked hash before, but he feels more numb than mellow. Maybe it's the Chartreuse. Maybe it's what Deonna said before he left. Charles pulls out into the street, and then stops before he knows why he's stopping. The flashing lights of a police cruiser race down the block toward him. It zooms past, siren wailing into the distance. His chest thumps.

He thinks back to Deonna slurring, tottering against an empty crate. "You were in rehab. You've got a record, bub. You were mixed up in a whole lotta nasty. Last thing you need is the Baltimore Police department snooping around your garbage cans, if you get my drift. You can keep your mouth shut, right?"

Charles nodded when she said this. He attributed it to ugly drunkenness; Charles had discovered a possibly damaging fact about her, and she was doing some risk management.

But now, thumping chest rattling his ribs, pounding in his ears, he remembers how they met: he announced that he had just left rehab, and then he wailed about the string of death and misfortune that trailed him. She offered him the job because she's a drunk and thinks he's one too – but now he sees a broader view. She believes she has found herself a patsy.

He doesn't want her gemstones or her greasy drugs, but she's too blind to see this. Charles may not know what he wants, but he knows what he doesn't want.

To be used. To be yet another woman's patsy.

He hopes he's sober enough to remember this in the morning. He puts the car back into gear and heads home.

Tick

by Lynn Beighley

My cat, Pollock, is an indoor cat. He'd prefer not to be, but I'd prefer him to not become a gray cat pancake on the busy street in front of my apartment.

His current favorite perch is on the back of my couch. It looks out on a tiny balcony I never use. Last spring, a pair of confused robins mistook the railing for a tree limb. They produced one perfect egg. Once in a while, I'd sit next to Pollock as he waited for mom and dad robin to stop by. Me, I'd stare at the blue egg. Instead of trying to decide what the TV watching public wanted me to do, or what Bill Plover would do next, or if I was out of wine, I'd look at the egg. My eyes would lose focus (more often when I wasn't out of wine) and the egg would go from being a small blue sphere and become an entire (often fuzzy) universe.

And then it hatched. I don't know exactly when. I've been distracted. I went out with my dad on Thursday to help him drink his sorrows away. His fiancée left him. She wasn't willing to fly to Vegas for a quick, cheap wedding after I refused to let the *You Tell Me* reality show people foot the bill in exchange for my and Bill Plover's attendance. I'm still seething that he asked me, and he still doesn't entirely understand why I didn't want to do it. But he didn't mind me buying him many drinks, and by the end of the evening, Dad was ready to admit that she was in it

325

for the fame. He probably doesn't remember that concession, but it's there, in his addled brain.

And Seamus spent last night here. Very distracting.

After he left this morning, I carried my bowl of cereal to peer out with a riveted Pollock, and my egg was gone, and in its place ...

Remember *Return of the Jedi*? This one scene? Our heroes, Leia in a gratuitous bikini, are with Jabba the Hut on this hovering spaceship platform thing, hanging out over the desert. Beneath them is the gaping maw of some kind of horrible creature that will take a very long time to digest them. I remember it's supposed to take a thousand years. Yeah, okay, whatever.

Anyway, that blue egg I adored has been replaced by the gaping maw beast. Granted, on a smaller scale, but horrific all the same. (The nasty creature is called a Sarlacc, in case you were wondering. And the good guys do avoid getting digested by it, surprise.)

I can't figure out how such an enormous mouth could have come out of that egg. I watch in disgusted fascination as mom and dad take turns stuffing worms and bugs into it. It never closes. Pollock waits for the parents, I can't look away from the chick monster's pie hole. Without looking, I reach over to scratch Pollock under his chin. I'm pretty good at this, and he helps. My fingers touch his jaw and brush across a small, hard bump that isn't supposed to be there.

I look and see that Pollock, my indoor cat, has a tick. I hate ticks. I am proud that I do not scream or squeal. I do run to the bathroom and scrub my hand.

How did he get a tick? Did it come in on me? Or Seamus? I'm not sure how I'm supposed to get it off him. I remember something about Vaseline, something about a lit match you blow out, something about the tick head not being a good thing to leave in the creature. I dig around for tweezers, a pair I don't like, but I can only find my favorite ones.

Armed with my best tweezers, a jar of Vaseline, a book of matches, a towel, a box of tissues, a couple Band-Aids, and an old ashtray, I approach Pollock. He knows I'm up to something and leaps off the couch and dashes into my room, to hide, no doubt, in my closet.

I wander into the kitchen to run the can opener and lure him out. I run the can opener and my phone rings. I answer it, hoping it's Seamus, hoping I can get him to come over and take over the tick removal for me.

And it is Seamus.

"Hey sweetie," he says, "listen, there's a guy from the show here and he has an idea for us to make a lot of money, and I know how you feel about all this stuff, but Jenn, honey, please hear me out."

Pollock stands at the entrance of the kitchen, looking at me. Without speaking, I quietly hang up the phone.

Moirologia

by Andrew Stancek

You are every child who believes in the "happily ever after." You are ordinary and everything that happened to you is extraordinary. You show that dreams come true, that the impossible is possible, that sense is not necessary.

You are Clark Kent and Peter Pan and an ordinary kid, sick and with a strange name, living in an ordinary home.

You speak with a squeaky voice and a stutter and you sweat under the hot TV lights and you cannot explain and you are more lovable and more believable.

You walk funny. Maybe it's the sickness with the wacky name or maybe the months in bed. You don't quite limp but when we replay the footage we see that every now and then your legs don't align and your walk is off-kilter and you are every funny-looking funny-walking kid.

You don't shill for money on TV, don't go on tour, don't sell subscriptions to your site. You don't have a site. You are free. Every inventor in the history of the world, every guru, every speaker has passed the hat to the admiring crowds but you don't.

Every one of them wants to convert you to their image, to harness you to their needs but you remain you.

Then we realize that you not only won't merge for them, you won't merge for us either. You turn away from us, too.

You leave us behind.

When it dawns on us that we will not become you, we start to hate you.

You cannot be known.

You cannot be understood.

You cannot be saved.

Really Weird Shit

by Rachel Ambrose

Frederico's into some really weird shit.

I've figured this out over the past three weeks. And maybe my definition of "really weird shit" is getting skewed, because the other day I looked at a painting of a baby angel making love to a girl baby demon and thought, "wow, how adorable," instead of, "someone should send that painter to a shrink."

"Yeah, and he's really mysterious, like he'll leave these giant gaps in his calendar and when I go to fill them in, he's like, just leave them open," I'm telling Isa as I get ready for the monthly open gallery show in September. "Like entire afternoons."

"Is he … I don't know, a serial stalker? A secret nudist?" Isa asks, munching on tortilla chips out of the bag as she stands in the bathroom doorway. "Maybe he has some super rare medical condition that makes it impossible for him to work for more than four hours a day."

"I dunno," I say, putting down my mascara and grabbing my lipstick. "Probably some standing sex appointment with his wife. When else would he have time? He makes me feel really smart, though, which is a new thing for me. Blake was always so condescending, like, yes baby-waby you got the answer right, good girl, want a biscuit?" I shake my head. "I can't believe I thought he was good for me."

"That's twice today," Isa remarks, and I frown at her from the mirror. "Twice today you mentioned Blake. That's down from three times yesterday, so that's progress!" She does a little victory dance and I smile. Getting this job and leaving Mrs. Hatfield were really the best decisions I've made in a long time. Keeping track of Frederico is an easy job for me, given my slightly obsessive nature. Right at this moment, I can tell Isa that he's probably finishing dinner with his family and aims to be at the gallery in half an hour to start on setting up for the show.

"Is it creepy that I always know where he is?" I ask.

"A little," concedes Isa, nodding. "But think of how good that makes you, as his assistant! I bet he never lets you go."

"We can only hope," I say, giving myself one last look in the mirror. "Okay, I think I'm ready to do this, I'll see you later!" I grab my purse and head out the door, making sure to remember the crackers and cheese I've promised to bring. One more good thing about this job is that it's made me far less absent-minded than I used to be. The first week I went around completely neurotic and sure I'd forget something, but when I did (I double-booked Frederico in two meetings at once by mistake), the world didn't end! He just frowned at me and told me, "Don't do it again." So I haven't … yet. It's amazing what you can accomplish when quiet excellence is expected of you. And I'm well paid for it, to boot!

I sweep into the gallery twenty minutes later, a bottle of white wine in my handbag, and start assembling the snacks. Frederico likes what he calls "little bits" – in food as well as in art. He'll pick up an origami swan that someone threw in the trash and turn it into the inspiration for Oscar De La Renta's next summer gown. I fan out the paper napkins and straighten the blue cheese as I wave to Edie, my coworker. She's a junior curator at the museum, and Frederico is her boss too. "Oh, have you seen the new watercolor that

Blake Easton put together?" she says, leaning down to mutter in my ear. I turn, startled. Damn Blake. Can't he just get out of my life for one night? "It's *awful*," she says gleefully, and I laugh in relief. Of course it is.

Cold Comfort

by Gill Hoffs

My sinuses feel as tight as a virgin's twat, I stink of menthol, and I have sex-doll lips parted in a chapped 'O' because I'm so bunged up I have to mouth-breathe.

But today's client is only in town for one night. And the only girl he wants for his dinner at Parasols 'n' Parsnips is mucoussy me. Delightful.

I feel like today *I'm* the one renting my body, and it isn't a comfortable fit.

I spend the day in a steam room near his hotel, dumping herbal waters on the coals until my eyes smart and stream and my chest aches and nipples tingle. Come five o'clock, I'm as clear of snot as possible and a cold shower beckons. I rinse the stink away, and can't help noticing the other women's glances at my crotch. This client's Canadian and it's autumn so my pubes are currently cropped into a maple leaf, dyed red, a treat for him tonight. Let them look. It's fabulous.

A quick dash to the office, where Zoe has my outfit and a mug of Lemsip ready and waiting, and I'm ready to go. My co-ordination's off and the heels don't help so I bang into the doorframes and ricochet down the corridor like I'm in a pinball machine on the way to the car. The driver opens the door for me, probably hoping for a squint up my skirt, and I bend over from the waist allowing the fabric to reveal my lack of underwear because why the hell not but then my usual poise deserts me and I clunk my head on the way in, and what started as sexy becomes stupid instead.

"Are you alright, love? I felt that meself."

I rub the side of my head carefully, trying not to muss my hair, and sniff back the snot that so annoyingly insists on accompanying anything that makes my eyes water. Like an Audi to the head, for example.

"I'm fine, I'm fine."

I don't mean to snap at him but I'm really not fine, and clouting my skull on the car didn't help. We settle into our seats, strapping ourselves in and pointedly not meeting each other's eyes in the mirror, then drive through the drizzle to his hotel. A doorman with hazel eyes and a scurfy moustache opens the car door and this time I manage not to make contact with anything I shouldn't on my way out. He touches his index finger to the brim of his fancy hat as I walk past him with a smile and the tiniest of handbags toward the elevator. The woman on the front desk gives me the side-eye as I sniff my way past, so I deliberately slow my walk and keep my movements calm and dignified so as to dispel any notion she has of me as a cokehead.

I make it to the lift unchallenged, step in, press button 21, and sneeze.

Fuck-a-doodle-do.

I have enough floors between me and my 'date' to blow my nose long and loud, wipe my upper lip, check my lipstick and bogie status in my mirror, and tuck the damp tissue back into my bag beside my Olbas oil, lozenges, and sachets of strawberry lube. Zoe's already arranged with room service to hide a bottle of maple syrup in the bedside cabinet, so we're all set for the pre-dinner activities. I hope.

§

We start off well. I sit on the desk where only this afternoon he signed some multi-national deal, spread my legs and hold my skirt high.

"A maple leaf, eh? I love it! Good girl!"

He stuffs a finger in and I smile and squirm and wish he'd had a manicure. Hangnails can *hurt*.

He scoops me up, both hands on my arse, and throws me on the bed with an "Oof", which makes me revise my estimate of his age (60s? maybe?) instead of how happy I am with my weight.

I wriggle out of my dress and throw it near the door as he unzips his easy-iron trousers – they're expensive and suited to a busy day of travel and deals but still, easy-iron, ugh – and frees his cock from stripy blue briefs. I hold up a finger and murmur "Wait ..." as I retrieve the bottle of syrup from the tiny cupboard where it lurks beside the Gideon bible, then hold it up where he can see it.

He actually claps, thrilled at the fun of it, I think – his notes said he was *very* patriotic – and watches while I pour a little on my crotch and breasts then dribble more from a height onto my outstretched tongue. I put the bottle back near the bible then he pounces and all I feel are whiskers, tongue, and teeth.

I'm alternately too hot and too cold. Fever is definitely upon me. I can retreat to my own bed in my own flat with a wheatbag and my cat and my softest comfiest pyjamas in just under seven hours. I'm desperate for a cup of hot sweet tea and a sleep. But there's maybe half a dozen 'orgasms' to get through first.

My being poorly is proving a turn-on for my client, though. When I shiver and tremble he interprets it as need. When my skin prickles and goosebumps, he sees only erect nipples and chews them like winegums. When I mouth-breathe, he thinks I'm getting off on his sticky fumbling.

Then he digs his hands under my back and hefts me on top of him as he rolls onto his. When he snogs me I taste myself and too much maple syrup on his teeth, and I can't mouth breathe which is a disaster for my nostrils. I shudder with another flash of feeling frozen to the core and disengage from his face before he notices the snot coursing down my upper lip. It's much easier to hide your face with a blowjob.

I suck and lick and try not to sniff too loudly.

"Bend over. I *need* to fuck that wee pussy, *right* now, eh?"

Shit, my head's not with it, the lube's out of reach in my bag over by the desk. Instead of wiping my nose on the bedding I pinch a slick of it from my nostrils and dab it on the head of his cock, drip some spit on it, and crawl off him on all fours. My joints are aching and my crotch doesn't want any visitors today, thank you. Every cell of my vagina is shouting "Closed for business!" but I've got a job to do and he's a repeat client, and a good one, so there's no way I'm bowing out.

He takes me from behind and I fall over.

Somehow I manage to keep my arse in the air and not look like a total idiot, splayed on the bed. He finishes off with a spurt and a squirt and a "Whooooo!" and slaps my bottom as I roll over and collapse next to him.

"Clean me up, gorgeous – we've got time to go again before dinner."

I smile, of course, and clamber over to his cock. I lick and slurp and sniff – the latter as quietly as possible – and feel the first prickling of a sneeze building in my nose. Fuck.

I try to switch to just hands for a moment until my nose clears and the crisis passes but as I draw my head away his hands push me back onto his cock and keep me there. I would redirect the head of it into my cheek, safely away from my teeth, but he's giving me no room to manoeuvre. I put all my energy into sucking him off, hoping – no doubt in vain – that he'll miraculously spunk in the next few seconds before my nose goes nuclear.

What other info did he have on his form? What can I do to speed him up? My head's so foggy I doubt I'd remember my mobile number at this point. Finger in the arse? Worth a shot. I squirm my pinky in past some crusty stuff I try not to think about, glad I can't smell a thing, and he groans and pants and clamps my head down harder.

On the plus side, he's clearly building up to blow.

The negative, however, is that his pubes are now tickling inside my nostrils.

I can't help it.

With his dick in my mouth and my nose full of snot, I sneeze.

The only plus side to this is that my teeth don't quite meet.

Saying "Gesundheit" really isn't enough.

Peter Pan Collar

by Susan Tepper

Fall was when they used to outfit him for school in freakish short pants and checkered suspenders and a white button shirt with a round collar. High socks and brown leather tie shoes. The other boys called him *Peter Pan collar* and smeared dirt and their own snot on his face. He cried every morning begging to stay home. Out came the belt. He ran out the back door with the neighbor's geese hot on his trail. Those geese came in a flock. Before he could head the other way, five or more blocking the road to the school bus. Beaks open. Squawking and snapping at his bare legs.

Taking the beer opener kept on the floor next to the brake pedal, using the sharp edge, he pares his fingernails. Car windows rolled down. It's a good day. Warm but not too warm. Over the summer he let his nails grow till they curled too: yellow and dirty. It felt right. He settles his weight in the car's bucket seat. Clock on the dash shows 11:03. In no time they'll be out for recess. The first bunch of little darlings. They'll run and shout and squeak and squeal. Fly if they could. Spread their arms and fly like Peter Pan. That's what gave him the idea to take a new name. Fresh. Start over. Fuck Kavanagh and all the fucking Kavanagh family. P. Pedersen. That is it.

If he can just nab one small boy his day will be complete. Tuck the kid in the trunk, set up all soft and blankety for ease of transport. Drive a few towns over, up

338

the hill behind the reservoir. Back where the pines make thick walls. Open the trunk, take him out and love him. Love him to pieces.

Pedersen feels a woody coming on. He smiles. Pets it. Same as he pets the white rat Swoon.

The Cross to Bear

by Jessica McHugh

News of his mother's stroke pushes Father Edward McKenzie toward Shady Grace Retirement Home faster than he'd expected. The head nurse greets him at the door, her rotund physique testing the limits of her faded violet scrubs. Roberta's wardrobe outside of the retirement home isn't much better. While her floral church dresses flirt with a wider color scheme, the bulky shapes are just as unflattering, squeezing and segmenting her flesh in all the wrong places. Edward often wishes he could bring out her natural beauty with a makeover.

Really, Edward, I don't think this an appropriate time to ponder this.

Grandma Eleanor is right, as usual, but her voice makes him realize it's the first time she's spoken since he received the call from Shady Grace. Betty is her daughter. In spite of the difficulties they shared while Eleanor was alive, he assumed she would have some sort of reaction to her daughter's stroke. Even if it were only the fear that Betty would soon join her in the afterlife.

Though she's adopted a more somber tone than usual, Nurse Roberta's sunshine can't be hidden behind the dark clouds of the day. As they plod to his mother's room, Edward wrings his crucifix throughout her explanation of Betty McKenzie's condition.

"Your mother suffered a Transient Ischemic Attack, also know as a 'baby stroke'," she says. "I know the nickname doesn't make it any cuter, but these attacks are thankfully mild. Ms. McKenzie is asleep now, but we expect her to make a full recovery. She's a tough old bird."

"Yes, I know," Edward says.

Betty was tough when she ridiculed him as a child, tough when she tried to "cane the fairy out of him" as a teenager, and even tougher after he took the cloth. She never thought it was appropriate for him to conceal his true desires behind God and the church, and he agrees now. But not so cruelly. Edward doesn't think it's wrong to hide a corset beneath his vestments; he's just tired of hiding.

Roberta opens the door into Betty's room, and the first thing Edward sees is the cardiac monitor, its screen marked with colorful squiggles and digits. His mother lies beneath a crisp white sheet, her skin more jaundiced than ever. The nasal cannula delivering her oxygen whistles. Roberta shuffles over to inspect it, but Edward stops her.

"I don't want to wake her yet."

Roberta nods as she pats his shoulder. "I understand. Take your time, Father."

She closes the door when she leaves. Only then does Edward notice the drippy stain on the back, like someone had hurled a liquor bottle at the door. Staring at his sallow mother in the hospital bed, he figures it's an all-too-accurate assumption.

Edward has seen folks in far worse circumstances at Shady Grace. More machines. Less consistent breathing. As a priest, he's compelled to sit beside Betty's bed like he does in those dire situations, to hold her hand, to ease her heart and mind by assuring her that she has a place in God's Heaven. But as her oft-abused son, he refuses to take one step in her direction.

Instead, he leans against her dresser, his gaze captured by the glimmer of glass in the top drawer. He grits his teeth as he removes and drops the empty vodka bottle in the trash. He pockets the other he finds, still sloshing with liquor. Some of the vodka has spilled in the drawer, staining many of the old photographs inside. Several are ruined, the alcohol distorting Betty's youthful face, but after pushing them aside, he finds unsullied pictures of his mother as a young girl, the unmistakable glint of hope filling her eyes.

May I?

He hands one of the pictures to Eleanor, who sighs.

"She was so full of life," Edward says, "So hopeful."

She was posing. After this picture was taken, she went right back to being who she was.

Eleanor digs deeper into the drawer and finds a photo of Edward as a child. Gazing at it, her face warms.

Now, this is someone who never poses, never pretends.

Edward snatches the photo from her, his jaw clenched. He can't remember the day the photo was taken, or how Betty had gotten him to smile – until he squints at the photo. Seeing his mother's ballet flats on his tiny feet, he sighs in remembrance. As a child, he would often slip them on while she was away, delighting in the crisp scrape of the leather against their splintered kitchen floor, and how the force of his clumsy pirouettes would occasionally toss them across the room.

He'd been unable to ditch them before Betty arrived home the day the photo was taken. She'd snapped it, ignorant of the shoes until he'd started shuffling away. Tearing them off his feet, she threw the ballet flats out the window, declaring them "tainted" before caning Edward's bottom bloody.

Dropping the picture back in the drawer, Edward whispers. "I never pretend? That's all I do, Grandmother. I've been posing for a picture all my life."

Not at the Paradiso Club.

"And we saw how well that turned out."

Staring at the sticky snapshots of a life misled, Edward can't muster one memory in which Betty appears as happy as in the pictures. Worse, he can say the same about himself.

He shuts the drawer with a sigh. Eleanor touches his shoulder, but it's not as comforting as it once was.

You aren't alone, Edward. You understand that, right?

Facing his grandmother, he nods. "I do. All too well."

Betty McKenzie snorts. Seeing her struggling to sit up, Edward dashes to her side, but she waves him away.

"How are you feeling?" he asks.

She narrows her eyes and croaks. "Oh, Edward, I feel so many things. About my failures, mostly." He sits beside her, pleased that the stroke has made her introspective until she adds, "I wish I'd never had a child. You, especially."

He lowers his head, twisting his crucifix as he says, "We can't choose who our children will grow up to be, any more than those children can choose their mothers. Or change them."

Edward tries to stop her as she wrestles with the nasal cannula, but she hisses, pulls it from her nostrils and hurls it at him.

"You shouldn't have come," she says. "This is all your fault."

"I think the empty bottle of booze in the trashcan is more at fault than I am."

She wheezes. "Maybe so, but I was drinking because of the rumor I heard about you. That you tarted yourself up, went out in public as a woman, and fucked some stranger."

Edward's innards tremble and twist. "Where did you hear that?"

"Geraldine Kitner. She said her son stopped into some homo bar for directions and saw you dressed as a woman, throwing your disgusting lifestyle in everyone's face."

As she shakily draws her yellowed face closer to Edward, her skin appears to sag even more. But beneath the wizened flesh, her attitude is hard and clenched. "Go on," she says. "Tell me it's not true."

Imagining the oversized ballet flats on his feet, Father Edward McKenzie smiles. His toes grip the soles of his shoes like he used to with the slippers, holding them to feet through illusory spins and high kicks.

"No," he says. "I didn't sleep with anyone, but I won't deny the rest."

Betty's stomach lurches, and she covers her mouth as she swallows hard.

"I'd say 'I have no son,' but that would probably make you happy, wouldn't it?" Wrapping her claw around his crucifix, she tears it from his neck. "This is a family heirloom. Since I have no child, it belongs with me."

"It's Grandma Eleanor's, and she wants me to have it."

"Eleanor is dead. She doesn't want anything anymore," Betty says. "Even when she did, I wasn't in the habit of giving her what she wanted."

Edward stands, his hand resting on his chest. Turning away from Betty, he says, "I'll tell Roberta you're awake. I'm certain she'll be disappointed."

He opens the door to leave, but the sound of two women asking the same question stops him. Together, Eleanor and Betty say, "You're not going to try to take it back?"

Standing beside her daughter's bed, Eleanor's face drains of its color. Her face creases in confusion, and her hands shake as she reaches out. Eleanor has always been infinitely kinder and more beautiful than Betty, but for the first time, Edward recognizes how closely they resemble one another.

"No," he replies, smiling at the crucifix. "I don't need it anymore."

The Displeasure Principle

by Shane Simmons

"Sorry it's been a while since we last got together. Girlfriend's been dealing with a family crisis and she really needed me." He looks rougher than usual and rubs his tired eyes.

In my presence, Callum says very little about his live-in girlfriend. But when he does there comes across an affection. On one hand, how can someone be quite willing to sneak around behind their loved one's back, and yet still seem to be entirely in love with that person? I've come to the conclusion that what they *have* and what we *do* are entirely separate beasts. And I suppose for him they can co-exist quite peacefully without rattling each other's cage.

For me, I've begun to crave something more.

"What was the crisis?"

"Her dad's been diagnosed with Parkinson's. He's only in his early forties." He twiddles his thumbs amongst the forest of hair covering his torso. "She's been pretty cut up about it."

A revolting pang of jealousy appears from out of nowhere. I push it down as hard as I can but I find myself remembering back, stood alone in the living room of the old house, two police officers before me. Telling me my parents had been involved in a crash. Their car had careered off the side of a bridge onto the road below. They told me the paramedics had tried their best to save them.

Their words blurred mid-air, passed right through me, slo-mo. Nothing registering. Slipping into shock, I'd begun to tremble.

I remember wanting no one other than Mark in that room with me.

I'd never felt so alone.

I give him a peck on his cheek. "She's lucky to have you."

He rolls over, already spent and I'm lying next to him, finishing myself off. I'm staring up at the ceiling, trying to think of something, anything to make this work. But I tug, pull, stroke, and nothing. If only he'd give me a hand (or even better, a mouth) but he lost interest seconds after he came.

I give up, my hands slide down limp at my side. I can hear his breathing next to me, in and out. His 'phone chirps from somewhere on the floor.

His eyes snap open, "Fuck," he says, jumping out of the bed, "sorry, you can't stay tonight."

"Girlfriend coming home?"

He's clambering to pull on his jeans. I'm reaching to pull on mine.

In the hall I pick up the rucksack I'd packed this morning with my toothbrush, some deodorant and fresh clothes for tomorrow. I turn to find he's already opened the door.

"I'll text you sometime soon."

As I retrace my route to the train station, in the back of my mind there's a niggling. I know what the deal is.

On the opposite platform is a heaving mass of bodies, tarted up, heading out for a night uptown. It's only just gone seven and the night is early, but when all working days begin blurring into one and you have no real plans, the arrival of the weekend is a non-event.

Going along with Sandra and her idea of 'fun' was maybe where this all went wrong. For her, simply having a lie-in lay is all the 'fun' she needs. She kids herself that it means something more, and yet she still never fails to seem far happier than myself.

And Callum somehow manages to have his cake and eat it. I suppose that makes me a bit jealous.

I step onto a train that will soon be heading in the opposite direction to the razzmatazz uptown. The carriage is crammed with city suits and briefcases, all heading home after work.

You see those people, the ones who get married and end up having affairs? And when they (inevitably) get caught, they always come out with that line, "But they meant nothing." It never soothes the wounds, but perhaps there's an element of truth. Maybe that 'other' person never really meant a thing beyond fleeting moments. And I no longer want to be that 'moment'.

Sandra thinks I need someone, anyone, and I don't think I do.

The only reason I bothered responding to Callum's texts and going out of my way to get up to his place was the nights spent playing Xbox games like a pair of teenagers, sharing a post-session takeaway and talking aimlessly about anything and everything.

I don't *need* Callum's body. And I don't *need* Mark, who's just a dying memory, slowly going out of view on the horizon. I don't *need* anyone. Not just yet.

Next month I turn twenty-three. Sandra had already talked about going out for my birthday do. In her mind she'd already invited herself, Marlon and Callum in tow.

Funny that, when it isn't herself being cheated on her morals on such matters really don't count for much … I don't *do* birthdays. I'd like to run away for the week. Do what I want to do, go where I want to go. A few seats free up on the train. I sit down and take out my 'phone, type 'city breaks' into Google.

Where could I go?

Looking down at my 'phone I find my eyes distracted by a shape under the taut grey sateen trousers of the suit opposite. I shake my head and get back to more pressing matters. Where could I go?

A text message interrupts my browsing.

"Sorry bout tonite. Msg ya 4 a hook up soon."

"I think it's for the best that we leave it there mate," I type into my 'phone. "Best of luck to you."

I'm smiling as I close the messages and return to looking over pretty photos of cities, cobbled streets by night, sunlit scenes, winding canals.

"Shit!" I jump up as I see the sign for my station sliding away from the train. Too late, no point in pushing through the people blocking the aisle, so I sit back down and wait.

Getting off at the next stop, I walk over the bridge to the opposite platform. Once again my 'phone calls for attention. It's Callum.

"????"

After hitting delete I go into my contacts and erase his number too. It's empowering, doing just what you feel. When I get in I'm going to order myself a Chinese. Put the 'phone on silent. Book myself a birthday break away.

"Yes, why the fuck not," I think to myself, as I step onto another train.

Sand

by Michelle Elvy

They arrive at the beach and Ellie parks the car. Stevie pays the meter – two hours. Manny unfolds from the back seat and stretches. Sylvie is already racing to the water, her small feet kicking up sand with each happy stride. A day at the beach. One last trip before Stevie heads south.

They've driven across the low flatlands of the eastern shore to get here – across the Bay Bridge and east, cornfields blurring, acre after acre. A trip Stevie has made a hundred times. He's feeling nostalgic today – Ellie at the wheel, Manny and Sylvie in the back, playing Go Fish on the seat between them. He and Manny played Go Fish when they were kids. Go Fish and Minecraft, Tomb Raider and Poker. They started stealing cars when they got bored with all the rest, but that only lasted a year or so. In January they veered way off course, all of them. They've been crawling their way back to the center ever since. Stevie has wondered all year whether that flight through the sky, when he was hurled from the car while the others tumbled and rolled together – Lucky going through the windshield and ending everything they knew up until then – put him on this outward-reeling trajectory and marked the beginning of his long goodbye. He can't fight centrifugal force. He has tried to come back to the center – graduating and getting into college, helping Manny graduate too. Even his relationship with Ellie is an effort to hold fast.

And yet he's leaving. Manny's running his dad's garage, Ellie's got an internship with the Chesapeake Bay Foundation – reasons to stay. But Stevie's deferred college for a year and in some ways is already gone.

Manny jogs down to the beach after Sylvie but Ellie comes around to Stevie's side of the car and leans into him. They kiss. She smells like summer, even now. Salt. Sugar. Sun. He will never forget this smell. He nods to the package lying on the front seat. "What is it?" He wants to open it and see the treasure Ellie has placed inside, but he also wants to keep it exactly as it is, neatly wrapped in its square box.

"It's for you. Something from here." He thinks she means here, as in *this place*, the geography they have all been born into, but as she says it Ellie's hand goes to her locket around her neck and rests near her heart. Stevie looks from the package on the seat to Ellie and thinks *What the hell, maybe I won't leave after all, maybe I'll stay here, maybe I'll get snowed in if I stay long enough, maybe I'll spend the winter plowing driveways or skating on a frozen lake or just holding Ellie's hand.*

His stomach churns at that small gesture. Hand on heart. Up to this moment, he's been pretty sure he's leaving forever.

"I'm not leaving forever, you know."

"You never know. Besides, you haven't read this."

Stevie unwraps the paper and opens the box. Inside is a book. A hard cover. He turns it over in his hands. "Ellie, this isn't just any book."

"I know."

"You can't give me this."

"Yes I can." She touches his shoulder, leans in, her forehead against his. She is exactly the same height and their foreheads and noses and then lips touch again. Her wind-blown hair tickles his cheek; her hand cups the back of his neck. Her breath is pulling him in, stilling the restlessness inside.

She inhales, pulls back. Stevie looks at the book in his hands. A first edition of William Warner's *Beautiful Swimmers*, with an inscription: *To Tom, one of the finest few.* Signed by the author.

One of the few things Ellie has from her grandfather, Tom. There are untold stories about Tom and his son, Ellie's dad, both part of a long line of fishermen. Ellie has always been connected to the Chesapeake in a way that Stevie only remotely gets. He feels the vague notion that this is where he's from, sure – with parents from DC and his own life playing out in its entirety in this low flatland of sorghum and corn, lacrosse and summer lightning storms. But for Ellie, this is where she *belongs*. Her grandfather Tom was a waterman on one of the last skipjacks of the Chesapeake. He dredged for oysters on his traditional boat, the *Maryanne of the Choptank*, all through the 1960s and 70s and even into the 80s. He gave countless hours to William Warner in a long series of conversations that eventually turned into the Pulitzer-winning book. He dropped dead of a heart attack the year Ellie was born.

Stevie knows Ellie is attached to her mostly missing family members more than those alive – her grandfather and father, also lost unexpectedly to the hard work of the mostly benign waters of the Chesapeake, and her uncle, a man who moved inland to raise cattle in an effort to escape his waterborne birth right and all the expectations associated with it, who was then crushed in a freak tractor accident. For as long as Stevie has known Ellie, her only remaining family, besides Sylvie, has been her mother, who is scarcely there, preferring vodka to raising two daughters and usually holed up with her weird cousin in a far corner of Pennsylvania. There have been glimpses of Grace, but they are never happy glimpses. Sightings, with cruel aftermaths – especially for Sylvie. Stevie has never asked but he knows there's a connection between addiction and the long line of watermen Grace married into. And he knows that, just as her mother has been driven away by her affiliation with the Tyler family, Ellie's life is just as intricately tied to the murky history of the sand and silt of the region.

He knows his story begins here but does not end here. He knows his story only briefly intersects with Ellie's. He knows his story is not about sand.

But this here, this small book in his hands – this is a piece of Ellie's history, her family, her heart. And now it's his.

"But this is your granddad's – your dad's. Yours." Stevie's throat catches.

Ellie shrugs. "You like to read."

Stevie suddenly feels himself spinning out from the tight circle they've all occupied for years. With one small breath, Ellie can pull him in and hold him close, but this is not Ellie reeling him back; this is a release, a gentle push. He feels the tenderness of this moment, this book: Ellie saying *go*, even as she draws a tentative line between their two paths, his course set for points beyond the wide mouth of the Chesapeake, hers standing firm on the ever-shifting silt of this mid-Atlantic region. He is sad and also grateful. He will cart this book with him the rest of his life. He will read it and re-read it and he'll even come back to the Chesapeake from time to time. He will carry Ellie's history with him, always. And he will be connected to it, too. But he will keep spinning outward, away, away.

"Come on," Ellie says, "let's go find some soft-shells."

§

They collect Manny and Sylvie from the beach and walk down the street to a pub where they sit at a long table covered in paper and order a half-bushel of jumbo crabs and two soft-shell sandwiches. Large glasses of lemonade, too. It's a hot September day and the mid-afternoon meal is succulent and sweet. Stevie bites into the white bread holding his soft-shell crab, sautéed just right, butter oozing, the tomato and lettuce and small dollop of tartar sauce exactly as they should be. Manny is handing over his crablegs to Sylvie, who is pounding them with vigor, the mallet large in her small hands.

Sylvie stops her banging and produces a small bottle from her backpack. She hands it across the table to Stevie.

"What's this?"

"Something from here," she says. It's not lost on Stevie that both sisters speak the same way, but Sylvie doesn't hold her heart; instead, she thrusts the bottle into his hand and laughs.

The bottle has a stopper cork and is filled with layers of color: grey, pink, black, even red, with a lighter shade of yellow on top. There are a few objects suspended among the grains, too, and a neatly tied yellow ribbon around the neck.

Stevie raises an eyebrow toward Ellie, who is sitting next to her sister. Manny leans in beside Stevie to look closer. Sylvie explains.

"The grey is the dirt from our back yard, near where we buried Yellow Bird." Stevie recalls the day they buried her canary together – his first introduction to this new friend.

"The shark's tooth is from Calvert Cliffs, where Ellie took me on my birthday. And the black is from the soil on the side of the house, where we plant our tomatoes. We add coffee grounds. They grow better that way. I love tomatoes."

Stevie and Ellie exchange smiles.

"The red is from Grandpa Harry's yard, in North Carolina. There's a tire swing in the tree. I have a box of dirt from there in my closet."

"I have weird shit in my closet, too," says Manny – an act of solidarity with the small child, but Stevie pokes him to shut up.

Sylvie ignores them both and continues, "The shells are from the last time I came to the beach, and the yellow – that's from today: sand."

Stevie chokes up, slugs his lemonade. Manny turns over his fifth crab to begin picking out the meat, and Ellie puts her arm around Sylvie.

Stevie is thinking of what to say when the bottle slips from his hand and drops. The cork pops off and the bottle rolls across the hardwood floor, its contents spilling out. It rolls further into the aisle, just as the waiter walks towards their table. In a moment of bad timing, the waiter steps on the bottle and it shatters.

Now Stevie's on his knees trying to re-shape the mess into a neat pile. He drags the edges of his hands together, cupping the sand and dirt. The layers are mixed now, the neat striations jumbled in a pile. He picks out shards of glass and scoops up some of it to bring back to the table, where the others sit dumbstruck by the misfortune.

"Shit, man, bad luck," says Manny, and Stevie is grateful that his friend has broken the silence because he's not sure what he would do with tears from either Ellie or Sylvie.

"Well, I got some of it."

Stevie hopes he can save the moment, say something meaningful to Sylvie. He glances at her, this small careful girl who has given him such a compact piece of her own story. He thinks she is pouting and refusing to look up at him when he realizes she is rummaging in the backpack in her lap. She produces a small bottle – one exactly like the one she so carefully filled for him, only this one is empty.

"Here." She uncorks the bottle and holds it out across the table.

Stevie clumsily sifts the dirt and sand through his fingers into the small neck of the bottle. Some goes in, but most of it falls onto the table. It's a small drab thing when he holds it up to examine it. Half full. He shoves the shark's tooth and some of the small shells on top and corks it.

"Sorry," he finally says.

"That's OK," says Sylvie, pulling on her braid. "I know where there's more sand."

Dirty Martinis

by Len Kuntz

I'm not broke, but I'm getting there. Besides, it's lonely on the road and strangers are never as friendly as you'd guess.

So I pull over at a truck stop near Nashville with a *Help Wanted* sign in the window. It's a bartending gig, something I know a little something about having spent my last year of college fixing drinks for drunk frat boys at a strip club called *Jiggles*. The manager here is an obese man who goes by the moniker Hercules. He's so huge that it's torture for him to breathe and any time he moves or even leans a little it's like hearing a vacuum cleaner going full blast.

Herc gives me a test run. He has me make an Old Fashioned, a Manhattan, Dirty Martinis and even a Dirty Girl Scout, which, by the grin on his face, would be his trump recipe, yet I nail the concoction with just the right amount of Bailey's and a dash of crème de menthe. The happy smirk on his face tells me he's impressed.

"Start now if you want," Herc says.

I work my shift and another late into the evening. Herc is low on bartenders, I learn, because almost all of them end up stealing from the till, which is pretty stupid since there are two low-hanging cameras in each corner.

No one ever orders a Dirty Martini, let alone a Dirty Girl Scout. Mostly it's gin and tonics, whiskey straight up no ice, or rum and cokes. And beer of course. Lots of beer.

I try to keep things clean in and around my work space but there's so much alcohol soaked through the floorboards after all these years that certain spots give up a tight squeal when you step there, like crushing a poor kitten, plus the air smells like a well-used urinal.

The patrons are mostly miserable, and they're all drifters, yet an hour before midnight a lady comes in and I feel my knees buckle.

She looks exactly like my wife, but with red hair.

"Hey there," she says.

I try to speak but I've got rocks in my throat.

She takes the center stool at the bar, staring at me, daring me to look away. For a minute we just look at each other. I feel sweat dripping down my ribs. My socks are damp with sweat as well.

"Do I know you?" she finally says.

I swallow and manage to say, "I'm not from around here."

"Me either."

She smiles and it's my wife's smile, the kind she'd give me when she was in the mood for some hanky-panky.

"What'll it be?" I say, feeling dizzy and out of sorts.

"Give me your best drink, you pick."

So I make her a Dirty Martini and when she says, "Why don't you join me?" I do as she suggests, making another for myself. It's late and there's no one else in the place, plus I'm thirsty and nervous, needing something to take the edge off.

When we clink glasses in a toast, she says, "To chance encounters."

I drain my glass in three quick swallows. She flashes that smile again. I make another drink and try not to down it all at once.

She says, "You look like someone who's had their heart broken in a million pieces."

"How do you know that?"

357

"Ah, so you have?"

I nod. It feels like there's a balloon swelling in my chest. Since I left home, I've done a pretty adequate job of not thinking about my wife, but now, here with this woman who looks and acts so much like her, nostalgia ensnares me and I feel as weak and defeated as I did when I found out she was cheating on me.

"Hey now, it's all right," the woman says, reaching across the counter and clutching my hand which is damp with what I now realize are my own tears. "It's like they say: Time heals all wounds."

"You think?"

"There are plenty of fish in the sea," she says, using her free hand to unbutton her blouse.

"Hey."

"Momma said there'd be days like this."

"What are you doing?"

She draws my hand across the counter and pushes it inside her bra, purring, "There's no place like home."

Her skin is creamy and warm, her nipple as rigid as an eraser.

I reach under her armpits and hoist her off the stool and onto the bar counter, climbing on it too, positioning myself between her wide open thighs.

As I enter her, she grabs a fistful of my hair and yanks my head to hers, biting my ear, saying, "A stitch in time saves nine."

We go at it furiously. She makes the same urgent, wounded animal noises my wife would always make. She's demanding. She bites my other ear.

It lasts a half hour or an entire day, I can't be sure, because I'm in a netherworld. Everything feels right and somehow restored. When I say, "I've missed you so much," there's a guy across the bar in hunting fatigues sucking on a toothpick who snarls, calls me a "Queer" and backs out of the bar.

358

I look around for the woman who resembles my wife, but she's not there. I'm leaning over the bar, fully clothed. The air smells of jasmine, the fragrance my wife loved, or maybe it doesn't smell like anything other than barley and hops.

Ninth Inning

by Michael Webb

I have to get away. The team, like so many do, has descended into backbiting and innuendo, the blame circulating like bad air on a plane. The manager overmanages, the pitchers over-throw, the hitters overswing, and 4 straight losses becomes dropping 8 of 10 and the thin reed of your playoff hopes snaps off entirely. We are playing out the string in Baltimore, games that no one cares about under leaden skies, obeying the dictates of the schedule before small, unhappy crowds.

After a dismal 8-1 shellacking, which I was no small part of, and a tense phone call from Angela about behavior problems from the kids and my wavering interest in another baby, I decide I need to get out. I walk far enough from the hotel that I shouldn't be found, stepping into a mostly empty chain restaurant for a beer and some appetizers.

I was trying not to look at the lowlights of the Oriole hitters beating me like a rented mule on the televisions overhead, staring at the bubbles in my beer, when I feel her presence next to me.

"Hey stranger," she says. It is Jen, the reporter from Comcast, the only member of the press corps I remotely get along with. She is dressed up, expensive looking black pants, tall heels, and a thin, low cut top. Not altogether different from work attire, but with a little more sparkle. Like she is trying 20% harder to look good.

"Oh Jesus, not you," I say with mock seriousness. "I didn't give you enough this afternoon?"

"Hey," she says, taking a step back. "I'm off duty. Promise."

"Alright," I say, trying to sound gruff.

"May I join you?"

"Of course," I say.

The bartender, a chunky blonde with a purple streak on the side of her head, brings me my wings. Jen orders a beer for herself. I watch her cross her legs, the leather of her shoe reflecting the too bright lights. Overhead, I glance at myself as I wind and throw and watch a triple fly into the right field corner. When you get hit hard, the home media delights in your misery.

"Drowning your sorrows?" Jen says softly. Her makeup is quiet, professional, but expressive, a little flashier than usual. She is pretty, with the wide, oversized eyes of someone who is at home in front of a camera. I realize that I've seen more of her in the last month than I have of Angela, and I don't have the first idea of her personal life.

"You saw it," I say flatly. "I was shitty. What do you think?"

"Yeah," she says. "Your slider was flat, and your heater had no life. You're not hurt, are you?"

My back tenses, as if her saying the word can summon an injury. "I thought you were off duty!" I say with mock seriousness.

"Sorry," she says. She looks away, across the bar. "Force of habit."

"What sorrows are you drowning?" I ask.

"Me? Oh. I was meeting an ESPN producer here, but they are ..." she says, looking around for a clock, "seventy-five minutes late."

"For work?"

"Oh, no," she says, shaking her head.

"Oh," I say teasingly. "A hot date!"

361

"You could say that," she says. She looks away, her eyes wandering towards the door. A flush spreads down her neck. I can see the flat expanse above her cleavage turning pink. I feel the distance from home and Angela and Madison and Dylan, suddenly, silently aware of the 3000 miles that feel like ten million. I try to picture Jen in a single hotel room, undressing for bed, her shoes lonely and useless on a tan carpet. Something clicks inside me, Angela's biting anger on the phone and the smell of hot wings suddenly making me flush in sympathy with her.

"Anyone who would stand you up is a damn fool," I say. She is still looking at the door, the twisting emphasizing her trim waist and firm breasts as the blouse pulls taut. She turns back to look at me, her eyes slightly wet, her face softening into a smile.

"Thanks," she says softly. "That's nice to hear."

"So what's plan B for you?" I ask.

"This," she says. She smiles a little wider. She is half turned towards me in the chair.

"I'll drink to that," I agree. We clink glasses. A fat man in a Ravens cap across the bar from us looks up at the sound. An idea is forming at the base of my skull.

We drink in silence for a moment. The TV above our head shows the Orioles celebrating after their win, then a glimpse of a Raven at practice. I pick up a chicken wing and gnaw some of the meat off of it. I taste the grease and the bite of the spices. My eyes water.

"So what about after," I say, trying to sound casual. My heart pounds slightly. It's against all the codes of both of our professions, but the need tugs at me. Angela is a moon circulating a distant star, and Jen is here, and real, her bare, elegant calf inches from my skin. I can picture it. I want it.

"Oh, just bed," she says. She takes another long draft from her beer. "I don't have time to go out trawling." She is looking down again. You don't have to look far, I think at her. I'm right here. Jen finishes her beer and tugs at her

362

pants, dusting off imaginary crumbs, preparing to stand. I look at her anxiously, trying to drain my own glass. She is fishing in a small leather clutch.

I stand. "Oh no," I tell her. "Let me," I say. "I make more money than you do."

"Oh," she says with surprise. I take out a credit card and lay it down, and the punk rock barmaid scoops it up like a carnivore on the savannah.

"Walk back with me?" I suggest.

"OK," she says. "Sure. We just can't go in together, you know?"

I understand. A group of professional athletes can gossip as well as any 7th grade class.

The barmaid comes back with the receipt, which I sign, adding a generous tip, and hand back. We walk towards the door. I don't know how to ask for her room number. Or will she ask for mine?

"Whoever he is," I say, holding the door as she makes her way into the September cool, "he's an idiot for standing you up this way."

"Yes," Jen says, the door shutting behind us. "She is."

High and Dry as Those Trapped Souls

by James Claffey

The top of the house overlooks the river and the surrounding countryside, and the Bird, as he sweeps the binoculars across the horizon, can name the neighbors who once were friends of his parents.

From his perch he can see across the tops of the houses to the distant farms: Hunt's, Lambert's, Delaney's, Keogh's, Mulvihall's, and Partridge's, all small farmers with ordinary cottages set in fine pastureland. When he was a boy his father and grandfather rowed across the fields to the houses cut off from the town by the overflowing river. His mother, one time, scanned the view for a sign of her husband and his father, who had taken Christmas packages to the isolated farmers, all trapped in their homes for weeks due to the terrific flooding that came like a Biblical plague at the end of one cold November.

"Where are you now, Mammy?" the Bird asks, the sun so strong his eyes are barely open. The room is mute, not even a spider moving in its web. "Ye've left me as high and dry as those trapped souls all those years ago," he says, wiping his watery eyes with a sleeve. Below, the CIE bus from Dublin pulls in and disgorges its passengers. Hard to make out, but the Bird knows by outline the names of a fair few of the passengers. It's been a long spell since he's had a day in Dublin, and he imagines taking a walk to the Long

Hall on South Great George's Street for as fine a pint as there is in Christendom.

A woman steps off the bus and holds her hand to her head, keeping her hat in place as the wind whips at her. Familiar frame. Ah, it couldn't be, he thinks. Melodie. Her height. Maybe even her hair, though he can't make out the shade, but the length is close. He throws the binoculars on the bed and flings himself towards the stairs. As he skitters down the staircase he feels the thump of his heart and says a quick Our Father that she's back in town. "Please God, let my luck be on the turn," he says, blessing himself before throwing open the front door and racing towards the bus stop.

At the stop, Melodie is arm-in-arm with one of the musicians from the band she played with the night he first saw her in Hogan's. A tinny feeling comes over the Bird and he totters backwards and almost trips over the leg of a chair. His chest is hollow, lacking in blood, and he slumps to a sitting position on a wooden bench by the window of Grace's Butcher's shop. Her name sticks in his craw and he unscrews the flask in his pocket and gulps down a mouthful of the burning drink. "Me ... Melo ..." he can't form the syllables of her name and simply witnesses the bastard kiss her hard on the mouth. The Bird retreats to the steps outside his house, the nun's house, and drains the flask in one go.

Inside, in the kitchen, he takes the plates drying on the table and holds them above his head.

"One for sorrow ..."

Crash.

"Two for joy ..."

Crash.

"Three for a girl ..."

Crash.

"Fecking hoor ..."

The last plate explodes on the linoleum floor and bits of china litter the place like confetti. Through the settings of bone china the Bird laments his lost love, sure that the man she is with cannot possibly give her anything like the attention he would. These are the dishes he pictured her filling with delicious French cooking, her hair pinned back in a bow, the apron tight about her waist, his little woman making their lovely home together.

"Bitch. Bitch. Bitch."

He yells so the windows shake and the nuns might hear his cries, but he doesn't give a fig for their reverence. More bitches, too, those bloody nuns and their insistence of not allowing their converts to choose their path in religious life.

The kitchen he leaves like a madhouse, the shards of china everywhere, the possibility of love shattered into so many impossible pieces as they send his heart straight to hell. In the bedroom the wardrobe door rattles and he shakes a head at such madness. "Leave me alone, Mother," he cries. "Go back to hell and leave me to this misery." The door opens and his mother leaps out and in a jiffy he's across the floor scooting his entire body into the relative safety of the nearby corner. "Bird, Bird, Bird. You soft touch. Didn't I tell you all women would be your downfall?"

"No, Mother! You promised me happiness. You promised me a life to enjoy, you vicious traitor."

The mother clucks and beckons him forward. "Filthy. You disgusting creature!"

He raises his eyebrows and summons up a mouthful of spit, which he gullies into her ghostly figure. Nothing. No response. Not even a "Goodness!" Instead of disgust, the creature folds in on herself and in moments is gone. The Bird cries as he beats his fists on the door of the wardrobe. All love is pointless, he thinks. The wardrobe door shakes and trembles, the curses stored by him for some time now fly from his lips as he directs his anger and hatred towards the remaining actors and stage people.

Misery loves company, and the Bird wishes he had the company of someone to drown his sorrows. He thinks a trip to McKettrick's might reveal Melodie and her musical lover, and he doesn't give a damn. If he gets the chance he'll let her know exactly who he thinks she is, in no uncertain terms. Yet, he knows this is a lie, and that he'll end up toasting her happiness and bemoaning his useless religion, which only seems to satisfy the people around him, and never himself.

Before he sets out for the pub he descends to the back storage room outside the kitchen. There he grabs several ancient planks of wood and a handful of nails. With the hammer firmly in his grasp, he bangs the planks across the wardrobe door, the nails splintering the polished wood of the piece. Each swing of the hammer brings another curse out of his mouth. "Rot. In. Hell. You. Dirty. Fecker." He swings the last hammer blow so hard the head of the tool disappears into the wooden splinters, opening the wardrobe for surreptitious viewing.

"Now, then. You trollop of a Frenchwoman, it's time I set my intention, once and for all." The door slam must rattle the windows of the entire town, for the barking of dogs and the mewing of cats fill the evening with plainsong.

My Suicide, Interrupted

by Gwendolyn Joyce Mintz

Mora will be angry. But I believe at some point she'll understand. I can't text that goodbye and certainly not to her. She's a glimmer of hope that won't die out. Why I love her. And why I don't trust her. She might call or text back and then what – my suicide interrupted?

Phone's off. Neither she nor the others can call or text to see why I'm not at the meeting.

It's time. It's time. It's past time.

It may take them a minute to understand why Lindsey arrives at the table with the glasses but I hope they smile when she tells them I made arrangements earlier and tonight the champagne's on me.

Undone

by Stephen V. Ramey

"Control-Z," I say. *Undo last change.* "Remember how I showed you?"

Frank leans over the keyboard. I lean over his shoulder. I've been trying to teach him Microsoft Excel for a couple of weeks now. He got it in his head to do his household budget on the computer though he thinks it's a magic box with evil intentions. His daughter bought it for him last Christmas.

A stream of "z" stretches through several cells.

"You have to push the keys at the same time, Frank." I reach past him. "Here, let me show –"

"No, no, I'll get it." He positions his left index finger precisely over the *Ctrl* key, his right over *Z* and mashes both down. The river of "z" disappears, followed by the mistake and the correct entry he made before it.

He lifts his hands, triumphant.

"Nice," I say, "only you don't have to hold the keys down so long. See how it erased the Mortgage amount too?"

Frank chuckles. "I wish it were that easy."

"There's a way to redo that," I say, but he's already pecking keys on the number pad.

"That works too."

Frank is an interesting fellow. He's reserved most of the time, but when he's hooked on a topic or focused on a task, he can be like a bulldog. Fortunately, we made a gentleman's agreement my first day here that we would not pry into each other's lives. Frank may be tenacious, but he respects a bond as much as any man I have met. I like him a lot.

We've come to depend on each other. I drive him to the grocery store and mow the lawn and he lets me use his computer for the draft of my novel. He knows I'm writing, but has yet to ask what or why I write so late at night.

I'm up to chapter seven and feeling pretty good. I do miss Anne, especially in the mornings. She used to brew coffee before she went to work and would leave a note reminding me of whatever needed reminding that day. I loved the way she signed *Anne* with a flourish, that final swoop leaping up into the text of the note. I loved Anne. I think I still do, but that must be wrong. How could I give her up so easily if my love was true? Cold turkey is for quitting drugs, not emotional involvement.

I feel healthier since I came to stay with Frank. Mostly it's the lessened stress, I imagine. I used to worry every night that Anne would hate me for letting her down, or obsess over what new horror the doctors would find. I still remember word for word the call in which Dad told me his cancer had relapsed. He'd been on an experimental regimen and the tumors were shrinking. Hope had resurfaced; I heard it in his voice, saw it in his eyes. And then, "It's back." A sigh. The liver tumor had expanded and a second emerged. *Inoperable.* "What about a transplant?" "It's in my stomach and lymphs." And though we talked a few times after that, that was the goodbye I remember, the exhaustion in his voice. "Love you, Dad," I said. "Make me proud," he said. A choke, a click, and life would never be the same.

"Did I do that right?" Frank says. He's pointing at a cell in the spreadsheet that shows $742.35. The cells above it are encased in a solid border, indicating they are included in the summation.

"That's perfect, Frank." I pat his shoulder and his face breaks into a smile.

"I guess it's never too late," he says.

"For what?" I'm thinking of Dad's profile against a glowing television screen. *His face is so thin.*

"It's never too late to see the light," Frank says.

My throat seizes up. Dad used to say something like that. *Hang in there, Son. It's never too late to learn the dance.* He'd say that when I confided that life was not so good, another rejection, Anne on the warpath, a failed attempt to install a bathroom ceiling fan. *Don't let the world shut you down*, he'd tell me. *You'll find your music, I know you will.*

We were never close until he got sick. I'd seen him as an ineffective authority figure, someone to ignore, even mock. The illness made things right between us, gave me the relationship I had (unknowingly) craved.

And then it took him down. *Cancer. Death.* Every wise thing he'd told me was lost to my heart, every ounce of love destroyed. He *was* weak; a stronger man would have lived, a truer father would have seen our healing complete.

The computer screen blinks off. Frank's chair pushes back. I move. Air resists me; I hear a river rushing. My hands curl into fists. My eyes find the keyboard, the keys *Ctrl* and *Z*. Index fingers extend.

"How's spaghetti for tonight?" Frank squeezes my shoulder and moves past me to the kitchen.

"Fine," I say, but it's another voice I hear. *Make me proud, Son.*

Guilt

by Gay Degani

Dr. Sam Martin finds himself on the sidewalk along the Old Road, his mind a jagged mosaic: the breeze smelling of barbeque – the days getting shorter – he should get rid of that stack of wood – why hasn't that stop sign, twisted by last January's windstorm, been replaced? And then, an image of Charmaine, hands on hips, belly beginning to swell – Charmaine smashing the new tile in the bathroom – Charmaine curled next to their aero-bed, her nightgown crumpled above her waist, the worn pine floor stained with blood. Why is he out here in front of his house on the wrong side of the gate with some old man poking him in the chest, raising his voice, "Hey, Doc! Doc?"

Frowning, Sam asks, "W-why are you shouting at me?"

"You okay, Doc?"

"Me? I'm fine – fine."

"You don't look fine."

Sam hones in on the old guy, then studies his dog. Al? Fred? Gus! The dog is Gus? No, the old *man* is Gus, the same one who helped him search the Trencher mansion for Charmaine. Sam says, "Gus, right? And Gracie?"

"No one forgets Gracie. Any news?"

When Sam reported his wife missing two months ago, after turning the neighborhood upside down, the cops asked if the remodeling was causing any stress, were they getting along okay, did she have a temper, did he have a temper? He explained the miscarriage and his wife's depression, and the older cop, the one with the bad hair plugs, muttered, "Uh-huh," in that cynical way people do. Sam felt guilty then. He still feels guilty now. Whatever happened to Charmaine, he should have kept her safe, helped her cope. It was his fault. He hadn't handled anything right when she lost the baby. When *they* lost the baby.

"Doc!"

"Sorry. Just can't remember why I came outside. You know the feeling."

"Not me." Gus taps his own forehead. "Mind like a steel trap. You know what strikes me is that we had someone at the bungalow disappear too. The night of the storm."

The line between Sam's brows deepens.

"Yeah," says the old man. "Not like your wife exactly because this one left with her two kids. Her husband was, well, what we used to call a wife-beater, at least according to Sybil, our landlady. Jamie was her name, packed her suitcase and when the storm happened, she took off."

"Charmaine wouldn't leave me, not like that. We – I'm not – like him."

"Oh, I didn't mean that. The thing is, after she left, she never called Sybil. They were close, so it's kind of surprising. And Jamie didn't take her suitcase. It got crushed by the oak when it landed on her house. Sybil's storing all her stuff in the garage."

Sam remembers the fallen tree. It had taken months to get the whole mess cleaned up and now it doesn't look like the bungalow is going to be rebuilt. "No one ever heard from her?"

"That's what I mean. Sybil still has her cleaning deposit too. You'd think she'd need the money if not her stuff. You haven't heard from your wife either, right?"

Flashes from the day Charmaine flipped out, taking a hammer to their bathroom, and hiding in the nursery of the deserted Trencher mansion next door kaleidoscope through Sam's mind. He pivots slowly toward the big Mediterranean looming over its unkempt yard. When she disappeared a few months later, he was certain that's where she'd gone, but she hadn't.

Gus yammers on. "… two women disappearing on the same street, but she'll be okay, Doc. You know how women are. Right, Gracie?" The old man tugs at the dog's leash, and the mutt cocks her head. "We gotta get going, don't we, girl? Keep the home fires burning, Doc. She'll be back."

Without another word, Gus turns and limps across the Old Road and taking the path down to the creek, he disappears into the growing dusk.

Sam deflates as if Gus's arthritic finger had left a pinhole in his chest. The gloom thins him almost to nothing, a thought, a vapor, the memory of a vapor. He plucks at memory and finds only fading shards. An early autumn chill prickles his neck as he steps toward the mansion.

After he'd reported Charmaine's disappearance, the police searched their house and because Sam claimed he'd gone inside the Trencher mansion to search for his wife, they'd searched that too. They knew the old man had gone inside with him and they'd scared away a squatter, some kid. Sam said it hadn't been his wife, and they believed him.

The window that had been his way in when he'd looked for Charmaine the day she disappeared, is locked. He uses his elbow to break the glass, not hearing its shattering sound against the evening quiet. He has to do this again, compelled to get into this house, doomed to repeat this experience over and over just to make sure she isn't waiting inside for him to find her. To take her home. To make another baby. To give him another chance.

Knocking away the remaining shards of the pane, Sam barely feels the sting of sliced skin as his hand rakes across a tooth of glass. Blood gushes warm, but he ignores it, reaching in to unlock the window, sliding it up. He hesitates, almost overwhelmed by what he knows is futility, but then he sighs and hoists himself up, puts a foot onto the sill, then heaves his torso through the opening, dragging his other leg behind. He falls inside, landing hard on his knees and hands. The scream, he thinks, is coming from deep inside his own chest, syncopating with the drumming in his ears. Pain shoots through his bloody injured palm, up his arm. He curls head to knees, cradling his hand, and in the new silence, he understands it isn't he who screamed.

He struggles to stand, the gloomy house spinning around him. He bellows, "Hey, who's here?"

The grim absolute silence of the house seeps into him, the smell of moldy decay. He pivots around toward the window, a muddy green square behind him, dusk coming on. And beyond the window he hears shouts and voices. And then as if suddenly compelled, the feeling of urgency sinking into his crotch, he leaps into the hall, into the kitchen, and throws open the bolt on the back door and heads out, circling the old mansion into the front.

Glimpsing his own weedy yard, he hardly recognizes it, distorted by shadows, a foreign landscape. Someone hollers, a dog barks, a mumble of voices, and as he swings around, figures move out onto the sidewalk, huddled together, and then in the distance, a siren sounds. Sam strides toward the crowd. A woman in some kind of a caftan turns toward him as he approaches and behind her, he spies someone sitting on the curb, the old man, Gus, his dog yapping.

"What happened?" Sam says. "Is he hurt?"

"No," answers the woman. She grasps his arm tight. "He found a – body – creek."

"What do you mean?" he asks, thinking dog, coyote, maybe a horse? There's a horse trail along the creek.

Streetlights flick on and he can see the woman's frightened face. He recognizes her as the owner of the bungalows. Her fingernails dig through his shirt.

Connections

by Sally-Anne Macomber

To: Milton Flaxmill, Red Cow Publishing
From: Trudy Polaris
Date: September 20, 2014 1:07 p.m.
Re: Do you know any fashion designers?

Dearest Milton,

We had some strange visitors yesterday.

At first I thought they were spies.

It was about 11.33am and I heard a knock on the door of our Tyrolean hideaway. I thought it might be one of the goats playing a practical joke, knocking on the door, and then I thought, no, wait a minute, if it was one of the goats I would have heard hooves on the stairs and the bell around its neck, ringing with each step.

"I think there's someone at the door," I said to my husband.

He looked up from the crossword in the *Kitzbuheler Anzeiger* and said, "So open the fucking door!" (Such a kidder, my husband.)

I opened the door and there on the doorstep stood a tall, thin man with a clipped moustache and wearing a blue and yellow t-shirt.

This is not such a strange thing, though, finding a tall, thin man with a clipped moustache and wearing a blue and yellow t-shirt standing on your doorstep. This happens a lot here in the Tyrol, usually tourists losing their way and wanting to know directions to the nearest Autobahn or skiers who took a wrong turn back in March still trying to locate the nearest piste or locals wanting to see for themselves the woman who almost bankrupted the local dairy industry with her wheeling and dealing in Bulgarian feta.

(Grooooaaan! Yes, the gossip still continues. Tyrolean dairy farmers have a loooong and unforgiving memory.)

The strange thing is, he started talking to me in English. Like he expected me to know English. "I am looking for the nearest Autobahn," he said, with not a trace of a Swedish accent. "We are lost."

He held a map in his hand and being the super-friendly person I am – I was, after all, voted *Person Most Likely to Give You Helpful Advice When You Are Lost on a Fishing Trip* at high school – I pointed out to him where we are on the map and where the nearest Autobahn is. He thanked me, still no trace of a Swedish accent, and then walked back to his car.

"I think they're spies," I said to my husband, as I sat in the window and watched the car (it had Swedish plates) still parked on the side of the goat track. The man was talking to his companion – well, I assume they were companions, unless they were both looking for the nearest Autobahn and had somehow, through extreme luck, met each other and discovered they were both lost in the very same way.

Soon I was slithering along the ground in my goat-milking uniform (industrial-strength leather apron and matching vinylette overalls), as these are the only real outdoor clothes I own, so I could spy on them. I wedged a stale slice of feta under one of the back wheels of the car with the Swedish plates – they still hadn't caught sight of me! And luckily for me, I have been inventing lightweight but durable building bricks out of the old Bulgarian feta we have just laying around the front yard – and with the impromptu tin cans attached with string I had made on a whim just that very morning (you forget I'm a scientist, Milton, my mind must be occupied with *something* while I wait to hear from you!), I pressed one against the back passenger door and listened with the other.

I couldn't make out much of their conversation, but the two words I did manage to hear were 'Prize' and 'Oslo'. So I can only assume I am being awarded the Nobel Prize!

I did not hear the words 'Literature' or 'Physics' but I am sure the prize will be awarded to me for one of them. When I find out, you will be the first (after my husband) to know.

After the tall, thin man with the clipped moustache and wearing the blue and yellow t-shirt stopped talking to his companion, he started the car's ignition and drove off in a cloud of dust (even I was surprised by how dusty the cloud was!) and I was left by the side of the road holding the can.

This will be great for publicity for the book. The latest bestseller from Red Cow Publishing, written by a Nobel Prize winner!

So now I am wondering if Red Cow Publishing has any productive connections with Scandinavian fashion designers. I am thinking a dress made of silvery-yellowish white, to represent nuclear fission, would be best, though I realise this is an unusual colour and perhaps not every fashion designer can work with such a distinctive shade.

Have you been to one of these events before, Milton? The Queen of Sweden attends and it is usually held on December 10th, so there is still some time (though not a lot) to have the dress designed and ready for my appearance in Oslo. (I read this on Wikipedia, about the dates and the venue.) And I'm sure most fashion designers would love to design the gown of the next winner of the Nobel Prize for Literature and / or Physics.

Is there some protocol for who I should thank at the publishing house? I know I have a tendency to rush things in social situations but you probably have a list of thankees your authors should thank on important occasions like this.

As always, looking forward to your reply,

Trudy Polaris.

To: Leonard Strauss Jr., Red Cow Publishing
From: Trudy Polaris
Date: September 20, 2014 3:52 p.m.
Re: Scandinavia

Dear Herr Strauss Jr.,

Even though I have not heard from you, I *do* have some big news! I can't say yet just exactly what it is, as I wish to avoid a Tyrolean media stoush.

(The locals here are so disapproving of attention-seeking behaviour and while your sister seems like a sweet old Frau – I mean, when she's not clearly avoiding me. There are, after all, only so many Tyrolean beech trees she can hide behind! – I can't guarantee that if I tell you and you tell her, she won't rush off and tell the science columnist at the *Kitzbuheler Anzeiger* and then *everyone* will know.)

But what I can tell you is it involves a glamorous dress, foreign dignitaries, the social whirl of Scandinavian academia and a big gold gong.

More soon,

Frau Trudi von Polarissen

To: Boy Polaris
From: Trudy Polaris
Date: September 20, 2014 8:27 p.m.
Re: your internship at Red Cow Publishing

If Leonard Strauss Jr. hasn't noticed you by now and given you your own desk and maybe even your own locker, it's probably because you're not wheeling down the corridors of Red Cow Publishing fast enough, making yourself visible.

And how can he give you a contract to sign if he's never clapped eyes on you?!

Put yellow highlights in your blue hair and double your whey powder protein shakes to build up your biceps so you'll roll down the corridors of Red Cow Publishing in your wheelchair quicker.

Otherwise, my only other advice is, suck it up princess!

Your loving mother

One Way or Another

by Mandy Nicol

Charlie and I went to Angela's wedding yesterday. Angela looked beautiful, in a sheathed mermaid type of way. She confided she had stacked on the kilos this past fortnight while fretting over whether she's doing the right thing, whether she really wants to settle down and live the rest of her life with one person.

It might have been that last comment or it might have been too much champagne but later, after the reception, something made me say yes to Charlie.

And so I had to tell Mum.

Mum is sitting opposite me at the dining table, glaring at the chocolate éclair I've placed in front of her. Seph sits on her knee, entranced, trying to inhale the éclair with her tiny busy nostrils.

I sip my coffee then say, "It's really not that bad."

Mum doesn't answer. Instead she reaches out to the plate, swipes a dollop of cream onto her fingers and offers it to Seph. The little pink tongue licks with rabid delicacy.

I want to throw my coffee at both of them.

"It's only three weeks, Mum. I haven't had a proper holiday since we all went to Wilsons Prom when Dad was still alive." God, that's twenty years ago.

Peregrine ambles over, sits down beside my chair and rests his head on my lap. I fondle his ears. I'd like to give him some of my vanilla slice but he's on a diet.

"I really don't understand what you're so upset about," I say.

Mum takes a deep, exaggerated, *it should be painfully obvious* breath and the dam breaks.

"I can't be trapped here all by myself for three weeks, Nadia. It's bad enough being here alone when you waltz off with Charlie for a weekend, and now you want to go away for three weeks? Anything could go wrong in three weeks. There could be a fire, or a power black-out and the generator won't work, I could fall over and hurt my hip again, or break a leg, an arm. My neck. There's the dogs to look after, and the chooks. What if there's a fire? What if the phone lines are down and I can't call for help? And what about bread? I'm not freezing bread, it's unnatural, and I can't very well make it ..."

I glance at the breadmaker on the kitchen bench, shoved in a corner under a stack of recipe books and appliance manuals. I look back at Mum and she won't meet my eyes so I look at the breadmaker again, for a little longer, and watch her out of the corner of my eye. She lifts her gaze straight back to my face.

"... Well what about milk?" she continues. "You won't catch me drinking that long-life rubbish." She contorts her lips as if her head is in a bucket of rotten yoghurt. "No, three weeks is too long Nadia, it won't work. You can't go."

She picks up her éclair with her Seph-cleaned fingers.

I don't stop her.

I wait until she finishes eating, then I say, "I wasn't expecting you to stay here by yourself Mum. We're talking about December and Anthony said he'd be home from New York well before Christmas. If he isn't here you could go and stay with Celeste in Melbourne. Or Celeste and the kids could come and stay here. Or we could ask the neighbours to keep an eye on you and do some shopping for you. We'll work something out."

She stares at me.

383

I stare back.
And I say, "One way or another, I'm going."

Dr. Stanley
Has a Date

by Margaret Bingel

Nora's foot taps on the ground as she sits on the park bench. Even though there is no chill of autumn yet, she pulls on the sleeve of her blouse, fingers tracing the seam. I could leave now, she tells herself. I can just get up, and go, and pretend this didn't happen and I can go back home. A stranger's laugh tears her from her thoughts, and she whips her head over her shoulder nervously.

When her son told her to go out and find herself a man, what Nora couldn't tell him was that she already had man problems; Dr. Stanley had been courting her for weeks. Flowers every Saturday, and a weekly phone call every Wednesday, as well the occasional coffee date, leaves no question in Nora's mind about Dr. Stanley's ("Please, call me Rob," he told her back in June) intentions. But all the attention made Nora very suspicious about the universe's sudden interest in giving her a husband. Having never married, with only a son to love, Nora doesn't think she has the backbone to take another man's hand. Am I too old for a romance? Nora asks.

Dr. Rob Stanley approaches the park bench behind her, carrying two sacked lunches and a tray holding two coffees. He watches the bun perched low on her head, her hair a soft brown, like a mouse. If there are grays in her lovely hair, he thinks, it'll only suit to match her eyes. He sits down next to her, and she turns to face him. The sun on

Nora's face makes it shine like a golden medallion, and Rob has to catch his breath. She is so beautiful, he thinks, while he offers her a coffee.

Nora takes one of the lunch sacks instead and pulls out a turkey sandwich. Spying an apple and a small bag of chips, she looks up and smiles.

"Thank you for lunch, Rob. You even got me a green apple. How did you know I like green apples?"

"Well Nora, they're tart and sweet, just like you. And since birds of a feather ..." Rob's voice trails off, and his eyes squint in the sun. "Nora, does Ned have a dog?"

Now it's Nora's turn to hold her breath. She doesn't like him asking so many questions about her son. It makes her feel like she's holding secrets, and she has always shared everything with Ned.

"Yes. Nadia. Why do you ask?"

Rob notes the trepidation in her voice and her furrowed brow.

"He offered me a dog treat during one of our Wednesday sessions. I just wanted to make sure that he wasn't eating them himself. It was liver and cheese flavored."

Rob laughs, and Nora chuckles along with him. She thinks he looks handsome when he lets himself actually smile, and not just smirk at her. She reaches her hand over and grabs his, looking deep into his eyes.

From a distance, Ned watches his mother kiss his physical therapist. He knows Dr. Stanley saw him, walking along the path by the pond, and he'll have a little talk with him real soon.

Nadia nudges Ned's leg, and tightening his hold on her lead again, he walks away from the blossoming couple, a small grin creeping across his face.

Big As Life

by Darryl Price

Hey. It's me. And I suppose by default it's you. Have I said that before? I've been feeling flat again lately. Like a piece of paper. Not part of any stack. We've talked about this before. I've been having a few thoughts going around like loosely rolling marbles racing past each other in my head lately. So I thought I'd run them by you. See if they're worth listening to.

Tell me, Doc, do we get to see the ones we loved again – the way they were when we loved them?

Will I feel anything when I'm gone?

Will I know myself?

I'm not sure where this line of questioning came from, it just came from somewhere, and it won't leave me alone, so I'm looking for an answer. Maybe that will help it find the front door, so to speak.

Hey, Doc, wait, did I tell you I met someone? At a bake sale of all places actually. It's an interesting story. At first all I heard was her voice, yeah I know not a good sign, but it attracted me, that sound. Turns out she was selling homemade cupcakes to raise money for something or other. They had pink icing on them, Doc, and it just turned something over inside me – that and her voice, which, if I may, sounded like a beautiful wild bird making happy noises in the highest branches of an extraordinarily beautiful blue sky kind of day. To me.

That about sums it up as far as the feelings go.

We started talking and she didn't run away and neither did I. We actually stayed in eye contact with each other in that moment in that room on purpose. It threw me for a loop, Doc. I thought I was pretty much all done with that sort of flirty thing, but you know what, Doc? It felt good. Natural. I liked her presence. It didn't scare me. Well, not right away.

Well, don't get me wrong – I hightailed it out of there pretty doggone quickly after that. I didn't want to ruin things right off the bat. But now get this, Doc, she'd written her phone number on the inside of the cake box flap. When I got home I decided to have a cupcake with a big old glass of milk and guess what, that's when I noticed it. Big as life. Hand-written. Like a beautiful ribbon.

I don't know. Maybe she writes that on every box top – to try to drum up business – but there was a smiling face next to it! And it said, "hope to see you again real soon."

Now that I think about it, it does seem a bit ambiguous.

Don't matter. I already called her up. We're going to go out to dinner some time. I didn't want to sound too anxious. I told her it would be likely pretty soon. Guess I can be just as ambiguous. Then all those questions started bothering me.

And so here we are. You and me. Like always. Together again. At least on paper. We are paper warriors of the heart, or is it worriers?

Are we friends, Doc? No, don't answer that – I don't want to know. Just help me if you can.

Stuck between a cupcake lady and a memory I can't ever forget.

Take a Leap

by Teresa Burns Gunther

It's Wednesday night. The days are shorting out to fall. The lights downtown are visible in my "view slice" through the houses across the street. My tea has gone cold in my surfing shark mug – a gift from my cousin, Susie. She followed Steve, Kevin's cousin, to LA and landed her dream job – a part in a daytime soap.

Susie's life is a minefield but she has a cellular abundance of hope. I have always stopped to analyze what's practical, doing what I want but making sure it makes sense. We both land on our feet but hers are more likely to end up in daisies.

I watch the last of the neighbors going in, collapsing strollers, dropping running shoes into front porch baskets, putting gardening tools away; the last car is jockeying for legal purchase before tomorrow's 6:00 a.m. street sweeping. So many lights and houses, all the lives that surround, but are so separate from mine. It used to make me lonely. But now I have Kevin. *And you,* I tell Stella and rub her with my foot, she moans and wags her tail.

It's hard to believe 2014 is 73.15% over.

Maybe it's the shark's teeth that remind me of another fall, when boys and possibilities for love seemed innumerable. I was 15, a junior in high school. My father dropped me off that day in his sports car, loud with rock music. His car attracted as many boys as my long legs in a short skirt. "You're a star," my father crowed as he sped off, the actor enjoying playing the rare role of father that morning.

Joey Markham was waiting in his leather jacket, leaning against the corner of the art building. His eyes were all over me. His curiosity was thrilling. As I drew closer I slowed down, setting one foot directly before the other. I looked right into his eyes, telling myself that I wasn't afraid of anyone, a mantra I repeated all the time.

He called me beautiful and I said *yes*.

He fell in step, checking me out from beneath his lank hair. "Yes, what?"

"You can take me out on Friday." I was glad for the bright sun that made him squint hoping he wouldn't see my heart rattling in my throat. He grinned and told me I was *something*.

He was a senior so I knew he'd expect more grown up activity than the boys I'd dated freshman year. On Friday, we went out for pizza and a movie. In the empty back of the theater, third row from the last, I let him touch my breasts, slide his hands under my panties, let him put my hand on his penis that was stiff and pointing at the screen. The sting of this pleasure fascinated me. *Next time*, I told him, when he asked for more. He took me to a party the following Friday night, and after serving me beer from a keg, after introducing me to his friends who were older, smoked pot and were more interesting than anyone from school, he pulled me into a back bedroom where posters of race cars and naked girls adorned the walls. This excited me, too. And I lay back, watching as he undressed me, ringing with titillation and desire and when he entered me I knew. On Monday he would tell all the kids at school.

Kevin thinks I'm something, too. He's what Gail, my officemate, calls a "mensch." He makes me believe in love and puts an X in most of the boxes on my man wish list. I'm smarter now. Stella is crazy about him and he likes her.

He's smart and kind, successful, he plays guitar and thinks I'm funny – funny good, not strange. Best of all he's tall! I believe things are *looking up! Ha Ha.*

My resolution for September is trust, take a *leap of faith.* Or as Susie would say: *take a walk on the spiritual side.* I'm not after any kooky-guru-lala-ram-das-crystals-incense trip, but something beyond the numbered, efficient order of my days. I've always been about fact and logic, my life ordered in black and white. I like a sharp pencil and a crisp lined pad where things add up. But as hard as I've tried to extend this calculus to my real life, it hasn't made the leap. Lives are hard to engineer. I'm trying to practice losing control, not an easy move for me. I want to know what it feels like to believe in the impossible, I want to stop making sense.

My phone buzzes with a text from Kevin, *b there in 2.* "Hmm ..." I sound the humming he sets off in me. It's scary to believe, with no other proof than how I feel inside. Scary because hope usually travels with its sad cousin: disappointment. I close my eyes, take a deep breath, I'm learning how to relax.

I hear his car whip around the corner and into my driveway. I watch him unfold from his car, all 6 foot 3 of him. Stella dashes down the steps, nearly knocking him over with her joy. He holds a pizza box high in the air and smiles up at me. He calls me *beautiful.* I call him *pizza man* and remind myself to just keep practicing letting things unfold without a plan.

Thursday

25

September
2014

Morgana Malone and the Mystery of the Secret Gift

by Matt Potter

"La Petite Fleurette Select Patisserie and Gifterie," I say into the receiver.

"Is that the Royal Rose Cake Shop?" a voice, sing-song wavery and uncertain, says on the end of the line. "I'm looking for the Royal Rose Cake Shop."

"Yes, we *were* the Royal Rose Cake Shop," I say, "we just have a new name. But it's the same service and we make the same cakes and we're at the same address."

"You haven't changed your range of cakes?" the older woman asks.

This happens two, three, seventeen times a day with Mum's old customers. And I curse Jane – my sister, who's still the new Susan (because I'm still the old Susan) – for changing the name of Mum's cake shop, hoping it will make the business more saleable when Mum decides to retire. Or when my sister decides it's time for Mum to retire.

I breathe in, and smell the sugary-sweetness of years of vanilla sponges and fruit cakes and cream puffs and lemon meringue pies and pavlovas.

"Oh good," the older woman sighs. "I always order a triple Victoria sponge for family birthdays and I need to order two. The family's getting so large now one triple Victoria sponge isn't enough."

I scribble *2 x triple Victoria sponges* and her name (which means nothing to me when she tells me but the way she says it, she obviously thinks it should) and her 'phone number on the order form – a newly-printed pad of them with the newly-minted *La Petite Fleurette Select Patisserie and Gifterie* at the top in pink curly-curly cursive – then tear if off the pad and place it in the *Orders – In* tray beside the 'phone. I want to ask her if, by *the family's getting so large*, she means in number or in size, but it's not always a good thing to ask a customer just how fat her family is, in case their weight *is* tipping the Richter scale.

"What's a *Gifterie?*" she says.

My face flushes and my armpits are suddenly sticky. I hate stammering the official "the *Gifterie* is an exclusive gift shop offering a select range of giftware." When instead I want to say *Hey, it's stocked with the stuff Jane / Susan ordered for her* NOT *Made in China shop that was accidentally made in China after all.*

So instead I say, "Thanks for your order," a little too loudly, and hang the 'phone back in its cradle.

And that's when I hear a voice, harsh enough to scratch glass on a rainy day. "I'm looking for Morgana Malone."

I step through the doorway, from the backroom into the main part of the shop, and sidle up to Mum behind the counter.

Mum's powdery face lights up, like she's forgotten I'm here. "There's someone to see you, love."

Mum's grey eyes are revealing … well, not a lot, really. What they *are* saying, is that she knows nothing of this woman. Who I see has long dyed-brown hair pulled off a face with no makeup, pulled back under a small blue headscarf. And is wearing a white blouse. And a longish skirt with small blue flowers spread across it. I don't know what she's wearing on her feet because I can't see over the counter but given the top half of her outfit, probably flat white sandals.

"Morgana!" she says.

And then I piece the voice and the blue eyes and the growing-back eyebrows together and realise that underneath the new hair and the 50's housewifey fashion statement it's –

"Zebadie," I say, clasping my hands behind my back.

I am *so* glad I'm standing behind the counter. Otherwise she'd rush over and throw her arms around me, pressing me against those massive … my God, no wonder I didn't recognise her! Her three and a half boob jobs are gone too! She's been gutted, filleted, her breastwork lipo-suctioned out of her and replaced by something new. Or maybe something old.

Standing against the spring sun shining through the shop window, she's almost … concave.

And then I remember the last time we met – the day of the wedding rehearsal when I was supposed to be her bridesmaid – she called me a *cunt*.

And I can't help it, it's so obvious I have to say something. And hand at my cleavage, "What happened to your –"

"Oh those old things," and Zebadie waves her hand in the air, like they're yesterday's news. "I had them refashioned after I got the hostess job on the Plymouth Brethren Home Shopping Network."

I'm about to say, *So once again you've used your breasts for a career move,* but instead, Mum draws herself up to her full height, which is just above my shoulder, and says, "So you're the one who called my daughter a *cunt*?!"

Zebadie smiles. "Look, I'm not here to talk about how cunty or how *uncunty* your daughter was," she says, "trying to steal my fiancé from on top of me the day before my wedding. But what I *am* here to tell you is that" – and here she pierces me with those blue blue eyes and I wonder, just *what* is she going to say now, when she says – "Grigor forgives you."

394

I stand there.

Just looking.

I don't know what to say.

It's not that I'm waiting for someone else to butt in – which is normal when my family is around – but my lips are dry and my armpits are sticky and my mouth opens and nothing comes out.

"He wants you to know that. And he's dropping all the charges against you, too," Zebadie adds.

"What *charges?*" Mum asks, eyes fierce and her chin indignant.

"Breach of promise and criminal intent to bankrupt," Zebadie recites, like she's reading off a charge sheet.

Mum leans over the counter, which is not too difficult because she's 73 and stooping comes naturally. "My daughter was over *Grigor*" – and she spits his name out like it's a rancid olive – "years ago. She's seeing a lovely young man now who comes from a very good family and he has wonderful prospects." And she pats the counter, like she's scored a point on a quiz show.

For the second time in as many minutes my face flushes and now the crooks of my elbows are sticky. My 73-year old mother is defending my choice of boyfriend. Soon she'll be saying the 24-year age difference between Seth and me is something to be cherished.

"Grigor is turning over a new leaf," Zebadie says, "and he's moving on. He'll be on parole in six months."

"*Parole?!*" says Mum.

Zebadie tilts her head and for a second I expect something to fall out of her ear. "The one thing the Plymouth Brethren Home Shopping Network has taught me," she says, "is Christian forgiveness. And pretty soon Grigor will have his Porsche out of the pawn garage and things will be good again."

Ah, so that's it, I think, as Zebadie turns around and heads for the door. She still wants the Porsche.

"Let's hope that while you're waiting for the Porsche," Mum calls after her, "the Plymouth Brethren Home Shopping Network teaches you some manners."

Zebadie smoothes her blouse over her breasts. And her eyes pop, like she's still surprised at their lack of contours. "I'm just the Messenger," she says. "But this is from me." And she points at my hair, the top half grey and brown and the bottom half faded orange. "Get your hair dyed again Morgana because you look like a bad drag queen! Ya cunt!"

We're having a cup of tea. As in, "Let's have a nice cup of tea," so it's Mum and me sitting at the table in the backroom. Mum sips tea from a fine china cup saying "Nothing like a nice cuppa" and "Good riddance to bad rubbish" and "I don't think the Plymouth Brethren Home Shopping Network knows what it's in for" and "She doesn't have the right-shaped head for a scarf, does she?" and "She does have a point about your hair colour though."

And I just sip tea.

Tingaling. The front doorbell rings again.

Turning her wrist to look at her watch, "That'll be the postie," Mum says, and putting her cup down on its saucer, she's through the door and saying "Thanks, postie," to the postman and back again, sipping from her fine china cup and a pile of mail sitting on the table between us.

And there's a large yellow envelope on top. *Morgana Malone, La Petite Fleurette Select Patisserie and Gifterie*, it says, in Seth's medical student scrawl.

Mum opens a drawer under the table and pulls out a letter opener, handing it to me. I slice the envelope open across one end and pull out a parchment.

Morgana Malone is written across the top.

And underneath that, *to be used for 12 Singing Lessons.*

Then *Marco Garibaldi School of Singing*, under that.

I shake my head. I don't know why –

"Maybe it's a present," Mum says, looking at me over the rim of her tea cup.

I stretch under the table for my handbag and dragging it out, reach in and pull out my mobile. And there on the screen, as I breathe in the smell of wheat flour and Demerara sugar and royal icing and wine-soaked sultanas and mock cream, is the tell-tale symbol of an unopened envelope.

It's from Seth.

I click the message open.

Can we meet tonight? We need to talk.

Letter to Q

by Gary Percesepe

Q,

I received your sweet email today and it made me cry. I have not been able to cry for a while (or write) so it was good to finally feel something.

But look – we are not very good with boundaries, you & I, are we?

I mean, we both know that I suck at keeping to established, agreed to boundaries, ground rules, whatever the hell we call them – but YOU – you suck too, it turns out.

I want to be honest here – I loved getting your three (count 'em, 3) emails since we agreed to have no contact. I love hearing from you, and knowing that you are thinking about me even as I am thinking about you. And this morning, in particular, as that magical hour approached, 9am–9:30, around the time we are always checking in with each other, getting caught up, encouraging one another in the new day, with the work – I felt a tug, a pull in your direction, and I KNEW you were thinking about me, and it was almost as if I was able to pull a response from you to my call, in my peculiar Aquarian Way, because – bam! – seconds later, there was your email today, at 9:37 am.

I love getting your emails, in spite of the fact that I explicitly asked you NOT to contact me, because it means that you are thinking about me, sure – but I also worry about it, because it demonstrates that we cannot keep boundaries, and this is not good news for you, or for me, or for your marriage. And when I am a healthy, fully functioning, generous, caring person (which I am NOT, these days – as I expected, I am having a VERY difficult time this week) – then I really really WANT for you to be safe and well and happy in your marriage, and not thinking about me.

Here is the problem: I somehow fell in love with you, and it was wrong and it is impossible and you are MARRIED with two young children, but it is too late – against my will I fell in love with you, and I had maybe two days of happiness but everything since has been torment and misery and terrible suffering and I cannot do this anymore. I just can't. I am in a very dark place, it is the worst time in my life that I can remember, and everything is falling apart around me. I cannot even count how many things in my life have gone terribly wrong, and I feel that I am making poor decisions, that I have some 'divorce brain syndrome' that just makes my mind lock up with grief and I say and do things that are inappropriate, and here is why I requested no contact with you this month: I DO NOT TRUST MYSELF AROUND YOU, AND I DO NOT WANT YOU OR ANYONE TO SEE ME THIS WAY!

I do wish I could get it back to the "friendship" stage – with laughter, much laughter – like we used to have, it was so fun, but I do not seem capable of that right now, and maybe never.

Love is a terrible, awful thing – it tears you to pieces.

I do not want to be torn to pieces. My life is a shambles and I cannot work. I cannot bear to think of the memoir – I want to delete it and throw my computer in the ocean. My novel is an unfinished, abandoned failure. I am half afraid of going to Amalfi because I have fantasies of flinging myself off the high cliff into the sea, my pockets stuffed with poems that will never be read – poems for you.

My life is like a scene out of *Moonstruck*. In one sense, it is really FUNNY. But who is laughing?

And there can be no happy ending for us. The boy does not get the girl.

I picture you reading this and shaking your pretty head and saying no no, and trying to argue me out of all this, telling me that the novel will be fine and the memoir will be fine, and JUST STOP THAT, but Q, you are so naïve – you don't really know anything about love, do you? Don't you think I WANT to stop feeling like this? Of course I do. Just tell me this: How does a person fall out of love? Just explain to me what the hell I am supposed to do with you, now?

Go on to another woman? Sure. Like Mary? We see how well that worked out.

Mary was the person who helped me the most when I was so fucked up that August day in Montauk, she told me that to keep the friendship with you I had to pour all my love and tenderness into the friendship and sublimate the rest. She was gentle with me, and she seemed to understand that I loved you first of all, and she accepted that. She was the ONE person on earth who SHOULD have been able to handle what she saw in the room that night.

And she couldn't handle it. She must have sensed something, she picked it up, it was electric. I have been trying to tell you this for months now. People feel it when they see us together, it cannot be hidden.

I think, in retrospect that Mary was REALLY hurt that night. I hurt her. I have to live with that truth. Just by showing up with you, just her seeing the two of us together, that hurt her. She responded inappropriately, of course, but she was upset and flustered and stuff just came out, and then later, when she had a day to think about it, and process what had happened, she just got her tail up and fucking stung me good, and warned me off her. And I have no desire now to ever contact her again.

What next? Go on to what you call "my androgynous poet?"

I laughed when I got that addled email from you about my "poet friend" who had contacted you and asked to be friends. And you asked me if I had suggested that she FB friend you. HA! As if.

Once I figured out you were talking about Rooney I was like – oh. So Q knows I am interested in this woman. But what does she know? Does she know I have not yet made a move to have her? Does she know I hesitate because of her, because of Q? Does she know that I hesitate because I want to prove to her, as I subconsciously and then consciously tried to prove with Mary, that, given a choice, I would choose her – choose Q, every time? And that it would be unfair to ANY woman, to be in relationship with them, because I would be unfaithful every day and every night of my life, with Q?

If I tried to be with Rooney, or with Mary, or with a thousand other women I might like or admire, Q – listen to me now – *I would still be searching for you in every woman.*

I would always seek to duplicate the connection that we had, that we have.

This is why I told you that with you something came to an end in me. I do not want to love again.

More importantly, I CANNOT ever love again. It is broken in me, that muscle. I simply cannot do it. This is it – I am going out on this one. There is a finality about it, a doomed sense of impossible love. No more. I have already told you this.

You tell me that this is untrue, you tell me that you really WANT me to move on to another woman, but I do not believe you. And even if I did, I cannot. It would not be fair to her.

I cannot be with another woman. At 9:30 in the morning I would feel what you feel – the urge to check in, to connect.

The only thing I can think to do is to disappear from the face of the earth.

To be in a place where you do not know where I am, or what I am doing. And where I have no dealing with you whatsoever. I don't want to see your emails, your FB messages, your tweets – they all cause me to suffer unbearably. I do not want to think about you or what you are doing or thinking or feeling. It tears me to pieces. I do not wish to be torn to pieces any longer.

Yesterday

Deep in the night I awakened with my new form of therapy, self-administered: I simply recite to myself out loud variations of this sentence:

I know Q loves me but she is married with two children

I know Q cares deeply about me but we cannot be together

I know Q adores me but she is a married woman, she has two young children

I know Q loves me, that is not in doubt – but we cannot be together so let it go, willya?

Q gives you all that she can give, it's just not our time, she told you that, so forget it.

Q, repeat, is married and has two young children at home, are you kidding?

Dude, it's not us, you said so yourself, Q cannot love you do not ask her to, let go let go

Today again

Ok – I was going to keep this letter going all month but I lost heart.

I can't go on, I'll go on.

g

The Clone Whores

by Nathaniel Tower

Samford has never been a one-woman kind of man, but he is longing for Sarah, the cloned girl with the tight ass he hasn't seen for a couple months. He hasn't thought of her much lately, mostly because he's been running from the government – or so he thinks.

Samford's burning desire has led him to a clone whorehouse called The Clone Whores. He wonders if this is some reference to a *Star Wars* movie he never saw. Samford fucking hates *Star Wars*. In fact, he thinks all science fiction is pure shit, especially the really dumb stories that have so little to do with science.

He doesn't know how he found The Clone Whores. Perhaps instinct has guided him here. He both hopes and doesn't hope he will find Sarah inside.

He knocks three times, as he was told to do. A woman in at least her late nineties opens the door and creaks, "You're welcome," out of her dying mouth.

"Are you a clone?" Samford asks, even though he knows it is too forward. He can't imagine the clones are really this old, but one never can tell. Truthfully, he doesn't understand how they clone the women at all. He learned a few weeks ago that men are cloned through sex. Watching himself birthed out of that blonde woman in the Motel 6 was quite the mindfuck. He also now knows that the man in bed with him that one morning was the by-product of his own reckless fornication with the brochure lady. He can't help but wonder how many Samfords are around.

"Yes," the woman whispers back.

Samford is not attracted to her at all, but her single croaked syllable elicits instant erection. He is a horny man, and he will happily fuck any clone that will have him. It's not just about the orgasm though. It's also the experimentation, and the knowing that another Samford won't surreptitiously emerge from the clone's vagina.

"Come in," the old woman beckons him. "There are many women waiting for you to mate with them."

"Mate?" Samford doesn't like the sound of this.

"Yes, mate."

"But I thought this was a house of clone whores."

The woman squeals with childish laughter, suddenly seeming half her age. "You have been misled, my boy." Her bony hand is suddenly resting on his penis, albeit through his pants and underwear. Even through the two layers, he feels about to come all over the skeletal hand.

"Do tell," Samford moans.

"The Cloning Whores are here to clone you more." She rubs her hand up and down with little passion, like she is dusting an old chest of drawers. It is the sexiest thing Samford has ever felt. His eyes start to roll back. The woman smiles. "My maker was a ferocious porn queen in the 70s."

Samford doesn't think he can take it anymore, but this isn't how he wants to go. He lifts her hand away from his crotch.

"You are a special woman," he says, "but I shouldn't be here."

"That's where you're wrong," she says. "You shouldn't be anywhere else. Come fuck my girls. They have been waiting for a man like you."

Samford doesn't want to go inside but does anyway. He is led into a giant room with a crystal chandelier as big as a hot air balloon. Only after admiring the chandelier and its sparkling beauty does he hear the moaning. He looks around the room and sees dozens of whores pounding away on top of men. They are all fornicating on chaise lounges, which Samford has always wanted. A quick scan tells him that none of the women are Sarah. Where the hell has she gone, and why does he suddenly want her so bad?

"You may take the open couch," the old woman says with a point.

As Samford walks toward the couch, he tries to divert his eyes. Although he is an avid lover of porn, especially the website www.clonedbitches.com, he doesn't want to watch these fuckers. But it's hard to look away when so much raging intercourse is happening right before one's eyes. Before he sits down, he spots a man who looks just like him. Then another. And another. Samford notices that every man in the room is his identical. The whorehouse is filled with Samford doppelgangers. One woman removes herself from a Samford-copy's penis. Within seconds, a new Samford bursts from between her legs. As if the birthing process has not even fazed her, the woman struts her naked body toward Samford's couch, leaving the new Samford squirming on the floor behind her.

"Take off your pants and give me your seed." Her voice is deep and horribly unsexy. Samford wants his penis to retreat deep inside his body, but it grows rapidly and bursts out of his pants, piercing through the thin fabric that hasn't been washed in weeks.

The woman does not engage in foreplay. There is no licking or kissing or petting. She mounts Samford's exposed dick and thrusts exactly seven times before he feels himself burst inside her. She is soon off him, and he leaps off the couch, not bothering to put his penis away before sprinting to the door.

"Come again," the old woman cackles as he heads out into the night. He looks back at her and flips the bird, his now flaccid penis still flopping about. She laughs harder, and he spots a woman who looks just like his lovely Sarah emerge at her side. It can't be, he thinks, but it is the only thought he is allowed to have before he collides with a body in his path. They fall to the ground together. Samford looks at the figure's face and sees the spitting image of his Sarah. He leans in to kiss her, but she doesn't taste like he remembers. He forces his mouth away from her and looks back at the other Sarah by the door. She is gone. Before Samford can protest, he realizes his cock has been inserted into the imposter Sarah, but he can't muster the strength for even a semi-erection.

"I'm all out," he tells her.

She spits in his face. "You humans aren't good for much, are you?"

Samford searches for a comeback as the Sarah pushes him away.

"What's your name?" he asks.

"Sarah," she says. "We are all named Sarah. Just as you are all named Sam."

"But my name is Samford," Samford protests.

The Sarah chuckles. "Keep telling yourself that, my boy."

Samford hears sirens. The police must be there to round up the clones. He slaps Sarah hard across the face and takes off running into the woods, his penis hardening just as he reaches full speed ahead.

Swallowed Whole

by Kimberlee Smith

She's breaking most of the rules. It's early, still dark, as Mum's hands hover over the Ouija Board. She's concentrating so hard to force a conjuring of what she wants to hear, that she's not allowing me to lead her. She's using the board, which was handed down to her by her mum, in the room where she and my bub will lay down their heads tonight. It's an open invitation to other spirits. Some that might not be quite as friendly as I am. Mum hasn't anyone except the bub there while she works the Ouija, and she knows there should be at least three people to manage the incoming spirit.

She doesn't ask me any questions. She's determined to control her own fate through the board, but I'm running interference and she's going to know it. She's been using the Ouija since she was a little girl – hid it from my daddy the whole sixteen years they were married, although I caught her using it now and then – so she has a false sense of security about it. It is not her friend.

Her eyelids are fluttering. She squints, peeks down at the parchment-color, stained board when the planchette slows and stops on *W*. There's supposed to be a person who writes down the message while Mum concentrates and keeps all fingertips on the planchette, but instead she lifts her right hand off and quickly scrawls the letter on a piece of scrap paper, then puts her fingers back on the black, heart-shaped disc.

I'm struggling with her. It feels like we're arm wrestling. Not literally going at it with phantom limbs, but spiritually, psychologically, emotionally. I'm going to win, because being in touch with letters, then words, then messages, is too great a desire I have to let her hopes take over when my energy can overtake her; I am certain of it. It takes nearly an hour for my complete message to get to her.

Waltz, Ma-til-da, home
Don't Tom Waits, make haste. We're all
Dead to Bro-ther Tom

My daughter Etheline, 8-and-a-half months old, claps her hands together and squeals, "Mummy!"

My mum, Maybell, sucks in a deep breath and all the color washes from her face.

"Now I know it's you, Melodie. Why won't you help me, darlin'?"

Mum puts her hands in her lap and weaves her fingers tightly together, like a church steeple. Then she unlaces them, picks up the gin bottle, swirls it around to check how much is left, which is never enough – the bottle is her only constant companion other than Etheline – and Mum fills her glass half-full. Liquid courage, I believe it's called. She reaches for Etheline's bottle of lime cordial, twists off the teat, and pours a splash in her drink.

"All I get is some cryptic, cheeky – what the heck was that message? A haiku? Five-seven-five. Our first communication and you're being *clever*? Tell me something nice, please, Melodie. Lord how we, how I, miss you." She wraps both her hands around her glass and lifts it to her lips, taking three gulps, and lowers it to where it nearly touches the table, but at the last second brings it back up to her lips for another swig.

I think the message I send is thoughtful, sentimental. We share a favorite song, albeit after my passing. *Waltzing*

Matilda. She discovered the Tom Waits rendition when she turned on the stereo in my old Jackaroo she's been driving on her cross-country trip to find my daddy.

Mum forgets to screw the teat back on Etheline's bottle. The bub squints her amber eyes and hisses long and slow. Serpentlike.

Mum twists the top back on the bottle.

"Baby, sometimes you scare the bejesus out of your sweet grandmum. I wish you wouldn't do that. If you have the ability to stop, please, please, do," says Mum as she locks eyes with the bub. Mum's are pleading; Etheline's are slitty, intense. Mum slides the bottle with all the premeditation of a well-conceived chess move toward Etheline, who snatches up the bottle while flickering her dry little tongue in anticipation. Her tongue is slightly forked. I watch her so closely so I am certain the split in her tongue is a very recent transfiguration.

I've paid Brother Tom, my daddy, and Mum's only husband, a visit, unbeknownst to him. Her curiosity bled over to me. I don't want her to see what I have. Brother Tom, founder of the Signs of Holiness Supreme Divinity Evangelical Church, has made himself a new home and a new family.

Brother Tom's aboriginal wife has conceived six babies. Five born, one every year, and one in utero. She's wobbling around off-balance like she swallowed a watermelon or two. Wait. She's pregnant with twins and doesn't know it. One of them is dead and she doesn't know that yet, either.

She has never been to a doctor and Brother Tom apparently prefers it that way. She's wearing a floral housecoat and a tight pair of mauve flats with bows, like the first pair of shoes she's ever worn in her life. A few of their littlies are running around with matted hair, in various states of undress. One is crawling; the fifth can't even crawl yet. It's an infant. The two youngest are naked. Not even wearing nappies. They all look like wombats. Dung-colored, thick, and bristly.

There is something up there in the Kununurra waterfalls that render some women very fertile. Brother Tom doesn't tell anyone, but I can see into his past and know he's brought his wife there over a dozen of times and forced her to swim in the freezing waterfall for the sake of procreation. For a man stuck to his religion, it's curious he would resort to mysticism outside his own to ensure she falls pregnant.

She looks bewildered and lost except for when she's by his side. He is the most rudimentary form of a Svengali. First he took Mum, who was only able to conceive me, then he took Alice – I believe she had a given name that sounds like the name of that band Kajagoogoo, but he renamed her Alice, as in Alice Springs. She is learning English slowly – he is succeeding in wiping out her aboriginal history and creating a new breed that more suits him.

Brother Tom doesn't know he has a granddaughter. Etheline's his first grandchild, and now I know she's not going to be his only.

Mum says *goodbye* (the golden rule of terminating a session with the spirit world), folds the Ouija board in half, places the planchette in a divot in the cardboard box just like it's a puzzle piece, puts the lid on the box, and stashes it away in her suitcase.

There are other pressing matters at hand and she wasn't keen on the message I sent.

I reckon she's going to ignore my advice. She settles the charge at the front desk, paying a spotty young bloke wearing a stiffly starched buttoned-up shirt with *Brolga Inn* stitched over his name. 'Tam,' it reads.

She puts the room key and a crumpled ball of bills on the counter and then smoothes them out with a flat palm.

"Checking out early, ma'am?" asks Tam.

"Apologies, Tam. We have a bit more driving to go before we reach our destination. Lovely spot. Sorry we aren't able to stay another night," says Mum nodding toward the bub, who's asleep with her head nestled in the crook of Mum's neck. So Mum did pay mind to the rule of not sleeping in the same room she uses the Ouija.

"Nice name, Tam. Reminds me of my favorite biscuits, you know, Tim Tams," says Mum, with a wink.

"Name's Tom. They made a mistake in the stitching. It's Tom," he says, shaking his head and looking at the squirrely stitching on his shirt.

"Ah. I see. *Tom.* Now, that's a good name as well. Good, solid name. Tom." Mum clears her throat and her face brightens. I can tell she's having foolish thoughts about Brother Tom. But I suppose there's no stopping her now.

She and the bub hit the road for a while and stop somewhere in the desert.

She realizes about a half-hour into the drive that she has no food left from her reserves and there're no shops around for kilometers as far as she knows. The lodge was only for sleeping, not offering provisions of any sort. She stops in the middle of nowhere and intuits there's a family of rock rats, which she senses are nearby in a crevice of a rock formation, and also picks up on a snake, a desert death adder, in the vicinity. Somehow she implores it to wind its way to the crevice to swallow the rock rats.

It obliges, swallowing three. I have a vision of Brother Tom swallowing his wife's aboriginal tribe whole. Without a single second thought, just pure second nature.

§

Mum has a slight trepidation in catching the snake, but of all the deadly serpents she's handled in her life, she never was bitten by even one. She's sensitive to them. She knows how to handle them.

After a while, the death adder, with a midsection distorted, bulging with the rock rats, slithers back out to bathe in the sun, but Mum grabs it right at its jaw with one hand. With the other, she takes one of her knives and slices it open as simply as if she were opening a brand-new suitcase. *Zip.* She reaches in and pulls out the flattened rock rats and plops them in a plastic bag. She shuffles around, eyes on the ground, picking up switches to use as skewers and then impales them, one rat to a switch. She cooks them over a tiny blue sterno.

The fur chars right off them. Those rock rats meet a similar end to what I believe Brother Tom deserves. If there's a Hell, and this is one time I hope there is, he's going to burn in it but good. For infinity.

Four Ounces, Plain

by Vanessa Weibler Paris

We're eating dinner when the phone rings. *Riiiing.* I look at
Iris expectantly.

"You really want to get that? To interrupt our dinner?"
she asks. "Really, James?"

Riiiing.

"Just this once?" I ask in my quiet voice. I can't even
remember the last time the phone rang.

She sighs. "Fine."

Riiiing.

I push myself up from the table with effort. Tonight's
dinner is poached chicken (four ounces, the size of a deck
of cards, no larger, plain), broccoli (four ounces, steamed,
plain) and iceberg salad (four ounces, chopped, plain).
We're "slimming me down," as Iris says, for her next big art
project. I spent my entire life being called "Slim Jim" and
hating it. Now, Iris calls me nothing but "James," which I
find myself hating even more. She has reduced me by a full
syllable. By half.

Riiiing.

"What's the project about?" I'd asked, once or twice,
but she covered my mouth, smiling, shook her head and
stroked my jawbone with both hands.

"When will it start?" I'd tried a different tack. "Not until
we reach two digits," she'd said. Two digits: 99 pounds. I'm
not sure how close we are now; she blindfolds me for our

nightly weigh-ins, which are followed by sex, blindfold still in place.

Riiiing.

Beside the phone, the flowers in the cheap-glass florist-shop vase are dead. Its card ("Get well soon, Jim! We miss you lots! xoxo, Linda, Barb & Dar"), perched on a plastic stick, is crumpled and stained, crooked, the ink smeared. I haven't been to work in weeks, a month, more. I have no energy. I'm not myself. I spend my days with Iris, dozing and talking. We move from bedroom to living room, as energy allows, and then back again.

Soon, I'll need a doctor's excuse or my work disability payments will stop. I should have sent them a thank-you note, the office ladies I used to lunch with every day. I should have called. "My cousin is a doctor somewhere in Canada," Iris had mumbled when I mentioned it. She was playing with her big box of shish kebab skewers again, wooden and pointy and ordered in bulk. Stacking, layering, arranging. "I'll have him write you an excuse for chronic fatigue syndrome. They can't disprove that."

Riiiing.

"Hello?" I say hoarsely, picking up the phone.

"Jim?" It's Bobby, my lifelong best friend. I haven't seen him in a while. Months. He got married earlier this year and that's what happens, right? When one friend gets married, and the other gets his first real girlfriend, who ends up moving in?

"Hi, Bobby," I say, trying not to sound out of breath. Bobby, Andy, Dougie and Jim: They used to call us the BADJers. Dougie even got us all BADJer t-shirts for Bobby's bachelor party. Dougie, who was diagnosed with testicular cancer the following week. He beat it, or so we thought. Bobby had left me a message a while back to let me know the bad news: it had returned. It was being treated. It was too soon to tell. But it'd be good, real good, if I could get in touch.

I should get in touch, I think. I should call. When I feel better, when I'm not so tired, I should call.

"It's Dougie," Bobby says in a voice that doesn't sound like Bobby at all. I wonder if there's something stuck in his throat, or if it's been so long I don't remember what he really sounds like. "Listen. It's not going to be long. You should come see him. He'd ... he wants to see you. You should come."

I should come.

I clutch at the counter. The vase crashes to the floor.

Eli and Damon

by Joanne Jagoda

Ah … I've got to stretch. I hate writing up these detailed reports.

"Here is your coffee Mr. Dangott."

"Thanks Susan. This Starbucks Cappuccino is the best. I'm going to miss it when I head back to Israel."

"Anything else sir?"

"No thanks Susan. I'll be going downstairs to the interrogation room in a few minutes."

What an incredible view of the San Francisco skyline, but I wish I could share it with my beautiful Dafne. I'd love to show her this city. I hate to deceive her. Even though she may be a brilliant math professor, she thinks I'm an international businessman working in Silicon Valley. I'm ready to get out of this dangerous game, maybe have a couple of kids and become the businessman that I pretend to be.

There's my cell. "I'll be right down."

They're bringing Damon Southeby to the interrogation room on the second floor. I'll be doing the final debriefing, though Homeland Security got most of the details of the kidnap plot from him. He made a deal because he didn't want to spend the rest of his life in an American prison. Agents will be taking him back to Great Britain on the 10pm British Airways flight. He'll be under the scrutiny of

417

Scotland Yard, but his terrorist employers will be hunting him down like he has a bull's eye on his back.

He is sitting quietly, his handcuffs attached to bars on the table with his feet shackled. He's acting like he doesn't have a care in the world, humming to himself with a stupid smile on his face, but he's pale and I see perspiration stains under the armpits of his rather unglamorous prisoner tee shirt.

"Officer, we can be in here by ourselves. I'm not expecting any trouble from him."

I'm going to rattle him a bit and pull my chair up very close. I can smell his sweat. "So Damon. You're looking a bit out of sorts."

"Well you would be too, if you had shit to eat and you had to sleep on a three inch mattress."

"Sorry, this place isn't up to your usual standards. I'm Eli Dangott, agent for the Mossad. I have to tell you I found your plot rather ingenious. I'm tempted to ask you to come to work for us."

Damon stares hard at me. I flip through the binder that has the details of the plot. "I've read what you told the other interrogators. Uh ... let's see ... first you snared Anne through your phony website setting up a blind date who didn't show up. Then you bumped into her at the Fairmont Hotel, meeting her at the bar by accident, as David Lewis. I was in the lobby by the way, observing you. When she finally contacted you a month later, you started your whirlwind romance, including the glorious weekend in the Napa Valley. I trailed you there. You took advantage of her, you asshole."

Damon strains his hands against the manacles, glaring at me. His face reddens in anger. "I recognize you now. I knew I was being followed. You're pretty good at this game, Dangott."

"And I was parked in front of your apartment for weeks. We figured out you had to get close to Anne to kidnap one of the twins to be held for ransom so that the grandfather, George Donaldson, would give up his plans for Project Octopus. Surely you must have known that my country had a vested interest in this anti-missile system for our security."

Damon spits out his words. "They offered me a ton of money. It was always about the money, not allegiance to their cause. I was going to retire after this operation. I had it all planned." He looks away in disgust, as if he can see his dreams of relaxing with a tropical drink under a palm tree evaporate.

"I suppose you never got over your uh, working class roots. We know everything about you down to your expensive cologne and the size of your imported boots."

Damon's dark blue eyes turn hard. *I know I've hit a nerve.*

"We know how your mother struggled to manage five kids and ironed clothes to make money. How your father, a boiler–maker, drank his wages at the pub and knocked around you and your *mum.*"

Damon's knee bobs up and down in an impatient rhythm. He snarls, "Well, so what arsehole. You did your homework."

"You were a brilliant student who got in to top schools on scholarship but never fit with the bluebloods. Then you got in trouble stealing lab equipment and computers and hooked up with the wrong element in jail."

"Has Anne asked for me?"

"Don't flatter yourself Damon. She hates your fucking guts. Let's focus on your operation. So you had your thugs, dressed as students, waiting at the Stanford Shopping Center. You picked up our agent Liat in the Apple store thinking she was Cassie."

Damon shakes his head, "She was a ringer for the girl."

"Yes, and you were rough on her, throwing her in the van, leaving her tied up on the cement floor, no food or water."

"I was ready to cut off her fingers one by one."

"You asshole, we wouldn't have let you touch her. She had transmitters hidden on her body and my team was close by."

"My people forced your Cassie double to call her mother at the mall instructing her to return home immediately and wait to hear from us. I made the ransom demand to Anne a half hour after she got home using a voice synthesizer. We weren't afraid to hurt her daughter to get what we wanted. She played her part well. She was hysterical when she called me saying she didn't know what to do. I had no idea she knew I was complicit."

"She was furious at you Damon. Go on ..."

"When I got to the house, I convinced her not to contact the FBI or police for Cassie's sake. She then called George relaying the ransom demands."

"And George was waiting by the phone with our agents who told him exactly what to say to Anne. He wanted to kill you with his bare hands. He supposedly called an emergency meeting of his top people. He told her he would have an answer in a few hours."

"I'll admit Dangott, I was pacing and jumping, waiting for his phone call. Robin stayed in her room. Anne was a basket case. Finally George Donaldson called and said someone from his company would have the specs delivered first thing in the morning. Anne convinced him that she trusted me, and I should be the one to take the plans to the drop site. I stayed overnight at the house. Anne locked herself and Robin in her bedroom."

"I was watching you with my cameras Damon, and Robin was giving me regular reports on her cell phone."

"That girl was always a little shit. Wait … you were the delivery guy who brought the plans. You had a Spanish accent."

"Si Senor."

"After you handed me three tubes of blueprints, binders of specs and a stack of computer discs, I left quickly, supposedly heading to the drop place but I took off for the airport. I had booked an 11am flight to London. I thought I was home free. After I got to the airport, I called Anne from the parking lot to say where Cassie was being held. I'm not a total bastard."

"My agents had already freed Liat and arrested the two punks who kidnapped her, but they didn't know what it was all about. We picked you up at the ticket counter of British Airways holding the tubes of plans and a carry-on with the rest."

Damon looks away and breathes resignedly. He looks at his hands attached to the table. "Now what? I've told you everything."

"Since you have provided us with the identity of who hired you, we are sending you back to London like we said. Scotland Yard will follow up with you."

"So I hear." Damon doesn't sound too concerned, but a line of sweat drips down his cheek.

"What will you do? You know your terrorist friends are going to hunt you down."

His voice is soft. "I'll disappear. I'm expert at that. And you might not believe this Dangott, but I could have really loved Anne. Tell her that for me, will you? She deserves better."

I'm surprised to hear the first sincere words from Damon Southeby's mouth. "I suppose I can do that, Damon."

I cross to the door and peer through the small glass window, signaling the agents. Two burly Homeland Security Agents enter and release Damon from the hand

and foot shackles. He rubs his wrists and shakes them out. They grab his arms and pull him to his feet, then one of the agents handcuffs his wrists together behind his back. They push him towards the door.

Damon turns and faces me. "I'm available if the Mossad is looking for *another* good agent." He chuckles as the guards push him through the door.

Authors

Rachel Ambrose is a twenty-something fiction writer from Connecticut. Her favorite season is winter, she enjoys well-made Manhattans, and she loves Southern fiction. Her work has appeared in *Crack the Spine*, *Exiles Literary Magazine*, and *The Colton Review*. Currently at work on her second novel, she blogs at http://victorywhiskeyjuliet.tumblr.com.

Lynn Beighley is a fiction writer stuck in a technical book writer's body. Her stories often involve deeply flawed characters and the unsatisfying meshing of the virtual and actual world. She has an MFA in Creative Writing and currently has 16 books published.

Margaret Bingel is just a writer, living in Manchester, New Hampshire. She spends her time working at her father's beer store, art modeling, and writing (when she can). She doesn't have a website or a blog yet, but who knows, maybe she'll have one in the future.

Guilie Castillo Oriard is a Mexican writer currently exiled in the island of Curaçao. She misses Mexican food and Mexican *amabilidad*, but the laissez-faire attitude and the beaches of the Caribbean are fair exchange. Plus, the bounty of cultural diversity inspires great culture-clash fiction. Guilie is currently revising and editing her first novel. Her short stories have appeared in *Fiction 365*, *Lady Ink Magazine* and *Pure Slush*. She blogs at http://guilie-castillo-oriard.blogspot.com.

John Wentworth Chapin lives and writes in Baltimore, where he is too frequently starting Project B before finishing Project A. John writes non-fiction as well as fiction. Find him on the web at http://johnwentworthchapin.com.

James Claffey hails from County Westmeath, Ireland, and lives on an avocado ranch in Carpinteria, CA with his family. He is the author of a collection of short fiction, *Blood a Cold Blue*. His website can be found at http://jamesclaffey.com.

Gay Degani has published online and in print including *The Best of Every Day Fiction* editions and her own collection, *Pomegranate Stories*. She is the founder-editor emeritus of EDF's *Flash Fiction Chronicles*, a staff editor at *Smokelong Quarterly*, and blogs at *Words in Place* where a list of her work can be found. She's had two stories nominated for Pushcart consideration and won the eleventh Annual Glass Woman Prize for her flash piece, *Something about L.A.*

Michelle Elvy is an editor and writer who has meandered from the shores of the Chesapeake to New Zealand's Bay of Islands. Michelle has published poetry, short stories and non-fiction about travel, faraway places, food, motorcycling, slow travel, the kindness of strangers and raising children in unusual places for numerous literary journals and magazines in the US, Canada, Australasia, UK and Europe. She edits at *Flash Frontier: An Adventure in Short Fiction* and *Blue Five Notebook*. She can also be found regularly at *Awkword Paper Cut*. More about manuscript assessment and Michelle's take on editing and writing at http://michelleelvy.com.

Gloria Garfunkel is a psychologist and writer with a Ph.D. from Harvard University in Psychology and Social Relations. A former psychotherapist, she has published many stories in literary journals and anthologies.

Teresa Burns Gunther has had fiction and non-fiction appear in numerous literary journals and most recently in *Northwind Magazine, Bookslut* and *Best New Writing 2012*. Teresa is the Editor of *The Lakeside,* an online literary magazine, and she founded Lakeshore Writers Workshop in Oakland, California where she leads creative writing workshops and classes and works one-on-one with writers. Find her work at http://www.teresaburnsgunther.com/.

Gill Hoffs lives with her family and an ever-dwindling supply of Nutella in the North of England. Find Gill on facebook or as @gillhoffs on twitter, email her a dirty joke at gillhoffs@hotmail.co.uk, or leave a clean comment at http://gillhoffs.wordpress.com/. *Wild: a collection* is out now from *Pure Slush Books*. Her non-fiction book *The Sinking of RMS Tayleur: the Lost Story of the Victorian Titanic* is also out now, from Pen & Sword. (See her site or http://www.pen-and-sword.co.uk/ for details.) Feel free to send her chocolate.

Joanne Jagoda of Oakland, California, took an inspiring writing workshop after retiring in 2009, and launched on a long-postponed creative writing journey. Since discovering her passion for writing, she has worked non-stop on short stories, poetry and non-fiction. Her work has appeared in a number of e-zines and print anthologies, including *Pure Slush* and *Idea Gems Magazine*, and she was a poet of the month for a Jewish news weekly in Northern California.

When not taking writing and poetry classes, Joanne enjoys being a writer-coach for ninth graders, Zumba, and visiting her three grandchildren in Jerusalem.

Len Kuntz is a writer from Washington State and an editor at the online literary magazine *Metazen*. His work appears widely in print and online. You can find more of his work at http://lenkuntz.blogspot.com.

Sally-Anne Macomber was born and raised in Toronto, Canada, and studied journalism at Concordia University in Montreal. Her work on high fashion and the demise of haute couture has appeared in various online and print publications in both Europe and North America. She turned to writing flash fiction in 2010, and hasn't looked back.

Jessica McHugh is an author of speculative fiction that spans the genre from horror and alternate history to epic fantasy. A member of the Horror Writers Association and a 2013 Pulp Ark nominee, she has devoted herself to novels, short stories, poetry, and playwriting. Jessica has had thirteen books published in five years, including the bestselling *Rabbits in the Garden*, *The Sky: The World* and the gritty coming-of-age thriller, *PINS*. More info on her speculations and publications can be found at http://www.jessicamchughbooks.com.

Gwendolyn Joyce Mintz is a fiction writer and aspiring photographer. Her work has appeared in various online and print publications. In other incarnations, Mintz is a writing instructor, a teddy bear maker and somebody's grand-mother.

h. l. nelson is Founding Editor/Executive Director of *Cease, Cows* lit mag and a former sidewalk mannequin. Pub credits: *PANK, Hobart, Connotation Press, Metazen, Drunk*

Monkeys, Red Fez, Bartleby Snopes. She's also editing an anthology which includes stories by Aimee Bender, Roxane Gay, Lindsay Hunter and other fierce women writers. Her MFA is currently kicking her ass. Tell her what you're wearing: heather@hlnelson.com.

Mandy Nicol grew up in Melbourne, Australia and made a tree change to country Victoria in the mid-nineties – the decade, not her age. She has various animals including a flockette of pet sheep that are thankful for her vegaquarian habits. She writes short stories and loves flash fiction. *Pure Slush* is the first venue to publish her work.

Derek Osborne lives in eastern Pennsylvania. His work has appeared in *Boston Literary Magazine, Bartleby Snopes, Literary Orphans, The Linnet's Wings, Pure Slush* and many others. To read more visit http://gertrudesflat.blogspot.com, or email him at derekosborne1@gmail.com.

Vanessa Weibler Paris lives in Erie, Pa., with a guy, a girl, a boy, a bunny rabbit and a dog. She writes things both real (for work) and pretend (for fun). Her favorite things include hot peppers, bad puns, small-world stories, and tales with a twist at the end.

Gary Percesepe is Associate Editor at *New World Writing* (formerly *Mississippi Review*) and a Contributor at *The Nervous Breakdown*. Author of four books in philosophy, Percesepe's poetry, fiction, essays, and interviews have appeared in *Story Quarterly, N + 1, Salon, Mississippi Review, The Millions, Brevity, PANK, Metazen, The Brooklyner*, and other places. His collection of short stories, *Why I Did the Grocery Girl*, is forthcoming from Aqueous Books. His poetry collection *falling* and his flash fiction collection *itch* were published by *Pure Slush Books* in late 2013. He has taught at Saint Louis University, Wittenberg

University, and University of Dayton. He lives in Buffalo, New York.

Matt Potter is an Australian-born writer who keeps a part of his psyche in Berlin. Matt has been published in various places online, and he is, rather amazingly, also the founding editor of *Pure Slush*. You can find more of his work at his website: http://mattcpotter.webs.com/.

Darryl Price was born in Kentucky and educated at Thomas More College. A founding member of L. Jack Roth's Yellow Pages Poets, he has published dozens of chapbooks, and his poems have appeared in many journals. He currently edits *Olentangy Review* with his wife Melissa.

Stephen V. Ramey is an American author from New Castle, Pennsylvania. His work has appeared in many places, including *The Doctor TJ Eckleburg Review*, *The Journal of Compressed Creative Arts*, and *A Capella Zoo*. *Glass Animals*, his first collection of (very) short fiction is available from *Pure Slush Books*. Find him and more of his work at http://www.stephenvramey.com.

Shane Simmons is a self-confessed coffee shop writer who believes that regardless of quality, each paragraph penned should be rewarded with sweet treats (cake, muffins, Belgian waffles, etc). London-born, he ran away to Glasgow ten years ago, expanded his waistline and now blogs at http://scribblingsimmons.wordpress.com/.

Kimberlee Smith is a writer whose poetry, essays, fiction, and creative non-fiction have been published in numerous literary journals and anthologies. She was awarded a residency to the Jentel Arts Program in 2013. She lives with her two daughters, two dogs, three cats, two rabbits, and nine chooks on her farm in rural Connecticut. She received her MA in English from the University of Sydney, a certificate in the Creative Writing Program through UCLA, and her BA in Journalism from the University of Southern California. She is enrolled currently in post-graduate studies at Columbia University in New York. She can do a headstand on a trampoline, kill a chook, and make hard cider from the apples in her orchard.

Andrew Stancek was born in Bratislava and saw Russian tanks occupying his homeland. His dreams of circuses and ice cream, flying and lion-taming, miracle and romance have appeared recently in print in *LA Review*, *Windsor Review* and *New Sun Rising: Stories for Japan*. Among the many online publications featuring his work are *Every Day Fiction*, *Gemini Magazine* (Flash Fiction Contest Grand Prize Winner), *fwriction*, *r.kv.r.y. quarterly literary journal*, *Tin House*, *Flash Fiction* Chronicles, *The Linnet's Wings*, *Connotation Press*, *THIS Literary Magazine*, *LA Review*, *Windsor Review*, *Thrice Fiction Magazine*, *New Sun Rising*, and *Pure Slush*.

Susan Tepper is the author of four published books of fiction and a chapbook of poetry. Her most recent title *The Merrill Diaries* (*Pure Slush Books*, July 2013) is a Novel in Stories that follow a young woman's adventures in love and lust on two continents, spanning a decade. Tepper has received nine Pushcart nominations, and one for the Pulitzer Prize in fiction. You can visit her website here: http://www.susantepper.com.

Nathaniel Tower lives in the Twin Cities with his wife and daughter. After teaching high school English for nine years, he decided to pursue a career in writing / publishing / editing. His fiction has appeared in over two hundred online and print journals. His first collection of fiction, *Nagging Wives, Foolish Husbands*, was released in 2014 through *Martian Lit*. Nathaniel is the founding and managing editor of *Bartleby Snopes Literary Magazine and Press*. You can find out more about Nathaniel at http://nathanieltower.wordpress.com.

Townsend Walker lives in San Francisco. His stories have been published in over fifty literary journals and included in seven anthologies. One story won the SLO NightWriters story contest. Two were nominated for the PEN / O. Henry Award. Four were performed at the New Short Fiction Series in Hollywood. He is associate editor at *Grey Sparrow Journal*. During a career in finance he published three books, on foreign exchange, derivatives and portfolio management. Educated at Georgetown, NYU and Stanford, his website is at http://www.townsendwalker.com.

Michael Webb is continually surprised anyone is interested in what he has to say, and he blogs occasionally at http://innocentsaccidentshints.blogspot.com.

Other 2014 compendiums
from Pure Slush

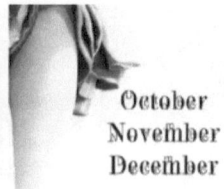

Jan Feb March 2014
ISBN: 978-1-925101-33-1

April May June 2014
ISBN: 978-1-925101-46-1

Oct Nov Dec 2014
ISBN: 978-1-925101-48-5

For the complete catalogue of
fiction and non-fiction
print books and eBooks
visit the Pure Slush Store at
http://pureslush.webs.com/store.htm

www.ingramcontent.com/pod-product-compliance
Lightning Source LLC
Chambersburg PA
CBHW020926020726
47495CB00002B/371